"CONGRATULATIONS, HE'S A BEAUTIFUL BOY."

"Thank you." The woman was beaming. "My husband and I are so happy."

Laura knelt down in front of the boy and gently pinched his chin. "And happy birthday to you," she said. He did not react at all.

The baby just sat still, oblivious to everything going on around him. He was small, Laura thought, smaller than one-year-olds should be. But something else about the baby struck her as odd. She didn't know exactly what it was, but something seemed unusual.

"He's so calm around people," another woman said.

"Yes, he is—usually," the mother said. She giggled and said, "Last month, while we were at the pediatrician's office, another little boy—a three-year-old—came over and tried to get Robby to play with him. All of a sudden Robby snapped at him, tried to bite him. I had to run over and pull him away, and it wasn't easy, believe me."

She looked down at her son. "You made the older boy cry, didn't you?" she said, sounding almost proud of it. She looked up at the other mothers. "I don't know where he gets his temper from. But he's still my little pride and joy."

THE
CLINIC

KIP LANGELLO

POCKET STAR BOOKS
New York   London   Toronto   Sydney   Tokyo   Singapore

This book is a work of fiction. Names, characters, places and
incidents are products of the author's imagination or are used
fictitiously. Any resemblance to actual events or locales or persons,
living or dead, is entirely coincidental.

An *Original* Publication of POCKET BOOKS

A Pocket Star Book published by
POCKET BOOKS, a division of Simon & Schuster Inc.
1230 Avenue of the Americas, New York, NY 10020

Copyright © 1997 by Kip Langello

All rights reserved, including the right to reproduce
this book or portions thereof in any form whatsoever.
For information address Pocket Books, 1230 Avenue
of the Americas, New York, NY 10020

ISBN: 0-671-55282-1

First Pocket Books printing April 1997

10 9 8 7 6 5 4 3 2 1

POCKET STAR BOOKS and colophon are registered
trademarks of Simon & Schuster Inc.

Cover photos courtesy of Science Source

Printed in the U.S.A.

For my parents,
Patrick and Grace Langello

PROLOGUE

———◆———

Today was the day. He knew it had to be done.

He waited by the kitchen window, watching his wife drive off to the market, then he walked to the pantry. On the top shelf of the cabinet was the container of lighter fluid. He brought it to the kitchen counter, then searched the drawer under the phone for the box of wooden matches. When he had everything ready, he stopped for a moment to catch his breath and steady himself.

His son was upstairs, alone. There had been no trouble for the last few days, but it would come, he knew. Next week or next month, or perhaps not until next year—there was never any way to tell exactly when. But it would definitely come. No question about it. What form it would take, he could never foresee, and this unpredictability made him dread every waking moment.

It had to be done, he told himself again, just as he had been telling himself for months. This was the last thing in the world he wanted to do, the one act he thought he could never carry out. But he had to disregard his paternal instincts. His emotions could not guide him now. He had to view this coolly, with detachment. This needed to be done. And only he could see it through to the end.

It was time.

He walked up the stairs slowly, his legs feeling heavy, his body slumped. Last night, having finally resolved that he must do this, he had not slept at all. Now the walk down the

1

hallway to the small bedroom was like wading through chest-deep water. Each step was a strain. With each step, he felt as though he were being pushed back, as if a force were trying to prevent him from doing this.

But he could not stop now. He had to go through with it. He should have done something after the incident with the dog. He should have seen it then, realized it then, understood then how bad it would get. If he had, he could have prevented what had happened at the day-care center. But even then, he hadn't acted. Now he was going to. Now, after what almost happened when the neighbor's little girl came into the yard. He shuddered at the thought of what had almost been.

Yes, now he was determined to act. The situation could not go on this way any longer. He could not bear to stand by and do nothing, and yet he knew that if he went through with this, he would not be able to live with himself. Either way, life was over for him, which is why he had decided to stay with his son. For that reason, and to make sure his plan succeeded.

He found his son sitting on the bedroom floor, staring at the wall. The boy was small for a 3-year-old, and he acted like a child who had barely matured since birth. Toys that his mother had bought for him lay near his feet, unused. Instead, he twisted a thread from the rug around his fingers. Another strand hung from the side of his mouth. Sunlight through the window caught the rivulet of drool on his chin. His eyes held not a glint of life.

The father walked in silently and took the boy's hand. The boy stood without resistance. He had come late to walking, learning less than a year ago. His stride was still unsteady and he had to hold onto his father to keep from falling, so together, the two of them made their way across the room, up the hallway, and down the stairs to the kitchen.

He put his son in the highchair, then set out a bowl of cereal. He watched for a while as the boy manipulated the spoon with little deftness, spilling milk and flakes with each mouthful. When he was convinced that his son was settled and suspected nothing, he removed his belt and slid it around his son's waist, then he fastened the buckle behind the chair, securing the boy in place. With minor curiosity, the boy looked up for an instant at his father. Then, as though nothing were wrong, he returned to his breakfast.

The father watched a moment longer. His hands started trembling. Over and over, he told himself that he must do this. *He must.* There was no other choice. He wished to God there was a way to keep him, but he knew otherwise.

He reached over and picked up the can of lighter fluid. Then he took the box of matches. For so long, he and his wife had wanted a child. Now he wanted only to rid the world of it.

1

For so long, they had wanted to have a child.

Laura Fielding rolled over in bed and gently shook her husband. "Dan," she whispered. It was still dark. The window was open a few inches, letting in the cool scent of juniper and dew. She heard a car drive past the house. A dog barked in the distance. New Orleans was slowly awakening.

"Dan." She shook him again.

He rolled over now and squinted to see the clock. "What time is it?"

"Six-thirty."

"You've got to be kidding. Wake me up at eight."

"Honey, today should be the last chance this cycle."

"Oh, Christ. I'm too tired," he said. "Do you know what time I got in last night?"

"The shoot ran late?"

"It took forever. Look, I need to get some sleep. We'll do it later. In a couple of hours."

"I have to get to the office."

"Go in late."

"I can't. One of my clients has an audit this morning and I have to be there."

"I'm too tired, Laura. Tonight, okay? We'll do it tonight."

"We have to go to that dinner party tonight, remember?"

"After that, then."

"You know we never get back before one or two in the morning. We'll be too tired."

"I'm too tired now. Tomorrow," he said. "We'll do it for sure tomorrow." And with that he buried his head in the pillow.

"Tomorrow will be too late," she said.

Yesterday, when she used the ovulation predictor kit, the test result came out positive. The LH surge meant they had only two days, tops. Since she and Dan hadn't made love last night because he had worked late, and they probably wouldn't make love tonight, they needed to do it now if she was to have any chance of getting pregnant.

"Honey, you know we have to do it before I ovulate or—"

"I know, I know. Spare me the gynecological lesson this morning, okay?"

Laura fell silent, hurt by his tone. She told herself that he was only behaving this way because he was tired, but lately he was always tired, always unwilling. He made her feel like she was forcing him all the time, like he was doing her a favor, like she was doing something wrong.

But both of them wanted to have a child. Dan wanted one just as much as she did. And like him, she was tired much of the time. She dreaded going through this with him every cycle, but she understood that if they were ever going to have a baby, they had to do this. So she accepted it. And she tried to make the best of it. Why couldn't he?

"Dan, you know that if we don't do this now . . ." she started to say.

"All right, all right, we'll do it," he said. "Just give me a minute, will you?"

He rolled out of bed and went into the bathroom. He left the door open and the light off.

Laura listened to him urinate, then watched him walk to the mirror and cough and spit into the sink. After a few minutes, he trudged back out, his body slouched.

"Whatever happened to spontaneity?" he murmured. "Christ."

He flopped on the bed and squirmed up onto her. His breath was hot and stale against her face. She kissed his neck, trying to make this pleasurable for both of them, but he barely reciprocated. He acted like he was performing a chore, no more enjoyable than taking out the trash.

He needed quite a while to get hard, and the delay only irritated him more. Laura surrendered any hope of feeling delight in what they were doing. Two years ago when they began trying in earnest to conceive, she had done her best to make it romantic, to make it sensual. But the act had lost all affection after so many months of having to do it on specific days, at specific times, regardless of how tired or rushed or stressed they were, even if they had been arguing moments before. It had become an obligation. Now both of them were going through the motions and little else.

Finally Dan entered her. His technique was mechanical. Laura sensed anger in each thrust. When it was over, he let out a breath of relief and went right to the shower without saying a word.

The dinner party was at the lakefront home of Huey and Tabitha Boze, friends of theirs from college. Tabitha sold overpriced real estate in Slidell; Huey was the operations manager for the Superdome. Also here tonight were fellow Louisiana State University alumni Joe and Becky Delgado, who drove up from Baton Rouge, where they owned a small bakery, and Ed and Missy Wilson, both of whom were professors at Nichols State University, outside Thibodaux.

The eight of them got together a few times a year to catch up on each other's lives since college, talk politics and literature, boast about their careers and families, and laugh at the forsaken idealism of their school days.

As they went outside onto the patio tonight to have coffee and dessert and watch the sailboats on Lake Pontchartrain, the conversation turned to the sad state of society.

"Lawyers are the real problem," Huey Boze said as he did every time they got together. He lit a cigar and flung the match into a planter of azaleas. Grinning at Laura, he said, "Present company excepted, of course."

"That's awfully kind of you," she said. "But I'm sure I don't deserve to be singled out."

"You know it's true about lawyers, Laura. Your profession has been the bane of society since Shakespeare's time."

"I guess that means we're going to knock lawyers again tonight. Any chance we could attack another profession for a change?"

"We could pick on doctors," Ed Wilson said.

Huey shook his head and puffed on the cigar. "No good. Doctors wouldn't be a problem if it weren't for lawyers suing the good ones and defending the bad ones."

"Don't we serve any purpose at all?" Laura asked.

Huey pondered it. "None that I can think of."

The others laughed.

Dan said, "Sure you do, honey. You give us someone to deride at dinner parties."

"Thanks for the support, honey."

Dan shrugged. "I gave it my best shot."

"Hey, I've got a good one," Huey said. "Lawyer goes into the bank, right?"

"Here it comes," Laura said. "Another lawyer joke."

"The old boy behind him in line starts massaging his back," Huey said.

"What bank is that?" Tabitha asked. "I'd like to open an account there."

The others laughed. Huey ignored her and continued.

"Anyway, the lawyer says to him, 'What in the hell are you doing?' So the old boy says, 'I'm a professional masseur. A good massage relaxes the muscles, makes people less tense. As a public service, I always massage the person in front of me when I'm standing in line.' So the lawyer says, 'Well I'm an attorney, but you don't see me screwing the person in front of me.'"

Huey waited for the burst of laughter. Instead he got only hisses and moans.

"Don't you get it?" he said. "The lawyer tells the masseur, 'You don't see me screwing the person in front of me.' Because lawyers screw people for a living. Get it?"

"We got it," Tabitha said. "We just didn't think it was funny."

Huey threw up his hands. "I'm stuck with a bunch of lawyer lovers. You people don't know funny when you hear it."

"Speaking of screwing . . ." Missy Wilson said.

"It seems we always get around to that eventually," Dan said.

"Speaking of screwing," Missy continued. "Did you hear that Liz and Jeff are having another baby?"

"Another one?" Tabitha said. "What does that make now? Three?"

"Four, I think."

"I must have missed the third one."

Becky Delgado looked at Laura and Dan. "So, when are you two going to start a family? You're the last ones without a baby, you know."

"The last ones in the whole world?" Dan said.

"You know what I mean. Of our friends."

"I think you need to make new friends."

"No, really," Huey said, joining in. "What are you waiting for? You've been married now—what?—ten years?"

"Longer, I think," Tabitha said. "It wasn't long after college that you two got married, right?"

"After Laura finished law school," Dan said. "Thirteen years."

"All right, thirteen years," Huey said. "That's long enough. You should have kids by now."

"We want to make sure the marriage is going to last," Dan said.

The others laughed. Laura forced a smile. This subject always came up and it always made her uncomfortable. Dan had become adept at deflecting the comments, avoiding any direct answers. Laura always withdrew.

As the conversation turned to the governor's latest embarrassment, Laura glanced across the patio at Dan. The brief look they exchanged was heavy with the frustration they both felt.

Laura suddenly realized Jenny was talking to her. "Hmm?" she said, looking up.

Jenny put down her coffee cup. "Okay. Out with it."

"Out with what?"

"With whatever is bothering you."

"Nothing's bothering me."

"I know you better than that. You've been distracted ever since we got here."

They were sitting outside the Café Du Monde, most of the wrought-iron tables around them filled with tourists. The sidewalk was noisy, families laughing and snapping pictures, studying maps, arguing about which sights to take in next. Laura never would have come here on her own, but Jenny liked their French coffee and beignets. Laura had never developed a taste for the pieces of deep-fried dough sprinkled with confectioner's sugar. Jenny ate them every day.

Jenny enjoyed just being in the middle of the activity of Jackson Square. She was a travel writer, and she thrived on being with "her readers," as she called them. Laura would rather have met somewhere quiet. Her mood was sullen this morning.

"Sorry," Laura said. "What were we talking about? You wanted to know if you could expense your computer instead of depreciating it, right?"

Jenny sat back and folded her arms. "Forget the computer," she said. "I want to know what's up with you. You can talk to me, you know that."

Jenny Hopkins had been Laura's first client at Beckum, Sterling, Gold. Over the 12 years they had known each other, Laura and Jenny had become close friends. Today, they were meeting to discuss Jenny's taxes, but Laura was having trouble concentrating on that.

"I went to the doctor yesterday," she told Jenny.

"Why? Is something wrong?"

"No, not the way you think. For the last two years, Dan and I have been trying to have a baby." She shook her head and spoke in a whisper. "I don't think it's going to work out."

"It can take longer than two years, Laura. Some couples try for many years before they conceive."

"We don't have many years."

"Why not?"

Laura hushed her. "Listen. Can you hear it?"

Jenny listened in silence for a moment, looking confused. "Hear what?" she asked.

"Tick, tick, tick," Laura said.

"Huh?"

"That's my biological clock running down. I'm not getting any younger, you know."

Jenny scoffed at that. "You've got plenty of time. Thirty-five is young."

"I'm thirty-*eight.*"

"That's still young."

"Not if you're trying to get pregnant, it isn't."

"This is the nineties. A lot of women these days wait to have kids until their careers are established. A lot of them don't get around to doing it until they're in their forties."

"And a lot of them have trouble, too."

"Laura, it'll happen. You'll get pregnant."

"What if I don't?"

"You will, don't worry."

"I am worried. This may sound silly, but I feel like—like I have a need inside me. It's as though I *have* to give birth. It's almost like I'm not complete if I don't. Do you know what I mean?"

"You're right. It does sound silly." Jenny took one last bite of her beignet, gulped some coffee, then got up and said, "Come on. Let's take a walk."

They went across the street to Jackson Square, the central area of activity in the French Quarter. In the middle of the square was the statue of Andrew Jackson, the hero of the Battle of New Orleans, and set up around it were portrait artists, jugglers, a mime, and a xylophone player with a bow tie and straw hat. Everywhere Laura and Jenny walked, they heard music, laughter, people hawking food and souvenirs.

"What are we doing here?" Laura asked.

"No one can stay depressed in the square," Jenny said.

"This isn't going to cheer me up."

"Who's talking about you? I'm the one who needs the cheering up."

Laura found herself chuckling.

Jenny put her arm around Laura and said, "Listen to me,

11

okay? In case no one ever told you, a woman's worth no longer comes from having babies. Maybe it did a hundred years ago, but it doesn't anymore. It's just not the most important thing in the world. My God, look at all you've achieved."

"I know all that. In my head, I know that, but in my heart, I feel differently. I spent so much time and energy on my career that I ignored everything else. And now my career is all I have, and that's not enough anymore. I look back at the cost"—she shook her head—"and I can't help asking if it was worth it."

"You can still have a child. You just have to give it time."

"Every day I'm not pregnant makes it harder for me to ever get pregnant."

"I think you're placing too much importance on this. I really do."

"Do you know what it's like every time someone sends me an invitation to a baby shower, or every time I get an announcement that someone I know just had twins, or when someone at the firm brings in a new baby to show off and then they all ask me when Dan and I are going to start our family? Do you know how that makes me feel? How that makes Dan feel? Do you know what it's like every time I take one of those pregnancy tests and Dan asks me what the result is? That look of disappointment on his face when I tell him. Do you know what that does to me inside? So yes, I place a lot of importance on having a baby," she said. "That's because it *is* important. I want to have a baby, Jenny. Is that so much to ask? Everyone else can have babies. Why can't I?"

They stopped at a bench at the edge of the Moon Walk, away from much of the noise and activity. In front of them was the Mississippi River. A barge passed slowly in the distance.

Jenny held Laura's hand and said, "I know it's difficult for you. And I want you to know that I do understand. When I was married, I couldn't have kids either. And I'm doing okay today. Your situation isn't as unique as you think. A lot of couples go through the same thing. *A lot.*"

Laura stared at the barge. "You'd think that with all the advances women have made over the last fifty years, we could have done something about this. I guess our bodies are still the same. We're just not made for having babies this late."

"Just don't give up hope," Jenny said.

"It's hard not to."

"You know my kid sister, Paula?"

Laura shook her head.

"Well, she's a couple of years older than you and she just had her first child."

"Gee, that makes me feel a whole lot better. It's always nice to hear about other women having babies when I can't."

"I'm just saying that it *is* possible."

"You haven't talked to my gynecologist."

"Doctors can be wrong. You should look for another doctor."

"Right. I'll find one who says I can get pregnant, and then magically I'll get pregnant. Is that how it works? Jenny, I don't need another doctor to tell me I can't have a baby. I've been there in bed with Dan all this time. I know we're doing it right. We've got the sex part down pat. And it's not working. The problem isn't my doctor."

She took a breath. It was difficult for her to talk about this. "I had a problem a few years ago," she said. "They found some cysts on my Fallopian tubes. They were able to remove them, and it turned out they weren't cancerous, but the procedure left scarring. My doctor thinks that's what's preventing me from getting pregnant."

"There are ways they can help you."

"My doctor's done everything she can think of. The only way to bypass the tube problem is to use *in vitro* fertilization, which we were going to try, but my doctor needed at least five or six eggs in order to give the procedure any chance at all of working. But all I could produce was one egg."

"Paula had the same problem," Jenny said. "Sometimes they can work around that."

"I've tried everything. I took the drugs. Clomid, Pergonal, Lupron. I've had so many tests I can't even count them anymore. I still don't make enough eggs. God knows why I bother."

"You need to see a specialist. A *real* specialist. Not an OB-GYN who sticks *infertility* under her name in the yellow pages. They really don't know the latest advances. You need to go to a doctor who does nothing but help women with problems like yours."

"It's not going to do any good," Laura said.

"You don't know that. Paula tried for the longest time, just like you; then she went to a clinic in Alabama, and within a month, she was pregnant."

"Why? Doctors in Alabama know more about having babies than doctors here in New Orleans?"

Jenny laughed. "The clinic she went to specializes in helping women who have difficulty getting pregnant. That's all they do. The doctor there—his name is Dr. Chyles— he's supposed to be some kind of miracle worker."

"Oh, a miracle worker! You should have said that in the first place. That makes all the difference in the world."

"You know what I mean. The success rate there is high, very high. I told you, Paula got pregnant, and she and her husband had all but given up hope. I'm telling you, the doctor up there is doing good things. You should go."

"Dr. Child?" Laura said. "A baby doctor named Child? Give me a break."

"It's Chyles with a *y* and an *s*, and it's on the level. His clinic is called the New Life Center. It's in Alabama. Not quite all the way to Montgomery."

"Montgomery? That's more than three hundred miles from here!"

"I said it's not *all* the way to Montgomery."

"Anywhere in Alabama is too far to go just to have this guy tell me I can't have a baby."

"He's not going to tell you that, I promise. Look, I'm going to get the address and phone number from Paula and give it you tomorrow. You call them. Okay?"

"I don't know," Laura said, not very hopeful.

"Do you want a baby or don't you?"

"Of course I do."

"Then try this place. What have you got to lose? From what Paula tells me, the women who go there are having babies. She said they have a saying up there. 'If your husband can't get you pregnant, Dr. Chyles can.'"

Laura found herself laughing again. "They do *not* say that," she told Jenny.

"That's what Paula told me. I really think you should try it. If you really, really want to have a baby, you should give this place a chance."

The rest of the day and into the evening, Laura kept thinking about what Jenny had said. She wondered if that clinic could be as good as Jenny claimed. Maybe seeing a specialist was worth a try. If Dr. Chyles had access to technologies that her doctor didn't, maybe he could help her. Maybe there was still a chance that she and Dan could have a child.

The next day, after Jenny phoned with the specialist's address and phone number, Laura called her own doctor and asked if she knew anything about the New Life Center and Dr. Norman Chyles in Collier, Alabama.

"I've heard of the place, yes," she told Laura.

"What have you heard?"

"Well, the center is relatively new. It's only been there a year or two. From what I understand, they specialize in treating patients who have difficulty producing an adequate number of eggs."

"Which is the problem I had when we tried *in vitro.*"

"Yes."

"My friend tells me that they've had a lot of success there."

"I've heard that, too. Quite a bit of success, actually. I would have mentioned it to you, but frankly, I assumed it was too far away. It *is* in Alabama."

"I know it's far, but putting that aside, do you think it would be worthwhile for me to go there, to talk to them?"

"Since they specialize in your particular problem, they

may be able to do things for you that I can't do here. If the distance doesn't bother you, I'd say try it. I guess it comes down to how badly you and your husband want to have a baby."

2

Laura and Dan left New Orleans at six o'clock Friday morning, stopped briefly in Mississippi for breakfast at a Waffle House restaurant off Interstate 10, then drove on into Alabama. Two and a half hours north of Mobile, they exited Interstate 65 and headed east. Thick woods flanked the two-lane highway. Occasionally, a house peeked through the trees, but mostly, the land was undeveloped. It was almost noon, and Laura noticed that Dan looked tired from driving.

"Do you want me to take over?" she asked.

He shook his head. "I just hope this trip is worthwhile. This is a long way from New Orleans."

"I know, but if they can help us, isn't it worth it?"

"That's a big if."

Neither of them spoke for a while as Dan negotiated the country roads, trying to follow the directions given Laura over the phone by the nurse who had made the appointment. The jazz station on the radio faded out now. Dan tried to tune in another station but could find only country music, so he turned the radio off. He looked at Laura. She saw that he had something on his mind.

"What is it?" she asked.

"We have to consider that it might not work."

"I don't want to think that way. I want to be positive. I want to believe it will work."

"That's all well and good, but the reality is that the doctor at this clinic might not be able to help us. And if that's the case, I think we have to consider that."

She didn't say anything. She didn't want to accept it.

"Us having a baby," he said, "might not be meant to be."

She looked away, still saying nothing.

He waited a moment, then said, "Laura, let's face it, eventually there may come a time when we'll have to let it go and move on."

"I want a baby," she whispered.

"So do I. But if they can't help us . . ."

"They can help us," she whispered.

"Laura—"

"They can. I really think they can. They helped Jenny's sister, and Jenny said she had the same problem we do. My doctor said this clinic has had a lot of success with couples in our situation. I think it's going to work this time. I really do."

Downtown Collier had some quaint shops, a grassy square, post office, and a tiny inn. Most prominent were the two churches, one on either end of Main Street. A sign indicated that the New Life Center was two miles ahead.

Once they were away from downtown, the landscape became mostly farms and woods. Few people seemed to live out here.

"Why would anyone build a clinic in the middle of nowhere?" Dan said. "You'd think it'd make more sense to open it in a city somewhere."

"I don't know; it's kind of peaceful out here," Laura said. "Maybe that's why. I read that stress has a lot to do with infertility."

Dan shrugged. "It's still an odd place for a clinic like this. How much business can there be out here? Who's going to come this far to see a doctor?"

"We did."

"That's because we're crazy. And desperate."

Laura laughed, but in the humor, she felt sadness, too. She tried not to dwell on their desperation, tried to maintain hope, however unrealistic it might be. But every now and then, pessimism would surface in her thoughts, and it would take all her strength not to despair.

Now, as Dan steered the car around a curve, he suddenly slammed on the brakes. Laura slid forward, bumping the dashboard. The car skidded and fishtailed, the rear tire sliding off the road.

"Are you okay, Laura?" Dan asked.

She sat back in the seat and caught her breath. "What happened?"

"I should have run the damn thing over."

"Run what over?"

"That damn cat."

Laura looked out the window. On the road a few yards in front of them, a cat had its back to the car and was concentrating on a squirrel splattered on the pavement. Not once did it look back at them as it gnawed at the rotting animal.

"That's real attractive," Dan said.

"Look at that poor thing. You can see its ribs. It must be starving."

The cat was mostly white with a few splotches of orange in its coat, and while that seemed like an unusual color to Laura, she sensed that something else about it was odd, though she couldn't quite identify what it was.

Dan blew the horn to get it to move, but the cat didn't budge. It didn't even look back at them.

"Just go around it," Laura said.

"There's no room."

On one side of the road, the pavement dropped off into a deep gully, black with swamp water. A stone wall bordered the other side, keeping back the woods.

Dan blew the horn again. The cat still ignored them. "He better move or he's going to end up like that squirrel," Dan said.

"Don't run him over."

"I'm not going to sit here all day. If he doesn't move, he gets run over. That's the rule of the road."

Dan hit the horn again, this time holding it down for several seconds. At last the cat turned slowly. A piece of flesh dangled from its mouth. It looked first to the right then to the left, as though scanning the woods to make sure no other animals would challenge its catch. Finally, it turned its head enough for it to see their car.

The sight startled the cat, as though it hadn't known that the car was here, even with the horn blaring. Its eyes sprang open wide, and Laura saw a strange reddish hue in them, an almost crazed, rabid look. She also noticed the sides of its head for the first time.

The cat darted across the road and into the woods so quickly that Laura wasn't sure she had really seen it. She turned to Dan for confirmation.

"Did you see that?" she asked.

"It's about time it moved."

"Didn't you notice?"

"Notice what?"

"It didn't have any ears."

"What are you talking about?"

"That cat. It didn't have any ears. It didn't move when you blew the horn because it couldn't hear it. Wow," she said. "I never saw anything like that before. A cat with no ears."

"If he keeps eating dinner in the middle of the road, you won't see it again, either. He'll be one dead cat."

As Dan drove on, Laura peered into the woods, searching the shadows for the cat. It was gone.

"Poor thing," she said quietly. No ears. Starving. Maybe sick. She doubted it could survive in the wild for very long, and the thought of it dying alone in the woods saddened her.

The clinic was a brawny, one-story, windowless structure of brick that looked like a fortress tucked into the woods. Notices hung from trees all around, forbidding hunters and trespassers anywhere near the facility. An insignificant sign marked the entrance, simple white lettering on brown wood: NEW LIFE CENTER, ASSISTED REPRODUCTION.

Expensive sedans filled the dozen or so spaces marked PATIENT PARKING. Noticing the license plates, Laura was impressed that the majority of the cars were not from Alabama, but instead places like Mississippi, Tennessee, Florida. There were even a few from as far away as South Carolina and Kansas.

"Look at all these cars," Laura said as Dan looked for a parking spot. "My doctor said this place was new. To have so many people coming from so far away, this place really must have a good reputation."

"Let's hope they can live up to it," Dan said.

The security guard in the lobby looked to be in his fifties. The roll around his midsection strained at his uniform, making him look like he was pregnant. Laura giggled to herself, thinking, *This place must be really good; even the men get pregnant here.*

She thought it odd that there would be a guard out here in the country, and an armed guard at that. It didn't fit the surroundings. But she decided that his main job was probably directing patients and visitors where to go, rather than securing the building. Besides, having him here just meant that the building was safe.

The nametag on his shirt said ROY HICKS. He showed them to the outpatient wing, where several other couples were waiting to see the doctor. Laura gave the receptionist the medical records she and Dan had gotten from their doctors in New Orleans. The receptionist handed them lengthy questionnaires to fill out, detailing their medical and personal history. Dan complained about having to answer all the questions; he thought most of them were unimportant or weren't anyone's business, so Laura had to fill out both forms.

After she finished and turned the forms in, an orderly came over. Tall, blond, broad-shouldered, he looked like he had been a local high-school football hero three or four years ago. The quarterback. He told them it would be a short wait before Dr. Chyles could see them, and offered to give them a quick tour of the facility in the meantime.

* * *

"We have our own maternity ward," the orderly explained as he led them through the building.

"That's unusual, isn't it?" Laura said. "How many patients choose to have their babies here?"

He looked at her as though the question were odd. "Why, all of them do," he said. "It is the best facility around. Wait until you see it."

The maternity ward comprised two corridors, each with eight rooms. A nurses' station was positioned at the intersection, overseeing both hallways.

"The ratio of patients to nurses here is two to one," the orderly said. "That's very high."

He showed them one of the unoccupied rooms, which impressed Laura. It looked more like a hotel suite than a hospital room. The colors were soft pastels. Paintings hung on the walls. Plants had been placed throughout. There was even a sofa by the window that converted into a bed for the husband, and a large-screen TV.

"We try to make it as comfortable as possible for our patients," the orderly told them.

"I think you've succeeded," Laura said.

"I noticed there's no phone in there," Dan said.

"That's right. Dr. Chyles feels it's important that the patients are not disturbed when they come in for delivery. A stress-free environment is one of his top priorities. Most women usually stay for no more than two nights, so they don't mind going without a phone for that long. Actually, a lot of them welcome it. They can't be disturbed by problems at work or other bothersome intrusions."

"Like their husbands," Laura said.

The orderly laughed. Dan didn't think it was funny. He sneered at Laura. She giggled and took his hand. They followed the orderly down the corridor to the neonatal intensive care unit.

"From the looks of this place," Dan said, "I'll bet it costs a pretty penny to have a baby here."

"I couldn't say. I don't know anything about that. But I do know that this is the best-equipped, most modern facility in the state. If a patient happens to experience any complications, this is definitely the place to be—not that there would be any complications, of course. But it's just nice to know that you're in such good hands. Did you know that Dr. Chyles's wife—she's also a doctor; her name is Dr. Acer—she's the anesthesiologist here?"

"We didn't know that," Laura said.

"She's a fabulous doctor herself. You're really going to like her. And Dr. Chyles, too. They're the best. They're just the best. You'll see for yourself."

As the orderly walked ahead, Dan whispered to Laura, "What he means is it's going to cost us a fortune."

"But if it means having a baby, isn't it worth it?"

"They haven't said they can help us yet."

The orderly took them to the entrance of the delivery area. A sign outside the double doors said STERILE AREA. AUTHORIZED PERSONNEL ONLY.

"We can't go in, but we can take a peek," he said. He opened the doors a few inches, just enough for them to look in. "We have two delivery rooms," he explained. "No waiting." He chuckled at his own joke, then added, "They're the best equipped in the state."

To one side of the delivery rooms was another door marked PATHOLOGY—PHYSICIANS ONLY. Laura asked the orderly what that was.

"That leads to the lab where Dr. Chyles sometimes biopsies the placenta after delivery."

"Why does he do that?"

"I'm not real sure exactly why, but I know that he's the most thorough doctor you'll ever find. He always does that little extra bit to make sure everything is just right."

"That's good to know."

Before returning to the outpatient wing, the orderly showed them the cafeteria and the gift shop, then led them down another hallway.

"There's one more thing I'd like to show you," he said.

He brought them to an observation window cut into the wall. On the other side of the glass was a large laboratory filled with state-of-the-art instruments. Half a dozen technicians were working inside, oblivious to the three of them standing in the hall, looking in.

"We do all our own testing right here on the premises," the orderly explained. "That makes everything quicker and we can control the accuracy much better. This is also where the *in vitro* fertilization process takes place. If all goes well, you'll be able to watch Dr. Chyles do that."

"I hear that the success rate is really high here," Laura said.

"I don't know the exact figures, but most of the couples who come here end up having a baby eventually."

Laura looked at Dan, feeling encouraged. He even smiled a little, showing optimism for the first time since they arrived here. As much as Laura was trying to remain levelheaded and realistic about their chances, she was genuinely starting to believe that it would work.

The orderly took them back to the waiting room.

"I'm sure they'll be calling you in to see Dr. Chyles soon," he said. "Good luck with your baby."

"Thanks," Laura said. "And thanks for the tour."

When the orderly left, Laura held Dan's hand and said, "I really feel good about this place. They seem to have everything right here and they seem to know what they're doing. I think we were right to come here. I really think it's going to work this time."

"Honey, don't get ahead of yourself. We don't know anything yet. Let's not set ourselves up for a big disappointment, okay? Let's just wait and see what the doctor says."

"I just feel like it's going to work this time. I'm sure of it."

The nurse appeared at last.

"Mr. and Mrs. Fielding?" she said. "Dr. Chyles will see you now."

3

When they walked in, Dr. Norman Chyles was sitting behind his desk, scribbling notes in a file. He took off his reading glasses and came around the desk to greet them.

"I hope I didn't keep you waiting too long," he said.

After they shook hands, he gestured for them to sit. Laura had expected an older man. Dr. Chyles looked to be in his early forties, with short black hair, his sideburns graying slightly. He was tall and thin, and he had prominent, almost avian features. She got the impression that he was thinking every moment, but he also came across as understanding and easygoing. He looked confident, she thought, and that instilled confidence in her. He had the air of someone who knew what he was doing.

His office was furnished elegantly, more like a CEO's office than a doctor's examination room. His desk was free of clutter. To the side was a computer; it was turned off now. In the corner behind him was a door to a closet or a washroom.

Three walls were adorned with enlargements of photographs. From the subject matter, Laura could tell Chyles favored seascapes. The most intense shot hung behind the desk, a powerful depiction in various shades of gray of waves crashing into a rocky coastline. It was a marked departure from the relaxing countryside outside the clinic, she thought.

The fourth wall was filled with medical diplomas, certificates, awards. As Laura sat in front of the desk, she glanced at the diplomas, curious about his credentials. She noticed his degrees were from some of the best schools in the country. He had certificates from the American Fertility Society and the Society for Advanced Reproductive Technology and was board certified in obstetrics and reproductive endocrinology. Immediately, she felt reassured. She had come to the right place.

"Well," Dr. Chyles said, "I've been reading through your file." He picked up the folder and skimmed through it again. Laura watched anxiously. He didn't seem to be in any hurry to get to whether he could help them. He read for a moment then looked up.

"You're an attorney?" he asked Laura.

"Yes."

"What kind of law do you practice?"

"Tax law."

"That must be a demanding profession, I would think."

"At times it can be, yes."

Chyles nodded and scratched his chin. His face showed concern. He looked at her again and said, "Will that be a problem if we are successful here?"

Laura felt a tinge of excitement hearing the word *successful*.

"A problem?" she asked. "How do you mean?"

"The assisted reproduction process we use places great demands on the patient's time. I think it'll be difficult for you to go through the therapy here while actively practicing law."

"I'm prepared to cut back my workload at the firm if necessary."

"Good."

Chyles looked down at the file again, reading for a moment. Something seemed to strike his interest. He looked up at Dan.

"I see you're a photographer," he said.

"That's right."

"What kind of photography?"

"Fashion, mostly."

"Really? I dabble myself," Chyles said, glancing at the photos on the walls.

"You took these?" Dan asked. "They're good. Real good."

"Well, I'm just an amateur."

"You have a good sense of perspective and you use light well. I'm impressed."

"Really? Thank you again."

Finally, Chyles turned his attention to the reason they had come to his clinic.

"I've been reviewing your test results," he said. "Dan, your ejaculate appears to be fine. Two point seven cubic centimeters of semen, which is midrange normal. The sperm count is approximately sixty million per cubic centimeter, which is high normal. Size, shape, behavior—all look good. I don't see any problem there."

Dan chuckled. "Hey, I do what I can."

Laura was too nervous to laugh. She watched Chyles, almost dreading what was coming next.

"I see you two tried *in vitro* fertilization last year."

"Yes," Laura said, "but the doctor couldn't harvest enough eggs to fertilize."

Chyles nodded. "That happens quite often." He scanned the file again and said, "No indication of endometriosis or uterine fibrosis. Good. No legacy of uterine scarring from the curettage."

"The what?" Dan asked. He looked at Laura. "What's that? Curettage? I never heard you mention that before."

Laura didn't know what to say.

She hadn't thought to tell her doctor in New Orleans to include in her record a note asking Dr. Chyles not to mention it to Dan. Now she didn't know what to tell him. Dan was staring at her, waiting for an explanation. She looked at Chyles. From his expression, she could see that he understood that she was hiding it from her husband.

She turned to Dan. "When I had the problem with my Fallopian tubes," she said, "they did a procedure to make sure there wasn't a similar problem with my uterus. That's all."

He nodded, and she was relieved that he believed her lie.

"*Was* there a problem there?" he asked.

"No. None at all."

"Oh. Okay. Good." He looked at Chyles. "Then that's not the problem, right?" he asked.

Chyles glanced at Laura. "The current difficulty," he said, then he looked at Dan, "appears to be due to the condition of Laura's Fallopian tubes, not her uterus—that and her inability to produce an adequate number of eggs for an ordinary *in vitro* fertilization attempt."

"Is there anything we can do about that?" Dan asked.

Chyles put down the file, folded his hands on the desk, and said, "I believe we can help you, yes." He looked at Laura and smiled. "We specialize in *in vitro* fertilization techniques for women in your situation."

"You really think you can help us?" Laura said.

"Yes, I do."

Dan said, "Even though her other doctors couldn't?"

"I can't speak for what other doctors can or can't do. I can only tell you what I believe we can do for you here, and I believe we can help you have a child."

His words sent shivers of joy through Laura's body. She looked at Dan and noticed that he was having as much trouble controlling his excitement as she was.

"That's great!" she said. She squeezed Dan's hand. "Isn't it, honey?"

He smiled at her with a look of love she hadn't seen in a long time, then he turned to Chyles and asked how they would proceed.

"First, we'd put Laura on a therapy of fertility drugs. I know you've been through that before, but we have to try to produce as many eggs as possible. That's always to our benefit. That will involve daily injections that you administer yourself at home. The husband usually assists with this part. You're not squeamish, are you, Dan?"

"I can stick her with a needle; that's no problem. I've done that before."

"Even if the drugs don't produce a large number of eggs, we've had a lot of success using only a single egg. We harvest the egg or eggs then fertilize them with your sperm in our laboratory." He looked at Laura. "Then we transfer them to your uterus. At that stage, we'll treat you with a progesterone supplement in order to help prepare your uterus to accept the egg."

"A progesterone supplement? What is it? Is it safe?"

"Absolutely safe. I wouldn't suggest it if it weren't. And whenever we do *in vitro,* it is definitely necessary. It would be impossible for you to maintain a healthy pregnancy without it."

"Are there any side effects?" Laura asked.

"There may be some minor discomfort at first, some bleeding or cramps, nothing dangerous. That passes fairly quickly, though."

"I should be able to put up with that. If it's safe and necessary, then I don't have any objections."

"I use it with many of my patients. That's why we've had such a high rate of successful births here—higher than most clinics of this type."

"What is the success rate?" Laura asked. As a tax attorney, she dealt with numbers all the time. Hormone supplements and the inner workings of her body weren't always easy to understand, but numbers were black and white. She needed the numbers to evaluate it properly.

"Since I came here from Miami two years ago," Chyles said, "we've had exceptional success. We're averaging close to seventy percent live births."

"That high?" Laura said. It was hard for her to believe it could be that high, but she wanted desperately to be convinced. "I thought the average success rate with *in vitro* was about forty percent."

"At other clinics, and in the past, that's true. First of all, you have to understand that that figure is for all the patients who come to be tested, not for the patients who actually qualify for treatment. There's a big difference there. Also, there have been significant advances in this field over the last year alone. We can do things we couldn't do just a short time ago. We really do know what we're doing here. We specialize in a particular type of patient, patients like yourself, and since that's all we do here, naturally we can focus all our efforts toward that one type of treatment, and that increases our success rate. Considering that you're under forty and healthy, the odds are very promising. Seventy percent is not an exaggeration. I honestly do believe we can help you have a child."

Laura looked at Dan. "Seventy percent," she said, growing more sure by the minute. She saw that he was starting to get swept up in the excitement, too.

"Oh, there is one other side effect that I need to mention at this point," Chyles said. "The process we use can sometimes make the delivery of the placenta afterward a little difficult. Rest assured, it doesn't endanger the child or the mother in the least. It's just a little more painful than I'd like it to be. What we recommend is after your baby is delivered, you receive general anesthesia so you'll be out while the afterbirth is delivered. The procedure is relatively minor and completely safe. It takes only a few minutes, but because of the discomfort, it's best that you're sedated. That's all."

Laura was a little concerned, never having heard anything like that before, but she had never heard about the hormone supplements that were going to help her finally have a baby either, so she assumed it was all part of the developing science. It didn't seem to be too big of a deal, especially considering what she was getting out of it.

"My doctor will know how to do it, right, when I deliver?" she asked.

"I should have mentioned before—you'll have to have the child delivered here."

"Here?"

"Yes. We have our own maternity ward on the premises."

"Yes, we saw it."

"It's better equipped than most hospitals."

"I'm sure it is, but I don't know about coming all the way up here when it's time to deliver," Laura said. "I mean, who knows when I'll go into labor. It's a long drive. I may not be able to make it."

"You don't understand. You'll already be here," Chyles told her. "I was just about to explain that the treatment requires extensive monitoring and testing. First, from the time we implant the fertilized egg until you become pregnant—a period of approximately two weeks—you'll have to come in for injections twice a day. And then after you become pregnant, you still have to receive hormone injections once a day. You couldn't possibly carry the baby to term without them. So you'll be spending a lot of time here. You have to be prepared to do that if this is to succeed."

"Every day?" Laura asked.

"Yes. Seven days a week. That's the reason we have our own maternity ward here. We have to treat you with the hormone injections right up to the delivery. That has a lot to do with our success rate. We have to be able to control your pregnancy to assure that you don't have any problems."

"But we live in New Orleans," Dan said. "That's a six-hour drive from here."

"I noticed that in your file. You have to decide whether that's going to present a problem for you."

"Can my doctor in New Orleans give me the shots?" Laura asked.

"This is a special procedure that I've developed, and it requires special expertise that your gynecologist simply doesn't have. We have to test you every day, see how you're responding, how your hormonal level is reacting, in order to make sure the dosage is correct, and then we modify it accordingly. The only way to do this properly, to ensure the highest possible rate of success, is to do it all here. I'm sorry," he said.

Dan looked at Laura. "Honey," he said quietly. "I don't see how you'll be able to do that. Driving six hours each way, twice a day. That's impossible."

Laura didn't say anything, but she knew Dan was right.

"If I may," Chyles said. "I suggest to all my patients who live a prohibitive distance from the clinic to consider renting a place nearby for the duration of their treatment and pregnancy."

"You mean move out here?" Dan said with a dubious laugh. "I don't think so."

"Well, of course that's up to the two of you. I can tell you that we have people who can assist you in finding a place if you decide that's what you want to do. The rents are very reasonable around here."

"It doesn't matter what the rents are," Dan said. "There's no way we can move out here. We both work in New Orleans and it's not practical to drive back and forth every day."

"That's something you have to take into consideration. Only you can decide how badly you want to have a baby and what sacrifices you're willing to make for it."

After leaving Dr. Chyles's office, Laura and Dan went to the clinic's financial counselor. The woman explained that each treatment cycle and *in vitro* fertilization attempt would cost $16,000, which Laura's insurance would not cover.

They spent the night at the Pickens Inn in town, staying up past midnight discussing what to do.

"I don't see how we can do it," Dan said.

"I've been thinking," Laura said. "I could easily work from home. All I need is a computer, a fax machine, and a telephone. I can do most of what I need to do from there, and whatever I can't do, someone else at the firm can take over for me. The partners are real supportive about pregnancy and maternity things. Last year, Kate Webb had to spend her whole last trimester in bed, and she worked from home. I should be able to work from here without any problem."

"You mean live out here?"

"It wouldn't be permanent. Just until I have the baby."

"Maybe *you* can work from home, but I can't. What am I supposed to do, drive back and forth to my studio every day? If I give up sleeping altogether, I can probably do it." He shook his head. "We have to be practical about this."

"What I meant is I could rent a place out here myself. You could stay in New Orleans and then on weekends come out here."

"I don't know about that."

"If it means having a baby, I think it'll be worth the inconvenience. Don't you?"

Dan blew out a breath of exasperation. "I don't know, Laura. This is a long ways away and you're talking about nine months."

"I know that. But I want a baby."

"I want one, too, but not if it means your living out here all alone for that long."

"I don't mind living out here. I really don't."

"*I* mind."

She took his hands in hers. "I know, and I'm going to miss being away from you, but if it means having a baby, I think it's worth it."

"What if it doesn't work?"

"Dr. Chyles seems to think it will."

"But it's not guaranteed. It's not one hundred percent."

"It's seventy percent, and that's pretty high. That's as good as it's ever going to get."

"I know, but if it doesn't work, I'm worried about your having to deal with that disappointment."

"I can't be any more disappointed than I already am."

"Laura, I've seen you in the past when we thought it would work and it didn't. I don't want you to have to go through that again. I don't want *us* to go through that again."

"Please," she said. "I really want to try. I really do. One last time."

He could see the resolve and desperation in her face. For her, there was no decision to make. This was clearly something she had to do.

He leaned over and kissed her. "We'll try it," he whispered. "One last time."

The next day, before driving back to New Orleans, they picked up the necessary medications from the clinic. They decided that if they budgeted themselves closely and maybe borrowed a couple thousand dollars from Dan's sister in Arizona, they could afford the medical fees and the extra rent.

For the next 10 mornings, Dan gave Laura two injections as instructed. When the ovulation predictor test showed the LH surge, Laura called the clinic, then she and Dan made another drive to Alabama. It was July second. Collier was preparing for its annual Independence Day festivities. Flags and banners hung all through town.

Chyles examined Laura, then scheduled her right away for the transvaginal oocyte retrieval to harvest her eggs from her ovary. The nurse brought Laura to another room and prepared her for the surgery. When Chyles came in, he was accompanied by a woman doctor, both of them dressed in teal surgical clothes.

"I'd like you to meet my wife, Dr. Acer," he said to Laura. "She'll be administering the anesthesia."

"It's nice to meet you," Laura said.

She shook Laura's hand. Her grip was firm, her palm warm and dry. She was tall and thin like her husband and carried herself like someone accustomed to wealth, yet she did not come across as conceited. Instead, she seemed pleasant and sure of herself. Laura felt comfortable with her.

"I want you to know, Mrs. Fielding," Dr. Acer said, "that I've reviewed your chart, and Dr. Chyles and I have discussed your situation thoroughly. We both feel very confident about this procedure."

"Absolutely," Chyles said.

"I never had husband-and-wife doctors before," Laura said with nervous laughter.

"Well, we've had a lot of husband-and-wife patients," Chyles said.

They scrubbed for the operation, then returned, wearing

latex gloves and masks. While the nurse draped Laura in sterile clothes and placed her feet in the stirrups, Dr. Acer started the IV drip.

"We administer the anesthesia at the last possible minute," she explained, "to minimize its effects on the eggs. We don't know that it has any effect, but we take every precaution possible to increase the chance of conception."

"The entire procedure should take less than half an hour," Chyles told Laura. "It'll be over before you know it."

That was the last thing Laura remembered before she lost consciousness.

When Laura came to, only Chyles and a nurse were in the room with her. Chyles said that he had been able to harvest only one egg, but he'd worked successfully with only one before. He explained that he would know soon if the egg was healthy so they could attempt to fertilize it. He had to go to the lab now to talk with the embryologist.

"Doctor, before you go," she said. "I, um—" It was difficult for her to come up with the right words. "I wanted to thank you." She spoke quietly, not wanting the nurse to hear.

"Why don't we wait until we see how successful the entire treatment is?" Chyles said.

"No, I mean—"

She was embarrassed mentioning this and she wasn't quite sure how to word it, but she felt she needed to say something.

"You didn't say anything to my husband," she whispered. "About, um—" She glanced over at the nurse, who was putting away instruments in the corner of the room. Lowering her voice even more, she said, "About why I had the curettage."

Chyles nodded, understanding now what she meant. He turned to the nurse and said, "Would you give us a moment?"

The nurse left, closing the door behind her.

When they were alone, Chyles said, "It was clear that your husband wasn't aware of the circumstances."

"I just couldn't tell him. When it happened, I didn't

realize it was going to be a problem, and then when my doctor told me that that's the reason I can't conceive—" She shook her head, the words hard to find.

"I just couldn't tell Dan," she said again. "When it happened, I wanted to, but . . . I couldn't. Now, after not saying anything for such a long time, if I told him, I'm not sure he'd understand."

"I can certainly appreciate your concerns."

"Am I wrong not to tell him?" she asked.

Chyles hesitated, thinking it over. Laura watched him closely, trying to read his face, but she couldn't tell what he was thinking. She hoped he would say that she was doing the right thing by not telling Dan. After all this time, there was no way she could break it to him without hurting him, without jeopardizing their marriage.

"That isn't what is affecting your ability to have children," Chyles said, and left it at that.

Laura sighed, relieved.

"Thank you again, Doctor."

He touched her shoulder and smiled.

In another room, Dan supplied a semen specimen to be used to fertilize Laura's egg. After he was done, a nurse brought him and Laura to the observation window that looked into the laboratory. From here, they watched anxiously as Chyles came in. He seemed businesslike, barely glancing up to acknowledge them.

He walked to the station where a young, balding man was sitting behind a microscope, peering through the lens. Chyles stood behind him, watching over the man's shoulder.

"What are they doing?" Laura asked.

"That's the embryologist," the nurse explained. "He's looking at the fluid Dr. Chyles aspirated from your follicle."

"Ooh. Aspirated from your follicle," Dan said. "Sounds dirty."

Laura ignored him and asked, "What is he looking for?"

"First he has to confirm that an egg is present, then he classifies the maturity of the egg. The best eggs are what we call preovulatory, or mature eggs. They're ready for fertilization immediately. Immature eggs we can sometimes incubate and try to fertilize later, but the success rate isn't as high as preovs. The postmature ones can't be fertilized at all, and they're usually discarded."

Laura and Dan watched anxiously. Chyles and the embryologist spoke tersely. Through the thick glass of the observation window, Laura and Dan were unable to hear their conversation. Nor could they read their faces; neither man showed much emotion. To these professionals, an egg was just an egg. To Laura and Dan, it was their future.

It seemed to take forever. Finally, Chyles came to the window and pressed the intercom button.

"It's preov," he said.

The nurse was the only one who immediately understood. She jumped in the air, excited. "That's great!"

Chyles smiled. Through the intercom, he said, "It looks like we're in good shape."

For a moment, Laura and Dan did not react, but then the initial shock wore off and joy swept through them. They hugged and kissed.

The nurse apologized for her outburst. Even after working here for two years, she explained, she still felt a thrill when the news was good. She pointed out another station in the lab where a woman in white lab clothes was examining a glass specimen container with milky seminal fluid.

"That looks familiar," Dan said. He winked at Laura and said, "I made love to that jar this morning."

The nurse giggled. Laura elbowed him in the ribs.

They watched as the woman worked on the semen specimen, adding chemicals and moving it from one container to another.

"She's washing it," the nurse explained.

"Why? Is it dirty?" Dan said.

"That's how we separate the semen plasma from the sperm. The sperm is what we need. The rest is discarded."

"Easy come, easy go," Dan said.

The nurse giggled again.

Laura said to Dan, "Easy, huh? It hasn't been easy come for you in years."

"Hey!"

The nurse turned her head, trying to keep from laughing.

"Don't believe her," Dan told the nurse.

Next, the woman in the lab placed Dan's sperm in a centrifuge and began spinning it.

"Won't the little guys get dizzy spinning around like that?" Dan asked the nurse.

"What they're doing is separating the best sperm, the motile ones, from the rest."

"All my sperm are top notch. Tell Chyles he can use any one of them. They'll all work fine."

The sperm had to be incubated overnight, so Laura and Dan checked in at the Pickens Inn. They made love leisurely in the afternoon, both of them thankful they didn't have to perform according to Laura's menstrual cycle anymore. Afterward, they joked about how it would be funny if they conceived now, before Chyles could fertilize the egg in his lab. When night fell, they watched the fireworks from the porch of the inn. The next morning, they returned to the clinic, nervous and giddy with excitement. They had never gotten this far before. They had never allowed themselves this much hope.

Standing at the observation window again, they watched the embryologist combine the sperm with the egg in a petri dish. Chyles stood behind the man, watching intently. The procedure was done quickly and without the least bit of show or drama. When it was done, Chyles looked toward the window and nodded, offering a confident smile.

"I always thought the conception of our child would be a little more romantic," Dan said.

"Oh, I don't know about that," Laura said. She put her arms around him and held him tightly. "I'm feeling pretty good right now. Aren't you?"

Filled with emotion, he kissed her on the forehead and held her close. They watched as the embryologist brought the petri dish to the incubator.

"That's our son in there," Dan said.

"Our daughter, you mean."

"Looks like a boy to me."

The embryologist made out a label and placed it on the shelf with the dish.

"I'm so glad we're doing this," Laura said.

"I am too. I just hope it works."

"It'll work. I just know it will."

5

The next part was the most difficult. They had to wait 48 hours to find out if the fertilization was successful. On Friday morning, while Dan was in the shower and Laura was putting on her makeup, the clinic called. Laura's hand trembled as she held the receiver to her ear.

"I have the results from the IVF we did on Wednesday," the woman said.

Laura felt her entire body quiver with an uneasy mixture of excitement and fear. She closed her eyes and crossed her fingers. "Yes?" she said.

"It was positive," the woman said. "Congratulations!"

Laura couldn't speak.

"Mrs. Fielding?"

"Um, yes, thank you," Laura said. Her voice cracked as she fought to choke back her emotions. "Thank you."

"The next step is to transfer the zygote," the woman said. "Dr. Chyles wants to let it incubate for another seventy-two hours before he transfers it."

"Zygote?"

"Once the egg is fertilized, that's what it's called. A zygote. After it implants in your uterus, it's no longer a zygote; it's called an embryo. And then a baby," the woman said, sounding as full of joy as Laura felt.

They scheduled an appointment for the following Monday.

When Laura hung up, she went straight into the bathroom. Dan was still in the shower. The room was full of steam and it smelled of shampoo and soap. Laura opened the door, startling him. Immediately, he saw she was crying.

"Honey, what's wrong?" He came closer and held her shoulders. "Are you all right?"

"The clinic just called," she said, tears streaming down her cheeks.

Dan misunderstood her sobs. "I'm so sorry, honey," he said. He held her gently. "It'll be all right," he said. "It'll be all right."

She put her arms around him and pressed her head against his chest, which was still wet and soapy. "It worked," she whispered. "It really worked."

It took a moment for Dan to comprehend fully. "You mean . . . ?"

She gazed up into his eyes. "I have to go to the clinic Monday to have the zygote put inside me."

"To have what put inside you?"

Laura laughed. "That's what I said too." She explained the terminology then said, "We're going to have a baby, Dan! We're really going to have a baby!"

He picked her up and pulled her into the shower with him. Under the spray of warm water, they celebrated the wonderful news. They both understood that she still wasn't pregnant, that the fertilized egg would have to successfully implant, but for the first time since they began this struggle two years before, they had reason to be hopeful.

Laura called the senior partners of her law firm at their homes to discuss her situation. Since she was not the first attorney on staff to have a child, they were receptive to the idea of her working at home and they did their best to accommodate her needs.

They decided she would take a two-week vacation, starting Monday. Nothing she was working on had to be taken care of immediately. If the procedure proved successful, she could set up an office at the rental house in Alabama and work from there. If the worst happened and she did not become pregnant at the end of two weeks, she would simply return to work and proceed as normal.

Next, she called Jenny Hopkins to give her the good news and thank her for suggesting Dr. Chyles.

"Didn't I tell you he was a miracle worker?" Jenny said.

"Well, I'm not pregnant yet."

"You will be. I just know it."

Laura reminded herself that she had to guard against being overly optimistic, but she couldn't contain her excitement. "You know what?" she said. "I really think this is going to work this time. I really feel good about this."

"I'm so happy for you, Laura."

"It's all because you told me about the New Life Center. I owe you a great deal."

"I know. And I've already decided how you can pay me back. I talked to an editor at *Together Woman* magazine. She wants me to do an in-depth article on this whole area of infertility."

"You're a travel writer. This isn't your kind of article."

"I'm a writer, period. If it has words and a story, I can write it. And guess who's going to be one of the subjects of the article?"

"You want to do a story on me?"

"Not just on you specifically. It'll be about women having babies later in life, the difficulties that waiting presents and the solutions that are available. I'm going to focus on you, and on my sister, and on some other women I know. Maybe I'll interview that doctor of yours."

"Sounds like a good idea."

"You didn't think I sent you up there for nothing, did you? We both make out. I get money, you get a baby."

"I think I got the better of this deal."

That evening, a handful of their friends and some of the lawyers from Laura's firm came over to throw a going-away party for Laura. They had cake and champagne. Everyone hugged her and wished her the best.

Even though Laura enjoyed the attention, she knew that

all the celebrating was a bit premature. She wasn't pregnant yet. For this to work, the transfer procedure had to be successful, then she had to carry the baby to term. A lot could happen in the next nine months.

As she went to bed that night, filled with anticipation and trepidation, she thought about the long road ahead. She wondered if she was setting herself up for disappointment again. With so much that could go wrong, she knew she should be cautious and not let her optimism get the best of her. But the more she thought about it, the more difficulty she had keeping herself from getting swept up in what was happening. This was the closest she and Dan had come to having a baby. It just had to work.

On Saturday morning, Laura drove to Alabama to meet with the real-estate agent and look over several houses available to rent. Dan had to shoot a department store layout that he couldn't reschedule, so Laura went alone. Since she was the one who would be living in the house, she figured she should be the one picking it out.

The first house the realtor showed her was old, but it was in good condition. It had a warm Southern charm with which Laura quickly fell in love. The siding was sky blue shingles. White shutters hung beside the windows. A large porch circled the entire house, with a wooden bench in front and two rocking chairs in back. A weeping willow shaded the side yard from the harsh July sun. From one of the branches hung a love seat swing. It looked like the perfect place to sit in the afternoon and read Eugenia Price. In the back yard, grassy fields rolled away from the house to the old-growth woods.

The only neighbor was in a ranch-style house across the street, tucked amid cypress trees.

"Mrs. Wheeler lives there," the realtor told Laura. "She's a patient at the clinic herself. I believe she's due in five or six months. She's very friendly. She's from Georgia. You'll like her. I take it your husband won't be joining you?"

"He'll be here on weekends. His work is in New Orleans. He can't leave."

"It's the same with most of women who rent from me. You and your husband needn't be concerned. Collier is about as safe and tranquil a place as you could find anywhere."

"I guess that's why Dr. Chyles decided to open his clinic out here rather than in a big city somewhere," Laura said.

"That and the tax breaks," the realtor said with a wink. "The county commissioners gave him all kinds of incentives to make sure he chose Collier. The closest hospital is almost an hour away, and they thought it would be good to have a medical facility nearby just in case of an emergency. Also, his clinic brought a lot of good jobs here, and that benefits all the local businesses. I can't complain myself. Rental business is booming for me. Besides," she added with a smile, "Dr. Chyles is certainly doing good things for young couples like you and your husband."

"We're keeping our fingers crossed," Laura said.

She signed a nine-month lease that afternoon, with what the realtor jokingly referred to as a "pregnancy clause." She included this clause in all her leases these days. It allowed the tenant to terminate the lease in two weeks if she didn't become pregnant.

"But not many clients have had to exercise that clause yet," she told Laura. "I understand the clinic has a very high success rate. The patients have a saying, you know." She lowered her voice. "They say, 'If your husband can't make you pregnant, Dr. Chyles can.'"

"Yes, I know. I've heard it."

Laura left for New Orleans that afternoon, feeling more hopeful than ever before. The next day, she and Dan loaded up both cars and moved her to what she hoped would be her home for the next nine months.

6

Dr. Chyles came in carrying a stainless-steel tray covered with a white cloth. He set the tray beside the operating table.

"How are you feeling this morning, Laura?"

"A little nervous."

"No need to be. We do lots of these procedures. There's very little chance of anything going wrong."

The nurse helped Chyles set out the equipment and check Laura's vital signs. While they were preparing, Dr. Acer came in, spoke briefly to Laura, then started getting everything ready for the anesthesia. Dr. Chyles explained how he would transfer the zygote, using a narrow plastic catheter inserted through her cervix and into her uterus. He made it sound simple and straightforward. As Laura listened to his steady, reassuring voice, most of her apprehension faded.

"After the procedure," he said, "we're going to give you a hormone injection formulated to aid the zygote in implanting. Altogether, it'll take less than an hour." He smiled warmly and said, "It'll be a piece of cake. You'll do just fine."

Dr. Acer started the IV drip. As she and Dr. Chyles left to scrub for the operation and the nurse prepared the instruments to be used, Laura gradually began to drift off. She saw the nurse remove the white cloth from the steel tray, revealing two syringes. They were quickly going out of focus. The nurse smiled at her and told her that everything would be just fine. Laura managed a nod. It was all Laura could do just to remain conscious.

A moment before Laura lost consciousness, Chyles and Acer returned to the table. "That'll be all," Chyles told the nurse. The last thing Laura recalled seeing as she succumbed to the anesthesia was the nurse walking out, leaving Chyles and his wife alone to perform the procedure.

Laura awoke feeling groggy and disoriented. It took her a moment to remember where she was, what had happened. Dr. Chyles was standing beside her, smiling. His wife was gone, but the nurse had returned.

"That wasn't so bad now, was it?" Chyles said.

"It's done?"

"All through. Now it's just a matter of waiting to see if the zygote implants. I'd like you to take it easy for the rest of the day. Most often when there's a failure, it occurs in the first few hours. Go home and lie down. Don't do any work; don't do anything strenuous or stressful. You'll have to come back here late this afternoon for another injection, but aside from that, don't do much of anything."

"I think I can handle that."

"My nurse will give you more specific instructions regarding food, smoking, alcohol, that type of thing. It's important that you follow them."

"I will," Laura said. "And Doctor, thank you. For everything."

"You'd better hold off on thanking me for another two weeks. The zygote implants in three to four days, but the pregnancy hormone won't show up in your blood in high enough levels for us to read for up to two weeks." He touched her arm in a fatherly way that made her feel safe, then left.

After she dressed, she followed the nurse back to the waiting room, where Dan was sitting impatiently. He stood up right away when she came in. She fell into his arms and they hugged.

"How did it go?" he asked.

The nurse said, "Very well."

"That's great!"

The nurse gave Laura instructions on what to do and what not to do for the following two weeks, then Laura and Dan headed up the hall to leave. When they reached the lobby, the security guard, Roy, was there, flipping through *Auto Trader*. He got up to open the door for them.

"Everything go all right?" he asked.

"Yes, thanks."

"I hope you have lotsa luck with the baby. I'm sure you will. Doc Chyles is real good."

"Honey," Dan said to Laura. "Wait here. I'm going to bring the car up to the door."

"That's not necessary."

"Yes, it is. The nurse said you have to take it easy, and I'm going to make sure you do. Now you just sit down and wait until I bring the car around."

She laughed, then kissed him. "My knight in shining armor."

As he left, he told Roy, "If she tries to leave, shoot her."

"Ten-four."

Roy went back to his *Auto Trader*. Laura sat on the bench and watched through the window as Dan rushed across the parking lot. She laughed to herself, watching him now. He looked like a nervous, doting father already. It struck her suddenly that their best days together were yet to come. A baby was going to make everything perfect, make their life complete. Much depended on this procedure being successful.

Just as Dan reached the car, Laura heard the squealing of tires. Startled, she turned quickly toward the sound. A green Mercedes sped across the parking lot and skidded to a stop in front of the clinic doors. The driver jumped out. He looked lost, frightened.

"What in the hell . . ." Roy said, dropping his magazine and getting up.

For a moment, the man outside just stood beside his car, looking around as though trying to find someone to help him. Roy started toward the door, but by now the man turned back to the car and pulled open the rear door. Leaning in, he lifted something from the back seat. It took a moment for Laura to realize he was holding a woman.

She lay in the man's arms, unmoving, her hands hanging down lifelessly, her hair spilling toward the pavement. The man carried her toward the lobby entrance. Laura got up right away. Roy ran outside to help the man, then turned around and hurried to open the door. When the man came in, he was breathing heavily and smelled of sweat.

"What happened?" Laura said.

"My wife!" He sounded frantic, confused.

Roy took the man toward the bench where Laura had been sitting. As they laid his wife down, Laura noticed that she was pregnant.

"Oh my God!" she whispered, her hands coming up to her mouth in dread. She couldn't tell if the woman was alive. She wasn't moving at all.

"Dr. Chyles!" the man said. "Someone get Dr. Chyles!"

The guard ran down the hall toward the outpatient wing. The man fell to his knees beside his wife and held her hand. Laura came closer to see if she could help, but she was afraid to look at the woman, dreading what she might see.

"What—what happened to her?" she asked.

The man didn't seem to hear her question. He gazed down at his wife, his face dark with worry. "Everything's going to be all right, Dana," he told her. "You're at the clinic now. Everything's going to be just fine."

Dana's eyes opened barely a slit. Laura could see she was in pain and was terrified, but at least she was alive. Laura began trembling, thinking about this woman and her baby, worrying that she was miscarrying.

Dana tried to say something, but all that came out was an unintelligible moan. It seemed to take all her strength to shake her head, which was all she could do to communicate.

"You're here now, sweetheart," the man said. "They're going to take care of you. You're going to be all right."

Dan rushed through the doorway now and came over to see if he could help. Roy raced back in, a nurse hurrying behind him. She took one look at the woman on the bench, then shouted up the hall, "John, get a gurney! Get a gurney over here!"

The nurse rushed over to the woman and began feeling her throat, touching her forehead and cheeks. She struggled for a moment to get out her stethoscope, then pressed it to the woman's chest and listened to her heart.

An orderly hurried over, wheeling a gurney. Everyone but Laura helped lift the woman from the bench and set her down on the white sheet. Laura stepped back and watched, afraid for the woman and praying that the baby was all right. Dan, sensing her distress, put his arm around her. Laura held on to him tightly. As the orderly started to wheel the woman away, Dr. Chyles arrived. Calmly but quickly, he examined the woman.

"What happened?" he asked Dana's husband.

"I don't know! I just found her like this when I got here today!"

Chyles turned to the nurse. "Bring her to OR-1, stat. Page Dr. Acer and have her meet me there. Go!"

The nurse and orderly rushed out, wheeling the unconscious woman away. Chyles started to follow, but the man grabbed his arm and stopped him.

"What's wrong with her, Doctor? Is she going to be all right? What about the baby?"

"I'll know better afterward. Let me stabilize her first, then I can examine her and see just what's wrong. It looks like toxemia, but I won't know for sure until I get her in the OR. I'll let you know as soon as I do."

Chyles was in a rush, but he could see that the man was shaken up, so he took a second to pat him on the back reassuringly.

"You did the right thing by bringing her here," he said. "Now just try to relax. Everything's going to be okay."

The man nodded, but he was still jittery. "She was barely conscious when I got to the house," he said. "She could hardly talk but she kept saying, 'The clinic, the clinic,' so I brought her here as fast as I could. God, I just hope I got her here in time."

Chyles had looked concerned from the beginning, but now he had a strange expression of uneasiness. "She was able to talk to you?" he asked the man.

"Yes, sort of. She was weak and could only mutter a few words, but I guess you could say she was talking, yes."

"Did she say anything else?"

"No. No, just 'the clinic.' No, wait," the man said, remembering now. "She did say something else: 'The other one'—something like that. 'The other one' or 'another one'—she said that several times. I'm not sure exactly what she was trying to tell me, but that's what it sounded like: 'another one.' Does that mean anything?"

Chyles shook his head. "No. I'm sure it doesn't mean anything at all."

"She kept saying it over and over."

"Look, why don't you go to the waiting room and try to relax. I'll come in to talk to you when we know more."

The doctor put his hand on the man's back again to reassure him. Then Chyles glanced toward Dan and Laura. In the instant before he turned and hurried away, Laura noticed his face. Something puzzled her about it. Was it the sudden calmness? No, not exactly. Something else. Something just short of satisfaction. She wasn't sure exactly what it was she saw in that brief moment, but she was sure that it was out of place.

Then he was gone. Laura saw the distraught man again, and her thoughts of Chyles vanished behind her feelings of sorrow for this man's wife and baby.

The man was devastated. For a moment, he just glanced around the lobby, not sure what to do or where to go. Then he turned and staggered down the hall toward the waiting room.

"They must have tried for so long," Laura whispered. "And now . . ."

Dan realized that she was afraid for their own baby, afraid that if she got pregnant, months from now she might lose the baby and that would destroy her.

"It's not going to happen," he said quietly.

She peered into his eyes, feeling vulnerable, fragile.

"I promise," he said. "It's going to be all right."

He held her. She was shivering so he rubbed her arm and shoulder to warm her, then he whispered, "Let's go home, sweetheart. The doctor wants you to rest."

7

Dan stayed with Laura in Alabama the rest of the day, treating her like a queen, not letting her do anything around the house. He made her stay on the sofa and gave her a magazine to read. Every 20 minutes or so, he came over and asked if she needed anything. Laura couldn't help but laugh to herself. She thought his attentiveness was sweet.

When she started to get up once, he rushed over and said, "Hey, what are you doing? Dr. Chyles said for you to take it easy and that's just what I want you to do. You stay right there. If you need something, I'll do it for you."

"I have to go to the bathroom. Do you think you can do that for me?"

"I could, but I don't think you'd get the same relief."

Later, Dan drove her to the clinic for her afternoon shots, then he made up the bed upstairs and prepared dinner for her. She was feeling queasy, which Dr. Chyles told her was normal after the first shots, so she didn't feel like having more than a small cup of soup and a few saltine crackers. Dan peeled and sliced an apple for her and left it in the refrigerator for later.

At six o'clock, he had to head back to New Orleans.

"I'm sorry to leave you alone like this," he said, "but I have to shoot that swimsuit layout at sunrise tomorrow. They scheduled it over a month ago."

"It's all right. I understand. When we decided to do this, I knew I'd have to be here alone. I'll be fine."

49

He explained that he had several other assignments scheduled throughout the coming week, so he wouldn't be able to return until Friday night.

"I'll be fine," she told him again. "You just be careful driving."

This would be the normal routine, she knew. Weekends, they would be together, but the rest of the week, his work would keep him in New Orleans. She wished they didn't have to be apart for so long, but they had discussed this several times over the last weeks. He had a business to maintain, and they were definitely going to need the money. It had to be this way. She accepted that.

But as she watched him drive away, she realized that she had not been prepared for this. A deep sense of loneliness began sinking in even before his car was out of sight. Tonight, more than any other night, she wanted him here.

The house seemed unsettlingly empty. Unlike their place in New Orleans, outside the windows here it was solid blackness, total silence. She felt peculiarly despondent tonight, so she went to bed early, hoping to sleep through this first night, yet she could not shake the feeling that something wasn't right.

She blamed much of her melancholy on Dan's absence and on the unfamiliar surroundings. But she also attributed some of it to the incident with the pregnant woman who had been rushed into the clinic that morning. Even though several hours had passed since then, Laura was still distressed about it. She could not stop thinking about the woman and her baby and hoping that they were all right.

The *in vitro* fertilization attempt might also have something to do with the way she felt, she thought. While Chyles hadn't said as much, she decided that her sense of disquiet was probably a normal reaction to the procedure or to the hormone injections. It would take a little while to adapt to all that had happened, she told herself. Time and a good night's sleep would help. In the morning, she would start to feel better; she felt confident of that.

But the good night's sleep did not come. She lay awake for hours, and as the night dragged on and her sense of anxiety grew, she began to feel an odd pulse of fear. It was a feeling she did not understand at all. Somewhere in the back of her psyche, she had a nagging thought that she had made a mistake in coming here, in trying to have a baby.

No. She quickly dismissed this feeling, attributing it to the new environment and to the potent medications Chyles had given her.

Part of it, too, she reasoned, stemmed from her anticipation of the major changes that would soon come to her life. It was only natural, she told herself, for her to feel reticent—natural but unnecessary.

Both she and Dan wanted this child desperately; this much, she knew for certain. And she felt confident that the procedure would be successful; everyone kept telling them how good Chyles was. They were doing the right thing. She told herself this over and over. Even though she felt a bit uneasy right now, time, she assured herself, would give her perspective on this, and soon, everything would seem proper.

For much of the night, she remained awake, thinking about the fertilized egg Dr. Chyles had placed inside her. Resting her hands over her stomach, she noticed an odd sensation, as though she could feel the zygote stirring in her womb. She knew it was all in her mind; experiencing such a sensation so soon was impossible. Still, she definitely felt that she was now physiologically different, a feeling of being altered in a way she could not describe and did not fully comprehend. Again, she attributed it to having undergone recent surgery. Regardless of how minor the operation had been, any invasive procedure takes its toll.

She spent the rest of the night wondering if the zygote would implant. For such a long time, they had tried to conceive a child. Now that they had new hope, it could not fail. It simply could not.

The next morning, while she was in the kitchen making toast, something moved just outside the window. It was only an instant of motion, a white blur, but it was so close and so sudden that she flinched back, startled.

By the time she looked up, it was gone. She caught her breath, then leaned over the sink and peered out the window. The back porch was right below the windowsill. The two rocking chairs were side by side out there. The paint on the railing was peeling. A few of the boards needed replacing.

Beyond the porch was a long expanse of open field. Farther back loomed forbidding woods. Laura looked over the entire area but could see nothing that explained what had flashed past the window.

She turned and looked toward the side yard and noticed the willow tree rustling, the bench swing swaying slightly. A hot breeze blew across the open fields this morning, so she thought that perhaps she had seen leaves blowing in the wind. It might even have been a bird. Whatever it was, it was certainly nothing over which she should be concerned. Things like that were just part of living in the country. She didn't give it another thought.

She was about to sit down and eat when the phone rang. She assumed it was Dan, since only he and her law firm had the number up here and it was too early for anyone at the office to call.

She picked up the phone and said, "Hi, honey."

The woman on the other end laughed. "Is this Laura Fielding?" she asked.

"Yes. I'm sorry, I thought you were someone else."

"For his sake, I hope you thought it was your husband."

Laura laughed, then asked, "Who is this?"

"Pardon my manners. I should have introduced myself. I'm Charlotte Wheeler. I'm your neighbor across the street, and a fellow patient at the New Life Center."

"Oh yes, Mrs. Wheeler. The real-estate agent mentioned you."

"Please call me Charlotte. I hope I didn't wake you."

"No, not at all. What can I do for you?"

"I just thought we ought to get acquainted since you and I are the only souls living out here."

"It's that remote, is it?"

"It sure is. It's nice, though. I think you're going to like it here."

"Do you mind if I ask you how you got my number?" Laura said.

"I got it from the same real-estate agent who told you about me."

"Really? She gave you my number?"

"I hope you don't mind. She thought you might be feeling a little isolated out here and would appreciate someone to talk to. I know I sure would."

"I guess I don't mind. To tell you the truth, I'm glad you called. I could use a friend up here. I don't know anyone in Collier."

"Well, now you know me. Why don't we ride to the clinic together this morning? That'll give us a chance to get to know each other."

"Sounds like a good idea."

"I'll pick you up in about an hour?"

Laura hung up, thinking that Charlotte sounded like a warm, friendly woman. She was sure the two of them would become close over the next several months—that is, if Dr. Chyles's procedure proved successful.

"Good morning again," Charlotte said when Laura climbed into the BMW.

"Good morning, and thanks again for the ride."

"It's my pleasure. I like the company, and besides I figured you'd be sick and tired of driving after coming all the way up here from New Orleans."

"How did you know I'm from New Orleans?"

"Same way I got your phone number."

"The realtor told you that too?"

Charlotte laughed. "You'll get used to small-town life pretty quick."

"I guess I don't have much choice."

As they backed out of the driveway, Laura noticed that Charlotte's pregnancy was showing. She was a petite woman and she looked awkward and uncomfortable with her new size.

Charlotte saw Laura looking at her stomach, and she smiled. "I'm really getting big."

"I'm sorry, I didn't mean to stare," Laura said.

Charlotte giggled and said, "I don't mind."

"Congratulations."

"Why, thank you."

"When are you due?"

"In a little more than three months."

"Really?" Laura thought she looked like she was much farther along than that.

"I know," Charlotte said. "Everyone says for this early I'm showing a lot. A lot of people think that means I'm going to have twins. But it's only one baby. Dr. Chyles said so." She smiled again. "A boy."

"Well, I'd say he's going to be a pretty big boy."

Charlotte responded with another proud grin.

Laura guessed that Charlotte was in her early forties. She had a refined, gentle manner that Laura found pleasant. They had only just met, but already, Laura felt at ease with her.

"The realtor told me you were from Georgia," Laura said.

"That's right. From Columbus."

"Then you're a long way from home too."

"About two hundred miles. I guess that's a long way. But my husband and I want a child, so . . . here I am."

"There must be fertility clinics in Georgia. Aren't there any closer to where you live?"

"There are a few in Atlanta. We tried two of them, spent a fortune there, and none of it did any good. It took coming here for me to finally get pregnant. Dr. Chyles is supposed to be the best, you know."

"So I've heard. Well, I hope he can live up to his reputation."

"Oh, he can." Grinning, Charlotte patted her stomach. "Trust me," she said.

"We'll know in two weeks. My husband and I are keeping our fingers crossed."

They drove for a few minutes before coming to another house. As they approached it, Laura noticed a man come outside and head toward the Mercedes in the driveway. This was the same man she had seen yesterday carrying his wife into the clinic.

He brought two suitcases to the car and loaded them into the trunk. A few smaller bags were already in there, making it difficult for him to fit the larger ones in. Laura noticed that the back seat was also full, packed with boxes, a lamp, some plants.

"They must be leaving," Charlotte said.

"You know them?"

"They're the Aarons. I don't remember his first name, but hers is Dana. She's a patient too, you know. She must have had her baby."

"I saw them at the clinic yesterday," Laura said.

"Then you met them?"

"Not really. I saw them come in, that's all. She was very ill. He had to carry her."

"Oh dear. That's terrible."

"Was she having any problems that you know of?"

"Not that I know of. She seemed to be doing fine. But then, she and I weren't the closest friends."

"No?"

Charlotte seemed to want to explain. "To tell you the truth," she said, "I thought she was kind of abrasive."

"Abrasive?"

"You know, loud and pushy and a bit of a troublemaker. But I guess that comes from her job. She's a lawyer, up in Memphis, and you know how lawyers can be."

Laura chuckled. "I'm a lawyer."

Charlotte turned red with embarrassment. "What I meant was *some* lawyers have a bad image. Sometimes they can be——" She struggled for a moment, searching for the right word, then just gave up the thought altogether. "But I don't mean you," she said quickly. "You don't seem to be that way at all."

"Maybe that's because you don't know me very well. Give me a little time. I'll get on your nerves eventually."

"No, I can tell. You're not like that. I'm sure you're nice. Dana was nice, too. Don't get me wrong. But she was just one of those people who's always stirring things up. You know how some women can be?"

"I don't think women have a monopoly on that trait."

"You're right about that. I don't have anything against Dana. It's just that sometimes she can rub you the wrong way, that's all. For instance, I used to go in for my morning shots right after she did. I can't begin to tell you how many days I'd have to wait past my appointment time because she was asking one thing or another about this or that. She wanted to know every little detail about the clinic, about what the shots were, about why something was this way and not that way."

"Some people are naturally inquisitive."

"I know, but really. Sometimes you can go too far. I would have thought she'd be happy just being pregnant. You'd think that'd be enough. It is for me."

"It'll be enough for me, too," Laura admitted. "If it happens."

"Well, not for Dana. You know, she drives the nurses crazy. You can see that. And I don't think Dr. Chyles cares much for her, either. He didn't say so, but you could tell."

"He seemed very concerned about her when I saw her yesterday."

"Oh, yes, he's very good that way. Very concerned. You say she wasn't doing too well? It must have been a difficult delivery for her. I hope everything turned out all right."

"To tell you the truth, it left me a little concerned," Laura said.

"Oh, you don't need to be. Dr. Chyles is the best. He's just wonderful. I've been here for five months now and I haven't had any problems at all."

"That's good to hear."

Charlotte touched Laura's hand reassuringly. "Don't you worry, honey. Everything's going to be just fine."

As the nurse checked Laura's temperature and blood pressure, weighed her, and prepared to draw blood, she said, "My name is Gail and I'll be the one putting you through this every morning from now on. If there's ever any problem or if you have any questions, feel free to ask me."

Laura had one question already. "I was here yesterday when Dana Aaron was brought in by her husband. I was wondering how she was."

Gail looked uncomfortable. She spoke quietly. "Mrs. Aaron passed away last night."

Laura was stunned. "What happened?"

"I'm really not supposed to discuss one patient with another one. And I really don't know much anyway—just that she had a severe case of toxemia and Dr. Chyles wasn't able to stabilize her."

"Does that happen often?"

"Never. That was the first case." Gail glanced nervously at the door to make sure no one was coming, then she whispered, "Apparently, Mrs. Aaron had a history of hypertension and some other problems that she didn't tell the doctor. That's what caused the complications yesterday. And that's why it's so important that the doctor know everything."

"That's really tragic, what happened to her."

"Remember, you didn't hear it from me. Okay?"

The nurse brought the blood specimens to the lab for testing, leaving Laura alone in the examination room, thinking about Dana Aaron, growing more concerned and fearful as she waited. Fifteen minutes later, Dr. Chyles came in.

"Well, everything looks good," he said. "The blood tests show that we're right on target with the hormone levels."

He prepared the syringes for her injections, then wiped her arm with a sterile solution.

"I'm going to administer your shots today," he explained. "But normally one of the nurses will do it. I'll come in once a week to examine you personally and check your progress. Of course, if you have any problem or if you want to talk to me, just tell the nurses."

"I do have a question now," Laura said.

"Sure. What is it?"

"If this works and I get pregnant, what are the chances that there will be complications afterward?"

"Well, there's always a chance of complications, with all pregnancies, not only for women using assisted reproduction techniques, but for all women. I can tell you, though, that with the extensive monitoring we do, the chances of complications here are much lower than in the population as a whole. Most of the time, we can catch whatever it is before it develops into a serious problem, and we can usually take measures to prevent it. The percentage of women who have successful births here is much higher than at conventional obstetric practices."

His calm voice and reassuring manner left Laura feeling a little more confident. She felt fortunate to have him as her doctor, but she was still worried about what had happened to Dana Aaron.

"It's just that—" she said, having trouble putting her uncertainties into words. "I'm a little worried about what happened to the woman yesterday?" she said.

"Woman?"

"Dana Aaron. I was here when her husband brought her in. I heard that she died last night."

"Where did you hear that?"

"I overheard someone talking about it. She had toxemia, is that right? What happened?"

"Please understand," Chyles said, "as a physician, I'm prohibited from discussing a patient's medical history. Just as I wouldn't discuss your individual situation with another patient, I can't discuss another patient's with you. I'm sure you can appreciate that."

"Yes, of course. I didn't mean for you to violate any confidentiality."

"What I can tell you is that Mrs. Aaron's situation was unique," he said in a reassuring tone. "I can't really get into it, but trust me, it was completely unrelated to her treatment here."

Laura nodded, remembering what the nurse had said about Dana Aaron's not disclosing her entire medical history. If Chyles didn't know everything, how could he care for her properly? Laura had told Chyles everything.

"You need not be concerned about anything like that happening to you," Chyles said. "I can't emphasize this enough. If I thought you were going to have any problems whatsoever, I certainly would have pointed it out to you and your husband when you first came in, and we would have begun doing everything possible to minimize it right away, even now, this early."

"That's good to know," Laura said.

"I believe you're going to have a successful pregnancy, Laura, and a very healthy baby." He squeezed her arm comfortingly. "I assure you, you have no reason to be worried."

8

Laura and Charlotte had lunch together at Libby's Dinette, a small, friendly restaurant in town. Afterward, they went for a walk up Main Street, looking in the shop windows, enjoying the mild day. When they reached the park, they cut across the grass and sat for a while on a bench beneath a dogwood tree. The air smelled of freshly mowed lawn.

"I think I'm really going to like this little town," Laura said. "I was thinking that it would be a nice place to raise a child."

"It would be. It's very tranquil, very safe. It's a little like Columbus that way."

"It's nothing like New Orleans."

"Your husband is still down there, isn't he?"

"Yes. He's going to spend the weekends with me, but he has to stay in New Orleans for his work. How about your husband?"

"He's in Columbus. We own a restaurant there, right on the edge of the Chattahoochee River, a really nice location, and one of us needs to be there all the time. That's just the way the restaurant business is. Richard comes here when he can, but it's hard for him to get away."

"You two don't mind being apart for so long?"

"It really isn't that long. Altogether, it's only nine months."

"That seems like a long time to me," Laura said.

"Well, when you've been trying to have a baby for six years, nine months is nothing at all."

"I guess that's one way to look at it. Dan and I have been trying for two years, and that seems like a long time. I can't imagine trying for six years. That must have been really difficult. All the drugs and tests, not to mention all the poking and probing the doctors do. Sometimes it seems like I've been penetrated by more medical instruments than by men."

Charlotte laughed.

They sat for a while in silence, just taking in the beautiful afternoon. Laura noticed that Charlotte's mood changed now. She looked sad as she stared off at nothing.

"Charlotte, are you okay?"

Charlotte sighed. "I just hope it works," she said, her voice a frail whisper.

"Sure it will," Laura told her. "You're already pregnant, right? It already worked."

Charlotte looked at her. She didn't say anything for a long moment, then she turned away, looking ashamed. Laura saw tears well in her eyes.

"Charlotte?"

"What I mean is," Charlotte said, struggling to get the words out, "I hope it makes things better between Richard and me."

Charlotte's gaze fell to the ground as though she felt too humiliated to look directly at Laura. The words came with great effort. "He blames me," she said in a hush.

Laura just watched her, not sure she should say anything. She had met Charlotte only this morning; they barely knew each other. She felt uncomfortable pressing Charlotte for more, but it seemed Charlotte wanted to talk about it with someone.

"He blames you?" Laura asked finally.

Charlotte nodded. She took a long breath, needing the air before she could speak.

"He's wanted to have a child for so long," she said. "Probably even more than I did. A boy. A son to carry on his name."

"That's not unusual for men," Laura said.

Charlotte peeked up at Laura for only an instant, and in that brief look she could barely keep from crying. She said, "He blamed me that we couldn't have a child."

Laura took her hand, then just held her, not sure what to say.

"Things . . ." Charlotte said, pausing to wipe her nose and swallow hard. "Things haven't been very good between us. For a long time. Because of—that." She gazed down at her stomach and gently touched it. "Now we're going to have a child," she said, her voice cracking with something between sadness and joy. "A boy," she said. "I hope it makes things right between us."

She looked up at Laura.

"It has to, don't you think?" she asked Laura. "It has to make things right again."

"I think so," Laura whispered, seeing how vulnerable Charlotte was. How could she say anything different?

"I think so, too," Charlotte said. A dim but hopeful smile came to her face. "Yes, I think so, too."

Dan drove up to Collier on Saturday morning. He and Laura had spoken on the phone several times during the week, but Laura was still grateful to see him. She missed waking up beside him each morning, missed going to bed with him at night.

In the afternoon, Dan lit the grill outside and Laura made shrimp kabobs and grilled corn on the cob. They sat in the bench-swing under the willow tree and talked for hours about possible names for the baby. Later, they strolled through the fields behind the house, holding hands and kissing like newlyweds. In the last few months, Laura had forgotten how happy they could be together. Now that they were so close to having a child, it felt like a great pressure had been lifted from them. It felt like they were falling in love all over again.

But all the while they were together, she kept thinking about Charlotte and the problems she and her husband were having. It was sad that Charlotte thought she *needed* to have a baby to save their marriage. Not only was it sad, it also made Laura uneasy. She wondered how close she and Dan had come to that same point in their marriage. Were they trying to have a baby because they *wanted* to, or was it because, like Charlotte and her husband, they *needed* to?

On Sunday, they slept late, went to the clinic for Laura's shots, then took a drive along the country roads and explored Alabama. They were an hour north of Collier when they decided to stop for gas and something to drink at a small country store. The store was the only sign of life on this long stretch of road, far removed from any towns, which was why as they approached, they were surprised by the black Saab pulling out of the dirt parking lot. They weren't surprised by the car itself, but by who was in it: Dr. Chyles and Dr. Acer.

"Do you think they live out here?" Laura asked.

"Can't be. It's too far from the clinic. They must be out for a drive. I guess we're not the only ones out here wasting gas."

The clerk inside knew right away that Laura and Dan were patients from the clinic. "The tags on your car, the way you dress, your age," he said with a friendly chuckle. "It's obvious."

"It's always nice to be reduced to a stereotype," Dan said.

"We're glad to have you here," the clerk said. "Louisiana money is as good as any to me. You know, your doctor was just in here."

"Yes, we saw them leaving," Laura said. "We were wondering if they lived near here."

"No, I don't think so. They just pass this way on the way to Montgomery. Come through two or three times a week."

"What's in Montgomery?" Dan said.

"Hell if I know. He don't say much, the doctor. Not one for talking, is he? They just stop, he pumps gas, she buys a Milky Way bar. Always a Milky Way. Then they're on their way again. Must have kin up in Montgomery."

Dan suggested it might be business.

"Don't think so," the clerk said. "Usually they come through nights and Sundays. So, what brings y'all out here today?"

The clerk talked so much that it took Laura and Dan 20 minutes to get out of the store. They followed a different route back to Collier. On the way, they found a roadside fruit stand set up in front of an orchard. No one attended the stand, but there were baskets of peaches and jars of freshly made preserves set out for people to buy. In the middle of the table was a wooden box with a slot cut into the top for putting the money in. Customers were on the honor system to pay for whatever they took and not steal the money left by others. Laura and Dan couldn't get over it.

"Can you imagine someone doing this in New Orleans?" Laura said.

"Yeah, right. The guy would sell out everything in ten minutes and make about a penny, if that much."

"I never imagined that people still live like this. I'll bet people leave their doors unlocked all the time and aren't afraid to go for walks at night. They probably don't have any real crime around here."

"Don't be deceived by the way it looks on the surface," Dan said. "They have their share of crime around here, just like anywhere else. They just keep it hidden better."

"You're just jaded by city life."

"And you're just blinded by the pretty scenery and the quaint way the people act. Trust me, Laura, this place has its share of murderers and rapists and God knows what else."

"I don't believe that."

"Believe what you want to. But I'm just telling you, I don't want you leaving the doors unlocked or taking walks at night."

Laura wrapped her arms around him. "You're so cute when you worry about me."

"You want to see cute, you should see me naked with a rose in my mouth."

Laura smirked. "That sounds like fun. Let's try that tonight."

"Play your cards right and you might be in for a treat."

They bought several jars of preserves and a couple of baskets of peaches, and when they got home, Laura baked a cobbler. She felt a welcome sense of tranquillity being so far removed from the stress and pressures of New Orleans, of her job, of the life she'd left a week before. Spending her days making the house livable, cooking, reading, taking walks along the shady lane in front of the house, made her feel domestic for the first time in her life—and it fit comfortably on her. She wondered if this was what it was like before women started working full time. She realized now just how much modern women had given up.

Dan left early Monday morning. Laura was sad to see him go. They stood on the porch and kissed as the sun came up. Laura watched him drive away. She waited until his car was out of sight before she went back inside.

Not once over the weekend had she considered that she might not get pregnant or might not carry the baby to term. Not once did she think anything other than that they *would* have a child. She was absolutely sure of it. She even believed she could feel it coming to life inside her.

The next weekend, Dan had to work, but he drove up early Monday morning so he could be with her when she learned the results of her pregnancy test.

This morning, Chyles himself came in to examine her. He instructed the nurse to draw two syringes of blood, then had Laura go behind the curtain in the corner of the room and give him a urine sample.

"We'll have the results in about an hour," he told her.

She and Dan waited in the cafeteria, sipping juice and saying very little. Laura felt frail and vulnerable. She couldn't stop worrying about what would happen, what the results would be. Dan reached across the table and wrapped his hands around hers. She was cold and trembling.

"Are you okay?" he asked quietly, as though the emotions they both were feeling were much too private for the half-dozen other patients in the cafeteria to hear discussed.

"I'm afraid," she whispered.

"It's going to be all right."

"But what if the results are negative?"

He shushed her. "It's still going to be all right," he said. "Okay?" She didn't respond, so he squeezed her hands and said it again. "Okay? It's going to be all right no matter what happens."

She nodded and held tightly to his hands. She wished she could believe that their marriage was different from Charlotte's, that theirs didn't need a child, but she had doubts. If having a child wasn't so important, wasn't absolutely necessary, they would not have come 300 miles and spent $16,000 to have one. Their problems might not be as obvious as the problems in Charlotte's marriage, but Laura did feel that she and Dan needed a baby to make things right.

At what point it had happened, she wasn't sure, but somewhere along the way, she and Dan had grown apart. They hadn't stopped loving each other—not exactly. Rather, they had stopped being an integral part of each other's lives. She had her world of work and friends; Dan had his. The world that was *theirs* seemed to have become steadily smaller until it was little more than the few hours each morning and each evening when they encountered each other on the way to and from their separate worlds. Sure, she still cared dearly about him and believed he felt the same way about her, but they shared nothing; they had a common stake in nothing.

A child would give them a new bond. A child would merge their worlds. A child—the age-old reason men and women wed—would fill the void that threatened to open wider, so wide they would not be able to close it again. She felt that without a child, their marriage would not endure.

Yes, they did need this baby. Their lives together came down to this hour.

"I love you," she whispered.

Dan leaned across the table and kissed her. "I love you too." And in his eyes, she saw the same desperation that was in her heart.

Holding hands, they walked into Chyles's office. He shook hands with them and gestured for them to sit. Laura felt unsteady, her stomach churning. She watched Chyles anxiously, trying to read the doctor's expression as he reviewed the computer printout on his desk. Dan put his arm around her and held her tightly. She was trembling.

Finally, Chyles looked up at them. "I have the results of your tests," he said. He paused and smiled. "They were positive."

Laura sank into Dan, overwhelmed with joy. "Thank God," she said, almost crying. She steadied herself, then thanked Chyles.

"I should point out," Chyles said, "that we can't be one

hundred percent certain of the embryo's viability until we do an ultrasound to make sure there's a fetal heartbeat. We'll do that in about five weeks. But right now, all indications are good. Congratulations!"

9

Now that she was pregnant, Laura began receiving daily injections of the hormones that Dr. Chyles explained were engineered specifically to assist the fetal development in "uncooperative hosts." Laura found it odd thinking of herself in those terms, but she realized that in the unemotional terminology of science, an uncooperative host was exactly what her body was.

A few minutes after the first series of injections, while she was still in the examination room getting dressed, she doubled over and threw up. Gail, the nurse, called an orderly to clean the mess and told Laura that vomiting was a normal reaction. The hormones just seemed to intensify normal morning sickness, she said, and added sympathetically, "All the patients learn to accept it."

Dr. Chyles made it a point to come back in after Laura was dressed and he assured her that she and the fetus were doing fine.

"The severity of your nausea should pass quickly," he said. "If it doesn't, let us know, but I'm sure you'll be feeling much better in no time at all."

Laura vomited again when she got home, and then again the next morning upon awakening. For the first week, this became part of her daily routine, but finally her symptoms settled down, and while the discomfort did not cease completely, it did become less severe. She still felt nauseated most days, but she didn't actually throw up as often. What got her through it was the realization that she was doing it for their baby. She could endure it for their baby.

Because she felt ill most of the week, she didn't get any legal work done. The next week, she called her secretary at the law firm and told her which files to send over. She also ordered a computer, printer, and fax machine from an office-supply superstore in Montgomery and had the phone company put in a second line for the fax.

When everything came, she set up the fax machine and plugged in all the cords for the computer and printer with no problem, but when she tried to turn on the computer, it would not work. Instead of booting up, a message flashed on the screen: SYSTEM DISK ERROR.

For the next two days, she worked without the computer until a technician came down from Montgomery. The man found the problem right away.

"It's your hard drive," he said. "The files the CPU needs to boot up are missing. That's what the system disk error message means." He booted the computer from a floppy disk, then entered a few commands. "Looks like your whole hard drive is blank," he said. "Did someone erase everything?"

"I sure didn't. I haven't even used it yet. The computer's brand new."

"Sometimes the factory forgets to preload the software. Doesn't happen often, but it does happen. If you have the disks, I can load it all on for you."

It took him two hours to load Laura's programs into the computer and fine-tune the settings. When he finished, it ran perfectly.

The next day, her secretary tried to fax her some contracts, but the machine jammed when the first sheet of paper went through. The repairman couldn't come again until the following Monday.

Laura didn't get much work done that week, either. Instead she spent much of the time sitting on the porch or under the weeping willow tree, reading, enjoying the tranquillity of country life. She and Charlotte met for lunch a couple times and on Thursday night went to the movies together at the only theater in Collier.

By Friday, Laura was feeling bored and lonely for her husband's company. Dan would be coming that evening to spend the weekend with her, and the anticipation of his arrival was the only thing that got her through the day.

Late in the afternoon, while she was at her computer, working, the phone rang. It was Dan.

"Where are you?" she asked.

"At the studio."

She looked at the clock. It was almost five. If he was still in New Orleans, there was no way he would get to Collier before eleven that night.

"I thought you left a long time ago. You'd better leave right away. You know how the traffic is on Fridays."

"Honey," he said in a voice that instantly caused her spirits to fall, "things are taking longer than I thought. I'm still shooting. I'm going to be stuck here awhile."

"No, don't say that," she said quietly.

"How do you think I feel? If I could have left earlier, I would have. You know that."

"I know." She sighed. "You go ahead and finish what you have to. I'll wait up for you."

"You're going to hate me for this, but I really don't think I can make it at all this weekend. The agency decided to change the whole concept for the ad we're doing, so now I have to reshoot. I mean, they're paying through the nose, but I'll have to shoot tomorrow and probably Sunday too."

Laura slumped back in her chair. "That's not fair."

"I know. I'm really sorry, but it just can't be helped."

"I wanted to see you."

"I want to see you too. But this is a good client. I really need to do this. And you know we can use the money."

"I know."

"You mad?"

"No. I'm just—" She sighed and said, "It's lonely up here by myself."

"It's lonely here too without you."

"It'd better be." She said it with a bitter tone, but then

she broke into a laugh and said, "If you know what's good for you, it'd better be. Are you eating okay?" she asked.

"New Orleans has one or two decent restaurants. I think I'll be all right."

"Smart ass."

They talked for another 10 minutes about how Laura was feeling and how everything was going at the clinic, then Dan had to get back to work. Laura hung up, dreading the long weekend alone but accepting that it was all part of the sacrifice necessary to have a baby. For the baby, she could survive another week without seeing her husband. For the baby, she could put up with quite a bit.

She worked for another half-hour at the computer, then started to go out onto the porch for a little fresh air and to watch the sunset. As she opened the front door, something moved past her on the porch, startling her. She jumped back and for a moment lost her breath. It all happened so quickly that she didn't see it clearly. All she saw was a white blur. She didn't know what it was, but she was sure something was out there, something small and quick, and it wasn't a leaf or a bird as she had assumed when she saw the same thing a couple of weeks ago. This time she was sure it was some kind of animal.

She heard a faint thud on the boards to the side, out of view from where she was standing. It sounded like an animal scurrying across the porch. Then there was silence. She stood frozen in the middle of the room, staring at the open door. A shiver arose deep inside her, one that triggered a keen sense of unease.

She had seen that thing before—whatever it was—and had dismissed it. But this time she could not ignore it. The door was open and the animal so near that it frightened her.

A moment passed before she could move. Hesitantly, she crept toward the door, fearing that whatever was out there might lunge in at her. When she was an arm's length from the door, she reached out and flung it shut, then rushed over and threw the latch. Only now could she breathe easily, feeling safe.

She caught a glimpse of herself in the mirror by the coat rack and had to laugh at the sight. *How much more foolish could I be?* she thought now. *Jumping at the sight of an animal outside the door, acting as though it were a monster.* Whatever it was, it was nothing, she realized, a raccoon or an opossum or one of the other harmless animals that lived in the nearby woods. She had no need to be afraid.

Even though she knew there was nothing outside for her to fear, she no longer wanted to sit on the porch and watch the sunset. She felt more comfortable now that she was inside, so she went to the kitchen to make dinner.

As she started to open the refrigerator door, she heard something jump onto the back porch, the same thudding sound she had heard in front. Instantly, her uneasiness returned, but she told herself it was nothing to fear. She had to stop being so excitable.

She went to the sink, leaned over so she could see out the window, and peered at the porch outside. There was nothing there. She looked a moment longer to see if whatever was out there would move into view, but nothing did. Shrugging it off, she returned to the refrigerator.

That's when the thing outside scratched at the door.

Laura wheeled around so fast she almost fell. The scraping sound frightened her. It was as if the animal's claws were scratching the bones of her spine. She heard three long scrapes. Then there was a pause, then three more scrapes.

One thought filled her head: *Whatever's out there is trying to come inside.*

Her first impulse was to call the police, but then she realized how foolish it would sound to them. You don't call the police when an animal scratches at your door. Perhaps you contact the Humane Society, but not the police. She assumed the Humane Society was closed at this hour. But even if they weren't, they probably wouldn't come out for something like this; it was insignificant. She kept telling herself that over and over: *It's insignificant. It happens all the time in the country.*

But no matter how many times she told herself that, no matter how irrational she knew her fear was, she could not shake it.

What kind of animal does this? she wondered. And she trembled to think of the answer.

She stared at the door, unable to move. Fear over-whelmed her, expelling all reason and rationality. The only explanation her mind could form was that the creature was trying to get inside so it could hurt her, and that made no sense to her at all.

The scraping continued for a moment longer, then sud-denly ceased. A silence followed, a silence as absolute as her recognition that she was completely alone. That realization left her even more nervous.

She waited more than a minute to see if whatever was out there would try again to come inside. The time passed slowly. The thing out there did not scratch at the door again. But instead of putting Laura at ease, the silence only heightened her anxiety. Since she didn't hear the animal move away, she did not feel the slightest relief.

She needed to know what it was. From the window over the sink, she couldn't see that part of the porch, so she went to the window close to the door. Gently, she brushed open the curtain just an inch and peered out. She had to get close to the glass to see the bottom of the door, and as she moved slowly toward it, she started trembling again. She kept thinking that the animal out there was going to smash through the glass and bite her face.

Her forehead was almost against the glass when she finally glimpsed the animal beside the door. The moment she saw it, she fell back in relief and once again laughed at herself.

It was a cat. A scrawny white cat.

When her nerves finally settled, she went to the door. A cat was not a threat, she told herself. What it could be, though, was company for her. And that was something she could use. With a lonely weekend ahead and a long week after that, she thought it might be nice to have a little pet around so she wouldn't feel so isolated.

She opened the door slowly, not wanting to scare the cat away. When the cat saw her, it did not budge. It just sat on the wooden porch, staring up at her.

Immediately, she recognized it, the white and orange coat, the emaciated body, the abnormal shape of the head—the absence of ears.

"I know you," she said.

This was the cat she and Dan almost ran over the first day they went to the clinic. It had been in the middle of the road, eating a dead squirrel.

"Remember me?" Laura said.

The cat's eyes had the same red cast that Laura remembered seeing weeks ago, but today, they did not look as feral, as threatening. Its oval head and lack of ears inspired only pity.

"You look lost," Laura said.

The road where she and Dan first encountered the cat was at least 10 miles away. Laura wasn't certain, but she thought that 10 miles was an awfully long distance for a cat to travel, especially one as small and malnourished as this one.

"You certainly do get around," she said. "But you look like you don't eat much."

The cat just stared up at her, not reacting at all to her voice.

"You don't belong to anyone, do you?"

The cat continued watching her, not moving.

"No, I didn't think so. How about something to eat? Would you like that?"

Laura backed away from the threshold, leaving the door open so the cat could come in if it wanted. She went to the cupboard and got one of the cans of tuna that she had bought in Collier last week. She emptied it into a soup bowl and set it on the floor just inside the doorway. The cat sniffed at the air for a moment, then got up and came inside, not showing the least bit of caution.

"You *are* hungry, aren't you?" Laura said.

The cat sniffed the bowl for a moment, then sat next to it and looked up at Laura, as though waiting for something better.

Laura chuckled. "That's all you're getting," she said. "Either you eat that or you find yourself another squirrel. It's up to you."

The cat held out a moment longer, watching her with an absent stare, as though it weren't really seeing her or perhaps didn't quite understand what it was that it was looking at. At last it stuck its head into the bowl and began eating. Within a minute or so, it devoured the entire dish of tuna.

"I guess you really were hungry."

Laura poured some coffee cream into another bowl, diluted it with water from the tap, then set it on the floor. The cat slurped it up right away. When the cat was finished, it sat on the floor and stared at her, waiting for more.

"That's it for now," Laura said. "We don't want to overdo it."

The cat remained behind the bowl, staring at her, waiting for more. With a sigh, Laura relented and poured in a little more cream. As the cat drank that, Laura thought that something was odd about this animal, something more than just the missing ears.

Perhaps it was the blank look in its eyes that struck her as strange. She wasn't sure. Or maybe it was that the cat did not purr. A lot of cats purr when they eat. This cat, however, made no sound at all beyond the chewing and slurping. Maybe that was it. Or maybe it was everything combined. Whatever the reason, she could not stop thinking how strange this cat was.

But its abnormalities only deepened the sympathy she felt for it: this poor, scrawny cat, alone in the woods, underfed, unable to hear. Surely it would die out there in the wild. Its deafness alone put it in jeopardy. It wouldn't be able to detect cars speeding down the road or catch predators sneaking up on it. She was surprised it had lasted this long.

"Hey, little fella," she said, squatting down in front of it. "Do you want to stick around here for a while? I'm all alone. You're all alone. We can keep each other company. What do you say? Does that sound okay?"

She reached out to pet it. As her hand stroked its back, its fur felt unusually coarse and cold. The cat did not react at all to her touch. It just stared off across the kitchen, as though it did not even feel her hand, as though she weren't even there.

"There's plenty of room for both of us," she said. "What do you say?"

Laura stood and walked to the door.

"You'd better speak now or forever hold your peace," she said.

She hesitated a moment, giving the cat a chance to leave if that's what it wanted. But it didn't budge. It stayed in the kitchen, so she closed the door and decided to keep it.

"Welcome to your new home," she said.

She went to the refrigerator and started to make a sandwich for herself. The cat walked to the window and hopped up onto the sill. There it sat and stared at her.

"How about Felix? Do you like that name? That's what I'll call you, Felix the Cat."

It acted cool and aloof, not at all a cuddly pet. But they were new to each other, Laura told herself. Felix would warm to her once it was here awhile, once it felt comfortable. And anyway, she thought, it was still company. Even as aloof as it was now, at least having it around would keep her from feeling so alone.

10

The next Saturday, Dan had to work again, but he drove up from the city that night so he and Laura could be together on Sunday. After a late dinner, they spent the evening catching up on what each of them had been doing over the past two weeks, then they went to bed. Dan was tired from the drive and from working all day, so they didn't make love that night. Instead they held each other for a while, then went to sleep.

Laura let him sleep late Sunday morning. She drove to the clinic alone to get her shots, and when she returned at 11:00, she woke him with a kiss.

"Ummmm." He licked his lips and gazed up at her. "That sure beats the alarm clock." He took her by the hands and started to pull her into bed with him.

"We don't have time this morning, sweetheart," Laura said. "We have to be at the birthday party at twelve-thirty."

"What birthday party?"

"I told you about it, didn't I?"

"Told me about what?"

"Dr. Chyles is having a birthday party at his house today."

"Isn't he a little old for that sort of thing?"

"It's not for him. It's for all the babies born at the clinic. It's been one year since the first baby was born, and Dr. Chyles is throwing a party for all the couples who had babies since then and for the couples like us who are expecting now. It should be fun."

"Sounds like a barrel of laughs." He closed his eyes. "Wake me up when you get back."

"Come on, Dan. All the babies will be there."

"So?"

"Don't you want to see the babies?"

"The only baby I'm interested in," he said, sitting up and putting his arms around Laura, "is this one"—he kissed her stomach—"the one in here."

Laura's body tingled. It had been a long time since she felt so much love from him. Having this baby was definitely going to make their marriage stronger. It was happening already.

Dan continued kissing her stomach, slowly working his way up her body. When he started to unbutton her blouse, she grabbed his hair and pulled his head away.

"I really want to go to this party," she said.

"We can have our own party."

She peered down at him resolutely. He knew he couldn't win.

"Let me take a shower first," he said.

"Better make it a cold one."

While he showered, she put on a light dress. It was the end of July. The party was supposed to be outdoors, and Laura knew it would be hot and humid. She was glad she had undergone the *in vitro* when she did; this way she wouldn't be her heaviest until winter arrived and the weather cooled.

It was too hot for a sports coat, so Dan wore a polo shirt and khakis. He smelled of cologne when he came over and hugged Laura from behind. The house felt very different with him around, so full of life. She wished he could stay all the time, but she knew it couldn't be. Eight more months, she told herself. It would pass quickly.

As they were leaving, they found a dead mouse lying on the porch by the front door, a thin puddle of blood surrounding it.

"How the hell did that get there?" Dan said.

"Do you think Felix could have put it there?"

"Who?"

"Didn't I tell you? I sort of adopted a stray cat last weekend. It gets lonely here and I thought it would be nice to have some company."

"Not if it's going to bring dead rats around."

"It's a mouse, not a rat."

"Laura, it's a rat, believe me."

"Well, maybe the mouse or rat or whatever you want to call it was already here and Felix just killed it for us. Did you ever think of it that way? He did us a service."

"I don't care one way or the other. I just don't want dead rats around here. They're full of germs. So are cats, for that matter. Having that thing around here, you could get sick."

"That's ridiculous."

"No it isn't. You have to start thinking about the baby now too, Laura."

Dan went inside and got yesterday's newspaper, then came back out and bent down over the rodent. As he was about to scoop it up, the cat leaped up onto the porch rail and hissed at him.

"You're already on shaky ground around here," Dan told the cat. "If you want to stick around, you'd better learn to keep your damn rats to yourself. Do you hear?"

The cat hissed again, a long, vicious hiss, teeth bared, eyes blood-red.

Dan looked over his shoulder at Laura. "Real nice kitty

you have, honey." Then he slid the newspaper under the rat and started to pick it up.

With a loud shriek, the cat flew off the rail and covered the length of the porch in two quick bounds. It was on Dan before he could react, clawing wildly at his shirt. When Dan swiped at it to knock it away, it scratched his arm, drawing three streaks of blood on his wrist. Just as quickly as it attacked, it snatched up the rat in its teeth and leaped off the porch, running across the yard and into the woods.

"Damn it!" Dan shouted, holding his arm. He turned to Laura. "I'm bleeding."

Laura was stunned. She had never seen this much animation in the cat before. "I don't know what got into him," she said. "He's never like that."

"That's one vicious goddamn cat you have, Laura."

"Are you all right, honey?" She came over and checked his hand.

"He cut me."

"It's just a scratch."

"My ass, it's just a scratch. It's a gouge. I'm bleeding. And look at what he did to my shirt. Jesus, Laura, it's torn."

"Come on inside. You can change your shirt. I'll wash your hand and put a bandage on it for you."

"Get rid of that cat."

"He's the only company I have up here."

"He's dangerous."

"He's not dangerous."

"Don't tell me he's not dangerous. And what if he has rabies? Did you ever stop to think about that?"

"He doesn't have rabies. He was just protecting his food, that's all."

"Bull. He's no damn good, I'm telling you that right now. Get rid of him, Laura, because if you don't and he scratches me again, or scratches you and it hurts our baby, so help me, God . . . "

To look at the expensive sedans parked on the street in front of Dr. Chyles's house, you would think it was the Slidell Country Club, not someone's home deep in the

Alabama woods. Most of the cars had license plates from out of state. Many had baby seats in them, a sight that brought Laura a shiver of anticipation.

Dan parked on the grass shoulder down the street from the house. It was shady here and Laura didn't mind the walk. They held hands like schoolkids.

Dr. Chyles lived in a sprawling antebellum mansion, tucked discreetly behind a wall of trees and shrubbery. Some scaffolding was erected along one wall, where renovations were under way. Lumber was stacked near the side. No one was working today.

Dr. Acer answered the door and apologized for the house's being unfinished. She explained that they had remodeled the entire place after moving in. "It was just unlivable when we bought it," she said, "but it had such charm and potential that we couldn't resist."

She took them through the house, showing off the work they had done. It was very modern inside, in contrast to the outside. The floors were marble and hardwood, the rooms large and full of light. Their bathtub looked like a small swimming pool. The kitchen belonged in a restaurant.

"Do you cook much?" Laura asked.

"I wish I could, but I don't have the time."

Laura thought the house was beautiful, no doubt about that, but with all the changes they had made, the charm Dr. Acer mentioned had definitely been lost. The flavor of Alabama a century ago was no longer here. This house could be anywhere.

When Dr. Acer discovered that Dan was a photographer, she made it a point to show him her husband's photographs. Several hung in each room, all of them shots of coastal cliffs, waves crashing against rocks, seagulls, murky beaches.

"Yes, very nice," Dan said about each picture, feigning a smile all the while.

"Aren't they just wonderful?" Dr. Acer said. "They're so emotive."

"Emotive—yes, that's it exactly," Dan said.

Dr. Acer didn't catch the sarcasm in his voice, but Laura did. She looked at him wryly when Dr. Acer turned to go into the next room. Dan chuckled to himself and followed the woman.

She took them to the study and had them sit while she showed Dan a photo album with more of Chyles's pictures. Dan flipped through them quickly, nodding approvingly. Laura, sitting beside him, kept saying *oh* and *ah,* hoping Dan would flip even faster.

When they reached the end, there was one photograph that was loose, upside down. Dan turned it over for a quick, obligatory look.

This picture was different from all the others. Instead of a seascape, this one was a shot of Dr. Chyles and his wife, sitting in front of a small house. Between them was a child, a boy no older than a year or so. A beautiful baby, Laura thought. Seeing Dr. Chyles's features in the boy's face, she asked, "Is this your son?"

Dr. Acer looked surprised that the photograph was there. She took the album from Dan and closed the picture inside it. "Yes," she said quietly as she put the album back on the shelf.

"How old is he now?" Laura asked. Chyles and Acer had looked younger in the picture.

"That was taken four years ago. Let me take you to the pool area," she said, eager to change the subject. "I'm sure you'd like to meet the other patients and see the babies."

Dan and Laura exchanged a silent look, both of them noticing Dr. Acer's discomfort when discussing her son. They did not mention the boy again.

The pool area was crowded with patients, eating and drinking, talking and laughing. Among them were a few senior staff members from the clinic. Laura recognized a couple of the nurses and one of the technicians from the lab. Dr. Acer pointed out the barn in the distance as she brought Dan and Laura outside.

"That's going to be our next project," she said. "We're going to convert it into a spa. There'll be a sauna, a hot tub, an exercise room, a tanning bed, everything."

"Yes, I can see it," Dan said. "The barn seems to be calling out for that, doesn't it?"

"Dr. Chyles and I think so."

Dr. Acer missed the sarcasm again. Laura elbowed him in the ribs. He chuckled and didn't say any more.

"Dr. Chyles puts in such long hours at the clinic," Dr. Acer said. "He needs a place like that where he can unwind afterward."

"Well, that should be nice," Laura said.

"We had one at our old house, before moving here. The sauna was especially nice in the winter, when everything was cold and damp. You can really appreciate something like that then."

"Yes, I can imagine so."

"We did so much work on that place I really hated to leave it." She forced a smile. "But I'm glad we're here now. I really like living here."

Laura could see that she was lying.

Dr. Acer left to greet another couple, leaving Dan and Laura on the patio, speculating on how much this place must have cost and how much Chyles must be pulling in from his practice. But Laura told Dan that as long as the doctor was helping couples have babies, it didn't make any difference how much he earned. Dan didn't say any more about it, but Laura could tell that the obvious wealth irritated him.

"Another thing," he said. "Did you notice how she kept referring to him as Dr. Chyles instead of Norman? What's with that?"

"That's just the way some people are. It's not unusual."

"I hate that kind of pretentiousness."

Looking at the other couples here, Laura noticed that most of the husbands gravitated to the liquor table, where a young man in a white shirt hastily mixed drinks and poured champagne. The women were content to leave the men to themselves and their talk of business and sports, opting instead to huddle around the mothers who had brought along their newborn babies to show them off like prizes.

While Laura and Dan were still taking it all in, Dr. Chyles came over and shook hands, thanking them for coming.

"We wouldn't have missed this for anything," Laura told him. "We really wanted to see the babies."

"One of us did, anyway," Dan said.

Laura elbowed him again.

Chyles laughed. "It's all right, Laura. It's always the women who want to see the babies. The men are usually dragged along kicking and screaming."

"Men have better things to do, that's why," Dan said.

Dan was trying to be humorous, but Laura detected an edge to his tone. Chyles didn't notice, fortunately. Or if he did notice, he didn't show it. He never stopped grinning, looking as proud of all the babies as the parents themselves were.

"You have a beautiful home, Doctor," Laura said.

"Thank you. My wife fixed it up nicely. She has a flair for that type of thing."

"She showed us your photographs." Laura looked at Dan. "They were good, weren't they, honey?"

"Yeah, they're good."

"You really think so? I'm not a professional like you are," Chyles said, "but I enjoy it."

The two of them talked awhile about camera equipment and darkroom techniques, none of which Laura understood. When they had exhausted the subject, Chyles asked them what they thought of the area, how Laura liked living here.

"It has its advantages and disadvantages," she said. "I miss all the activity of New Orleans, but it's nice living out in the country for a while too. The pace is much slower. If you can get used to it, it's very relaxing. Oh," she said, remembering, "did I mention that we saw you and your wife one day while we were out for a ride? Remember, Dan?"

"Yeah, that was a couple weeks ago, wasn't it?"

"That's right." She looked back at Chyles. "We were about an hour north of here. I don't know exactly where it was, what it was near. Do you, Dan?"

"No, I don't remember."

"Anyway, we stopped to get gas and just as we were pulling in, you and your wife were pulling out. I guess you didn't see us."

"No. No, we didn't."

"The clerk at the store said you go by there quite a bit on your way to Montgomery."

"Yes, we travel quite a bit."

Chyles glanced around, looking restless. Laura assumed he must have noticed new arrivals whom he needed to greet.

"You two must be hungry," he said. "There's plenty of food and drinks over there. Help yourselves. And Laura, remember, only nonalcoholic drinks for you."

He thanked them again for coming, then left to greet other guests.

"You two have a lot in common," Laura said to Dan.

"Give me a break."

"What do you mean? The way you two were talking about photography, it looked like you were really hitting it off."

"Honey, I was just being nice. He's not a good photographer. He doesn't know half of what he's talking about. He should stick to doctoring and leave photography to people who know what they're doing."

Laura was surprised. Dan acted like he was angry.

"I don't know," she said. "I thought his pictures were pretty good."

"That shows you how much you know."

The sharpness of the remark stunned her.

"What's wrong with you?" she said.

He forced a chuckle and kissed her on the cheek. "Just kidding," he said. "About you. Not about Chyles. I mean for God's sake, all his pictures are the same thing, the same shot. His subject matter is the whole thing. Give a two-year-old a Nikon, you'll get the same picture. It's impossible not to get a good shot of a coastline like that. The ocean does all the work. The photographer doesn't have to do much of anything. It's all point and shoot, nothing to it."

"I never thought of it that way."

"See, I know what I'm talking about. Trust me."

Laura shrugged. "Well, they're still powerful images."

"Credit Mother Nature, not your Dr. Chyles."

Laura didn't say any more about it. It wasn't worth fighting over. But Dan had still more to get off his chest.

"Chyles is a pompous ass, if you ask me," he said.

Laura shushed him. She looked around to make sure no one could hear them, then asked, "Why do you say that?"

"He's so full of himself it's sickening."

"I don't get that impression at all. He seems like a nice man. I'd say he's proud of his work. He's confident, but not arrogant."

"Honey, let's face it, you're not able to be objective about him."

"What's that supposed to mean?"

"You're pregnant."

"What does that have to do with anything?"

"It's simple. You credit him for your pregnancy, so you view him favorably. It's only natural. You don't see the real person."

"And I suppose you do?"

"As a matter of fact, I do."

"Oh yeah? How many times have you seen him? Four times? I've seen him a lot more than you have, talked to him a lot more, so I think I have a little better handle on the man than you do."

"Why are you defending him?"

"I'm not defending him. I'm just pointing out that you don't know him as well as I do. And for you to say——"

"Yeah, okay, whatever," he said. He tried to act like he didn't care one way or the other, but Laura could tell he was a little perturbed that she wouldn't agree with him.

"Look, I need a drink," he said. "How about you? Some club soda or juice or something."

"No thanks."

"I'll see you in a little bit," he said and walked away.

Laura watched him go to the bar, still struck by his strange behavior. He clearly had a problem with Chyles, but she couldn't imagine why.

Charlotte Wheeler came over now and saw Laura watching Dan.

"Is that your husband?" she asked. "He's cute."

"I wish I could say the same about his disposition today. I don't know what's gotten into him all of a sudden."

"I'll bet I know. He doesn't like being here. Right?"

"It's more than that. Out of the blue, he doesn't like Dr. Chyles. I don't understand it."

Charlotte dismissed it with a chuckle. "Laura, honey, you shouldn't let that bother you. None of the husbands like Dr. Chyles. Didn't you know that?"

"What are you talking about?"

"It's not hard to figure it out. Remember the saying here at the clinic? 'If your husband can't make you pregnant, Dr. Chyles can.' Well, look at it from the men's perspective. Dr. Chyles is the one who made their wives pregnant. They didn't do it themselves—another man did it, and that bothers the heck out of them."

"That's ridiculous."

"I know that, but it's a macho thing."

"That's stupid."

"That's men," Charlotte said. "They know it took going to Dr. Chyles for us to get pregnant. What's more, they know that *we* know it, and that's a threat to their manhood. It's almost like we cheated on them with Dr. Chyles."

"Oh, come on."

"And what's worse, they had to *pay* Dr. Chyles to let it happen."

Laura laughed about the whole thing, but in the back of her mind she admitted to herself that there might be some truth to Charlotte's explanation. Nothing else made sense.

Charlotte changed the subject now.

"Have you seen the birthday boy yet?" she asked.

"Not yet."

"Oh, you just have to see him."

She took Laura by the hand and led her to a group of women gathered around a mother and her child. "Come closer and take a look," she said, pulling her toward the middle where the child was.

The mother appeared to be about the same age as Laura. She was sitting on a patio chair, balancing a young boy on her knee. For a 1-year-old, the child had difficulty sitting upright; his mother had to support him. Charlotte, who had already met the woman, introduced Laura.

"Congratulations," Laura said to the woman. "He's a beautiful boy."

"Thank you." The woman was beaming. "My husband and I are so happy."

Laura knelt down in front of the boy and gently pinched his chin. "And happy birthday to you," she said. He did not react at all.

The baby just sat still, oblivious to everything going on around him. He was small, Laura thought, smaller than 1-year-olds should be, but she noticed that his mother was a small woman and just assumed that it was in the genes.

But something else about the baby struck her as odd. She didn't know exactly what it was, but something seemed unusual.

Another woman came over to see the child, so Laura moved away. She watched the woman pat the boy on the head, a gesture that reminded her of someone petting a kitten or puppy.

"He's so calm around people," the woman said.

"Yes he is—usually," the mother said. She giggled and said, "Last month, while we were at the pediatrician's office, another little boy—a three-year-old—came over and tried to get Robby to play with him. I was talking to the nurse, so I don't know what the other boy did, but all of a sudden, Robby snapped at him, tried to bite him. I had to run over and pull him away, and it wasn't easy, believe me."

She looked down at her son. "You made the older boy cry, didn't you?" she said, sounding almost proud of it. She looked up at the other mothers. "I don't know where he gets his temper from. His father never loses it like that. Neither do I. But he's still my little pride and joy."

She wrapped her arms around the boy and squeezed him. Turning him around so that he was facing her, she kissed him on the cheek, a tenderness to which he did not respond at all. He didn't kiss her; he didn't make any delightful baby sounds; he just sat and stared, as though nothing had happened.

"You're my pride and joy," the mother said to the boy, kissing him again. "You're so adorable I could just eat you up."

What struck Laura so clearly now as she stared at the boy's vacant face and his small, awkward body, was that he looked remarkably *un*adorable. He just sat on his mother's knee, almost inanimate, hardly moving, barely alert to all the commotion around him. Laura couldn't picture him acting the way his mother said he had acted in the pediatrician's office. Women kept reaching out to stroke his hair and rub his cheeks, but he remained indifferent to it all, staring with a blank gaze that appeared focused on nothing in particular.

Laura thought that his expression, his manner, the dullness in his eyes, his diminutive size, everything about him seemed—what? The closest word she could think of was *underdeveloped.*

He looked as though his thoughts were elsewhere, she noticed too. Then she realized that no, that wasn't it. More accurately, it was as though his thoughts were altogether absent.

Laura waited until she and Charlotte were far enough away from the other women to speak privately.

"Did you notice anything about that baby?" she whispered.

"What do you mean?"

"I'm not sure exactly. Doesn't he look kind of—I don't know—kind of odd?"

"Odd?" Charlotte thought about it for a moment, then shook her head. "What's odd about him?"

"For one thing, he's small, isn't he?"

"Small isn't odd, Laura. It's just—just small. A lot of babies are small. It's inherited."

"There's more to it than that. He looks like he's almost—" She selected her words very carefully now. "Like he's almost—I don't want to say retarded, but he looks like he almost is."

"Retarded?" Charlotte sounded shocked. "No," she said in utter disbelief. She glanced over at the child again and for a moment considered what Laura said, then she looked at Laura, her face creased with doubt. "Do you really think so?" she asked.

"I don't know. It's just that it looks like there's something wrong with him."

A woman Charlotte had met months ago at the clinic, before Laura had arrived, called them over to look at her newborn. Cradled in her arms was a 2-month-old girl. She looked adorable. Laura came close, knelt down, and touched her chubby face. Her tiny hand closed gently around Laura's finger, and in that instant she forgot all about the disturbing look of the other baby. All she could think about now was having her own child, one that would be just as irresistible as this little girl.

"I don't know if I can wait nine months for mine," she said.

"That's the hardest part," the woman told her. "But it's worth the wait. You'll see."

Just then, there was a loud noise from the direction of the house—what sounded like a crash—followed by shouting voices. Laura turned to see what it was.

The French doors to the living room flew open, hitting the wall and almost breaking the delicate panes of glass. A woman who looked to be a few years older than Laura struggled to come outside. Dr. Acer was holding her arm, trying to keep her in the house.

The woman screamed something now, the end of which sounded like "—not fair!" Then she pulled free of Dr. Acer and rushed out onto the patio. She had an almost crazed look in her eyes as she glared across the pool area at Dr. Chyles.

"My baby!" she screamed and started toward him.

Two men who worked at the clinic put down their drinks and rushed over to grab the woman before she could get near the doctor. She fought and screamed, but they managed to get her back into the house.

All of the other guests watched in silence. When the woman was finally brought inside and Chyles's wife closed the door, a soft murmur of voices carried through the pool area. Dr. Chyles looked around, embarrassed. He managed a nervous smile, then he headed across the patio toward the house.

Laura and Charlotte were in his path, and as he passed them, Charlotte said, "Dr. Chyles, what happened?"

"Poor woman," he said quietly. "I feel sorry for her. She wanted a baby so badly. I did all I could for her, but I can't always guarantee it's going to work out."

He shook his head in disappointment and hurried inside.

11

After the party, as Laura and Dan were driving home, they came upon a line of cars barely moving.

"A traffic jam way out here?" Dan said. "Give me a break. What is this?"

"Something must have happened."

"Good deduction, honey."

As they inched around the curve and over the rise in the road, Laura saw flashing lights in the distance ahead. Several sheriff's cars and an ambulance blocked one lane of the road. Deputies and paramedics were gathered around a car that had gone off the pavement and crashed into a tree. The front end was crushed, the windshield smashed. Even from back here, Laura could tell that it was serious.

As the people ahead of them drove up on the scene, slowing down and staring at the wreck, Laura noticed that most of the cars had been at Dr. Chyles's house earlier, people from the party. She wondered if the people in the damaged car had been at the party too.

She noticed that the wrecked car was a plain white compact, different from the expensive sedans and sports cars that most of Chyles's patients drove. She didn't remember seeing this car parked at Chyles's house, but she realized she could have missed it.

As she and Dan came closer, she noticed that the car had a bumper sticker that said AVIS—WE TRY HARDER. The car was a rental, someone from out of town, which led Laura to believe that it must have been a former patient of the clinic who flew in for the party. She wondered if it was someone she had met.

Then a horrifying thought occurred to her. Could a child have been in the car? The possibility that a baby could be hurt made her ill.

The paramedics gently removed someone from the driver's seat now. Laura saw the person only for an instant before more emergency personnel crowded the area, blocking her view. And in that brief moment, what she saw were vivid red streaks of blood and the face of a woman.

Laura didn't see the woman well enough to know if they had met this afternoon, but she did see clearly the way the woman's head and arms dropped flaccidly as the men moved her. She looked like she was dead.

Dan steered the car around the wreck, following the gestures of the deputy directing traffic. When they reached the deputy, Dan lowered his window and stopped for a second.

"What happened?" he asked.

"Woman lost control of her car."

"Is she hurt badly?"

The deputy nodded. The dark expression on his face filled in the rest.

Laura leaned across the seat. "Was there anyone else in the car?" she asked. "Any children?"

"No. Just the driver."

Dan drove on, and Laura sank back in her seat, relieved that no children had died, but still affected by the sight of the woman.

The next morning, Dan had to leave early for New Orleans. He slept for only a few hours before waking up at 2:30. As he made his way across the dark bedroom to the bathroom, he bumped into the foot of the bed, then into the dresser, then into the chair, cursing each time. Laura had a hard time holding in her laughter.

"Nobody in his right mind gets up this early," he said.

"Come back to bed," Laura said, half asleep.

"I can't. I have to shoot at the Moon Walk today. The light's best first thing in the morning."

Laura dragged herself out of bed too. Since she wouldn't see Dan for a week, she wanted to spend as much time as possible with him before he left. While he showered and dressed, she made coffee and put a couple of frozen bagels in the toaster. She heard the van that delivered the local newspaper come up the road. Thinking Dan might want to read it while he had his breakfast, she went outside and got the paper.

When he came downstairs, Dan was still groggy and irritable. He plopped down at the table and gulped the coffee.

"Take your time," Laura said. "You're going to get heartburn."

"We've got to figure out some other way to do this," he said. "I can't leave at this hour every Monday."

"Maybe you shouldn't schedule morning shoots on Mondays."

He dismissed that idea right away. "I have to do them when I have to do them. I can't always pick when. No, the only thing to do is leave Sunday afternoon from now on."

"Then we lose a whole night together," Laura said. "We only have three as it is, and sometimes just two when you can't make it up here until Saturday, like this weekend. If you leave on Sunday, I'll hardly get to see you at all."

"What can I do, Laura? I can't keep getting up this early. I'm exhausted. You want me to fall asleep on the road?"

"Of course not." Laura came over and hugged him. "I just like to have my husband around. Is that so bad?"

He twisted his head around and kissed her. "No, it's not. It's nice."

Laura poured herself some juice and sat with him. She offered him the newspaper, but he said he had neither time to read it nor much interest in the local news. Laura started to put the paper aside to read later, but she noticed the photograph on the front page. It looked like a driver's license picture. Laura recognized the woman right away, the one who had come out of Dr. Chyles's house yesterday screaming about how it wasn't fair that she couldn't have a baby.

"Look at this," Laura said, turning the paper around so Dan could see the picture.

"Yeah?" he said, giving it a quick glance. He obviously wasn't interested.

"Don't you recognize her? That's the woman from yesterday. From the party. The one who made such a scene."

He took another look at it. "Is that her?"

"It looks like her, doesn't it?"

Dan shrugged. "I guess so."

Laura flipped the paper over and read the caption under the photo. It said CANADIAN WOMAN KILLED ON HIGHWAY 3. "It can't be the same woman," she said. She turned the paper over again and checked the picture. "But that's definitely her. You remember that accident we passed on the way home? That was her."

She gave Dan the paper and he skimmed through the article, shaking his head sympathetically. "That's too bad," he said. He read it a moment longer, then shrugged and gave the paper back to Laura. He finished his bagel and gulped down the last of his coffee.

"I've got to get going," he said.

He put his cup in the sink, then kissed Laura good-bye. She reached up and brushed his cheek, but her attention was on the paper.

"Her name was Erin Archembeau," she said. "It says here that she was only forty-one."

"Yeah, I saw that. It's a real shame."

"Can you believe it? We just saw the woman and then a few hours later, she's dead. God, that's real creepy."

"Well, the way she was acting, out of control and all, she was probably going down that road a lot faster than she should have been. Listen, I want you to take it easy driving on these roads, do you hear?"

91

Laura nodded, but she was still reading the article.

"Talk about strange," she said. "Did you see where it says that her husband died a few weeks ago?"

"No, I didn't get that far."

"That's what it says. He died in Canada. Vancouver. It doesn't say how, though. Just that he died five weeks ago. And they had a son—a three-year-old. And he—" Laura stopped, shocked.

"What?" Dan said.

She peered up at him. "The boy just died too."

"You're kidding. How much misfortune can one family have?"

Laura put down the paper and walked with Dan to his car. It was pitch black but already warm. The air was still and bugs were flying all around. Laura, barefoot, walked down off the porch and onto the gravel driveway. The pebbles hurt her feet, but she went with Dan to the car anyway.

"Go on inside," he told her, swiping at the insects buzzing around his head. "You're going to get eaten alive."

"I'm okay."

He kissed her and said, "Now go in. The baby doesn't like bugs."

"Call me when you get home."

"I'm not going home. I'm going straight to the studio and then to the Moon Walk."

"Call me from the studio, then."

"If I have time."

"Call me, Dan. It'll only take a second. I just want to know that you got there all right."

He chuckled and said, "Don't worry, I'm not going to have an accident like that woman in the paper. I'm a big boy. I'll be okay."

"Just call me."

"Yeah, all right."

They hugged again.

"You know what's odd?" Laura said.

"What?"

"Didn't Dr. Chyles say she couldn't have a baby?"

"Who couldn't have a baby?"

"That woman in the paper, Erin Archembeau. Didn't Dr. Chyles say that about her?"

"I don't know. Did he?"

"I'm pretty sure that's what he said."

Dan shrugged. "I didn't hear him say anything."

"I guess you weren't with me when he said it. I must have been with Charlotte. Anyway, I'm sure that's what he said. She couldn't have a baby. They tried, but she couldn't."

"So what? What difference does that make?"

"The paper said she had a son. The one who died recently."

Dan shrugged. "It's probably her husband's kid from another marriage. Or maybe they adopted. Or maybe she had one kid but something happened in the delivery that made it impossible for her to have a second one. That happens. It could be lots of things."

"I guess," Laura said, "but I don't know."

"Look, I'd love to stay here and discuss it further."

Laura laughed. "Yeah, I'll bet you would."

They hugged and kissed one more time, then Dan got in his car and backed out. Laura went back to the porch and watched the car pull out. She swatted away the bugs until he drove up the road, out of sight. She dreaded the long week alone but knew it couldn't be helped. It wasn't easy for him, either, she told himself. Making that six-hour drive back and forth each week, plus all the hours he was putting in at the studio so they could afford to have the baby. They were both making sacrifices. They both wanted a child desperately.

When she turned to go back inside, she saw Felix sitting in front of the door. The cat hadn't been around since yesterday morning, when he had snapped at Dan.

"Where have you been, little fella?" she said.

She stooped down to pet him. Felix stared up at her with lifeless pink eyes. On his whiskers were brown flecks of dried blood.

"Have you been eating mice again?"

The cat sat deathly still, not reacting at all to her touch. Its fur felt bristly beneath her hand—and cold, as though its body did not generate the least bit of heat.

Felix followed her into the house, then hopped up onto the window sill. There, it just stared through the glass, never showing the slightest amity toward her, barely even showing any sign at all that it was alive.

12

Laura spent the week trying to draft a trust for one of her clients, but she found it difficult to concentrate on work. All she could think of was her appointment at the clinic on Friday morning. When Chyles told her that he wanted to schedule a sonogram to verify that there was a fetal heartbeat, it was the first time she admitted to herself that the procedure still could fail.

By Thursday, she was an emotional wreck. Dan drove up so he could be with her for the sonogram, and he did his best that night to reassure her that everything would be all right, but nothing he said put her at ease. She couldn't help but fear the worst.

They drove to the clinic Friday morning in silence. Dan went back with Laura, first to the examination room where she got her regular hormone injections, then to the special room where the sonogram would be done. Gail instructed Laura to drink four tall glasses of water.

"A full bladder raises the uterus so the doctor can see it better," Gail explained, "and it provides a wall to bounce the ultrasound waves off."

It took Laura five minutes to finish all the water.

After about 20 more minutes, Chyles came in. He dismissed Gail, not needing her assistance to perform the sonogram. He applied a special gel to Laura's midsection, then dimmed the lights and placed a hand-held transducer against her abdomen.

The ultrasound device looked strangely out of place in the clinic, Laura thought. In the weeks that she had been coming here, she had been impressed with the equipment. Chyles used only state-of-the-art instruments. But this ultrasound machine was an old black model that looked more antiquated than the one Laura's obstetrician in New Orleans had before she replaced it last year. When Laura mentioned this to Chyles, he laughed and said:

"I know, but this one has sentimental value. My parents bought it for me when I started my own practice. It was the first piece of equipment I had. It may look a little . . . experienced, but take my word for it, it still works perfectly. And I think it brings my patients luck," he said with a wistful wink. "I think it's going to bring you two luck today."

Dan stood behind Chyles and watched as he carefully moved the transducer over Laura's abdomen, searching for the fetus beneath. Alongside the examining table, a tiny monitor glowed dimly with the nebulous image of Laura's uterus. The image was poorly defined; to Laura it was like looking at an indistinct formation of clouds, not a human form. But Chyles seemed to make sense of it.

"There," he said, finally holding the instrument steady. He pointed to the monitor, to a tiny flutter in the gray image.

"Is that . . . ?" Laura started to say, but a rush of emotion kept her from finishing the question.

Chyles beamed proudly. "That's the heart," he said. He looked first at Laura then over his shoulder at Dan. "Do you see it beating?"

"Is that what that is?" Dan said, stunned.

"That's the heart. A beating heart."

"My God!" Dan said. "That's incredible! Laura, do you see it?"

She felt a warm flush of delight tingle inside her, a sensation she had never experienced before. Goose bumps rose across the entire surface of her skin. She suddenly felt a heightened sense of her own existence, of the miracle of life inside her.

"It's alive," she whispered.

"Very much so," Chyles said.

Dan took hold of Laura's hand. Leaning close, he kissed her and whispered, "I love you." Laura's joy came out in a gasp of laughter. Then a tear streaked down her face. She bit her lip to keep from crying, but her emotions overcame her and she started to weep through a euphoric smile.

Laura and Dan left the clinic that morning feeling closer than they had felt in a long time. Now they were sure that it was really going to happen, that they were really going to have a child. They made love that night as though it were for the first time. The pressure-filled nights of the past two years, when they had been trying so hard to conceive a baby, were forgotten now.

Laura was sad to see Dan leave for New Orleans Sunday night, but he promised her that he would be back next Friday so they could repeat the joy of this weekend.

On Monday morning, as Laura sat down at her computer and got back into the flow of work, Jenny Hopkins called. They hadn't spoken since Laura had called her last month to tell her about the successful egg fertilization.

"How's life in the boonies?"

"Peaceful. The scenery's beautiful. All in all, it's very relaxing."

"Translation, please?"

Laura laughed. "It's boring as hell."

"Feel like some company?"

"Are you kidding?"

"I have to come up there tomorrow. I thought I'd stop by and see how fat you've gotten."

"Sorry to disappoint you, but I'm not showing yet."

"*Yet* being the key word. Enjoy your figure while you can, because if your pregnancy is anything like my sister's, they're going to hang a bell around your neck and call you Bessie."

"That's something to look forward to. Thanks for the encouragement."

"Hey, that's all part of the miracle of childbirth."

The next day, they met for a late lunch at Libby's Dinette. Laura was thankful that the place was air-conditioned.

"So, what brings you to Collier?" she asked Jenny. "I mean besides me."

"Same thing that brought you here. The clinic."

"Don't tell me you're going to try to have a baby?"

"God, no. That magazine article I'm doing, remember? About you old hags trying to have kids after you've blown your youth on your careers."

Laura laughed. "I forgot about that."

"I'm here to do some research for it, to interview Dr. Chyles."

"How did it go?"

"He couldn't spare much time. When I made the appointment with him, I thought we'd have at least half an hour together, but it turned out to be more like five minutes. He passed me along to an orderly, who gave me a quick tour of the place."

"Dan and I took the tour the first time we came up here. It impressed us."

"I was hoping for something a little more in depth. I mean, the orderly was cute, but cute I can find in New Orleans. I wanted more time with the miracle worker himself. Unfortunately, Chyles said he had too many patients. He couldn't spare any more time."

"He is pretty busy."

"No kidding. Just from the looks of the waiting room, I'd say he has one hell of a practice here. I'll bet he's making a fortune."

"I'm sure he is," Laura said. "You wouldn't believe what Dan and I are paying him. But we really don't begrudge him the money. I don't, anyway. If he can help women have babies—which he obviously is doing—then he deserves to get paid for it, and that should be whatever the market bears."

"Well, the market bears a lot," Jenny said. "I've learned that assisted reproduction is big business. I'm talking *big* business. Getting pregnant is supposed to be a natural thing. You'd think with all the teenagers out there having kids so easily, it's no big deal conceiving a baby. But it ain't so."

"I could have told you that," Laura said. "As a matter of fact, I did tell you that."

"Yes, but you didn't tell me why. The reasons couples can't conceive are endless. The woman doesn't produce any eggs or healthy eggs. The husband's sperm count is low or they're irregular or just plain lazy. I think that's why my ex and I couldn't have kids. Everything else about him was lazy; I'm sure his sperm was too. Anyway, there's all kinds of diseases either the man or the woman can have that can make you infertile. And get this—your immune system can even produce antibodies that attack your husband's sperm the way they attack a virus, killing the sperm so they can't fertilize your eggs. I think my ex and I might have had that going against us too. I couldn't stand the guy; I'm sure my antibodies felt the same way about his sperm."

Laura laughed. She was glad that Jenny was here to break the monotony.

"So there are hundreds of things like that," Jenny said, "and the older the woman gets, the more obstacles she faces."

"Listening to you, I think it's a wonder that any of us ever get pregnant."

"Well, modern science is doing its damnedest to see to it that anyone who wants to have a baby can have a baby. Some of the things doctors are trying these days are mind-boggling. Did you know they have a procedure now where they drill a hole in the woman's egg so the sperm can get inside to fertilize it? I mean, these eggs are so small you can't even see them, and doctors are drilling holes in them. It's amazing how far science has come. Did you know that they're at the point now where they can clone embryos? *Human* embryos."

"I think I remember reading something about that."

"Two scientists at George Washington University did it back in 1993. They took a human egg and fertilized it with human sperm in the lab. Then when it divided into two identical cells the way fertilized eggs normally do, they dissolved away the protective coating and split the two cells apart. So now they had two identical human embryos. They coated both of them with an algae that acted like the original coating, and what do you know, the cells began to divide just like with normal embryos. They did it. They actually cloned a human embryo."

"Why even do that in the first place?"

"To prove it could be done, for one thing. You know how *men* are."

Laura laughed. "I think there's probably a little more to it than that."

"Well, they claim that the procedure will someday be used to help infertile women have babies."

"How?"

"See, the whole trick with helping woman who have difficulty conceiving is to start with as many fertilized eggs as possible. That way the chances are better that at least one of them will implant in the woman's uterus. That is, if the man has the juice. If he doesn't, it's a whole different ball game. But if he does, the more eggs you have, the better your chances. That's why doctors always prescribe Pergonal and Clomid and drugs like that to increase the number of eggs you produce."

"I know all about that."

"But a lot of women can't produce many eggs, even with the drugs. You, for instance. Now, if doctors can clone the eggs, make identical copies, make as many of them as they need—for instance, turn two eggs into sixteen—then the odds that the woman will get pregnant go way up."

"Yeah, but pregnant with what?" Laura said.

"A normal baby, they say."

"I doubt that."

"They claim that the cloned embryos are identical to the original ones."

"That seems too much like manufacturing babies, and you can't manufacture life."

"Want to bet? They've done it with animals for a decade. Agricultural researchers have been implanting cloned embryos in livestock. It's a different process than what the two scientists at George Washington University used. What the animal people do is pluck cells from one embryo and inject them into unfertilized eggs that have been stripped of their own genetic material, but the results are basically the same. They claim there's no difference between one of the cloned animals and one of nature's own."

"You can't tell with a cow or a pig or a rabbit," Laura said. "You can't measure its personality, its intellect, its soul. It's an animal, for God's sake. Humans are altogether different. You can't clone a human baby—I don't care what they say."

"If you ask me, it's only a matter of time before someone tries."

"That can't be legal."

"Guess again."

"You mean it *is* legal?"

"Put it this way—it's not *il*legal. The technology is way ahead of the laws on something like this. There aren't effective laws that can cover everything scientists can do. Besides, there's too much money involved. Did you know that more than ten percent of all couples have difficulty conceiving?"

"That's more than I thought."

"And the number is going up all the time as more couples wait longer to have their first child. And because so many are having trouble, more of them are going to fertility specialists for help, and they're paying through the nose for it. The average per treatment cost, when you add in all the tests and the drugs to stimulate ovulation and all the rest, is close to ten grand."

"That doesn't surprise me. It costs more than that here."

"I know. My sister told me. When you add it all up, it's a two-billion-dollar-a-year industry. That's major-league money. And do you know what the kicker is?"

"No, what's the kicker?"

"Get this. The success rate, on average, isn't even that good. Some agencies say that only a third of the couples get pregnant and carry the baby to term. Some consumer groups say that figure is inflated. They claim it's more like half of that, fifteen percent. There's no way to know for sure which is right because nobody really regulates them; nobody keeps track of that kind of information. Like I said, there's plenty of money involved in this and not a lot of government oversight, and when that's the case, money always rules."

"I don't think doctors could get away with lying about something like that."

"No, of course not. Doctors are above lying."

"You're too cynical, Jenny."

"And you're too trusting, especially for a lawyer. I guess when it comes to having babies, reason goes out the window."

Laura chuckled. "Yeah, desperation has a way of tempering reason."

"Couples like you and Dan are paying at least ten thousand dollars a pop at fertility clinics and that's for a fifteen percent chance of success. That's incredible."

"You wouldn't look at it that way if you were trying to have a baby and this was the only way. Anyway, Dr. Chyles told us that the rate here is a lot higher than fifteen percent. The figure just seems low when you include all the couples who come to be tested but don't qualify for the treatment, plus the ones who aren't healthy, the ones with all those problems you mentioned a minute ago, women who wouldn't be able to carry a baby to term no matter what. Sure, when you factor in all of them, the success rate sounds low. But for healthy couples with a particular problem that can be circumvented with drugs or *in vitro* or one of the technologies they have, then the success rate is much higher. Averages can be deceiving; you have to keep that in mind."

Jenny looked unconvinced. Laura felt she needed to defend her position, to defend the New Life Center.

"Since I've been here, as far as I know, there's only been one patient who wasn't successful," she told Jenny. "Just one. I admit I don't know all of the patients, but from talking to the other women and watching patients coming in and out, I've only heard of one woman who couldn't have a child here."

"Who's that?"

"Her name was Erin Archembeau. She was from Canada. Vancouver."

Jenny took a notepad from her purse. "Vancouver, huh?" she said, writing it down. "That's a long way to come. I think I should have a little chat with her."

"You can't. She died in a car accident in July."

"Just my luck. Did you know her?"

"Not really. I saw her an hour or so before she died."

"No kidding? That must feel weird. You meet her, and an hour later, she's dead."

"Yeah, it is kind of disturbing."

"I'll say. Maybe I can interview her husband," Jenny said. "I want to get the perspective of the ones who didn't have success along with the ones who did."

"Her husband died a few months ago, the newspaper said. They also had a son. He died too."

"You can't be serious."

"That's what the newspaper said."

"Either that's the unluckiest family in the world or I don't know what. No wonder she didn't have success here. And she's the only one you know of who couldn't get pregnant?"

"There was one other woman. She did get pregnant, but she had medical problems that she didn't tell anyone about and that caused complications. Her name was Dana Aaron. The day I had my *in vitro* procedure done, her husband had to rush her into the clinic. She died that night."

Jenny made note of that too. They spent the rest of the afternoon talking about things other than having babies. Laura tried to get Jenny to stay for the night, but Jenny had to get back to Louisiana. She left just before dark.

As Laura drove home, with the woods darkening around her, she thought how much she had enjoyed the time spent with Jenny. It reminded her that she missed the city, all the activity there, her friends, work. Staying out here in the country was pleasant at times, certainly less stressful than life in New Orleans, but she was feeling strangely and increasingly restless, anxious. She attributed it to loneliness, to being in an unfamiliar place, and she tried not to think about it. Still, whenever she was by herself and her thoughts were unoccupied, an uneasiness crept into her mind. She wished she could understand why.

13

The weeks passed slowly.

By September, Laura wasn't yet showing, but her clothes were starting to feel snug. She had to loosen the seat belt in the car. Stairs left her winded. The baby was growing.

Dan missed several weekends because of Saturday and Sunday shoots. Each Friday when he called to say he couldn't make it, Laura felt more lonely and depressed. She kept busy by working, and even though she talked often on the phone with people at her law firm and with clients as well as her friends in New Orleans, she felt isolated up here, cut off from the world. Originally, she had thought she would become accustomed to staying here all alone, but instead, she started resenting it more and more.

By the beginning of October she could no longer wear any of her clothes, so she and Charlotte drove to Montgomery and bought a maternity wardrobe. Whenever she stood in front of a mirror, the sight of her stomach brought mixed feelings. Inside her body the miracle of a child was coming true, and for that she was overjoyed, but she was rapidly losing her figure, making it increasingly difficult for her to think of herself as attractive.

When Dan came up in the middle of October and the two of them lay in bed together, he opened his hand wide and placed it over her stomach, making a comment about his "cute, chunky wife." Laura knew he wasn't trying to insult her, but it added to the insecurity she was feeling.

It rained on and off the entire weekend. Laura had hoped that they could take a drive in the country, remembering how much fun they had months ago when they rode around and bought peaches and preserves. She wished they could repeat it, rekindle those feelings, but the bad weather forced them to spend the weekend indoors.

Dan watched part of the football game on Saturday afternoon between Louisiana State and the University of Florida. When it was obvious that his LSU Tigers were going to lose, he turned off the TV and took a nap. Laura did some laundry, made dinner, then worked at her computer for a couple of hours. It was almost like spending the weekend alone, she thought.

On Sunday, Dan did a little yard work, then he and Laura went over some of the bills that he wasn't sure about. They watched half of a Bette Davis movie together before Dan had to leave for New Orleans.

Laura stood on the porch, watching him back out of the driveway. He waved and blew her a kiss, not paying attention to what was behind him. Laura heard a sickening thud and saw the rear end of the car jolt up slightly. From where she was, she couldn't see the back of the car, but she was sure that he had run over an animal.

He stopped and got out to see what it was. Laura came down off the porch and walked toward him. When Dan saw what he had run over, he sank back against the car, looking disheartened.

"Oh, Christ," he muttered.

Laura came closer. "What is it?" she asked.

"Don't come over here, honey."

She didn't heed his warning. When she reached the end of the driveway, she saw white fur on the road behind Dan's car. It stood out vividly against the dark asphalt and the shallow puddle of blood. She recognized it instantly. Felix lay dead.

She turned away quickly. Dan came over and held her.

"I'm so sorry," he said. "I didn't see it there."

"I know," she whispered. "It's not your fault."

He stayed with her for a moment, neither of them saying anything. Then he said, "Why don't you go inside."

She barely nodded.

He helped her up the driveway to the porch, then went around back and found a shovel. Laura watched as he scooped the dead cat off the road and carried it to the trash can beside the house. The thud as he dropped it in echoed in the pit of Laura's stomach. Dan placed the lid over the can, put the shovel away, kissed Laura good-bye, and left.

As darkness settled in that evening, Laura was still feeling bad about losing Felix. She heated some leftover chicken from yesterday and made a salad. The house seemed especially empty tonight. She missed the cat more than she thought she would have. Even as unaffectionate as it had been, she still thought of it as her pet. It was the only company she had. Now she had nothing. She knew she would get over it, but it would take time. Maybe a new cat would make it easier, she thought as she sat at the kitchen table, alone. She figured she could go to the Humane Society tomorrow and see if they had a cat to adopt.

When she finished eating, she started to get up to do the dishes, but then she heard a faint noise outside. The sound startled her. She froze on the chair and just listened. The wind had picked up with nightfall and she heard it hissing through the trees. Branches creaked as they bowed in the gusts. She wondered if that was the sound she had heard a moment ago.

Then she heard it again, and she realized it was not the trees. It was close to the house, and it sounded like it came from something animate.

She heard it again—movement, a hissing, dragging sound. It was even closer now, coming from the back porch.

She sat dead still and stared across the kitchen at the window. Behind the sheer curtains, blackness had overtaken the night. It was so dark outside now that she could not tell if someone was standing there, peering in.

The noise again—scratching on the porch, close to the door. She turned her glare in that direction and stared at the door. It suddenly seemed flimsy. She searched her mind for a memory of having locked it.

Again, the noise, even closer.

She noticed this time, as the sound seemed to echo through the empty house, that it did not seem to be coming from something large, from something the size of a man. It sounded, she thought, more like an animal.

Or, she thought, morbidly, like the sound of a crawling baby.

Again she heard the sound, closer yet, scratching the wooden surface of the porch.

Then silence.

For a long moment, she heard nothing out there and wondered if it had left. But then it started scratching the door, a desperate sound that reached into the house and made Laura tremble.

She remembered that Felix used to scratch at the door that way when he wanted to come inside. But Felix was dead.

It scratched again, harder, louder. Whatever it was, it wanted to come in.

A shudder of uncertainty ran through her. She wondered if whatever was on the porch had the facility to open the door and come in. She got up and, quivering, moved closer to check the latch.

She didn't feel much relief even when she saw that it was locked. The night air, damp and chilly against her skin, crept in as a draft under the door, making her shiver, keeping her breath tight and uneasy. The windows rattled in the wind.

She needed to see what was out there so she could decide what to do. She reached for the switch that turned on the porch light. It felt cold against her finger. When she flicked it on, the curtain glowed, but she still could not see outside. Gently, she parted the curtain and peered out.

Weak, yellow illumination leaked across the porch. Beyond it loomed the solid blackness of the woods, unaffected by the house light. Laura leaned close to the window and strained to see below.

It came into view so suddenly that it startled her, taking her breath away. The familiarity of it only made the sight more shocking. For a moment, she couldn't react. What she saw made no sense at all.

Peering up at her from outside, with lifeless red eyes and a spiritless expression, was a cat—her cat, the same white and orange earless feline she had adopted three months ago. The same cat Dan had run over earlier tonight. The same cat that a few short hours ago had been very much dead.

Bewildered, Laura just stared at Felix, not sure what to do. Several seconds passed before she reluctantly opened the door and let the cat in. She knelt down to examine it. Nowhere on it could she find blood or marks where Dan's car had hit it. Felix was uninjured. It didn't make sense.

Felix let her look at him for only a moment before he walked across the kitchen and headed into the other room. Laura noticed that he didn't have even the slightest limp, and she wondered how that could be.

The cat disappeared into the living room, as though nothing had happened. Laura stood in the kitchen, staring, still unable to make sense of any of this. She distinctly remembered seeing blood on the road this afternoon. And she could not forget the sickening sound of the tire hitting the cat, or the lifeless thud when Dan dropped the cat into the trash can. It should not be alive right now, she told herself, let alone in perfect health.

Laura followed the cat into the living room and watched it for a few moments before she went back to the front door. She had to try to understand this.

The night seemed to have gotten even chillier than it had been just a few minutes earlier when she had opened the kitchen door to let Felix in, chillier than it should be for the middle of October. She shivered as she stepped out onto the porch and looked toward the trash cans near the corner. The one Dan had put the cat in was still upright, its lid still in place, which didn't make sense. If the cat had freed itself, it would have had to knock the lid off and probably even tip over the trash can. But there it was, undisturbed.

Laura looked back into the house. Felix stood in the middle of the room, staring at her. He turned away now, walked to the window, and jumped up on the sill where he usually stayed. He continued watching her.

She looked at the trash can again. Definitely, the lid should be on the ground, she told herself. This did not make any sense at all.

Shivering more now, she walked down the steps and made her way through the darkness. A little illumination from the porch light reached over here, just enough for her to see what she was doing. The night was quiet except for the wind shaking the trees. The sound it made reminded her of the tail of a rattlesnake, and that thought added to her uneasiness.

As she came closer to the corner of the house, she noticed that something inside the can smelled rotten. She could smell it even through the lid. She dreaded touching it, but she needed to look inside. She grasped the metal handle. It felt like touching ice. She shuddered suddenly, which left her legs unsteady.

She pinched closed her nose and forced herself to breathe through her mouth, making it a little easier for her to tolerate the stench. Then she slowly removed the lid.

Flies were buzzing around. The smell was so rank now that bile began to rise from her stomach. A dim glow from the porch light settled into the trash can, just enough for Laura to see: lying on the bottom of the can, absolutely still, with blood on its coat, was a white-and-orange earless cat.

The phone inside the house started ringing. Laura assumed it was Dan calling to say that he had gotten home all right. She stared at the dead cat a moment longer, then put the lid back on and hurried to the porch. The only explanation she could come up with was that there were two cats, identical twins. That's the only thing that made sense. But still the whole thing left her feeling strange.

When she went inside and closed the door, she glanced at the cat on the window sill. Was this Felix? she wondered. Or was the dead one outside Felix? The thought of letting the wrong cat inside her house made her uncomfortable. She couldn't help thinking of it as an intruder.

That's just foolish, she told herself as she walked across the room to answer the phone. That had to be Felix; he was lying where he always did. But even if it wasn't Felix, it was just a cat. If its twin brother had been all right to have in the house, so was this one.

She picked up the phone, eager to tell Dan about the cats,

but instead of hearing his voice, she heard the frantic cries of a woman on the other end.

"Help me, Laura! Help me!"

It was Charlotte Wheeler.

14

Laura had been waiting for more than two hours now, and still no one had come out to tell her how Charlotte was doing. She paced the corridor. The clinic was nearly deserted tonight.

She walked to the end of the hall and stopped at the double doors where the sign said STERILE AREA—AUTHORIZED PERSONNEL ONLY. She stood by the doors for a while, then started up the corridor again, back toward the waiting room. She hadn't gone far when a nurse came down the corridor from the maternity ward. Laura hurried over to her.

"How is she?" Laura asked.

The nurse looked a little confused.

"Charlotte Wheeler," Laura said. "I brought her in at eight o'clock. They had to call Dr. Chyles to come. Don't you remember?"

"Oh, yes, I remember now. Dr. Chyles is in with her right now."

"She's been in there for two hours. What's happening?"

"I'm sure the doctor will let you know as soon as he can."

"Is she all right?"

"I honestly don't know. I'm on the maternity ward, not

the OR. You'll have to wait until someone familiar with that patient can come out and speak with you."

"Has anyone called her husband yet?"

"I couldn't say."

"Someone should call him. He should know. Maybe I should call. I don't know his phone number. Do you have it? He lives in Columbus, Georgia."

"No, I don't have it."

"It must be in her record."

"I don't have her record. I'm not the OR nurse. I'm sorry, but I can't help you. I really have to go; I have other patients to take care of. I'm sure someone who knows what's going on will be out shortly to talk to you."

The nurse left her.

Laura started pacing again. She thought about Charlotte's husband in Georgia and wondered how she could get his phone number. Directory assistance might have it.

She remembered that there was a phone near the waiting room and she started back up the corridor to call, but then she reconsidered whether she should even call him. First she should get some answers, find someone to tell her what was going on, then she could call Charlotte's husband, when she knew better what Charlotte's condition was.

She returned to the double doors and waited for several minutes. Finally, she couldn't wait any longer. Ignoring the sign, she eased open the double doors and peeked down the hall toward the two operating rooms.

Dr. Acer was just coming out of one of them. She was wearing teal scrubs, latex gloves, her mask partially untied and lowered to her neck. Obviously, she had just come from surgery, and Laura wondered if Charlotte had been the patient. Dr. Acer didn't notice Laura standing at the doors. Her attention was on something in her hands. She was carrying a stainless-steel tray covered with a white towel. Laura thought it strange that the doctor would be removing something from the room. It seemed more likely that a nurse or an orderly would do it, but the night shift was on and the clinic staff was small. Laura didn't give it another thought. Her main concern was still Charlotte's welfare.

Laura was going to call out to Dr. Acer and ask her about

Charlotte, but before she could, Dr. Acer hurried to a door marked PATHOLOGY—PHYSICIANS ONLY and went in. Laura waited, thinking that Dr. Acer would come right out. But before Dr. Acer could reappear, Dr. Chyles came out of the operating room. He, too, was in scrubs, although he had taken off his gloves and mask. He summoned two nurses from the maternity ward and directed them to the operating room. Looking tired, he started toward the same door his wife had just gone through, but Laura called out to him.

He looked surprised to see her peering through the doorway. He came over and led her back outside into the hall.

"I didn't know you were here, Laura. Is something wrong?"

"I came with Charlotte Wheeler. I'm concerned about her, Doctor. Can you tell me how she's doing? Is she all right?"

"Oh yes, she's just fine. I didn't know you were waiting. I apologize. I would have come out sooner."

"That's all right. As long as Charlotte's okay."

"She's doing just fine." Chyles's voice had such sureness that he quickly put Laura at ease. "I just finished delivering the afterbirth," he said.

It took a moment for Laura to realize what that meant. "You mean she had the baby?"

"Yes. It was a little premature, but everything went well."

"And the baby's all right?"

"As healthy as can be. Mrs. Wheeler is the proud mother of a beautiful baby boy."

"That's wonderful! She and her husband wanted a boy so badly."

Chyles chuckled and said, "We aim to please here. The nurses will move her to a room in a little while. As soon as she's awake and settled in, you can join her."

"Can I see the baby?"

He smiled. "Of course."

The nurse carried in a tiny infant, its skin bright pink and wrinkled. He was wrapped in a white cloth, so all Laura could see was his face, but she thought he was the most adorable baby she had ever seen. Charlotte started crying as soon as she saw him.

"Let me hold him! Let me hold him!" she said, holding out her arms.

The baby lay absolutely still in the nurse's hands. She brought him over to Charlotte and with delicate care lowered him into her arms. The baby wasn't crying or gurgling or making any infantile sounds at all. He kept his eyes closed and just lay in Charlotte's arms, without a hint of animation on his face.

Charlotte cradled him close to her chin, clinging to him as though he was the most valuable possession she had ever held. And indeed he was, Laura realized. He was the child Charlotte and her husband had been denied for so long; he was the missing element that was to make their lives perfect.

Charlotte continued crying as she rocked the baby in her arms and kissed his chubby cheeks. Laura, seeing Charlotte so joyful, thought about her own baby. She could barely wait for the day when she, too, would cradle it in her arms.

"Isn't he just the most beautiful thing you've ever seen?" Charlotte said. She squeezed him and brushed her nose against his face. "I'm just going to love you to death, you little miracle, you. I'm just going to love you to death."

Charlotte's husband drove up at the end of the week and took her and the baby back to Columbus. Laura was sorry to see her leave, but she was happy that everything had turned out well for them.

The realtor rented Charlotte's house right away. The young couple moved in the following Monday. Laura knew as soon as she met them that she and they would not become close friends the way she and Charlotte had. The wife was from the Philippines and barely spoke English. The husband was a commander in the navy. They lived in Pensacola, Florida.

Since Laura didn't know any of the other patients very well, she spent more of her time alone, working. Dan had to work the next weekend. When Laura complained about it, he reminded her that he had driven up just the last weekend.

He had to work this weekend because they needed the money.

"The clinic isn't cheap," he said, "and neither is raising a child."

In early November, Dr. Chyles scheduled Laura for another ultrasound—plus an amniocentesis—to make sure the fetus was developing properly and to test for possible birth defects.

Laura lay in the dark ultrasound room, straining to see the image on the small, dim monitor.

"Here's one arm," Chyles said as he manipulated the transducer over Laura's stomach.

"Where?" She had difficulty making out any distinct images. Chyles pointed to a dark outline on the monitor. It took a moment, but finally she recognized the shape of an arm.

"I see it now!" she said. "I see it!" She couldn't contain the sudden rush of excitement she felt with the sight of her baby. "That's the baby's arm?" she asked.

"That's one of them. Let's see if there's another," he said. The lightness in his voice took away any worry that the other arm wouldn't be there. He manipulated the instrument over her stomach until he found it.

"And here's number two," he said. "Can you see the hand here?" he asked her, pointing to the monitor.

"I think I do."

Chyles continued moving the transducer. As it produced an image of the baby's head, it looked out of proportion, as big as the rest of the body. Chyles told her that the oversized head was normal for a baby in the womb. Even for the first few months after it was born, its head would be disproportionately large. That was normal, nothing to worry about.

Next, the screen showed the baby's torso. Laura noticed a tiny flutter in the gray image.

"That's the heart, isn't it?" she said.

"Yes, it is."

"I can see it beating!"

Chyles continued manipulating the imaging instrument across Laura's abdomen. She thought she saw the baby's body in another position now, but Chyles said that what she saw was only an echo from the placenta. He said that was the one drawback of his old machine.

When he finished, he told her that everything looked just fine, the baby was developing quite well, and he saw no indications that she or the baby would have any problems.

Immediately after the sonogram, Laura was to undergo amniocentesis. Gail returned to prep her for the "tap." She cleaned a small section of Laura's abdomen thoroughly, removing the gel Chyles had applied for the sonogram, then she wiped the area with a sterile solution to reduce the risk of infection from the amniocentesis needle. Chyles injected local anesthesia into Laura's abdomen, gave it a few minutes to take effect, then, using the ultrasound equipment to guide him, inserted the long, thin needle through Laura's skin and into her uterus. She felt a sharp, momentary sting, about as painful as her daily hormone shots. Chyles left the needle in for almost a full minute, drawing out amniotic fluid, then he removed it, put a Band-Aid over the puncture mark, and that was it.

"That wasn't so bad, now was it?" he said.

"Not at all."

"We have to wait for the culture to grow before we have the results. That can take a week or two, depending on how quickly or slowly it grows."

"I have to wait that long?"

"Some of the big hospitals do it more quickly, but we use a special process here that's far more accurate. It just takes a little longer. Don't worry, the time will go by quickly."

"Maybe for you, but not for me."

"You're not worried, are you?"

"A little nervous. I keep thinking, what if there's a problem?"

"There's no reason to expect that there will be. Everything has been going just fine so far. This test is just precautionary, really. It's standard for a woman your age to have amnio, but the chances that we'll discover any congenital abnormalities are slim to none. It's always best to be safe, of course, which is why we do it, but if I were you, I'd just forget you even had it. Everything's going to be just fine." He told her to go home and take it easy for the next few days.

His assurances eased some of her anxiety. He seemed so confident, so definite. He had been right about being able to help her get pregnant; she had to believe he was right about this too.

15

Thanksgiving was a little more than two weeks away. Laura was getting large now and moving around was becoming a chore. The sight of her body in the mirror made her cringe. Her back ached all the time and her feet swelled so much that it pained her to wear anything tighter than slippers, but she learned to accept the discomfort. It was all part of supporting another life, all a function of the baby growing inside her.

As she was just returning from the clinic one afternoon, she came in the house to find the phone ringing. She had to hurry across the room to answer it. Out of breath, she flopped onto the sofa.

"Hello?" she said.

The woman on the other end spoke in an anxious whisper. "Laura?"

It took her a moment to recognize the voice. "Jenny? Is that you?"

"It's me." Jenny Hopkins sounded distraught. "I've been trying to reach you all morning," she told Laura.

"I go to the clinic in the morning for my shots. What's wrong?"

Jenny hesitated.

"Jenny?"

"We need to talk, Laura."

"Are you all right?"

Jenny didn't answer.

"Is something wrong?" Laura asked.

After another moment of silence, Jenny said, "Yes."

Laura waited for Jenny to elaborate, but Jenny didn't say any more. She remained silent for so long that Laura began to wonder if Jenny was still on the line.

"Jenny? Are you there?"

"I'm here."

"What's going on?"

"I've been away," she whispered.

"Away?"

"Canada. Vancouver. I found something there."

"I don't know what you mean."

"It's important that we talk."

"Of course. What is it?"

"Not over the phone. Can we meet?"

"I guess so. Sure. Where?"

"I'm flying up to Montgomery tonight. I'm going to rent a car and I'll drive over where you are tomorrow."

"What's in Montgomery?"

"A place called Woodridge. I've got to go there, see someone, see if I'm right."

"Right about what?"

"I'm pretty sure it's all part of it."

"Part of what?"

"I'll explain it all tomorrow, when I know for sure."

"Jenny, what's going on?"

"We'll talk tomorrow. It's too much to tell you over the phone and I've got to run to catch my plane."

"All right, whatever you want. Let me give you directions to my house."

"No, not at the house. Do you remember where we had lunch last summer when I came up there?"

"You mean at—"

"Don't say the name!" Jenny said quickly.

The panic in her voice sent a shiver through Laura's body.

"You know what place I mean, right?" Jenny said.

"I know it, yes."

"We'll meet there tomorrow."

"Okay. What time?"

"Three o'clock. And Laura," she said, her voice heavy with what Laura realized was fear. *"Be careful."*

When Laura walked into Libby's Dinette at 2:55 the next day, Jenny hadn't yet arrived. She took a table by the window. Outside, a brisk wind blew leaves through the town square, but the sun was shining brightly and the warmth felt good against her face. There were only a few other customers in the diner. A thin woman was sitting by herself, eating salad and reading a book about pregnancy. At a nearby table, a young couple was discussing whether to undergo the treatment at the New Life Center. The wife was reluctant to move up here; the husband was concerned with the finances.

Laura told the waitress she wanted to hold off having anything to eat until her friend arrived, but she ordered a glass of juice and sipped it while she waited for Jenny. Ever since the phone call yesterday, she had been trying to figure out what Jenny wanted to talk about. Her first thought was that it was a tax problem. Jenny was not the type to overreact, but notices from the IRS have a way of unnerving people. What Montgomery, Alabama, and someplace called Woodridge had to do with an audit, Laura could not imagine, but she was sure Jenny would explain it all this afternoon.

Half an hour passed without Jenny's showing up. Thinking that Jenny must have miscalculated the driving time from Montgomery, Laura ordered another glass of juice and continued waiting. By 4:15, she began to worry.

Jenny certainly should have showed up by now, she reasoned. The phone call from Jenny came into Laura's mind now. She remembered how Jenny's voice had sounded: cautious, fearful. Jenny had been reluctant to say much, as though she thought someone was listening in. And then when she told Laura to be careful, as if there were some danger, she certainly sounded more concerned than someone facing a tax audit. And now she was more than an hour late. Laura feared that something was wrong.

She left word with Libby that if Jenny came in, she was to tell her that she had gone home. When she got to the house, she called Jenny's apartment in New Orleans and got the answering machine. Next she called her own law firm. No one there had spoken to Jenny in months; no one knew anything about an audit.

She wanted to call someone else, call some place where Jenny would be, but there was no one to call. Then she remembered the name Jenny had told her, dialed directory assistance in Montgomery, and asked if they had a listing for Woodridge. They gave her a number and she called.

"Woodridge House," a man's voice answered.

From the name, Laura thought it might be a hotel. It could be where Jenny was staying. "Could you tell me if there's a Jenny Hopkins there?" she said.

"I'm sorry, miss, but we don't have any residents by that name here."

"This isn't a hotel?"

"No. It's an assisted-living facility."

Laura wasn't sure what that meant. She thought it must be a nursing home, a senior center, something like that. She had no idea why Jenny would have gone there.

"She would have been a visitor," Laura said.

"I'll check the visitor registry. Who was she visiting?"

"I don't know."

The man let out an annoyed breath then said, "One moment." A minute later, he came back on the line. "No. No one named Jenny Hopkins visited here today."

Laura thanked him and hung up. She didn't know where else to try, didn't know what hotel Jenny had stayed at, so all she could do was wait.

She tried to work on a client's will through the evening but found it difficult to concentrate. Her thoughts kept returning to Jenny. It was very strange that Jenny hadn't called, very unlike her.

Before going to bed, she called Jenny's apartment one

more time and again got the answering machine. She slept fitfully, waking several times, worried. The next morning after returning from the clinic, she called Jenny's apartment, sure that Jenny would be there now, determined to chide her for making her worry so much. But a man answered the phone instead.

Laura had never heard his voice before. She wondered if she had dialed the right number. "Is Jenny Hopkins there?" she asked.

The man hesitated. "Who is this, please?"

"Laura Fielding. I'm a friend of Jenny's. Who is this?" Laura asked.

"My name's Roger Kincaid. I'm Jenny's brother-in-law."

"Oh, I see. Is Jenny there?"

He hesitated again. When he spoke, the words came with difficulty. "Um, Mrs. Fielding, there's—there's been an accident."

He paused, and the silence in Laura's ear brought a shiver of panic. Her legs felt weak and she had to brace herself against the armrest.

"What—what happened? I mean—how is she? Is she all right?"

"I'm afraid that Jenny is—she died."

"No," Laura whispered.

"She was in a car accident," he explained.

"When? How?"

"Last night. Apparently one of her front tires had a blowout and she lost control of the car. She hit a tree, head on. She was in Alabama."

"She was coming up here to see me," Laura said, feeling a sickening wave of guilt.

"She was? I didn't know that. I'm sorry. You two were close?"

"I've been her lawyer for years. And her friend." Laura began to feel dizzy and nauseated. She sank down on the sofa. "Where did it happen?" she asked.

"The state police said it happened just outside Montgomery. Is that where you are, Montgomery?"

"No. No, I'm in Collier," Laura said almost absently, thinking about Montgomery, remembering that Jenny mentioned she had to go there first. No wonder they didn't have her name at Woodridge. She never made it there.

"Collier?" Roger Kincaid said. "Are you the Laura at the New Life Center?"

"Yes."

"Jenny mentioned you."

Laura realized now that this was the husband of Jenny's sister, the one who told Jenny about Dr. Chyles. She felt a connection to him because of the clinic, but she was much too disturbed over the news of Jenny to talk about it.

"Is there anything I can do?" Laura asked.

They spoke very briefly about Jenny's legal affairs, her will and trusts and what needed to be done. It could wait until after the funeral, she told him. He and Paula could call the law firm when they felt ready to deal with it. Laura said she would call ahead and have another lawyer there prepare to meet with them.

After she hung up, Laura sat on the sofa and wept. Her dear friend was gone. The woman who made it possible for her and Dan to have a child would never even get to see that child. And Laura would never again hear Jenny's sarcasm, never again have such a soulmate to confide in.

16

Dan drove up to Collier as soon as Laura called and told him what happened. He stayed with her through the weekend. She couldn't have kept herself together without him.

The funeral was set for Monday afternoon, so after Laura went to the clinic for her shots that morning, they dropped her car off at the train station, then she and Dan drove back to New Orleans together. He took her to the church and stayed for the memorial service. Jenny's friends gathered afterward at a restaurant around the corner, but Dan couldn't accompany Laura; he had to finish the layout he had been shooting last Friday when she called. By now she felt strong enough to go to the restaurant alone. She told him she'd get a cab home later.

The Mississippi Grille was quiet when Laura went in, the atmosphere subdued, respectful. Jenny's parents had died long ago and Jenny didn't have any children of her own, so the only family Laura saw were the brother-in-law she talked to on the phone, Roger Kincaid, and Jenny's sister Paula. They were sitting at a table in the corner of the restaurant, enduring a steady hail of condolences. Laura preferred to leave them with their grief, but she knew it was expected of her to go over and say something. She waited until they were alone, took a breath to steady herself, then approached their table.

"Paula?" she said. "Hi, I'm Laura Fielding."

Paula offered her hand. Up close she looked devastated. Laura wished now that she hadn't come over. She told Paula how sorry she was about Jenny's passing and how wonderful a woman Jenny was. Paula nodded in appreciation. Her husband seemed to be coping much better. He shook Laura's hand and thanked her for the kind words, then he said: "You're Jenny's lawyer, right?"

"Yes. You're Roger? We spoke on the phone a few days ago."

"Yes, I remember."

Roger turned to his wife. "Honey, this is Jenny's friend, the one who went to the New Life Center."

"Oh, you're *that* Laura," Paula said. A little color came to her face now. "I didn't make the connection right off. Yes, Jenny told us that she recommended the New Life Center to you." Paula seemed relieved to be talking about something other than Jenny's death. "I see Dr. Chyles was successful," she said.

Laura put her hand on her stomach. "I have Jenny to

thank," she said. "And the two of you for telling Jenny about the clinic."

"We're glad it worked out well for you," Paula said.

Roger congratulated her, but in his face Laura detected a hint of concern.

"How's your pregnancy coming along?" Paula asked.

"Just fine. My back isn't thrilled about it, but all in all, everything is going well."

Paula chuckled. "You don't have to tell me. I remember well."

"When are you due?" Roger asked.

"Not for another four months."

He looked surprised. Laura laughed and said, "I know, I'm really big for five months. Everyone thinks so."

"Paula was big, too," he said. "Remember, hon?"

"Yes, everyone thought I was going to have twins. But I just had one baby—a girl. But believe me, one is plenty. She's all we ever hoped for."

"You look very pleased," Laura said. "I'm happy for you."

"We wanted a child for so long. Now we have one. It's a blessing."

Roger just watched his wife, saying nothing. He nodded finally, but there was no affirmation in his gesture. In fact, Laura thought she detected something discordant about his gaze. It seemed he wanted to say something to her, yet he remained silent.

"We tried for three years," Paula said. "We went to every doctor we could find. I don't know what we would have done if we hadn't found Dr. Chyles. But thank God we did." She squeezed Roger's hand. "A blessing," she said quietly.

"How old is your daughter now?" Laura asked.

"Eight months. They grow up so fast."

"She's doing well?"

"She's just fantastic. Knock wood." Paula tapped the table, then turned to Roger, looking to him for confirmation. He smiled and nodded, but Laura noticed again the troubled look on his face, what appeared to be hesitancy or doubt.

They chatted a short while longer, then Laura offered her condolences once again and left them. She spoke briefly with a few other people she knew, all the while making her way toward the exit. She retrieved her coat from the front and was about to leave when Roger came over.

"Mrs. Fielding, do you have a moment?" he said.

"Of course. What is it?"

She could see that he was uneasy. He glanced around, looking concerned that someone might hear him, then he took Laura by the arm and led her off to the side.

"I haven't said anything to Paula," he said in a nervous whisper. "She's a worrier and I don't want to give her any more problems. She has enough on her mind as it is, what with Jenny's death and with Alyssa's problems."

"Alyssa?"

"Our daughter."

"She's not feeling well?"

"That's not it—exactly. She's been—" He struggled for the right word, finally settling on one. "Lethargic."

"Is she all right?"

"I'm probably just being an overly concerned parent."

"I guess it's hard not to be."

He shook his head, clearly bothered by what he was thinking. He seemed to want to tell her more, but he looked like he wasn't sure he should. He looked around again for a moment, then wiped his sweaty palms on his pants. When he turned his attention back to Laura, more than anything else he seemed confused and distracted.

"It's just that sometimes she seems so . . . lifeless. She just sits there most of the time like she's out of it altogether, except for the times when she . . . she just sort of explodes."

"Explodes?"

"Sometimes—I don't know what sets her off—but she just all of a sudden gets . . . violent. I mean really viciously violent. I don't know why. I don't know if she's developing some kind of a . . . a deficit or something. I just don't know." He shook his head, clearly confused and disturbed. "How can you tell at her age if there's something wrong?" he said. "Kids usually grow out of things like that, don't they?"

Laura didn't know how to answer. "Have you had a doctor look at her for that?" she asked.

"We take her to the pediatrician all the time. I mentioned it to him and he did tests, but he didn't find anything wrong. He doesn't think she has any developmental problems. He thinks it's just part of her personality. He's probably right. I'm sure it's nothing; just a phase. She'll grow out of it," he said, and when he did, he seemed to be talking more to himself than to Laura.

They stood in silence for a moment, Laura wondering why he came over.

"Is there anything I can do for you or Paula?" she asked.

He hesitated a moment, then said, "Jenny took a trip last week."

"Yes, I know. She told me she had been away."

"She went to Canada. Vancouver. She called us while she was there. What was strange was that she didn't want Paula to know that she called."

"She didn't? Why?"

"I don't know. She wanted to talk to *me*. She asked if I knew how many zygotes we had when we went through the *in vitro* fertilization treatment at the New Life Center."

"Why did she want to know that?"

"I don't know. She didn't say. I didn't even know what a zygote was. She had to explain it to me. It's the fertilized eggs—you know, the embryos that become babies?"

"Yes, I know."

"I didn't. And I didn't know the answer to how many Paula got. I still don't know. I think it was just one." He lowered his voice and added, "Paula had difficulty producing eggs. Anyway," he said, "I don't know why Jenny called all the way from Canada to ask me that. I thought maybe— you being her lawyer and all—she might have told you something."

"No, she didn't."

"Do you know what she was writing?"

"The last time I talked to her, she was doing an article on infertile couples and on the clinics that help them. I don't know if she was still working on that."

"I didn't know that. I guess it sort of makes sense then,

her asking about the zygotes. But that seems a long way to go to research infertile couples. You'd think there's enough of them around here."

As he said this, Laura remembered her conversation with Jenny that day last summer when they had had lunch together in Collier. Laura had told her about the woman who came to Dr. Chyles's house during the party, the one who screamed that it wasn't fair that she couldn't have a child. She had been killed in a car crash shortly afterward. The newspaper had said her name was Erin Archembeau and she was from Vancouver. Laura wondered if she was the reason Jenny had gone there.

"When you talked to Jenny that day on the phone," she asked Roger, "the day she asked you about the zygotes, did she mention the name Archembeau? Erin Archembeau?"

"Archembeau? No. But she did ask me about someone else. Someone named Nefayre."

"Nefayre?"

"Yeah. I told her I didn't know anybody by that name."

"Who is that supposed to be?"

"She didn't tell me. All she said was that it was connected to the story she was writing. I don't know how it figures in, but I guess it has something to do with why she went to Vancouver."

"And she didn't mention Erin Archembeau?"

"No. Why? Who is that supposed to be?"

"A woman she was interested in finding out about. She lived in Vancouver."

"Oh." Roger shrugged. "No, she didn't mention that name. Just Nefayre."

Nefayre. The name echoed through Laura's head along with the memory of Erin Archembeau. That day at the party, Erin Archembeau had screamed *not fair.* But now Laura wondered if she could have been mistaken about what Erin Archembeau had said. Could the woman have been screaming *Nefayre?* Why would she yell that at Dr. Chyles's house? Saying *not fair* made sense. It was not fair that Chyles couldn't make her pregnant. It was not fair that she and her husband couldn't have the child that they surely wanted. It was not fair that nature dealt them such a cruel blow. Her saying *not fair* was something Laura could understand. But it didn't make any sense at all for Erin Archembeau to say *Nefayre*.

"Jenny didn't say who Nefayre was or what the name had to do with the article she was working on?" Laura asked.

"No. I have to tell you, it was a pretty weird conversation," Roger said. "It really didn't make a whole lot of sense. That's kind of why I brought it up. I wondered if you knew more than I do, since you were her lawyer."

"No, I can't say that I do. Jenny did call me the day before she died to tell me that she wanted to talk to me about something, but she didn't say what it was. It sounded important, though. At first, I thought she was being audited, but that turned out not to be the case. I still don't know what was troubling her. She did say she had to stop in Montgomery, a place called Woodridge—it's a nursing home or something like that. That was part of whatever she was doing. Do you know if she knows anyone there or why she would go there?"

"No, I don't. When we found out about the accident, I asked Paula if she knew if Jenny had friends in Montgomery but Paula didn't know of any. She doesn't have any idea why Jenny would go there."

The phone conversation Laura had with Jenny kept playing in her mind. Laura could still hear the urgency in Jenny's voice, and she remembered the fear too, Jenny's insistence on taking precautions, her hinting that there might be danger. Jenny had been reluctant to explain much over the phone. The entire call had been very mysterious.

And now Jenny was dead.

A shiver ran up Laura's neck. The state police had determined that Jenny's accident had been caused by a blowout. They were convinced it was an accident. But Laura remembered that Erin Archembeau had died in a car accident as well. She kept telling herself that there was nothing sinister about either death, but she could not dismiss this thought completely. Jenny had feared that she was in danger. And then on that very same night, she died.

Laura remembered how Jenny had sounded on the phone and she considered whether Jenny's anxiety may have contributed to her losing control of the car. And Erin Archembeau had been visibly upset the day she died, too, which also could have contributed to her crash. On top of that, the roads up there were narrow and curvy. Both accidents could be innocent.

Could be. But Laura still wondered. No matter what justification she came up with, doubts remained. She kept thinking, *Could Jenny's death have been something other than an accident?* And if it was, were Erin Archembeau, the trip to Vancouver, the magazine article, the reason Jenny went to Montgomery—were all of those things involved somehow?

She looked at Roger Kincaid. "Do you know if anyone cleared out Jenny's apartment yet?"

"No, we haven't. It'll be a while before Paula feels up to doing that. Why?"

"Do you think Paula would mind if I took a quick look at what Jenny was working on, the notes for the article she was writing?"

"Why would you do that?"

"I'm not sure, exactly. I'd like to see if I can find out what Jenny wanted to talk to me about. It sounded important."

Roger considered it for a moment. He glanced back at Paula, sitting at the other end of the restaurant, then he turned to Laura again. From his pocket, he took out a single key.

"This is to Jenny's apartment," he said. "You won't disturb anything, will you?"

"I promise not to. I just want to look around her desk a little."

"Jenny spoke very highly of you. I don't think Paula would mind, you being Jenny's friend and her lawyer. Go ahead. See what you can find."

Laura had an eerie feeling when she unlocked the door and walked into Jenny's apartment. She felt as though she did not belong here, as though she was intruding into her friend's private life.

Jenny lived in the French Quarter, in a small one-bedroom apartment above an antique shop. The place was furnished sparingly. Two wooden rockers flanked the French doors leading to the iron-festooned balcony. Laura walked outside. On the street below, tourists milled about, shopping in the quaint stores, sampling the spicy foods of Louisiana. A horse-drawn buggy plodded by, hooves clattering on the road. In the distance, she saw the Mississippi River. This afternoon, the *Creole Queen* paddle boat was out on the water. She heard the faint brassy sound of the jazz band onboard.

She came back in and closed the doors. Above the sofa was a painting of Venice. Bookshelves took up most of the other wall space, and nearly every inch of tabletop was covered with magazines or half-read books. Noticeably silent was the small cuckoo clock hanging from the wall. The weight chains below it had not been pulled since Jenny's death. The hands were frozen at 8:27.

The air in the apartment held a trace of Jenny's perfume. It felt as though Jenny had just stepped out for a moment and would be returning any second. This thought, more than anything else, even more than the funeral, brought home to Laura the tragedy of her friend's death.

On the other side of the room was Jenny's workspace, a large mahogany desk, green banker's lamp, and leather chair. To the side was a smaller desk where her computer was, and alongside that was a table holding a stack of reference books. In the back was a wooden file cabinet. Laura walked over.

Except for a bin on one corner of the desk, the top was clear of papers and notebooks or anything having to do with Jenny's writing. Laura skimmed though the contents in the bin but found only bills and bank statements, nothing related to the article about infertility. Nothing, either, related to her trip to Vancouver.

Laura pulled back the chair and sat down. Placing her palms gently on the desktop, she drew a breath to steady herself. A small snapshot inside a brass frame was propped against the lamp. Laura pulled the chain on the lamp, illuminating the desk, then picked up the photograph.

She recognized Paula and Roger in the picture. They were on a sofa at home. Sitting between them was a baby, a girl, wearing pink pajamas. Laura assumed it was their daughter, Alyssa. Paula and Roger were beaming happily, holding the child and smiling at the camera. But Alyssa seemed completely oblivious to what was happening around her. She was staring up at the ceiling, her mouth slightly open, spittle running down her chin.

The thing Laura noticed in particular about the picture was the girl's expression. She had an absent, lifeless opacity to her eyes. Her face was set in a blank, vacant cast. One word came to mind when Laura looked at this girl: *empty.* It was as though there was nothing there, nothing beyond the outside shell of her body.

Laura noticed, though, that Alyssa looked somewhat familiar. For a moment, she thought back to whether Jenny had ever showed her any pictures of her niece. No, she was sure Jenny hadn't. Maybe Paula and Roger had brought the girl to Chyles's party last summer. Laura doubted that; surely they would have called and introduced themselves if they had. Jenny would have insisted on it.

Still, Laura was sure she had seen this girl before, and this thought nagged at her for a long while, until finally she understood.

It was not that she had seen Alyssa before, she realized. The familiarity she sensed was not so much from her features but from her expression. What Laura had seen before was the dullness of the eyes, the flat, shallow bearing, the vacant look.

Yes, she had seen this before—not in Jenny's niece, but in another child. In the boy at Chyles's party. Even though that had been months ago, Laura remembered that boy vividly. Something odd about him had struck her then, and now she saw the same quality in Alyssa. It had stayed with her all this time because it was so unusual, she thought, so incongruous in babies. She had always thought of children as being full of life. These babies, though, seemed almost catatonic. And that's what stuck in her mind. That's what was so unusual. That's what was familiar.

Staring at the photograph of Alyssa and thinking about the boy at the party last summer, Laura wondered if it was possible that these babies shared some common defect. She thought about how children with Down syndrome all look similar. These babies didn't quite look like that, but they did seem to share a similar quality. She allowed that she might be mistaken, but she could not stop comparing these two children.

And she thought about the article Jenny was writing and wondered if Jenny could have found something along these lines. She wanted to read Jenny's notes more than ever now and see if she could find some answers.

She turned her attention to the desk drawers, opening each one and searching the contents for anything relating to Jenny's research. She found nothing that seemed connected, just office supplies, unfinished articles on other subjects, a collection of receipts. Where would Jenny keep the material she had been working on for the last few months? Laura wondered. The desk seemed like the logical place, but there was nothing here.

Laura went through the file cabinet next, finding chapters from a novel Jenny had begun and abandoned, along with some old rejection letters, copies of contracts, a copy of a trust Laura had drawn up for her, articles with her byline that she had clipped from magazines. But she found nothing having to do with the fertility story.

Suspicion began deepening in Laura, leaving her uneasy. Jenny had obviously been deeply involved in researching the fertility article, so much so that she flew all the way to Canada to follow up on one aspect of it. There should be notes or correspondences or photocopies of things she had been researching somewhere around her desk. But there was nothing.

Laura swiveled the chair around and faced the computer. Perhaps Jenny had typed all her notes on the word processor and thrown away the paper. It didn't seem logical that there wouldn't be even a single piece of paper relating to infertility here, but Laura held open the possibility that everything might be on disk.

She pressed the power button and waited a few moments for the computer to boot up so she could run the word-processing program and see what was there. But instead of booting, the computer flashed a message: SYSTEM DISK ERROR. Laura turned the computer off, waited a few seconds, then tried to start it again. Again, the same message came on the screen: SYSTEM DISK ERROR.

At first she didn't understand what was wrong with the computer, but then she remembered last summer when the new computer she had ordered arrived at the house in Alabama. When she had tried to turn it on, this same message came on the screen: SYSTEM DISK ERROR.

The technician told her what it meant, but she couldn't recall exactly what he said. It had something to do with the hard drive, she remembered that much, but she couldn't recall—

Like a sudden gust of icy wind that took her breath away, Laura remembered. The message on the screen meant that the hard drive was blank. The files were gone. And it did not take much thought for Laura to realize how that had happened.

Someone had erased them.

17

"You don't know that someone erased the files," Dan said.

It was almost 2:00 A.M. He and Laura were lying in bed in their house in New Orleans. She wasn't able to sleep, so Dan stayed up and held her. She had hoped that being home tonight, in her own bed with her husband beside her, would bolster her spirits, set her mind at ease, but whatever comfort she gained from the familiar surroundings was lost under her grief and the many questions surrounding Jenny's death.

The missing files troubled her. That, more than anything, was keeping her awake. She was trying to make Dan understand why this bothered her so much, but he didn't seem to think it was as serious as she did. Maybe if Jenny had been *his* friend, maybe if he could have spoken to her the day before she died, maybe then he would share her sense that something was wrong.

"I'm not a computer expert," he said, "but I know that computers malfunction all the time. Hard drives crash, files get wiped out. That's just part of owning a computer. That's why a lot of people back things up on disks."

"I looked through Jenny's apartment for backup disks, but I couldn't find any."

"I didn't finish. A lot of people back up their files, but a lot of people don't. How many times have you heard about people losing whatever they're working on because they didn't back up? It must happen at your law firm."

Laura admitted that it did happen, occasionally, but that wasn't the point.

"That *is* the point," Dan said. "Jenny probably didn't back up either. She probably figured it couldn't happen to her. There's nothing suspicious about that."

"I couldn't find *any* disks in her apartment. None at all. And I know that's not right."

"There could be lots of explanations."

"Not any that make sense."

"Well, that's a matter of opinion."

"In my opinion, they don't."

He sighed, sounding exasperated and tired, but he didn't complain about being up this late. He pulled the blanket up to make sure she was warm, then said, "Honey, you've been through a lot the last few days. Why don't you try not to think about it so much."

"There's just so much that doesn't make sense."

"Give it time. I'll bet it will."

"Did I tell you what Jenny's brother-in-law told me?"

"No. What did he tell you?"

"He said that Jenny called him all the way from Vancouver to find out how many zygotes Chyles transferred to his wife."

"Why did she ask that?"

"I don't know and neither does he. He said Jenny didn't explain."

"How many did you have?" Dan wondered. "I think it was just one, right?"

"That's right."

"So how many did Jenny's brother-in-law say his wife got?"

"He didn't know how many."

"See, I'm a better husband," Dan said with warm grin. "I take an interest in my wife's uterus."

Laura chuckled, feeling a moment of ease. They lay in silence for a while. The sounds of city life outside the window were strange to Laura after sleeping in the stillness of the country for so long. Even at this hour, New Orleans was alive with activity.

"The point is," she said, thoughts of Jenny continuing to haunt her, "it's just a strange thing for Jenny to ask, to call all the way from Canada to ask about her sister's zygotes."

Dan laughed, then apologized for it. "The way you said it, it just came out funny."

"And Jenny wanted to know if they knew anyone named Nefayre."

"Who's that supposed to be?"

"All I know is that it has something to do with Vancouver, but I don't know how it fits in. The reason I thought Jenny went there was to find out about Erin Archembeau."

"I really feel like I'm out of the loop here. Who's Erin Archembeau?"

"You remember the woman who came to Chyles's birthday party last summer? The one who burst in screaming? When she left she crashed her car and died?"

"Oh, yeah, I remember it happening, but I don't remember her too well. Was that her name, Erin Archembeau?"

"Yes. And I thought Jenny went to Vancouver to find out more about her for the article she was writing. But when she called her brother-in-law from Vancouver, she didn't mention Erin Archembeau at all. All she asked about were zygotes and someone named Nefayre."

Dan shrugged. "Well, that doesn't really sound as odd as you're making it out to be. So, she asked about zygotes and someone named Nefayre. Zygotes are all part of the infertility thing—nothing unusual about that. And Nefayre, well, that could be anyone."

"Do you remember what Erin Archembeau screamed at the party that day?"

"No, not really."

"I thought she said, 'It's not fair.'"

"If you say so. I don't remember what it was."

"No, I don't *know* if that's what she screamed. That's what I *thought* it was. But I've been thinking about it. Maybe that's not what she said after all. Maybe what she actually said was Nefayre. That sort of sounds like 'not fair,' doesn't it? Nefayre, not fair—they sound alike."

Dan considered it, then shrugged and said, "I guess so. If you say that's what she said."

"I don't know if that's what she said, but let's just say it is. Why would she scream Nefayre? Why would she go to Dr. Chyles's house and do that?"

"I give up. Why?"

"I don't know, but I think Jenny might have known. She must have found out something in Vancouver, something to do with Erin Archembeau and someone named Nefayre, and something about zygotes. And whatever it was, it really scared her. When I talked to her on the phone last week, I could tell she was scared."

"Maybe that's something you're reading into it now, after what happened."

"No, that's what I thought then, when I talked to her. I mean, I've never heard her sound that way before. It scared me, the way she sounded."

"She didn't say why she was scared?"

"She was going to tell me the next day. But then—" Laura didn't finish saying it. She took a moment to gather herself, then said, "It's really bothering me, the fact that there's no notes, no way to tell what it was that Jenny knew, what she wanted to talk to me about. And then her dying in a car accident, the same way Erin Archembeau died."

"Wait a minute. It sounds like you're saying you don't think it was an accident."

"I'm not sure."

"I thought you told me before that the state police in Alabama investigated it and concluded that it was an accident, that she had a blowout and that caused her to go off the road."

"But how can they know for sure?"

"They can tell things like that."

"Not always. What if it wasn't an accident?"

"Oh, come on, Laura. You're letting your imagination get the best of you. Look, we both know how bad those roads are up there. You remember the first day we drove up to the clinic? *We* almost crashed. Remember? Jenny's having an accident isn't suspicious at all."

"You didn't talk to her the day before she died."

"No, I didn't, which is probably why I can look at it more objectively than you can. If there had been anything suspicious about the accident, the state police would have found it."

"Maybe they missed something."

"Laura, the only thing state troopers do is give out tickets and investigate accidents. They would have noticed, believe me. It was an accident. Your friend lost control of her car on those roads, which are terrible to begin with, and she hit a tree. It's horrible that it happened, and I feel bad about it, I feel bad for her and I feel bad for you, but, honey, things like that happen all the time. They're tragic, but they do happen."

"There's just too many questions," Laura said. "Too much doesn't make sense."

"It doesn't make sense to you right now, but I'll bet if you give it a little time, give yourself a chance to get some perspective on all this, it'll make sense to you, as much as the death of a friend can possibly make sense."

"You really think so?"

He held her more tightly. "I'll tell you what I think," he said. "I think you're the most caring, loving person I've ever met. You're the best friend anyone could ever ask for. And because you care so much, it's hard for you to accept that Jenny is gone. I know it hurts you, it hurts you so much that the lawyer in you is taking over as a defense mechanism, and the lawyer in you is concentrating on the smallest of inconsistencies and blowing them all out of proportion. Not everything in life makes sense to us all the time. Some things we can't understand. Some things we're not supposed to understand. At least not right away. But I really think that in a week or two, when you start to get some distance from all this, you'll see that it isn't what you think. I honestly believe that."

Laura snuggled closer. "I hope so," she whispered. She closed her eyes and drew in a deep breath of the warm scent of his body. She felt safe with him. Everything was all right as long as she was with him. If only they could stay together, instead of living six hours away from each other, things would be so much better. But she knew she had to leave in the morning, she had to return to Collier and continue her daily shots. She had to go back, stay by herself, deal with all of this alone. She had to do it, for the baby.

"I just want it to be over soon," she whispered.

He hushed her and stroked her shoulder tenderly. "Try to get some sleep, sweetheart. Try to get some sleep."

Early the next morning, Dan drove her to the train station. They kissed on the platform as other passengers boarded the train around them.

"I'll be up Saturday," he told her.

"I'll be waiting."

"Listen, I want you to take it easy driving. I want you to be careful. Remember, you've got my whole family with you and I don't want to lose any of you."

"You won't."

"I love you very much," he said. "Don't forget that."

She smiled. "I won't." They kissed again and she whispered in his ear how much she loved him, then she boarded the train and watched him through the window as he waved from the platform while the train pulled away.

18

Though she was tired from the trip, Laura drove straight from the train station to the New Life Center. She needed to have her daily blood tests and get her shots before the outpatient wing closed for the evening. Since she had missed her normal appointment this morning, the nurses had to fit her in between other patients. As she sat out front, waiting for them to call her, she chatted with a woman who was just beginning her therapy here. The woman had undergone *in vitro* on Monday and was nervous about whether it would be successful. Like Laura, she had the same difficulty producing eggs, until she came to Dr. Chyles.

"Dr. Chyles says he's had a lot of success doing *in vitro* with only one zygote," she told Laura. "We're keeping our fingers crossed that we'll finally have a child."

When Gail, her regular nurse, called Laura back, she was still thinking about the new woman and her zygote. The conversation she had with Jenny's brother-in-law was in her thoughts as well, particularly what he told her about Jenny's interest in the number of zygotes Paula had. After Gail weighed Laura and took her temperature and blood pressure, Laura said, "I was wondering if you knew how many zygotes Dr. Chyles transferred in the *in vitro* procedure I had back in July."

Gail laughed. "That's a strange question."

"My husband and I sort of have a bet about how many it was," she said, forcing a chuckle, trying to act casual about the whole thing. "I told him it was only one. He said it was more. Maybe you could settle it for us. There's a lobster dinner riding on the outcome," she added, laughing again.

Gail laughed too and started to prepare the syringes to draw blood. "I wish I could help you, Mrs. Fielding, but I don't know how many you had."

"It must be on my chart," Laura said, gesturing toward the folder on the desk.

"Not in that one. That just has the results of your daily blood tests and your exams since you became pregnant. Everything that came before, including the number of zygotes, is in the doctor's record."

"Would it be too much trouble to check that for me?"

Gail thought about it a moment, then said, "Well, I'm really not supposed to go in the doctor's office, but I'll tell you what: while we're waiting for the results of your blood test, I'll see if I can take a peek."

"That would be great. Thanks."

"Don't thank me yet. It may cost you a lobster dinner."

Gail left. As Laura waited, she found it difficult keeping awake. It had been a long day—a long few days, really. Since Jenny's death, she hadn't gotten much sleep. Mostly, these last few nights, she had lain awake thinking about Jenny. She hoped tonight she could finally get some rest.

Bored, impatient for Gail to return, Laura looked around the room for something to hold her attention. The folder was still on the desk where Gail had left it. She thought about taking a look inside, but decided that Gail wouldn't have lied about the information's not being there.

On the wall above the desk hung one of Chyles's photographs. It was another seascape, which is what all his pictures seemed to be. A different one was displayed in each of the examination rooms. It was drizzling in this picture; the sky was gray, and so was the water. The rocks were a darker leaden shade of gray. Rising from the sand were jagged cliffs. There were no people in the shot, no sea birds, no vegetation, just the harsh surfaces of the rocks and the waves crashing violently against them.

Doctors' offices should have relaxing pictures, she thought, soft colors and warm images to put patients at ease. Chyles, however, liked to display these. Laura wondered if it had something to do with his ego—showing off his creations, just like that party he threw last summer to show off the babies he had given to so many couples. Ego probably did have a lot to do with it, she decided, but that didn't make it wrong. Chyles had done something good for many couples and he was proud of it. It was understandable that he wanted to show off his accomplishments. He must also be proud of his photography. Even though the pictures weren't as important as his efforts to help couples have children, displaying them was a small concession to his ego.

As she stared at the photograph now, she had a strange, vague feeling that something about it didn't fit. But what didn't fit about it? she asked herself. Why did it look so wrong?

There was a tap on the door. Laura turned and expected to see Gail return with the needles and the information about the number of zygotes, but instead Dr. Chyles came in.

"Good afternoon, Laura," he said.

"Dr. Chyles. I didn't expect to see you until Monday."

"Well, the nurse told me that your blood pressure had been higher than normal the last few days, and that you looked especially tired today. I wanted to make sure you were feeling all right."

"I appreciate your concern, but I'm fine. I lost a friend a few days ago, and I guess that's just taken its toll."

"I'm sorry to hear that."

"I went down to New Orleans for the funeral yesterday and took the train back this morning. The traveling took a lot out of me."

"Traveling like that isn't really a good idea in your condition, Laura. I'd like you to try to take it easy as much as possible. Of course, I understand about losing your friend and going to the funeral."

"Well, I don't plan any other trips anytime soon."

"That's good."

"I feel pretty good otherwise, all things considered. I appreciate your concern, but you really didn't have to come in and check on me."

"Probably not, but since I'm already here, let me take a quick look."

He put a blood-pressure cuff on her arm and measured her blood pressure, then checked her pulse and listened to her stomach with his stethoscope.

"Everything seems good," he said. He put away the stethoscope and circled around to the front of the table. "The results from the amnio should be in in a few days," he said. "I'll know the baby's sex then. Do you and your husband want to know or do you want to wait and be surprised when the child is born?"

"We'd like to know ahead of time. But I want to wait until Dan comes up before you tell us. We'd like to find out together."

"That's a good idea. It's much nicer that way."

As he guided her feet into the stirrups, he asked, "Was it someone close?"

"Pardon me?" she said.

"The friend who passed away," he said, putting on gloves. "Was it someone close?"

"It was a woman I've known for many years, yes. She was my first client when I joined the law firm I'm with now. You met her once."

"I did?"

"Her name was Jenny Hopkins. She was a writer. She came up here during the summer to interview you for a story she was doing on fertility clinics."

Chyles glanced up at her, and Laura thought she saw recognition in his face, but he shook his head and said, "I don't think I remember her."

"She said you were busy that day and couldn't spend much time with her."

He nodded. "That could be true. I see so many people in the course of a day. If it was only a one-time meeting months ago like you say, and I didn't talk to her very long, I probably wouldn't remember her."

He turned back to the examination now and neither of them spoke much after that. As Laura lay in silence, feeling oddly uncomfortable with the doctor today, she had a strange sense that something was wrong.

It wasn't until Chyles finished the examination and looked up at her that she realized what it was. She watched as he wheeled the stool back and began preparing the injections, certain just from the look on his face that when he had spoken of not remembering Jenny, he had been lying.

19

Charlotte Wheeler phoned that night to tell Laura that she was taking the train in from Georgia tomorrow and to ask if Laura would pick her and the baby up at the station. They were only going to be in Collier for one night. Laura insisted that they stay with her.

Laura's appointment at the clinic the next morning was at 10:30, allowing her just enough time to pick up Charlotte at 9:45, drive her home, then go to the clinic for her shots.

When Charlotte got off the train, she carried the baby in a car seat and had him wrapped in a heavy blanket to shield him from the wind. Laura felt a rush of emotion, seeing her friend again and seeing the newborn. The sight gave her an even stronger sense of the child she was carrying inside her.

They hugged, then Laura said, "It's so good to see you. I missed not having you around. How's the baby doing? Let me see him."

"Michael's growing up so fast," Charlotte said.

She had him bundled snugly to keep him warm. She opened the blanket just enough for Laura to take a peek at him.

The baby looked like he had just awakened. He stared up at Laura with groggy blue eyes. He lay very still in his mother's arms.

"He's beautiful," Laura said.

"Isn't he just the most darling baby you've ever seen?"

"He sure is."

"Remember how tiny he was when he was born?"

"I remember. He's grown quite a bit since then."

Charlotte gazed lovingly at her baby. "We're so lucky."

Laura took the overnight bag from Charlotte and they walked to the car. Michael remained unfazed by all the people and noise and movement around him. Laura turned the heat high to keep him warm. The car filled quickly with the powdery scent of the baby. It was the most wonderful smell Laura could imagine.

"Before we leave," Charlotte said, "do you mind if I feed Michael?"

"Of course not."

"Some people get offended."

"Hey, I'm going to be doing the same thing myself pretty soon. How could I possibly be offended?"

Charlotte opened her blouse and positioned the baby at her breast. "You won't believe the way this makes you feel inside," she said. "It's incredible. It's like my body is all that's keeping him alive. Everything he needs to live and grow is right in me. And then when you feel his little hands holding on, and he looks up at you with those eyes of his, it really makes you feel like you've done something special."

"I've got four more months. I don't know if I can wait that long."

"I know exactly how you feel. I didn't think I could wait nine months, either."

"You didn't have to. Remember?"

Charlotte smiled. "I got lucky." She gazed down at the baby. "I wish I had done this ten years ago. Richard does, too."

"Your husband's happy?"

"Are you kidding? I never saw him like this before. He acts like a kid when he's around Michael." She lowered her voice and blushed. "When he and I are together," she said, "it's like we're on our second honeymoon. We haven't been this close in years. This baby is the best thing that could have happened to us."

"You little tramp," Laura said.

Charlotte blushed, smiling contentedly.

"So what brings you back to Collier?" Laura asked. "Tell me you came just to see me."

"I did want to see you."

"But . . . ?"

Charlotte beamed now. "We're going to do it again."

"Do what?"

"Richard and I are going to see if we can have another baby."

"You're kidding."

"Nope. I have an appointment with Dr. Chyles this morning at eleven to see if he thinks we can."

"But you just had Michael."

"And he's what made us realize how much we want another child."

"Don't you want to wait a little while before you go through this all over again?"

"Laura, I'm forty-one years old. I don't have time to wait. It's now or never. I thought you'd be happy for me."

"I am. Very much. You just caught me by surprise. If that's what you want to do, I think it's just great. You don't mind spending another nine months up here?"

"For another child, I don't mind at all."

"That's wonderful, then. I hope Dr. Chyles has good news for you."

"Maybe this time it'll be a girl."

Charlotte looked down at Michael. "I think you've had enough for now," she said. She started to ease the baby away from her breast so she could strap him into the car seat so they could leave, but he let out a loud, feral scream that made Laura cringe. His tiny fingers clawed desperately at Charlotte's breast.

Charlotte tried again to pull the baby away, but he screamed louder. His tiny fingernails dug into Charlotte's skin; he would not let go. With his mouth wide open, he bared his gums in what Laura could only describe as an animalistic snarl. For an instant, his eyes looked as though they rolled back into his head, leaving only vacant white apertures in his face.

Charlotte didn't know what to do. Panicked, she drew the baby against her breast and allowed him to continue nursing. He calmed down instantly.

"Is he all right?" Laura asked.

Charlotte's breathing was strained. She nodded. Then she forced a chuckle and smiled and said, "He's just overly hungry after the long trip." She tried to act as though nothing were wrong, but Laura could see that she was upset.

"Are you okay, Charlotte?"

"Oh, I'm fine. Really. This is nothing."

The outburst had come so suddenly, and now, just as suddenly, it was gone. Witnessing this strange scene left Laura bewildered.

As the baby suckled calmly, Laura saw that his face had a strange impassive cast. He looked as though he didn't even realize what had just happened. Laura was about to ask again if Michael was all right when she noticed that there were several pink streaks on Charlotte's breast where Michael had scratched her. One of the marks had a thin bead of blood on it.

"My God, Charlotte, you're bleeding," Laura said.

Charlotte quickly wiped the blood away, looking embarrassed. "It's nothing," she said, "just a scratch."

"Are you sure? Are you okay?"

"I'm fine. I told you, it's nothing."

Laura shook her head, still surprised by what had happened a moment ago. "Michael did that?" she said. "Has that happened before?"

"Really, Laura, it isn't anything." Charlotte was trying to act unaffected, but her voice was unsteady and her face was red. She was obviously uncomfortable discussing this. "It's nothing at all," she said. "Nothing. Really."

Laura didn't say any more about it. But as they waited for Michael to finish nursing, she could think of nothing else but what that baby had just done and how strange it all was.

For 10 minutes the three of them remained in the car at the train station while Michael continued to nurse. Only when he had his fill and was willing to relinquish his mother's breast did Charlotte dare to put him in the car seat so they could leave.

Watching this, Laura remembered what Jenny's brother-in-law had told her after the funeral, about his daughter's sudden violent outbursts. Is this what he was talking about? she wondered.

She couldn't help but think that this certainly was not normal behavior.

By the time they arrived at the clinic, Laura was a few minutes late for her appointment. Gail took her back right away. Laura was still thinking about what happened in the car when Gail said, "Oh, by the way, I checked on the number of zygotes for you. Remember you were asking about that yesterday? Well, I checked. It was two."

"Two?"

"Yup, two. Who wins?"

Laura didn't understand.

"The bet you and your husband had?" the nurse said. "About how many it was. Who wins?"

Laura remembered now the story she had told the nurse the previous day. "He did," she murmured, but her thoughts were on the number of zygotes. She was certain it was only one, that it *could* only be one. Chyles had harvested only one egg; that's what she remembered. That's what Dan had said too. "Are you sure?" Laura asked the nurse. "You must be mistaken."

"I'm sure I'm not," the nurse said. "I looked in the file in the doctor's office. It says it right there that he transferred two zygotes."

20

—•—

When they arrived home, Laura helped Charlotte get settled in. Michael needed changing and Charlotte was tired, so Laura offered to do it. As she wiped and powdered him, expecting to feel a surge of maternal emotion, she was surprised that she felt a strange sense of detachment instead. It wasn't because Michael wasn't her own; it was much stronger than that. She didn't know exactly what it was that made her feel unsettled, but she could not deny this strange feeling.

She looked down at Michael, trying to understand. He remained perfectly still the whole time, not reacting at all to what she was doing. He didn't seem to care that she wasn't his mother. In fact, he didn't seem to notice her standing over him at all. When she touched him, he didn't react in the least, as though he couldn't feel her hands against his skin. He just lay on his back, staring up at nothing in particular, his arms and legs motionless.

Laura felt uneasy holding him. She thought his body was colder than normal. She rubbed his arms and legs to warm him, but her touch still did not elicit the slightest reaction. If it weren't for his eyes being open, she might have thought he was asleep. No, it was a stronger feeling than that, she realized. It was almost as if the body in her hands was not even alive.

As she put the new diaper on him, she found herself staring at him again and she began to think that something about him looked familiar. It wasn't until she was almost finished that she realized what it was.

In many ways, Michael bore a strange resemblance to Jenny's niece Alyssa and to the boy at Chyles's party last summer. It was not his actual features, not something so much physical as it was . . . essential, intrinsic. She saw it mostly in his eyes, more specifically in the look *behind* his eyes, something internal, something almost innate. She wasn't exactly sure what it was, but he definitely resembled those other babies, and that recognition troubled her.

Like them, he had vacant eyes. And he seemed to move infrequently, and when he did move, it was slowly and awkwardly. His reactions to the world around him were withdrawn, spiritless.

Except for that instant earlier today in the car when he'd become suddenly violent. And even then, when it was over, he'd acted as though it had been nothing, as though he had no feelings about it at all, no guilt, no remorse, no—

That's foolishness, Laura told herself. *He's only an infant, for goodness' sake. At that age, children don't feel guilt; they have no sense of right and wrong. That's something they develop later.*

Laura wanted to believe there was nothing wrong with Michael. And she wanted to feel the same exhilaration and vitality that Charlotte felt when she was with her newborn son. But Laura could not dismiss the thought that Michael was not normal, and even if she could convince herself that he was, she still could not bring herself to feel anything for him.

But Michael isn't my baby, she told herself. *That's why I don't feel deeply for him. That's all it is. Surely that's all it is.*

But when she looked at Michael now, she found herself thinking the same thing she had thought when she had looked at the picture of Alyssa, when she had looked at the boy at the party last summer. The same word came to mind now: *empty.* She could not stop thinking that these children looked as though they had nothing inside.

In that sense, in that odd quality, the three babies seemed

related. And that did not make sense at all—unless the babies shared some common condition. But what might that be? she wondered. And what did it mean to their well-being? To that, she did not know the answer, but she did know one thing, one thing that kept coming to the front of her thoughts, one common bond shared by all three babies: all of them had been born at Chyles's New Life Center. That truth she could not erase from her mind.

When she finished changing Michael, she gave him to Charlotte, who put him to bed for a midday nap. Laura went downstairs and made egg-salad sandwiches, then she and Charlotte sat together in the kitchen, talking and having lunch.

"How did it go with Dr. Chyles this morning?" Laura asked.

"He was very encouraging. He thinks having a second baby is a good idea."

"He thinks he can help you conceive again?"

"He said there's no reason we shouldn't be able to. We just have to go through the *in vitro* procedure again, and the chances are good that it'll work just as well. We're going to wait until after Christmas. Then he's going to start me again on Pergonal and see how many eggs we'll get for the *in vitro* this time."

"I'm really happy for you. I hope it works out."

"I'm sure it will."

"Speaking of how many eggs," Laura said, "do you remember how many you had the first time, when you conceived Michael?"

"Just one. Why?"

"I thought that's what I had too, but today the nurse told me that she checked the record and it was two."

"What difference does that make?"

"A friend of mine was writing an article about fertility clinics and she was interested in that, the number of zygotes Chyles uses. I don't know why, though."

"She won't tell you why?"

"She . . . um—she passed away last week, before she could tell me."

"Oh, I'm terribly sorry for you, Laura. No wonder you

look a little peaked. I should have realized that something was bothering you. I'm so sorry. Can I do anything for you?"

"Thanks, but I'm doing okay. Just having you here for a visit is a big help."

"I wish we could stay longer, but Richard's parents are coming up from Tampa and I really have to be there."

"I understand. That's fine. I'm much better now."

"Are you sure? You looked kind of distracted."

"I've been troubled by a lot of things related to Jenny's accident. She was looking into a few different things and they were sort of related to the clinic here, and I was just hoping to make sense of it all."

Charlotte reached across the table and held Laura's hand. "It's hard when someone close to us dies. I know, because I lost my mother two years ago. It takes time to get over it, but we go on. And pretty soon, you'll have your baby and that'll be the only thing you'll think about. Take it from me, I know. Everything will be okay, Laura. You'll see."

"I hope so."

Laura was grateful for Charlotte's company. They stayed up late and talked about what it was like having a child. They caught up on everything that had happened to each of them since Charlotte had moved back to Georgia. The baby cried every few hours, needing to be fed, and each cry brought the return of Laura's mental questions about what might be wrong with Michael.

Laura did not sleep well that night, unable to shake the sense of uneasiness about Michael. The more she thought about him, the more she believed that something *was* wrong with him. Perhaps he was ill. She could not understand it, and she didn't know whether to say anything to Charlotte.

The next morning, Laura got up early to fix breakfast. Charlotte and the baby were still asleep. She poured a bowl of milk and set it outside on the back porch. Felix, or his twin—she still wasn't sure—was waiting by the door to come inside.

"You'll have to stay out until they leave," Laura said. She didn't think it was a good idea for the cat to be near the baby.

As the cat moved to drink the milk, Laura started back inside, then suddenly stopped, struck by what she saw. She stood in the chilly morning air, staring down at the cat. Her thoughts, however, were not so much on the cat alone. What she suddenly realized, what stunned her to the core, was the similarity between the cat . . . and Michael.

The cat never reacted when she petted it, never showed the least bit of affection. She remembered yesterday when she changed Michael's diaper that Michael responded the same way. The cat, even after all these months, gave Laura the impression that it stayed around solely for the food and shelter, having no interest in her company beyond that. She had only spent one day with Michael, but she could not stop thinking that the way the cat felt toward her was the same way Michael felt toward Charlotte.

And like the cat, Michael had a peculiar look—not a physical defect, nothing as blatant as the cat's absence of ears, but something else. It was something vague, something perhaps inside, a facet of his personality, of his nature. Something about him was definitely abnormal.

When Charlotte came downstairs carrying the baby, Laura said very little. She could not get past the feeling of uneasiness. They ate in quiet, then left for the train station.

Realizing that she might not see Charlotte for a while, and needing to confirm what was nagging at her thoughts, Laura carefully broached the subject of the baby.

"I never did ask you what Dr. Chyles said about Michael."

"What do you mean?"

"He must have examined him after he was born, right?"

"Sure. He's a very thorough doctor. He even examined him yesterday. He said he always likes to check on the babies' development when he has the chance."

"How does he think Michael is doing?"

"Michael is doing just great."

"That's what Dr. Chyles said? He said that?"

Charlotte looked confused. "Of course Michael is fine. I can tell that myself."

"Dr. Chyles said so too?"

"Of course he did. But I didn't need him to tell me that.

Why are you asking me this, Laura? It almost sounds like you think there's something wrong with Michael."

Laura was surprised that Charlotte hadn't noticed anything unusual about her son. Laura didn't feel comfortable telling Charlotte that her pride and joy didn't appear to be as perfect as she thought. But she was concerned about her friend and she felt she had to say something.

"I just wanted to make sure he was doing okay," Laura said. "I was worried after what happened in the car yesterday."

"Why? What happened?"

"You remember. When you tried to stop feeding Michael."

"Oh, that." Charlotte dismissed it with a wave of her hand. "That was nothing. That was just because of the long trip and because I had to get him up early yesterday morning. He was a little irritable, that's all."

Laura just nodded.

"No, Michael's just fine," Charlotte said. "He's as healthy as a baby could be."

"I'm glad to hear that. Really, I am."

As they drove through town toward the train station, Laura kept glancing at the baby in the car seat. Charlotte was making loving faces at him, touching his fingers, rubbing his nose. She was completely absorbed by her new son.

What struck Laura as she watched them was how unloving the baby was toward Charlotte. And how *unlovable*. He was beautiful; Laura could not deny that. But she did not find him at all lovable. *He's like a toy,* she thought, *like a doll that is a pleasure to look at but not something you can feel deep emotion for.*

And as she thought back to Chyles's party and the baby boy there, and thought back to that afternoon in Jenny's apartment and the picture of Jenny's niece, a disturbing notion entered her mind. Unconsciously on both of those occasions, she had experienced the same reaction, thought the same thought, about how unlovable these children were. In an inscrutable way, they *were* unlovable.

She shuddered as a frightening thought entered her mind. *Is this how my baby will be?*

Laura realized that this was not the first time this thought had come to her. She had been fighting to suppress it ever since yesterday—or perhaps even earlier, since she saw the picture of Jenny's niece, perhaps ever since she saw that first baby at the birthday party last summer. But now the notion of giving birth to a child she might not be able to love forced itself to the surface, and she felt a chill of uneasiness. She realized that this was what disturbed her the most about Charlotte's baby and about the other babies she had seen. She was afraid that her baby would be as lifeless as these others.

"Charlotte," she said quietly.

Charlotte looked up from her child, smiling blissfully. Laura wasn't sure how to word this, but she had to try. She had to ask.

"Don't take this the wrong way, okay?"

"Don't take what the wrong way? What's the matter, Laura?"

Laura hesitated, searching for the right words. Finally she said, "Do you remember that party we went to last summer? The one at Dr. Chyles's house?"

"The birthday party? Sure, I remember."

"Do you remember that baby, the first baby, the one-year-old?"

"Vaguely. Why?"

"Did you notice anything about him?"

Charlotte shrugged. "Like what?"

"I don't know exactly." Laura hesitated, then finally said, "It seemed to me that he was kind of apathetic. Did you get that impression?"

"Apathetic?"

"It was like he was almost—" Laura took a breath and hoped this didn't sound too harsh. "Almost abnormal," she said. "You know what I mean, don't you?"

"Not really. Abnormal how?"

"Kind of listless. You didn't get that impression from him?"

Charlotte shook her head. "To tell you the truth, I really don't remember him that well. Why do you ask?"

"Well, it's just that I think of babies as being so full of life, so inspiring. But that baby didn't seem like that to me. Did he seem like that to you?"

Charlotte thought for a moment then shrugged. "I really don't remember, Laura. It was such a long time ago. And there were several babies there."

Laura took another breath and tried to select her words carefully.

"I've noticed," she said, "with other babies born at the clinic that they're—they seem kind of—I'm not sure what you'd call it. I think I'd describe it as . . . impassive."

"Impassive?"

This was turning out to be more difficult than Laura had expected. But she continued anyway, trying to express her feelings subtly but clearly.

"I mean they're not emotional or affectionate or anything like that," she said. "The only time they show any real signs of life is when they're angry. Then all of a sudden they just get . . . sort of wild. I don't know if you remember, but the woman at the party told a story about how her son attacked another boy at the doctor's office. Remember that? And I talked to another couple, the sister and brother-in-law of a close friend of mine. Their baby girl is the same way. Her father said that most of the time she's very quiet, but then all of a sudden it's like something snaps. This may sound ridiculous, but it seems to me almost like there might be something wrong with them."

Charlotte just looked at Laura, not saying anything. Her expression changed from confused to somber, then to suspicious. The silence in the car became unbearable. Laura thought Charlotte was holding her son's hand more tightly now, clinging to it more protectively.

"What are you saying, Laura?" she asked defensively. "*Exactly* what are you saying?"

The sudden change in Charlotte's demeanor made it even more difficult for Laura to continue. This was not what she had intended. She wished she had handled it differently, wished she hadn't even brought it up, but it was too late to stop now. She had to try to make sense of it all. She just hoped she could make Charlotte understand.

"I told you about my friend who died," Laura said.

"You told me."

"She's the one whose sister and brother-in-law had a baby here, the girl I mentioned. Did I tell you that my friend was doing research for an article she was writing about fertility clinics?"

"You said something like that. So?"

"She went to Canada, to Vancouver, to find out about a woman who was a patient of Dr. Chyles's. I don't know what she found, but whatever it was frightened her. It had something to do with the number of zygotes used and with someone named Nefayre and with a place in Montgomery called Woodridge. I don't know exactly what it all means, but when I looked for her notes on her computer to see what she was doing, they were gone. All her disks were gone and everything was erased."

"Why are you telling me this?" Charlotte said, her tone sharp with anger now.

"I'm trying to explain why I—"

"I don't care about Vancouver or anybody out there and I don't really care about your friend's magazine article. I care about my baby. That's all. And it sounds to me like you're saying something is wrong with Michael."

"I didn't say that."

"Not in so many words, but that's what you're implying, isn't it?"

Laura didn't answer, but Charlotte could see by the expression on Laura's face that she truly believed that something was wrong with Michael.

"Just because he was irritable when I stopped feeding him?" Charlotte said, the anger in her voice now tempered with desperation.

"It's not just that, Charlotte."

"You don't have any right to accuse Michael of being anything less than a normal, healthy baby."

"Just listen to me for a minute."

"No!" Charlotte was fighting back tears now. "I won't listen to you. I listened to my doctor. He knows. He said Michael is just fine, and that's good enough for me."

"Charlotte, please—"

"I didn't think you were like that, Laura. That's the way Dana Aaron was, always making trouble. But I never expected you to be like that."

"I'm not trying to make trouble for you or anyone else."

"What do you call it, then? You make a sweeping statement like that, calling all the babies abnormal. That's a terrible thing to say."

"That's not what I meant."

"What did you mean, then?"

Laura let out a weak breath, confused and feeling overwhelmed. "I'm not sure," she said.

"Then you shouldn't say anything at all if you're not sure."

"I'm just trying to find out if there's something wrong with the babies being born here. That's all."

"There's nothing wrong with Michael."

Laura hesitated a moment, hoping Charlotte would calm down. Charlotte turned away and stared out the window, avoiding Laura's gaze.

"Charlotte," Laura said.

Charlotte didn't look or acknowledge her in any way.

"I'm really sorry, Charlotte. I didn't mean to hurt you. Honestly I didn't."

Charlotte turned slightly but still wouldn't look directly at her.

"If Dr. Chyles says the babies are fine and the parents say the babies are fine, why can't you just accept that the babies are fine? You haven't spent time with any of them. For goodness' sake, you saw Michael awake for only a few hours. That doesn't qualify you to make any kind of judgment about how healthy or normal he is. My goodness, Laura—"

Charlotte had to stop as tears streamed from her eyes. She wiped them away and let out a thin sigh. She faced Laura now. Her anger faded, replaced by a frightened, pleading look.

"All you have to do is take one look at Michael," she said. "Anyone can tell that he's a perfectly healthy baby boy. Whatever you're thinking, you're mistaken. There's nothing wrong with the babies being born here. There's nothing wrong with Michael."

Charlotte suddenly looked weak, fragile. Laura realized that it was useless to pursue this any further. Charlotte would never accept it, and if Laura tried to force her to see the truth, it would surely devastate her.

"I'm sorry," Laura said. "I didn't mean to hurt you. I didn't mean to say that there's anything wrong with your son. I'm sorry if I hurt you. Honestly, I am."

Charlotte nodded. She needed a moment to compose herself. Finally, she looked at Laura and spoke in an anguished whisper.

"Women are coming here and they're having babies. Before, they couldn't. There's nothing bad about that, Laura. That's a blessing. That can't possibly be anything but good."

21

Charlotte's visit had intensified Laura's fears and suspicions. She needed answers to her questions. At the clinic that morning, she sat in the examination room, waiting for her injections, staring absentmindedly at Chyles's photograph of the rocky coastline, trying to understand what had happened. Afterward, as she drove home, her thoughts remained on Jenny's trip to Canada, and she kept asking herself what Jenny could have learned there. What did it have to do with the babies?

Determined to find answers, Laura hurried into the house and sat at her desk. The cat, lying on the window sill, watched with little interest as she picked up the phone and called directory assistance in Vancouver. She asked if there was a listing for Erin Archembeau.

"That number has been disconnected," the operator said.

"Do you have any other Archembeaus listed?"

"I have a listing for Dean and Helen Archembeau."

Laura thought they might be related to Erin's husband. She dialed the number, but as it started to ring, she realized she wasn't sure what to say.

A woman answered. "Hello?"

"Mrs. Archembeau?" Laura asked.

"Yes."

"You don't know me. My name is Laura Fielding. I'm calling from Alabama. I'd like to ask you a few questions about Erin."

The woman said nothing.

"Mrs. Archembeau?"

"Yes."

There was heaviness in the woman's tone, caution. Laura was sure that this woman was Erin's relative. From the voice, she sounded much older than Erin, so Laura guessed she was Erin's mother-in-law. She wondered how close this woman had been to Erin and whether the four months since the death was enough time for her to feel comfortable talking about it.

"You are related to Erin, aren't you?" Laura asked.

The woman hesitated a moment, then said, "Are you another writer?"

"No. No I'm not."

The mention of *another writer* made it clear to Laura that Jenny had spoken to this woman, and this encouraged Laura to continue. It meant she was closer to discovering what Jenny had learned—and what had frightened her.

"I'm not a writer, Mrs. Archembeau," Laura said. "I knew Erin."

It was not exactly a lie, Laura told herself.

"You knew her?" the woman asked, still cautious.

"Yes. We met here in Alabama. You are related to her, right?"

"She's my daughter-in-law," the woman said. "What was your name again?"

"Laura Fielding."

"Miss Fielding, I'm sorry to have to tell you this, but Erin was in an accident a few months ago."

"I know, and I'd like to offer my condolences."

The woman hesitated. "Thank you. Um, if you knew about the accident, why did you call?"

"I was hoping I could ask *you* a few questions."

"What kind of questions?"

"This will only take a moment; it's very important to me," Laura said. "Erin went to a fertility specialist some time ago. I was wondering if you knew anything about that. His name is Dr. Chyles, Norman Chyles."

"Is he the one from the clinic?"

"The clinic? You mean the New Life Center? Yes, that's the doctor I mean."

"No, that's not what it was called. Narrows Point Reproduction Clinic, something like that. The one in Burnaby, you mean?"

"No, I'm talking about the clinic here in Alabama." Then Laura considered that Erin could have been Chyles's patient before he came here to Collier, so she said, "Or it might have been in Miami, Florida."

"Erin and Elliot never went to the States to see a fertility doctor. Certainly not all the way to Alabama or Florida."

"You must be mistaken."

"I know for a fact that they didn't. They've been to Washington and Idaho, but not to see a doctor, and they've never been as far away as Alabama or Florida. No, the first time Erin ever went to Alabama was when she had that accident. And I don't even know why she went that time. She didn't tell me. She didn't tell anyone. She hadn't been herself since—"

The woman didn't finish the thought. Laura waited a

moment, hoping the woman would continue, but all she heard over the line was silence.

"Mrs. Archembeau?" Laura said at last.

"I have to hang up," the woman said. Her voice sounded unsteady now. "I have to go."

"Can I ask you one thing? You talked to a writer a few weeks ago, right? A woman named Jenny Hopkins?"

The woman didn't answer.

"This is very important," Laura said. "Can you tell me what you and she talked about?"

"You *are* another writer!" Her voice had an edge of anger to it now.

"No, I'm really not."

"You listen to me," the woman said. She lowered her voice to a harsh whisper; her tone was clearly defensive. "My son didn't kill Tyler. Do you hear? I don't care what anybody else says. He loved that boy. There's no way he could have killed him."

The woman had to stop, choked with emotion. When she spoke again, defeat replaced the anger in her voice. She said, "Elliot didn't kill that boy, and that's all there is to it. Write that in your story." She hung up.

Laura sat at her desk, staring at the phone, the dial tone bleating in her ear. Hearing the woman mention Erin's husband killing his son shocked her. She couldn't help but think about Jenny's death, and again she wondered, *Is it possible her death wasn't an accident?*

For a few moments, she replayed in her memory the conversation with Erin Archembeau's mother-in-law. Nothing made sense. But she had found Jenny's trail, and now she had hope that she was getting close to uncovering what had frightened Jenny so much.

Could it have been the murder of the little boy? she wondered. That still didn't explain Jenny's interest in zygotes or Montgomery or someone named Nefayre, but at least it was something to go on.

Laura called her law firm in New Orleans next. She asked her secretary if they had dealings with any firms in the Vancouver area.

"Not in Vancouver, but we've used a firm in Seattle quite a bit to take care of matters for us in Canada."

"I'll try them. Let me have their number."

When Laura called, she spoke with an attorney named Catherine McKay. After exchanging a few pleasantries with her, Laura said, "The reason I'm calling is to see if you can look into something for me. By the way, this is to be billed to me directly, not to the firm."

"What would you like us to look into?"

"I'd like you to check out some people. Their last name is Archembeau. The first names are Erin, Elliot, and Tyler. They're from Vancouver."

"Do you have an address?"

"No, but that wouldn't do you any good because they're all deceased. Erin died last summer; Elliot and Tyler apparently died a few months before that. I need to know whatever you can find out about the deaths of Elliot and Tyler."

"We've worked with an investigator up there a number of times," Catherine said. "He's good. He should be able to get something for you. When do you need it?"

"Yesterday."

Catherine laughed. "Of course. Why did I even ask?"

"It *is* very urgent," Laura said.

"What's this all about?"

"I'm not exactly sure yet. I'm hoping your investigator can tell me."

"I'll see what I can do."

She hung up, then shuffled through the papers scattered about her desk, searching for a phone number. Laura wanted to find out about Jenny's trip to Montgomery. The place to start was Woodridge. She found the paper on which she had written the phone number last week when she was trying to find Jenny. She dialed it now. A man answered.

"Woodridge House."

"Can you give me directions how to get there?" Laura said.

22

The sign in front said WOODRIDGE HOUSE—DIGNIFIED ASSISTED LIVING. The building was 200 feet from the road, partially hidden behind pine trees. It looked more like a large private home than a care facility. Surrounding it were areas of open lawn, several gardens browned by winter chill, a grouping of benches in a shady patch of trees, birdbaths, a fountain.

Laura drove up the driveway and parked in front of the building. A dozen or so cars were parked here. It was 5:15. Dusk was beginning to settle in. The wind blew as she got out. She hesitated a moment before going inside, not really sure what she was doing here, what she expected to find, but she had come too far to turn back. She had to see what had drawn Jenny here.

When Laura walked into the small lobby, she noticed the heavy odor of disinfectant in the air. Soft music played from speakers in the ceiling. To the side of the lobby, a middle-aged woman was sitting on a sofa, talking quietly to a young girl with Down syndrome. They both looked at Laura and smiled.

A nurse's aide walked by, pushing a cart of soiled linens. She disappeared down one of three corridors leading off the lobby. At the end of the lobby was a receptionist's counter. Behind it, there was an office with the door open. No attendant stood at the counter, but Laura noticed a man in the office, talking to an elderly couple, assuring them that

Beth would be comfortable here. When Laura walked to the counter, he spared her a quick glance and mouthed to her that he'd be with her momentarily, then he went back to the couple.

Waiting at the counter, Laura noticed a notebook to the side. A typewritten note taped to the counter next to it said: ALL VISITORS MUST SIGN IN. She remembered that when she had called last Thursday, the man had checked the visitors register and had said Jenny's name was not there. Of course it wasn't there, Laura knew now. It couldn't possibly be there because she had died Wednesday night.

But what was here that Jenny had wanted to see? Laura wondered. Who was here that she had come all this way to talk to? Laura still didn't know how she was going to find out. If only Jenny had had a chance to come here before the accident. At least then Laura would know who—

It suddenly occurred to her that maybe Jenny had made it here after all. She had arrived in Montgomery Wednesday afternoon. Surely she didn't sit in her hotel room all evening, doing nothing. That wasn't the type of person Jenny was. She would have gone out. She would have kept active. Could she have visited this place Wednesday night? Laura wondered.

She glanced up at the man in the office. He was still engrossed in his conversation with the elderly couple. She turned her attention back to the notebook and opened it to the page marked WEDNESDAY, NOVEMBER 13. She ran her finger down the page, skimming the names. Near the bottom, she found the familiar signature of her friend.

The sight of Jenny's name took her breath away. She began to tremble at the thought that Jenny had indeed been here.

Beside Jenny's name in the book was the time she had signed in: 7:40 P.M.—only a short time before her accident. Jenny had died immediately afterward, Laura realized, and this thought sent a shiver of uneasiness through her.

She traced her finger across the page to the name of the person Jenny had visited. Printed in Jenny's handwriting, the name stood out clearly from the rest of the scribbling on the page. *Jeremy Nefayre.*

"Good evening, Miss."

Laura looked up and saw the man from the office standing across the counter, staring at her.

"Is there something I can help you with? I'm Mr. Sorenson, the assistant administrator."

"Um—yes." Laura closed the notebook. "I'd like to visit Jeremy Nefayre. What room is he in?"

"Room 118. It's down that corridor. The last room on the left."

"Thank you."

"Have you already signed in?" Sorenson asked. He opened the notebook to the page marked with today's date and didn't see her name. "You'll have to sign in here," he told her.

Laura picked up the pen, hoping Sorenson didn't notice that her hand was unsteady. She hesitated, not sure what name to write. She felt Sorenson watching her and was sure he noticed her hesitation, sure he suspected something was wrong. Finally she scrawled the first name to come to mind: *Erin Archembeau.*

Sorenson took the notebook and read it. "Are you a relative, Mrs. Archembeau?"

"I'm a close friend of the family's."

"I don't believe I've ever seen you here before."

Laura tucked her hands in her coat pockets so the man wouldn't notice that they were trembling. She drew a breath and hoped her nervousness didn't show as she said, "I don't live in the area. I'm just in town for a short time and I wanted to see him."

Sorenson studied her for a moment, his face showing concern. Laura thought he suspected she was lying, wondered what she could have said that gave her away. A quiver of fear ran down her back. She turned away so her uneasiness wouldn't show and started toward the corridor.

"Perhaps I should accompany you," Sorenson said, coming out from behind the counter. He looked back at the couple in the office and said to them, "Why don't you take a few minutes to read through that brochure. I'll be back shortly." Then he walked over to Laura. "I'll take you to Jeremy's room."

"That won't be necessary," Laura said. "I'm sure I can find it."

"Just the same, I think I should go with you."

"Is there something wrong?" she said sharply, hoping to intimidate him.

He didn't answer right away. Finally he said, "How long has it been since you've seen him?"

She wasn't sure how to answer, how long Jeremy Nefayre had been here. The more vague the answer, she decided, the better. "Quite a while," she said. "Why?"

"Well, sometimes it can be a little . . ." He chose the next word carefully. "Disheartening," he said.

Laura didn't understand.

"I think it might be more comfortable for you if I went with you," he said.

Laura didn't want him with her, but his warning made her uneasy about what she would find here.

"If you think it's necessary," she said.

"I think so."

The wing Jeremy Nefayre was on had six rooms on either side of the corridor. Most of the doors were open as Laura and Sorenson walked by, but the lights were off in all but one room. Laura glanced into that room and saw an aide cleaning one of the beds. She didn't look long enough to see the resident.

Sorenson took her to the last door on the right. The only light came from the flickering glow of a television set. The volume was off, leaving the room in silence. Even out here in the hallway, Laura smelled the distinct odor of feces and urine unsuccessfully masked with disinfectant.

Sorenson went in first. Laura hesitated, fearful that when Jeremy Nefayre saw her, he would tell Sorenson that she wasn't a friend, that she didn't belong here. She considered leaving right now. She had come here to find out whom Jenny had visited, and since she already knew the answer, it might be best to leave before she got herself into trouble.

But she didn't know enough yet, she admitted to herself. This facility, this person named Nefayre, this was what brought Jenny here. But what Laura still did not understand was *why* Jenny had come this far, who Jeremy Nefayre was, and how it all fit in with Erin Archembeau and zygotes. And she still didn't understand what had frightened Jenny. She needed to find the answers. The risk was necessary. She had to go into the room. She had to see what Jenny had seen.

Pausing to collect herself, she glanced out the window at the end of the hall and saw that night was coming quickly. The darkness unnerved her even more. The air seemed to be getting colder by the minute. She shook off a shiver, took another breath to calm her nerves, then walked into Room 118.

"He's asleep," Sorenson said, speaking in a normal tone.

"Don't wake him," Laura whispered. She didn't want their voices to rouse him.

"You don't have to whisper." Sorenson walked toward the TV, leaving Laura alone by the door. "He won't hear us. He's completely deaf now. That's why the sound is off on the TV."

Laura wondered if his deafness was something she should have known about as a close family friend. She worried that this slip-up gave her away. But Sorenson didn't seem distracted by it, so she dismissed her worry. She reminded herself, however, to be careful what she said from now on.

She peered deeper into the room. The furnishings were cheerful and comfortable. A bright-colored easy chair filled one corner. Near the window was a cherry-wood dresser. Posters of baseball players hung on the walls. The bed was the only thing that reminded Laura that she was in a medical facility. The base had motors and hydraulics for lifting and lowering the mattress. On either side of the mattress were aluminum safety rails, both of which were raised and locked in place.

"He can't see very well either anymore," Sorenson said, "but he still likes the TV. I'm not sure how much he can comprehend, but it seems to mollify him, so we leave it on when he's awake."

Laura just nodded. She started to direct her attention now to the figure lying in the bed, illuminated by the blue flicker of the television, but Sorenson turned it off before she could see Jeremy Nefayre clearly. The one thing she did realize an instant before the room fell into near darkness was that Jeremy Nefayre was a child.

Sorenson walked over to the bed and peered down at the boy for a brief moment. He let out a quiet sigh and shook his head sympathetically, then gestured for Laura to come over. She walked toward him reluctantly, her eyes fixed on the dark figure in bed that was gradually coming into focus.

Even with little light in the room she saw that there was something very wrong with the boy's features. The bridge of his nose was sunken, which made his eyes, already larger than normal, appear even larger. His mouth was parted to allow room for his tongue, also abnormally large. The wide space between his teeth gave his mouth a surreal look. His neck was so short that his head appeared to be resting on his shoulders. The remainder of his body was hidden by blankets, but even covered, the body appeared horribly malformed.

The sight of this handicapped child brought a sudden wave of nausea. Laura saw her own baby in this boy. She trembled, realizing that her child could be born like this. After wanting a child for so long, so desperately, what if he were born with similar deformities? The thought frightened her. She closed her eyes and tried to clear her head of the disturbing image of her baby being anything less than perfect.

When she opened her eyes again, she detected something strangely familiar about this boy. Her eyes were accustomed to the darkness now and she saw him more clearly. She knew she had never seen him before, but something about him struck a chord. She didn't understand why she felt this way, but she couldn't bear to look at the boy any longer. She wanted to study him in hopes of jogging her memory, but his deformities truly frightened her. She turned away.

Sorenson noticed her uneasiness. "I guess Jeremy's gotten worse since you last saw him?"

Laura could only nod, too disturbed to speak. She heard the boy's steady rasping breath beside her.

"All things considered," Sorenson said, "he's actually doing better than we had anticipated."

Sorenson's words conflicted drastically with Laura's perception of this child. She couldn't imagine him being any worse.

"He's doing better, you say?" she asked.

"Most definitely. Children with Hurler syndrome don't normally survive beyond five years of age. Early cardiac arrest and pneumonia are symptomatic of Hurler, but Jeremy's six now and his heart has actually gotten stronger since the treatments."

"Treatments?" Laura said.

"The transfusions. He's had four of them, I believe, in the last fifteen months or so. Each transfusion seems to help quite a bit. His father told me that he's scheduled for another one in a couple weeks. We're all hopeful that he'll continue to improve."

"I don't understand. You said that most children with Jeremy's condition die very young. The transfusions don't work for them?"

"Jeremy's transfusions are just experimental. I don't know how many other patients, if any, are undergoing them. But Jeremy is in a unique position."

"He is?"

"You know, because of his father."

"Oh, yes, of course," Laura said, not wanting Sorenson to suspect that she really didn't know anything about the boy, about his father, about the *unique position* he was in. But she wondered why Jeremy was the only child getting transfusions. If they could help others in this condition, why weren't they all getting them?

More than that, though, she wondered why this boy had been of such interest to Jenny. Hurler syndrome—whatever that was—wasn't what she was writing about. Laura could not imagine what all of this had to do with Jenny's story on infertility.

"Why don't I give you a few moments alone with Jeremy," Sorenson said.

Laura didn't want to be alone with the boy, fearing mostly that he would awaken and force her to cope with him, which she was not sure she could do. But she did want a few minutes without Sorenson watching. She thought that if she looked around, she might find something that would clear up some of the questions she still had.

Sorenson walked out, leaving the door open. Laura listened to the clap of his shoes on the floor as he went down the corridor back to the lobby. When the sound faded and she was confident that he was gone, she glanced down at the boy to make sure he was still asleep, then she walked over to the dresser.

The top was clear for the most part. A hand mirror sat on one end, and a can of disinfectant sat in the far corner, but that was it. Laura opened the top drawer, still uncertain of what she was looking for. Tiny children's underwear was folded neatly in here. She didn't touch anything or try to look under the clothes. That seemed too invasive. She felt uncomfortable searching in this boy's room. This was his life—she was intruding.

But it involved Jenny too, she told herself. And Jenny was dead and Laura needed to understand.

She opened another drawer and found more clothes. The third drawer had a few toys in it; most looked like they had never been used. She wondered if Jeremy was even able to play. She imagined him lying in bed all day, staring at the silent TV. The image saddened her.

She glanced back at him. He was still asleep. But again she found herself thinking about her own baby and what the chances were that it would be born handicapped like Jeremy. She wondered if that could be what Jenny Hopkins had been thinking. Had she found something about babies being born with abnormalities?

Laura's whole body shook as this thought quickly took root in her mind. *My God, could that be it?*

Suddenly, she was having trouble breathing and the nausea she had felt earlier when she first looked at the child returned. She felt weak and had to hold on to the dresser for support. Gasping for air now, needing to get out of there, she turned to leave when through the window, a flicker outside caught her eye.

It was the dome light of a car coming on as the doors opened. The car was parked in the lot in front of the building, close enough that Laura could see the two passengers as they got out. It was a man and a woman. She couldn't see their faces at first, but then the man turned to close his door. The white glow from inside the car illuminated him clearly. In the brief moment before the door closed and the light went out, leaving the man's face in darkness, Laura was stunned at what she saw.

The man was Dr. Chyles; the woman with him, Dr. Acer. They came around the car and headed toward the entrance of the building.

Laura couldn't imagine why they were here, until she turned and saw the child again, and in that instant, it occurred to her. This boy must have been born at the New Life Center. What she thought was familiar about him was the same apathy she had noticed in Charlotte's son, in Jenny's niece, in the boy from the birthday party.

The next thought that entered her mind brought with it a fear that she felt all the way to her womb. This boy's deformities were due to Dr. Chyles's therapy. That's what Jenny had uncovered.

The images of Charlotte's son and Jenny's niece flashed into her head and she wondered if those children too would end up like this.

And would her own child?

Laura didn't stand by the window long enough to think that through. She needed to get out of here quickly. She didn't want Chyles to know she was here.

She hurried away from the window, glancing only briefly at the boy as she passed the bed. Again the notion of familiarity teased her. Did he really look like the others? she questioned. She wasn't sure. She just assumed that was it, but she really wasn't sure.

She hurried through the doorway and started up the corridor toward the lobby. The sound of the front doors opening blew into the building with the night wind. Then she heard footsteps move across the tile floor of the lobby— the heavy thump of a man's shoes along with the quick clip of a woman's heels.

She stopped, realizing she couldn't go that way—but that

was the only way out. As she looked behind her toward the end of the hall, then turned again toward the lobby where Chyles and Acer were, her fear became so fierce that she could feel her heart racing.

She saw Sorenson come out from behind the counter and move across the lobby, extending his hand. He didn't look up the hall, didn't see Laura. His attention was on the man and woman entering the building. Laura still couldn't see Chyles and Acer, but she saw their shadows coming deeper into the lobby. She had only a few seconds before they would see her.

She looked behind her again. There was a small window at the end of the corridor but no door, no exit. She looked back toward the lobby. Chyles and Acer stepped into view now. Sorenson greeted them as though he had seen them many times before.

Laura only had an instant to react. Her heart felt like it was going to rupture.

Beside her was the open door to another room. The lights were off and she heard the thin rasp of someone's snoring. She darted into the room, and as she did, she caught a glimpse of Chyles turning toward her and starting up the corridor. She expected to hear him call out to her, hear him run up the hallway, but none of that happened. He didn't notice her.

In the darkness of the room, she strained to see the bed a few feet away. A teenage girl was asleep. As Laura's eyes adjusted to the lack of light, she saw that the girl was deformed. Thoughts of her own baby ending up in a place like this rushed into her head, frightening her more every moment. She looked away and tried to clear her mind, but the dreadful thoughts would not relent.

She could not shake the notion, either, that Jeremy Nefayre looked familiar, but as her thoughts flew from him to Jenny's niece, to Charlotte's son, to the boy at last summer's party, she realized that something didn't quite fit. She was missing something. What she saw in common among those other three was not the same thing she saw in this boy.

She heard Chyles, Acer, and Sorenson start up the hallway now and suddenly she stopped drawing breath. The three of them were still talking. At first, their words were unclear. They were speaking quietly so they wouldn't disturb the other residents. But as they drew closer, Laura heard Sorenson say, "She's in with Jeremy right now."

"Who is she?" Chyles asked, his voice sharp with anger.

"Her name is Erin Archembeau."

"That can't be," Acer whispered, fear in her voice.

"She said she's a friend of the family."

Chyles sounded angry, threatening as he said, "She isn't a friend of the family and she isn't Erin Archembeau."

As they drew nearer, Laura stepped deeper into the darkness and pressed herself flat against the wall. She watched them walk by, then disappear from view. She hesitated a moment to make sure they weren't going to stop, then she moved carefully to the doorway and looked out.

"I'm sure we can clear this all up right now," Sorenson said as they approached Jeremy Nefayre's room. And then he addressed Chyles by name, and when he did, his words struck Laura like a hammer blow inside her brain. He said, "Rest assured, we will take proper action, Dr. Nefayre."

Chyles was Nefayre! Laura realized. Then that meant that the boy in that room was—

Suddenly she understood why the boy looked familiar. He didn't resemble the other babies—she realized that now. *He resembled Dr. Chyles.* More than that, though, he was familiar to her because she had actually seen him before. Then came the memory of the photograph she and Dan had seen at Chyles's house the day of the birthday party, the one Dr. Acer unintentionally showed them, the picture of Acer and Chyles with a young child. The boy in that picture was Jeremy Nefayre.

Laura didn't know what it all meant. Her main concern was just getting out of here.

Sorenson led Chyles and Acer into Room 118. As soon as they were in the room, Laura slipped out and hurried up the hallway, fighting the urge to run. A few other people were in the lobby, and she didn't want to draw anyone's attention. Just as she reached the lobby and darted around the corner, she heard Sorenson's voice as he stepped from the boy's room.

"I don't understand," he said. "She was just here."

Laura didn't hear the rest of what he said. She hurried across the lobby and out the door. The cold night air hit her like a slap in the face. She realized as she rushed down the stairs, almost stumbling on the bottom step, that she was wet with perspiration and yet she was shivering violently.

She was eager to get away quickly. Breaking into an awkward trot, struggling because of her size, she raced to her car, fumbling first with the door handle and then again when she tried to put the key in the ignition. As she pulled the car out of the lot and headed up the long drive toward the road, she looked in the rear-view mirror and saw Chyles come out of the building. She hoped her car was too far away and the night too dark for him to realize who she was.

To her relief, he did not follow her. He just stood outside the entrance, glaring at her car's taillights. Laura sped to the end of the drive and turned hard, bounding up onto the curb as she pulled out into traffic. A car blew its horn, almost hitting her. She sped off, still trembling, still perspiring in the cold night. Even after the two-hour drive back to Collier, she had not calmed down.

23

As soon as she got home, she rushed to her desk and called Dan. He wasn't at home, so she left a message on the answering machine for him to call her as soon as he got in, then she called his studio. He wasn't there either. She checked the time. It was a little before 8:00. He was probably on his way home right now, she thought. She would try to call him again in a few minutes.

The night was a deep black now and the only light in the house came from the small lamp at Laura's desk. The darkness made her feel uneasy and cold, so she went around the house turning on all the lights. Then she went to the couch and sat in the corner, scrunched up in a ball and shivering like a frightened child.

Her head ached. She felt exhausted from the long drive, confused by what she discovered in Montgomery. She wished desperately that she could make sense of it all, make sense of Chyles's lying about who he was, of the tragic condition of the boy at Woodridge who evidently was Chyles's son, of the babies from the New Life Center, Jenny's niece, Charlotte's son, the boy at the birthday party. Perhaps it wasn't all related. Perhaps Chyles—or Nefayre—was just unfortunate enough to have a handicapped son. But then why was Jenny dead? Why was Chyles calling himself Nefayre?

She called Dan again. It was 8:15 and still there was no answer at the house. Thinking about the babies, she wondered if the treatment Chyles had given their mothers could have caused the abnormalities—that is, if the babies really were abnormal. She considered whether she might just be imagining it. After all, no one else saw it. Maybe Charlotte was right: if the parents didn't see it and the doctor didn't see it, maybe there was nothing wrong with them.

But there was definitely something wrong with Jeremy Nefayre. Even so, the other babies weren't the same as he was. If they were abnormal—she was trying hard to believe that they weren't—but if they were, they were abnormal in a much different way, in a much more subtle way.

She called New Orleans again, but Dan still wasn't home. Feeling even colder, she hurried over to the closet and grabbed her overcoat, then returned to the couch and covered herself.

Questions about Chyles's identity filled her head now. Was he was really Dr. Nefayre, lying about who he was to the patients at the New Life Center? Or was he in fact Dr. Chyles like he told his patients, and the people he was lying to were the ones at Woodridge? Whichever it was, why was he deceiving either of them about his identity?

Laura wondered if that was something Jenny had found out. Jenny must have discovered that Chyles was Nefayre, Laura reasoned, but did Jenny know why he had two identities?

And if Jenny did know, was that why she had her . . . *accident?*

Laura tried to call Dan again, but still he did not answer. Angry now, she slammed the phone down. *He should be home,* she thought. *He should be there when I need him.* She felt isolated up here, with no one to talk to, no one to help her figure this out.

The cat wobbled out of the kitchen and looked up at her, the way he always did when he wanted to eat.

"Not now," Laura said.

The cat stared at her for a few moments, then leaped up onto the window sill and stared at her from there. She thought how much he reminded her of Charlotte's son: the way he looked at her half the time as though she weren't even there, the way he ignored her except when he wanted food, the way he seemed empty inside. Dead inside—dead like the other cat, his twin brother, the one Dan had run over. Felix. Or was this one Felix? Whichever one he was, tonight his presence made her very uncomfortable.

The state police had said that Jenny's death was an accident. They had found no evidence to believe otherwise, but Laura had doubts. The missing files had made her suspicious initially—that and the fact that Jenny had been frightened when they talked on the phone. But what had frightened her? Not Woodridge or Jeremy Nefayre, surely. They weren't enough. What, then?

Jenny had never mentioned Chyles. Laura found it difficult to imagine Dr. Chyles having anything to do with Jenny's car accident. He didn't seem like the type of person who could kill someone. At the clinic, he showed so much concern and compassion. He dedicated himself to helping couples, to making life, not to taking life away. He wasn't a killer. Laura couldn't accept that he had anything to do with Jenny's car accident, or with Erin Archembeau's accident.

Laura thought now about Erin's mother-in-law and what she had said about her son Elliot not killing Tyler— another tragic death that she didn't understand.

She called Dan again, but still no answer.

The throbbing in her head was becoming unbearable, so she went into the bathroom and got a cold washcloth for her forehead. She was feeling lightheaded from exhaustion. Shivering, she returned to the couch and covered herself with the overcoat. Again, she dialed her home in New Orleans, and again Dan didn't answer. *He should be home by now,* she thought. *Something bad must have happened.*

Relief from her worries came only as she finally succumbed to her exhaustion and fell asleep. She didn't awaken until the sun shone through the living-room window, stinging her eyes.

She held up her arm to shade her face from the glare. Blinking the bleariness from her vision, she focused on her watch. It was 7:45 in the morning. She sat up slowly, feeling weak. She had slept for more than 11 hours, but she was still tired. Her headache hadn't faded completely, but it wasn't as painful as it had been last night. She was still confused, but the warmth and light of morning had chased away some of her fear.

There has to be a reasonable explanation, she told herself. She didn't know all the facts; something was missing that would clear this all up. If she thought it through logically, she believed, now that it was morning, it would make sense.

She called home in New Orleans, deciding that if she and Dan could discuss this whole situation calmly, she would feel better. She was also concerned that Dan hadn't been home last night, that he hadn't returned her call. In the back of her mind was the fear that something had happened to him. She needed to dispel that.

On the third ring, Dan answered the phone. "Yeah, hello?" He sounded impatient.

"Where were you last night? I was trying to reach you!"

"Oh, Laura, hi. I got your message. Sorry I didn't call you

back, but I didn't get in until late and I didn't want to wake you."

"You should have called anyway."

"It was almost two when I got home. There's no way I was going to wake you up at that hour. Besides, I was pretty much out of it myself."

"Where were you all night?"

"You know Nigel, the kid who goes to Loyola and helps me out on some of the shoots? Well, he popped the question to his girl yesterday and she said no. He took it kind of hard, so I took him out to drown his misery in scotch. I did a bit too much drowning myself. I feel like hell this morning. I overslept too. I was supposed to meet three models at the studio an hour ago. I hope they didn't leave."

"I have to talk to you, Dan. I found out some things, and I need to see if you and I can figure out what it all means."

"Honey, can we talk later? I'm really late. Look, I'm driving up there this afternoon. I'm going to stay right through until after Thanksgiving. I'll be there for a week. Can we do this when I get there tonight?"

"This is important, Dan."

"Are you all right?"

"I'm just a little confused. It's about some of the babies and about Dr. Chyles. I don't know where to begin."

"Is there something wrong with the baby?"

"No. That's not it."

"And you're okay? Medically, you're all right, aren't you?"

"Yes."

"That's a relief. Look, are you sure this can't wait until I get there tonight? I really don't have a lot of time right now. I promise you, you'll have my full attention when I get there. On top of that," he said with a chuckle, "I won't be as hung over as I am now, so I'll be much more helpful."

"We *have* to talk about it tonight, okay? Without fail."

"Absolutely. I'll be there about seven."

"Can't you make it earlier?"

"I'll try, but I can't make any promises."

"Make it earlier, Dan. Please."

"Honey, are you sure you're all right?"

"I'm just a little scared," she whispered.

"Why are you scared?"

"I don't know. That's the thing. I'm not sure."

"Look, do you want me to cancel today's shoot and come up there now?"

"No. You go ahead and do what you have to do there. We'll talk tonight. It can wait a few more hours."

"You're sure?"

"It can wait."

"Whatever it is, honey, I'm sure it's not as bad as you think."

"I hope you're right."

"Everything is going to be all right," he said. "I promise. Okay? It's going to be all right."

"I know it will."

"That's my girl. I love you, Laura."

"I love you too."

"See you tonight—early," he said, and hung up.

Talking to him left her feeling a little stronger. Whatever was wrong, it *would* be all right, she told herself. Together, she and Dan would figure it all out tonight. She was sure that by tonight, it would all seem like nothing.

She noticed the time. If she was going to make her appointment at the clinic, she had to go upstairs and shower and get dressed. She delayed only a moment, considering whether to go for the shots today. If they were causing children to be born handicapped, maybe she shouldn't be getting them anymore.

But it was only three babies, she rationalized. The other baby at the party, the little girl, had seemed perfectly fine. And Laura didn't even know for sure that there was anything wrong with the three other babies. Surely if there was a problem with those babies, someone else would have noticed by now.

She had no proof that getting the shots would jeopardize her baby. But she did have reason to fear that skipping them would. If she were imagining this whole thing, and Dr. Chyles was only what he claimed to be, she needed the shots.

She made up her mind that she would go to the clinic. She felt only the slightest bit of trepidation about her decision.

24

When Chyles knocked on the door and walked into the examination room this morning, what Laura felt more than anything was sympathy for him. Thinking about his handicapped son in Montgomery filled her with compassion. She still wondered why he went by the name Nefayre at Woodridge and Chyles down here, but she couldn't help think about the mental anguish he must suffer each time he visited his son, each time his thoughts dwelled on what had become of his only child.

"Good morning, Laura," he said.

"Good morning, Doctor."

"How are you feeling today?"

"I'm fine."

He didn't seem to act any differently from the way he did all the other times he had examined her, she thought. He didn't show the least bit of suspicion toward her. She decided that he didn't know that she was the one who had been at Woodridge yesterday. With that out of the way, she could breathe much easier. She did think he looked a little sadder this morning, but she attributed that to her own perception, to her new knowledge of his son's condition.

"I have the results from your amnio," he said.

Her body became tense when he said this. The amniocentesis would tell if her child would be born with any genetic abnormalities, if it would be like Jeremy Nefayre. She looked up at him, waiting nervously for the results.

"Everything looks just fine," he said. "You're going to have a healthy baby."

Laura let out a long sigh. She hadn't even realized that she had been holding her breath until then. She laughed, a little embarrassed, and said, "That's great news, Doctor."

"I'm sure it is. Now, about the baby's sex. You wanted to find out when your husband was here, right?"

"Yes. Dan is coming up tonight. I'll have him come in with me tomorrow morning. Can you tell us then?"

"No problem."

Chyles listened to her heart, lungs, and stomach with his stethoscope, then guided her legs into the stirrups and examined inside her. As she did every time during this part of the exam, Laura turned away and concentrated on the photograph hanging over the desk, hoping it would take her mind off the examination.

She had stared at this photograph many times before, the gray drizzle on a rocky coastline, and thought little of it except that it was a powerful image that managed to some degree to distract her. But today, with shocking clarity, the photograph took on new significance.

Chyles had several photographs similar to this one hanging in the clinic and in his home: rocky shorelines, waves, cliffs. She remembered Chyles and Dan discussing camera techniques. And she hadn't thought much of it then. She hadn't given it a second thought until this morning. Now she couldn't stop thinking about it.

Laura turned nervously from the photograph and looked toward Chyles. He was staring at her, which she hadn't noticed until now. How long had he been watching her? she wondered, a slight tremble running through her. She felt like she shouldn't have been looking at the picture, like he knew what was in her thoughts.

He looked away finally and resumed examining her. It took her a moment to regain her composure, then she said, "That's a nice photograph."

Chyles glanced over at it, then looked up at her and smiled. "Thank you."

"I noticed that you have a few others that are similar."

He chuckled. "I guess I favor beach scenes."

"They're very good," Laura said.

"I'm sure they don't compare to the pictures your husband takes, but I enjoy doing it when I have the time. Lately I've been pretty busy, though."

"And there's no coastline around here," she said.

"That's true."

"You must have taken them before you moved here."

He nodded, and Laura noticed a sudden change in his manner. He became quieter, almost tentative. He watched her for a second, then turned his attention back to the examination.

Laura remained silent until he finished and moved over to the desk to make notes on her chart. She needed to probe a little further; she needed to be sure.

"That doesn't look like Florida," she said, hoping she wasn't too obvious.

Chyles looked up from the notes he was writing, his concentration broken. "Hmm?"

"That picture," she said. "That's not what the beaches are like in Florida, is it?"

"You're right," he said. He looked down at the medical chart, and as he started writing, he casually said, "I took that one in Maine. My wife's family lives up there and we used to visit quite a bit. Not so much anymore, but we used to go there a few times a year."

"Oh, Maine," Laura said.

"The coast up there is very different from Florida's. I think it lends itself better to photographing—at least the type of photography that I like."

Something about the way he had said it told Laura that he was lying. That wasn't Maine. That wasn't the Atlantic Ocean at all. She was sure it was the Pacific—more specifically, the Pacific Northwest: Canada—Vancouver, Erin Archembeau's home town. The place Jenny went, the place she discovered whatever it was that had frightened her.

She remembered Erin's mother-in-law telling her that Erin went to a clinic in Burnaby, wherever Burnaby was.

The woman had been certain that Erin never went to Alabama or Florida, never saw a fertility doctor in the United States. But last summer at the birthday party Chyles had told Laura that he had tried unsuccessfully to help Erin conceive. The only way that could be true was if he had practiced in Canada. He claimed to have practiced only in Florida before coming here. He had to be lying.

She looked at him as he finished writing the notes in her file. She considered asking him about Canada, but something deep within her, a fear that she didn't fully understand, kept her silent.

Chyles looked over at her. "I've been thinking," he said, "about your baby's sex and how you and your husband want to find out together."

"Yes. We think that'll make it more special."

"I agree, but I think I have a better idea than making you wait until tomorrow. You said he's coming up tonight?"

"That's right."

"Tell you what I'm going to do."

He opened the drawer of the desk and took out an envelope. The New Life Center's return address was printed in the corner. Chyles picked up a sheet of paper out of Laura's file, folded it in three and slid it into the envelope, then he sealed it and wrote Dan's name across the front. He handed it to Laura.

"Give this to your husband when he gets in. This has the results in it. Have him open it tonight, when you two are together. Maybe have a couple glasses of champagne along with it—nonalcoholic, of course. I think that might be nicer for you two."

"That does sound romantic," Laura said.

She was struck by Chyles's sensitivity. It was hard for her to believe that such a caring, dedicated doctor would lie to her. But she knew he was definitely lying about Canada, about his name—maybe about other things as well. Still, there had to be a logical, innocent explanation, she told herself.

Chyles began to prepare the syringes now. As she watched him insert the first needle into the tiny bottle and extract the clear liquid, she trembled slightly. She thought she felt a quickening in the fetus, and now it became difficult for her to breathe.

What if those injections are harming the babies? she thought. But she was sure they weren't. Then again—how sure was she?

The image of Jeremy Nefayre filled her mind.

With the syringe now ready, Chyles came over and wiped her arm with a sterile solution.

"Are you feeling all right?" he asked. "You look a little pale."

She stared at the needle for a moment, then looked up at him. He seemed concerned, sympathetic. *Harmless.*

"Just a little tired," she said.

"I want you to try to take it easy today. When you're carrying a baby, you need more rest than normal."

"I know. I will."

He stuck the needle into her arm now. She winced, the pain sharper than it had felt all the other mornings. As he depressed the plunger, she felt an odd sensation, as though she could actually feel the serum streaming through her body, finding its way to her womb. She closed her eyes and imagined her baby trembling inside her as the hormones Chyles injected began attacking it.

She snapped opened her eyes and flinched, that image too much to bear. Chyles noticed.

"What's wrong, Laura?"

She took a deep breath before answering. "It just hurts a little," she said quietly.

"Sorry. It's just about over."

He gave her the second shot. The pain wasn't as bad, but the image of her baby drowning in acid continued to torment her. She felt a sickness in her stomach and took deep breaths until it passed. *It's all in your head,* she told herself. *The baby is fine. The shots are not hurting it, they're keeping it alive.*

"You had a busy day yesterday?" he asked as he was depressing the plunger.

The question caught her by surprise. "Pardon me?"

"Yesterday? Were you doing a lot, more than normal? Is that why you're tired?"

She wondered now if he suspected that she had been at Woodridge. She looked into his eyes but could not tell.

"I guess so," she said. "A lot of tax work."

He nodded and said no more about it.

Chyles withdrew the needle. "There, that wasn't so bad, was it?"

Laura managed a weak smile. "Not for you, but you ought to try it where I'm sitting."

He laughed. "Remember, take it easy today. Don't do too much. You want to be well-rested," he said and pointed to the envelope he gave her a few minutes earlier. "For the surprise tonight."

25

Laura took the suggestion Dr. Chyles had given her. On the way home from the clinic, she stopped at the liquor store in town and bought a bottle of nonalcoholic champagne. She went across the street to the market and bought a pound of veal and some fresh asparagus tips.

She was still concerned about all she had learned, but she convinced herself that when Dan came, they would make sense of it all. And they would do that tomorrow, not today. She wanted tonight to be special because they would always remember it as the night they learned the sex of their baby. She didn't want to spoil it.

Before she drove home she made one last stop, at the

Collier Public Library. In the reference room, she found a medical encyclopedia. She wanted to have as much information as possible when she and Dan discussed what she had learned about Chyles, so she looked up the condition that Chyles's son in Montgomery was suffering.

HURLER SYNDROME
(Also known as GARGOYLISM or MUCOPOLYSAC-CHARIDOSIS)
Hereditary disorder involving a defect in the metabolism of mucopolysaccharides. Caused by a deficiency of the α-iduronidase enzyme and transmitted as an autosomal recessive trait. Onset occurs within two years of birth, affecting both sexes with equal frequency. Symptoms include severe mental retardation and extreme somatic and skeletal changes. Individuals exhibit cardiovascular defects, enlargement of liver and spleen, joint contractures, opacities of the corneas, deafness, dwarfism, clawed hands, wide-set eyes, heavy brow ridges, widely spaced teeth, hairiness [see Hirsutism]. Children suffering from this disorder require institutionalized care. Death often occurs in early adolescence, usually resulting from heart failure.

Laura closed the book and for a moment just sat there, unable to move. What she just read disturbed her deeply. She thought about Jeremy Nefayre and how much that little boy must be suffering. His father too must be in such pain. She felt great sympathy for Dr. Chyles. It must be extremely difficult for him, she thought, having to care for a son in Jeremy's condition. How he maintained any sense of hope, she could not imagine, but he always put on a cheerful front at the clinic. With all that he was doing to help infertile couples, it was a shame that someone could not do something to help him and his son.

She left the library saddened by what she knew, but she

was still concerned about what she did not know and what impact that might have on her baby.

When she got home, the cat greeted her on the porch. "You have to eat early and go out for the night," she told him. She'd never told Dan about its appearing after its "twin" died—and tonight was not the night to broach the subject with him.

The cat followed her into the kitchen, nibbled at the canned food she gave it, then stopped eating and sat in front of the bowl, watching her prepare the veal.

"Oh, no," she said. "At twelve dollars a pound, this isn't for you. You eat your own food or you go hungry—take your pick."

The cat didn't eat, so Laura put the bowl of food outside on the back porch and put the cat out for the rest of the afternoon.

The phone rang. She hoped it wasn't Dan calling to say he couldn't make it or that he'd be late. She answered it reluctantly.

"Hello?"

"Laura Fielding?"

"Yes?"

"Hi, this is Catherine McKay of Conner, Lipman, in Seattle. You called me yesterday about checking on some people in Vancouver."

"Yes. I didn't expect to hear from you so soon."

"I have the information you wanted. Do you have a few minutes to talk?"

"Sure. What did you turn up?"

"Well, I had my investigator in Vancouver look into the Archembeaus. He just faxed me what he found. I don't know if it's what you were looking for."

"Can you sum it up for me?"

"Sure thing." Laura heard her shuffling paper on the other end of the line. "Okay, Elliot and Tyler Archembeau," Catherine said. "Elliot was the father, Tyler the son. They both died on March twelfth of this year. The boy was three."

"How did they die?" Laura asked.

"That's not exactly clear. There was a fire at their house, that much is known. The investigator's report says that the two of them were in the house alone. The fire started in the kitchen. The fire inspectors found a container of lighter fluid near the bodies and they think it was used to start the fire."

"Who do they think started it?"

"They don't know. My guy hasn't had enough time to dig too deeply into that, and I wasn't sure how much money you wanted to spend on this."

"I'm not sure myself. Tell me what you have so far."

"Unofficially, some of the investigators with the fire department think that the father set the fire. They believe it was a murder-suicide."

Laura remembered what Erin Archembeau's mother-in-law had said: *My son didn't kill Tyler. I don't care what anybody else says. He loved that boy. There's no way he could have killed him.*

Laura tended to believe her. If Erin and her husband had gone to a fertility clinic to conceive the child, obviously they wanted him desperately. It didn't make sense that the father would kill him.

"Why do they think that?" Laura asked.

"This is all speculation on their part. Officially, the case is still open, the cause of the fire still unknown."

"I understand. Go on."

"First, no one can figure out why the father and son didn't leave the house once the fire started, unless the father started the fire himself and didn't want to leave. The fire occurred in the middle of the morning. They were both awake. There were plenty of doors and windows they could have escaped through. They were on the ground floor. They should have gotten out."

"Unless they were overcome by smoke."

"Their bodies were found a few yards from the kitchen door. The boy was still belted in his chair. They had time to get out if they wanted to. But it's more than just that. People who knew the family said that the father had been acting strangely the last year or so leading up to the fire."

"What do they mean by *strangely?*"

"He quit his job, for one thing. A few months before the fire, he just stopped showing up for work. He told one of his co-workers that he needed to spend more time with his son. After that, he almost never left the house. We're talking about a man who used to be very outgoing, from what his friends told the fire inspectors and the newspaper reporters. He used to bowl, golf, play softball. He and his wife were always at parties and functions. Then they had the baby and practically disappeared—the father in particular."

"It isn't unusual for a couple to want to stay home with their newborn, especially after having tried for so long to have a baby. I can understand that."

"I'm just telling you what people who knew him said. They said his personality changed. He began acting weird. And they say the son was that way too—weird."

"How was the son weird?"

"One neighbor had to call the police on him."

"On who? The son?"

"That's right. On the boy. On a three-year-old boy."

"Why in the world would anyone do that?"

"The guy claimed the boy killed his dog."

"This isn't making any sense," Laura said.

"I said the same thing when I heard it, but that's what happened. And that part isn't rumor either. I saw the police report. The neighbor called the police because this little boy killed his dog."

"That's not possible."

"It was only a puppy, a tiny little poodle, but still it does sound unbelievable. If it weren't for the witnesses, I wouldn't believe it either. But a couple of kids saw him do it. They also said the boy was known to fly into sudden rages—just all of a sudden blow up and go wild—then just as suddenly become calm again. Most of the time, though, they say he was pretty unemotional."

Charlotte's son immediately flashed into Laura's head: the time Charlotte pulled the baby away from her breast, how he went into a frenzy, and how unemotional he was otherwise.

Just like the baby at the party. Just like Jenny's brother-in-law said his daughter was.

"The neighbors said that most of the time when they saw the boy, he would just sit and do nothing," Catherine continued. "He never talked. He couldn't talk very well, apparently. Even at three years old, he could say only a few words. But the neighbors swear that the boy killed the dog."

"How do they say he killed it?"

"He strangled it. Someone said he tried to eat it too, but the paper said that was nonsense, which I tend to agree with. Things like that get blown out of proportion quickly. Anyway, there's more too," Catherine said. "Another incident, at a day-care center the parents had the boy in for a short time."

"What kind of incident? With a dog, you mean?"

"No. With another child."

"What happened?"

"They found a little boy dead at the day-care center."

Catherine said it so bluntly that Laura was stunned. "Dead? My God," she whispered.

"Somehow the boy hit his head. The parents blamed the center's staff and sued them. But the staff said Tyler Archembeau hit the other boy with a toy truck. No one actually saw him do it, but he was alone with the boy when it happened. When they found the dead boy later, Tyler was sitting right beside him, acting as though nothing had happened."

"Did he do it?" Laura asked.

"No one knows for sure. The center lost the civil suit with the dead boy's parents and they went out of business. Nothing ever happened to the Archembeau boy. No one could prove anything. But then there's the *really* strange part."

Laura felt a shiver run up her back. "What do you mean?"

"When they found the dead boy," Catherine said, hesitating momentarily, "he had bite marks on his arms and face. Yeah. Several of them. Deep enough to puncture the flesh."

"How did he get them?"

"The people from the center claimed that Tyler Archembeau did it. Bit him. *After* he was dead."

"Are you serious?"

"That's what they claimed. The Archembeau boy's parents said that that was ridiculous, that their son didn't do it, that a dog did it. One of the workers had a little puppy, a chow, I think. She used to bring it in with her and let the children play with it. Anyway, the Archembeaus said that the dog bit the boy. The coroner up there said the bite marks didn't look like they came from a dog, but they didn't look like they came from a human either, so they never really determined what happened."

"Are you sure about all this?"

"I have copies of the police reports. Kind of hard to believe, isn't it? It is for me too, but I'm telling you exactly what happened. Anyway," she said, "the father, Elliot Archembeau, was really affected by all of it. He wouldn't let the boy outside the house after that. He quit his job. His wife, Erin, had to support the three of them. And then— well, the fire happened."

Laura hesitated a moment, her thoughts moving from child to child, Tyler Archembeau to Michael Wheeler to Jenny's niece, Alyssa Kincaid, to the birthday boy at Chyles's party.

"Do you have a picture of the boy?" she asked.

"Yes. The newspaper ran a photo."

"Is there anything unusual about him?"

"What do you mean?"

"About the way he looks. Anything at all that strikes you as, I don't know, odd or abnormal."

"Not that I can see from the picture. Why?"

"I'm just trying to see if there's a connection."

"Connection to what?"

"Someone else I know."

"You know, now that I look at him," Catherine McKay said, "he does look a little—not odd, exactly. Maybe *distinct* is a better word."

"Explain what you mean."

"It's hard to say exactly. It could just be the picture—it's not the best quality. But he looks sort of expressionless, if that makes any sense to you."

"It does," Laura said, speaking almost in a whisper.

"I guess you could say it looks more like a bad painting than a photograph. The face is flat. He has kind of a vacant look. Like he's almost—I want to say retarded, but that's not it exactly."

Catherine McKay paused, searching for the right word.

"Like he's not whole," she said finally. "Like something's missing. That probably doesn't make any sense to you."

"It does."

Laura realized that Catherine McKay's description fit perfectly. *Not whole. Like something's missing.* That was it precisely. That was what she had felt when she had looked at the birthday boy last summer, when she had examined the photograph of Alyssa Kincaid, when she had changed Michael Wheeler's diaper. Their handicap wasn't as blatant as Jeremy Nefayre's, but it was just as real.

"It looks almost like there's nothing inside," Catherine McKay said.

Laura felt her own baby stirring, and that made her shudder as she asked herself, *How whole will my baby be?*

"I'd like you to check into something else for me if you could," Laura asked. "There's a place called Narrows Point Reproductive Clinic, something like that. It's in Burnaby. I don't know where that is exactly."

"I do. It's near Vancouver."

"See what you can find out about it. I believe they specialize in helping infertile couples. Also, see if a Dr. Norman Chyles ever practiced in the area. Norman Chyles. He might have been associated with the Narrows Point clinic."

"I guess you want that yesterday too?"

"As soon as possible."

"It'll have to be after the weekend, but I'll make sure to get back to you before Thanksgiving. Will that be okay?"

"Yeah, that'll be all right. Just as soon as you get anything, fax it to me here." Laura gave her the fax number, then said, "Oh, one more thing. Check on one other name for me, too. I don't know the first name. But the last name is Nefayre. Dr. Nefayre."

26

Laura was waiting by the window, watching for Dan, when headlights came up the road and turned into the driveway. It was 6:15, already dark. A windowpane rattled in the wind. Laura hurried out onto the porch to greet him. He looked tired as he lugged his suitcase up the steps. She fell into his arms.

"I'm so glad you're here," she said.

"Are you okay, honey? What's wrong?"

"I don't know."

He held her tightly and felt her shivering. "It's going to be all right. I'm here now. Whatever it is, we're going to take care of it. Everything's going to be just fine."

The warmth of his body and the confidence in his voice quickly eased her anxiety. She didn't feel so alone anymore, didn't feel so confused. Together they would figure it out, determine what to do. Dan was right: everything was going to be just fine.

She gazed up at him and managed a smile.

"That's my girl," he said. He kissed her and said, "You sure are a sight for sore eyes."

"You're going blind. I'm getting so fat, it's disgusting."

"You're not fat, and you're not disgusting. You're carrying my baby, and I can't think of anything more beautiful than that."

They kissed again, then went inside. While Dan went upstairs for a quick shower, Laura finished preparing dinner. After she set the table, she lit two candles and filled their glasses with nonalcoholic champagne. Then she got the envelope Chyles had given her this morning and placed it on Dan's plate.

He came downstairs in jeans and a polo shirt, smelling of shampoo and soap. She turned on the radio, found a jazz station from Montgomery that barely came in, then dimmed the lights and led him by the hand to the dining room. She handed him one glass of champagne, then picked up the other for herself.

"What's going on?" he asked. "What's this for?"

She pointed to the envelope. "For when we open that."

"What's that?"

"The results from my amniocentesis. Well, not all the results. I already got most of them this morning. Dr. Chyles said everything looks good. What's in the envelope is the part about whether we should paint the baby's room pink or blue."

"He didn't tell you what sex the baby's going to be?"

"I didn't let him. I wanted us to find out together."

He kissed her and said, "No wonder I love you so much."

"Open the envelope. I'm dying to find out."

Dan picked up the envelope and handed it to her. "You open it."

She pushed it back to him. "It has your name on it. You have to open it."

"Are you sure?"

"Shut up and open it, will you?"

He laughed, set down his glass and tore open the flap. "I feel like I'm a presenter at the Academy Awards," he said. He slid out the paper slowly, deliberately. It was folded three times, so he couldn't see what was written on it.

He said, "And the winner is . . ."

He unfolded it and started reading. It was difficult for him to see in the darkness. He had to hold it near the candle. Laura waited anxiously. It was taking him longer than she had expected. She peered over his shoulder and could see that there was a lot of writing on the paper, but she couldn't see it well enough to read it.

Dan remained silent. The expression on his face began to change, but Laura didn't understand what his look meant. Finally, she couldn't take it any longer and said, "Well, come on, what does it say?"

He peered back over his shoulder at her. In the darkness, she couldn't see his eyes clearly, but she thought she detected something like anger.

"Do you want me to read it out loud?" he said, his voice low, steady.

Something was definitely wrong, she realized. She leaned closer to see the paper better. It had the clinic's name and address on the top. Below that, it said OUTPATIENT RECORD. It was a preprinted form with separate sections for the patient's information, test results, and physician's comments. The bottom quarter was filled with Chyles's handwriting.

"Yes, read it," Laura said. "What's the matter, Dan? Tell me what it says."

He took a breath, then started reading.

"Patient, Laura Fielding. Week twenty. All vitals normal. Weight gain within acceptable range."

Dan's voice became steadily lower as he read on, lower and angrier. Laura did not understand what was wrong and that frightened her.

"Examination reveals no indication of infection or placenta previa," he said. "Fetus developing normally. Except for fatigue, patient doing well."

He paused now and looked back at Laura. What she saw in his eyes made her tremble. The flame from the candle turned them red. The anger she had seen before was now much more malignant. He glared at her a moment, then turned back to the paper and continued reading.

"No . . . apparent . . . complications," Dan read, hitting each word deliberately, harshly, "from . . . prior . . . surgical . . . abortion."

He stopped.

His words echoed through the silent room. Laura felt like

she had just been hit in the face by a shovel. Her mind would not function. Confusion swept through her. Then shame. Finally fear—fear that Dan would not understand. She didn't know what to say, how to explain. For several seconds, he just stared at the paper. Finally, he turned to her.

"This says you had an abortion."

She avoided his glare and said nothing.

"Is that true?" he asked.

She looked up but still could not speak.

"Is it true or not?" he said, raising his voice for the first time.

She managed to nod.

"When?" he asked.

She walked over to her chair, the movement feeling very awkward, and she sat down. Dan remained standing, staring down at her.

"When did it happen?" he said, speaking quietly, but his voice was still sharp with anger.

"A year after I graduated from law school."

"After law school? *After?"*

She nodded and stared at the table setting, unable to withstand his hurt, angry eyes.

"After we were married?" he said.

She nodded.

"Who—" he said, pausing to take a breath and control his anger. "Who was the father?"

"You, of course," she said right away, first thinking that her admission would mitigate what she had done but then quickly realizing when she saw his face flush with anguish that it might have hurt him less if she had lied and said that the baby hadn't been his.

"Me?" he whispered, his voice breaking.

"Dan, we both agreed it would be better if we waited."

"Waited while you were in school, yes! But not afterward! We agreed to wait until you graduated to get married! We never said anything about afterward! Never!"

"It was understood, you know that."

"Understood that you'd get an abortion if you got pregnant? And you'd do it without asking me, without telling me? That was never understood!"

"Neither of us wanted a baby back then. You know that. We weren't ready. I wasn't, and neither were you."

"Don't tell me that."

"It's true, and you know it. Both of us were just starting our careers and we didn't have the kind of time that parents need to devote to a baby. You said yourself many times that we couldn't afford a child."

"I never—*never!*—said to have an abortion! That was my baby as much as it was yours! How could you do that? Goddamn it, Laura, how could you?"

"I did what I thought was best at the time."

"And to hell with me and what I thought. Is that it?"

"No, that's not it."

"You should have asked me first."

"I was the one who was pregnant, not you!"

"Don't give me that feminist crap. It was my baby just as much as it was yours. I'm not some one-night stand you met at a bar and never saw again. I'm you're goddamn husband. I had a right to know. I had a right to say whether I wanted to keep *my* baby or not. You should have told me. For God's sake, it's been thirteen years, and you still haven't told me. If I hadn't read that report, I wouldn't know now either, would I? When were you planning on telling me, anyway? Never?"

"You have to understand the position I was in."

"No, I don't have to understand. I can't understand. What I understand is that you aborted our baby and you didn't give a damn what I wanted. And you lied to me. And Chyles lied to me. He knew all along and he never told me. You told him not to tell me, didn't you?"

"No, I didn't tell him that."

"The hell you didn't."

"Dan, please believe me: I'm sorry I did it. I really am. Maybe I didn't handle it the best possible way, but I was young and I thought I was doing the right thing. I didn't mean to hurt you. You have to believe that."

"How many other times did it happen?"

"What are you talking about?"

"Abortions. How many other ones did you have?"

"I didn't have any others. You know that."

"How do I know that? You had one and I didn't know about that. How do I know you haven't had others? How do I know you're not going to abort this baby now?"

"Now you're talking foolishly."

"I don't think so. You seem to think that when you get pregnant, it's your baby and not mine. How do I know you're not going to decide that this isn't the right time to have this baby and so you go somewhere and have another abortion?"

"I'm not even going to answer that," she said. She got up too quickly and had to brace herself against the table for a moment until the dizziness stopped.

"I can't believe you did that to me, Laura. I honest to God can't believe that."

"Obviously, you can't think rationally right now, so I'm not even going to try to explain to you."

She felt a little steadier now, so she went into the kitchen and turned off the oven. She had no appetite, no desire to sit down to a romantic dinner with him.

"When you're ready to discuss this like an adult," she said, making her way to the stairs, "come upstairs and get me. Until then, I'm going to lie down."

"Until then, go to hell!" Dan shouted.

"You go to hell."

He grabbed his car keys off the table in the living room. "I'm not sticking around here for this, that's for goddamn sure."

"Where are you going?"

"Back to New Orleans."

"Don't be childish. You're not going to drive all the way back there. You just got here, for God's sake."

"Don't tell me what I'm going to do."

"You want to drive all the way back? Fine. Go ahead. Act like a baby."

"So you can abort me like you did the other baby?"

His words finally hit home. Laura could barely keep in the

tears. "You bastard!" she said, biting her lip to keep from crying. Then she rushed upstairs to the bedroom, slammed the door, and fell onto the bed.

She heard the downstairs door slam shut, heard Dan's footsteps stomp on the porch, then heard the car door open and close. The engine started and the tires spun in the gravel. She heard squealing as Dan's car sped up the road.

27

That night, Laura was sure Dan would return in a few hours. When he didn't come back, she went to bed expecting him to call from New Orleans in the morning. He didn't call while she was dressing to go to the clinic, nor did he call after she came back. She wondered if he would call before the weekend was over, call and tell her he was sorry for what he had said to her. Then they could discuss the abortion rationally.

By late Sunday night, Dan still hadn't called. She didn't feel she should be the one to call him and apologize. It wasn't her fault that he had said what he did and run out. She was willing to explain the abortion and even apologize for it, but first he had to make amends for his behavior Friday night. He wasn't the only one with hurt feelings. What he had to understand—what he should have given her a chance to explain—was that the abortion had been as painful for her to go through as it was for him to find out about it, probably more so. If there were some way she could undo what had happened more than a decade earlier, she would. But she couldn't change the past, and she suffered from that every day. That was enough punishment; she didn't need Dan to add to it.

She hoped that this pregnancy would relieve some of the pain she felt from the abortion, alleviate some of her guilt. And she was optimistic that after the baby was born, it would do the same for Dan's anguish. They needed this baby now more than ever.

This realization heightened her concerns about the health of the babies being born at Chyles's clinic. Since she hadn't been able to discuss it with Dan, she was going to have to make sense of all this on her own.

She thought about what Chyles did, putting information about the abortion in the envelope, and she wondered if he had done it intentionally. Maybe he suspected that she was the one who had gone to Woodridge, so he did it to create tension between her and Dan, distract them away from him and his son and his clinic. Was that possible? Could he really be that devious?

Monday morning, when she was sitting in the waiting room before going in for her blood test and shots, she overheard the receptionist telling another patient that Dr. Chyles had been called to delivery unexpectedly and would not be able to see her for her weekly checkup until the afternoon.

With Chyles in a different part of the clinic, Laura saw this as a good opportunity to see if she could get some answers, determine if there really was anything wrong with the babies and find out why Chyles had two identities.

Then Gail called Laura back. While she was checking Laura's vitals, Laura casually asked if this clinic was affiliated with any other centers.

"No. This is an independent facility."

"It's not connected in any way to any reproductive specialists anywhere else, say in Canada?"

"Canada? Goodness, no. They have a completely different system up there, you know. Socialized medicine. The government pays for everything; they regulate everything differently. Up there, couples have to wait forever to go to a clinic like this. No, we're not affiliated with any centers in Canada, or anywhere else. Why do you ask? You're not planning on leaving us, are you?"

"No. I was just asking for a friend."

"She lives in Canada? You know, a lot of patients come here from quite a distance away. Your friend might consider that."

"She can't travel this far—too many commitments up there."

"That's too bad. Well, I'm sure she'll find a place that can help her. Would you like me to ask Dr. Chyles if he can give you a referral?"

"No, don't do that."

Laura said it so quickly, so adamantly, that Gail looked at her strangely.

"I was just asking out of curiosity," Laura explained, not wanting Chyles to know that she was checking on him. "It really isn't that important."

Gail nodded and smiled, satisfied, then prepared the syringes for Laura's injections.

"Have you ever heard of anyone named Nefayre?" Laura asked. The question came out sounding much more significant than she wanted.

"Nefayre? Is that a patient?"

"No. Maybe someone who works here?"

Gail thought a moment, then shook her head. "No, nobody named Nefayre works here."

"You've never seen the name on any mail or anything like that?"

"No. Of course, I don't see the mail; that comes to the clinic's post office box, and Dr. Chyles or Dr. Acer usually pick that up. Why?"

"I just thought I heard the name mentioned in connection with the clinic."

"Maybe it's a patient. If she didn't make it past the *in vitro* attempt and didn't go through the complete therapy, I wouldn't know her. Maybe that's who it is."

The shots stung as Gail administered them. They had hurt for the last few days now. Laura couldn't help thinking about her baby each time the needle pierced her flesh, couldn't clear her mind of the image of those other *imperfect* children.

"Have you seen many babies born here with . . ." Laura tried again to sound conversational. "With any sort of problems?"

"What kind of problems?"

"I don't know. Any problems at all. Have you noticed anything about any of the babies that gave you any concern, even just a little?"

"No. But then I only deal with the babies *in utero,*" Gail said. "The staff in the maternity ward would know better, but I haven't heard anything. Why?"

"No reason."

"You certainly are full of questions this morning, Mrs. Fielding."

Laura forced a nervous smile. "Just premotherhood jitters," she said.

"That's only normal. You shouldn't be worried. The amnio came back fine. Everything seems to be going along nicely." She squeezed Laura's hand reassuringly and said, "Sweetheart, take it from someone who's seen dozens of these. You and your baby are going to be just fine."

When Gail was finished, she left Laura alone to get dressed. Laura put on her clothes quickly, then peeked out the door to see if any of the nurses were around. She heard the low chatter of voices coming from the reception area and heard a nurse reassuring a patient in one of the other examination rooms, but the hall itself was empty.

She looked toward the end where Chyles's office was. It took her only a moment to make up her mind. Checking one more time to make sure no one was watching, she slipped out into the hall and hurried to Chyles's office. The door was closed, but when she tried the knob she found it unlocked. She glanced back once more to make sure no one was looking, then pushed open the door and went inside.

The room held the subtle scent of Chyles's cologne, reminding Laura that she did not belong in here. She had to move quickly, find what she was looking for, and get out before anyone realized she was missing.

It was very quiet in here, she noticed as she moved across the room, a quiet that added to her nervousness. The first thing she checked was the door in the corner behind the desk. If it was a closet, it might contain medical records, she thought, but when she opened the door, she saw that it led to a washroom. At the far end past the sink was another door, an exit out into the hallway, she assumed. She decided there was nothing of any significance in there.

She went to the desk and began opening the drawers. The bottom one on the right was filled with patient files, in alphabetical order. She flipped through them until she found her own file and took it out to examine. Nervously glancing at the door every few moments, she opened it and read through the notes.

Much of it she didn't understand. There were a lot of medical terms and code numbers. But she saw where it said "July 7, patient received two zygotes"—the same number of zygotes the nurse had said. Then she looked earlier in the file to the notes concerning the harvesting procedure on July 2. It said the number of eggs harvested was two.

She was certain it had been only one. She tried to remember back to that day in July when she had undergone the procedure. She had been a little groggy from the anesthesia, but she recalled standing with Dan outside the window of the lab, and she thought the embryologist and Chyles had said there was only one egg. Now she wasn't sure anymore.

She looked up at the door again, worrying that someone might come, then she scanned the rest of her file. From what little she could comprehend, there was nothing in it that seemed unusual—just the number of eggs. She put her own file away and turned her attention to the others, flipping through the K's until she found the file for Paula Kincaid, Jenny's sister.

She checked the number of eggs harvested in her procedure. Three, but only two were preovulatory, usable. And the number transferred: two. That seemed normal. She put Paula's file away and looked near the back of the drawer for Charlotte Wheeler's file. In it, Chyles's notes indicated that he had harvested two eggs from her and transferred two zygotes. Laura pulled out another file, not even looking at the name. Two eggs harvested, two transferred. Another said three eggs harvested, two transferred. All of them were in the same range.

When Gail had told Laura that Chyles had transferred two zygotes in Laura's *in vitro* attempt, she must have been right.

Footsteps came down the hall toward the office now. Panicked, Laura closed the drawer and dropped to her knees behind the desk. She remembered that there was another exit in the washroom and she was about to crawl away when she heard the footsteps in the hallway trail off, leaving silence again.

She sank to the floor and just sat for a moment, catching her breath. *What the hell am I doing in here?* She realized how foolish she was being.

She composed herself and got up to leave, but then she noticed the computer beside Chyles's desk. She remembered Jenny's computer in New Orleans and how much importance she had placed on the information stored inside it. Everything had been erased from Jenny's computer, but maybe there was something in this one that would explain why she thought she had received only one zygote while her record said that it had been two. It would only take a moment, she told herself. She had come this far already . . .

She moved closer to the computer and turned it on. She had to wait for it to boot up. It seemed to take forever for it to go through its start-up routines. Finally, a database program came on the screen. Laura took hold of the mouse and clicked on the OPEN FILE icon. A dialogue box flashed on the screen, prompting her to enter the password.

She realized that Chyles had secured the files, requiring anyone who wanted to look at them to know his password. She wondered why he would do that, what could be in them that he wanted to protect. He hadn't even locked the drawer to his desk or the door to his office. Why lock these files?

The message ENTER PASSWORD kept flashing on the screen.

Laura glanced at the door, making sure no one was coming, then, still standing behind the desk, she typed CHYLES.

On the screen appeared INVALID PASSWORD.

She typed in NCHYLES.

INVALID PASSWORD.

She checked the door, then tried NORMAN.

INVALID PASSWORD.

She stood back and stared at the monitor for a moment, trying to figure out what the password might be. She tried to remember if Chyles had a dog, and if so, what its name was. People often used pets' names for passwords. But thinking back to the birthday party at his house last summer, she didn't recall seeing a dog, and the house didn't have the smell of animals. She didn't know when his birthday was, so she couldn't try that. Since there were about a billion possible passwords, she didn't have much hope that she could—

Then it occurred to her. She pulled up the leather chair and sat down. Her hands were damp with perspiration and her fingers stiff as she set them on the keyboard again. Her fingers moved slowly, deliberately, punching out the letters.

N-E-F-A-Y-R-E.

She hit the Enter key.

INVALID PASSWORD.

"Damn it."

She had been sure that was it. Realizing it was hopeless, she reached for the switch to turn off the computer, then thought of one more possibility. She typed in JEREMY and hit Enter. A list of files appeared on the screen.

"Yes!"

She was in. She scanned the list and found one file named FIELDING.DBF. Using the mouse, she pointed to the file and double-clicked. FIELDING.DBF opened, displaying a template that resembled the notes in the file folders inside Chyles's desk. She clicked on the scrolling bar to the right and searched through the file for notations on how many eggs had been harvested and how many zygotes transferred.

She found the information quickly and for a moment just stared at it, bewildered. It said that one egg had been harvested on July 2. That egg was designated E1. Just below was the number of zygotes transferred six days later: two. Their designations were $E1^a$, $E1^b$.

"That's not possible," she whispered.

How could Chyles have transferred twice as many zygotes as he had eggs to begin with? She read that section of the file a few times, thinking that she must have misread something, but no matter how many times she reread it, it still said the same thing. Chyles started with one preovulatory egg and transferred two fertilized zygotes.

She scrolled down the file, hoping to find something that would clarify what she read, certain that she had just misunderstood it, that it really did make sense. She came to a section with the heading SPLITS. Below it were a series of numbers:

She recognized the top number as correlating with the number designation of the one preovulatory egg Chyles had harvested on July 2. The bottom two numbers were the designations of the zygotes he transferred on July 7. But she still did not understand how he got from one egg to two zygotes.

She studied the numbers on the screen intently. It seemed to indicate that E1 *became* E1^a and E1^b—*split*, as the section heading indicated. That word, *split*, continued to roll through her thoughts until it suddenly struck her what it all meant.

For a moment, she couldn't breathe. She couldn't believe what she was thinking. She must have misunderstood what Jenny had told her—not during their phone conversation recently but months earlier when they'd met for lunch in Collier. Jenny had used that very same word—*split*. She had been talking about the two scientists at George Washington University and how they had successfully—

". . . for another half-hour," Chyles was saying, his voice coming from the hallway. Laura heard the tap of his shoes on the floor as he walked toward the door. "I don't want to be disturbed until then."

Laura hesitated, paralyzed with panic. When she could finally move, all she thought about was getting out, getting away before Chyles saw her. She quickly turned off the computer, then rushed into the washroom, closing the door behind her just as Chyles opened the office door and came in.

28

Listening at the door, Laura heard Chyles walk to the desk. From the sound, he seemed steady and calm, not rushing, not alarmed. She was sure he hadn't heard her or seen the washroom door close. As she listened to him sit in the leather chair, she hoped he wouldn't notice that it was warm from her having sat in it, hoped he wouldn't notice that it was out of place. She heard a click as he turned on the computer, then the hum of the fan inside the CPU.

He was going to stay in the office for a while, she assumed, recalling what he had said in the hall about not bothering him for half an hour. Surely during that time he would want to use the washroom, she thought. She had to get out before he found her.

She moved across the bathroom to the other door, stepping softly so he wouldn't hear her. She gently turned the knob and eased open the door.

She expected to see the hallway that led to the examination rooms but instead found darkness. At first, she thought she was in a closet and shuddered as she realized she was trapped. Then she noticed that the darkness seemed deeper than that of a closet. Her eyes slowly adjusted and she saw that this was a hallway, but a different hallway. The only light was a very dim glow coming from several yards in and to the right, low to the floor. Straining to see, she spotted stairs leading down. That was where the light was coming from. That was the only way she could go.

She descended slowly, pausing at each step and listening for any sign that someone was down here. She couldn't hear anything, but the smell coming from below was peculiar. The air held a trace of chemicals—and something else too. She detected the scent of something organic, but she couldn't identify what it was. A wave of nausea swept over her. She waited a moment for it to pass. Whatever it was made her uneasy.

But she had to escape before Chyles found her, and since this was the only way out, she continued down the last few steps. She stopped at the bottom. There was another narrow hallway, only one way to go. The light source came from straight ahead. She listened for a moment, heard nothing, then started down the hall.

The floor was covered with white tile, the walls solid concrete block, newly painted white and unblemished. She thought there should be water pipes and electrical conduit running along the ceiling, but instead, the hall was finished off like the main floor of the clinic. It did not seem like a basement down here, like the clinic's power plant, a place only maintenance personnel used, but she did not dwell on that thought for long. Her main concern was finding the way out. Once she was safely away from here, she could sit down and rationally figure out what to do next, in light of what she had found in Chyles's computer.

The hallway turned right, into a well-lit room. Laura stood in the doorway, surprised by what she saw. It was a laboratory, smaller than the lab upstairs, the one where the *in vitro* procedure had been done last July, but it appeared to be equally well equipped. Fluorescent lights hung overhead, glaring off the stainless-steel tables and shiny metal instruments. Everything looked sterile.

Shelves covered the walls, and on them, neatly arranged,

were dozens of vacuum jars. Some contained dull red liquid that looked like diluted blood. Others were filled with yellow fluid. Something was floating in each of the jars, but from this distance Laura couldn't tell what was in them.

She stepped into the laboratory. There were two other doorways leading from this room. One of them surely would take her to an exit, she reasoned, but that was no longer her first concern. She wanted to know what this place was, why a lab like this was in the basement.

She approached one section of jars and took a closer look at what was floating inside. It took a moment for her to identify what she was looking at, but the instant she realized what it was, a shiver of fear ran down her back and into her legs. She felt faint.

She struggled to breathe. For a few moments, she couldn't move, she couldn't think. Finally, she collected herself enough to stand up straight, face to face once again with the jars. Understanding what was in them, what the smell was that permeated the air, made inhaling difficult. It took all of her courage to stare at the tiny body parts suspended in the fluid: *baby* body parts.

She felt her own baby stirring inside her womb. A chilling fear crept into her brain. How could there be baby parts here? All reason suddenly seemed out of balance. This wasn't what the numbers in Chyles's computer meant, she told herself. This wasn't what she had determined he was doing. This was— What was it? She could not make sense of this at all.

The deathly silence unnerved her. Being in this room alone with all these dismembered body parts made her tremble. Suddenly it felt unbearably cold down here. She needed to get out right away.

She chose the better lit of the two hallways leading from the lab. There was a bright light at the end of the hallway— maybe sunlight, she hoped. As she moved slowly toward it, she passed several doors, all of them opening into darkness.

From one of these rooms, she thought she heard the hum of refrigerators. She hesitated at that doorway only long enough to confirm that there was no exit in there. Continuing down the hall, she came to a room that emitted an odor much stronger than that of the lab. It smelled like animals, she thought, animals and animal waste.

Cautiously looking in, she had the feeling that something or someone was in there. She detected movement, but she couldn't see well enough to tell exactly what it was. She was eager to leave the building without being caught, so she didn't stay long enough to find out what was in the room. She just wanted to leave, and leave quickly.

She continued up the hall toward the light, realizing now that it was fluorescent light coming through the doorway at the end of the hall, not sunlight. As she approached, she eased up carefully to the doorway and looked inside.

More medical equipment and steel tables filled this room. This wasn't a lab, though. This room resembled an operating room, she thought. The air held a scent similar to that of the outer lab, but in here it seemed more—more what? Not stronger. The closest she could come to describing it was more . . . *alive*.

She could see only part of the room from where she was standing. She started to reposition herself to see the whole room, when suddenly, she heard the sharp clang of metal against metal, like something steel falling onto a steel surface. She turned quickly toward the sound and was surprised to see a person standing by an operating table.

The person was looking in the other direction and was unaware that Laura was at the door. Dressed in a surgical gown, mask and gloves, the person was deeply involved with something on the table. Laura saw the gloved hand set a scalpel onto a steel tray. The light caught the flat part of the instrument for only an instant, but in that brief moment, Laura clearly saw blood running down the blade.

The person, continuing to work on the object on the table, shifted position. Laura recognized her immediately, even with the mask on. It was Dr. Acer, Chyles's wife.

Laura's eyes fell to the operating table, and as Dr. Acer stepped to the side, exposing what was there, Laura could barely suppress her shock at what she saw.

Instinctively, she brought her hand up and covered her mouth, then fell backward into the hallway and collapsed against the cold stone wall. She closed her eyes and shook her head, but she could not rid her mind of the scene she had just witnessed. She couldn't believe it was real. It couldn't be. *It just couldn't be.*

She felt bile churning in her stomach and was sure she was going to vomit. She had to get out of here, get away from this place, before they saw her, before they realized that she knew their horrible secret.

She started to stagger up the hall, when she heard a door open and close in the distance ahead, where Chyles's office was, then footsteps hurrying in her direction.

29

Until then, Laura had never really feared that Dr. Chyles would hurt her, but after all she had just discovered, she knew that he was dangerous.

She ducked into the darkness, leaving the door open. Since all the other doors were open, it would surely attract Chyles's attention if she closed this one, she reasoned.

She heard him cross through the lab and start down the hall toward the operating room where his wife was. Moving slowly and quietly, Laura crept deeper into the darkness. The stench of animals quickly filled her lungs, making the dull nausea in her stomach a sharp, stabbing pain. She noticed as she moved that something sloshed beneath her shoes. From its odor, she realized it was urine.

A shadow passed in front of the doorway and Laura froze. Suddenly Chyles came into view. Like his wife, he was wearing surgical clothes. Laura remembered the receptionist explaining to another patient that he had been in delivery this morning. He must have gone from the delivery room to his office while his wife came straight down here. Dr. Acer had to be the one who had brought the baby.

Standing there in the dark, Laura could still see the image of that naked newborn on the operating table, its gray skin covered with blood, the umbilical cord hanging across its torso. The baby's eyes had been open, but its arms and legs had been motionless. Laura was certain it was dead. She needed to believe that it was dead—dead now—dead before Acer had used the scalpel.

In that one instant when she had looked at the baby laid out on the stainless-steel table, Laura had clearly seen the incision in the baby's skull and the white brain tissue beneath.

It seemed so unreal. All of this was not real. She told herself, *This can't be happening. I must be home sleeping, dreaming this. But dreams don't have smell; dreams don't have the texture of that stone wall; dreams don't leave you nauseated. No, this is no dream. This is real.* As impossible as it was for her to believe, this was very definitely happening.

Chyles moved past the doorway without stopping. She listened to him walk to the operating room where his wife was doing— Doing *what?* Dissecting the baby? That's what it appeared to be.

Then Laura thought maybe she was wrong. Maybe all they were doing was operating on it. *Helping* it. It had been born with some brain abnormality and they were performing surgery to improve the baby's chances.

But why perform surgery in the basement? Why not in one of the operating rooms upstairs? They were the best equipped in the state, everyone had told her. It didn't make sense that they would come down here. And it didn't make sense that just the two of them would perform the operation, with no nurses to assist them, no specialists to make sure everything went right. It did not make sense at all.

No, that's not what they're doing, she realized. *They're not trying to save the baby.* The baby's skin was already gray; it was already dead. Laura's mind insisted that the baby had been dead before they had even brought it down here.

It was stillborn, she told herself. *Yes, that's it.* The baby had been born dead, and the two doctors were doing an autopsy to determine the cause so they could reduce the possibility that other women would lose their babies. This must be the pathology lab, she reasoned, remembering the doorway she had seen near the delivery rooms. Yes, that's it. Nothing horrible was happening here, only good things. After all, women were having babies. Women who couldn't conceive before were now having babies. Charlotte was right—it could only be good.

Laura heard Chyles's voice now.

"How far have you gotten?" he asked his wife as he entered the lab.

"Ready for the extraction."

"Let's get to it, then."

Laura heard them moving around, heard the clatter of instruments, the scuffing of shoes on the concrete floor. *This is the time to leave,* she thought.

As she moved slowly toward the door, she noticed breathing around her. This unsettling impression that she was sharing the air with something else grew more vivid with each breath she drew. Her eyes began adjusting to the darkness now and she saw cages around her, many of them, stacked one on top of the other from floor to ceiling. The smell of animals she had detected earlier was just that, she realized—animals. One by one, their forms started to come into focus.

In one cage were several puppies. They were furless, she noticed. They looked to be only a few days old. The cage beside theirs held an adult dog, lying listlessly, cramped in the small space. It was looking at her, but she got the distinct impression that it didn't understand what it was seeing. Its stare was familiar. It watched her the very same way her cat watched her.

She turned and looked at the cages on the other side of her. The first one immediately caught her attention. She couldn't believe what she was seeing. There in the darkness was a pair of red eyes peering back at her. The white fur that surrounded the eyes was difficult to see without light, but she did make it out, just as she made out the splotches of orange in its coat.

Another pair of red eyes blinked into view from the rear corner of the cage, another white-and-orange head turned toward her. Then a third pair. These eyes were lifeless, empty, little more than holes in the darkness.

Even in the darkness, she was able to discern the distinct shape of their heads: smooth, oval, feline heads—each of them without ears.

They were identical to the cat at her house. Identical to the cat Dan had run over months ago. Identical to the cat they had seen in the road the very first time they had visited the clinic.

Clones of that cat, she realized, remembering what she had seen in Chyles's computer, the embryos that had been "split," remembering what Jenny had told her about the two scientists at George Washington University who had successfully cloned human embryos.

Chyles was cloning animals. That was the only explanation Laura could think of for these cats. Quivering with fear, she asked herself, *Is he also cloning babies?*

She already knew the answer.

Thoughts of the operating room at the end of the hall filled her brain again: that gray, lifeless baby that Chyles and Acer had dissected. It seemed that they not only were cloning embryos, they were also killing babies.

Acer's words to her husband echoed through Laura's mind: *ready for the extraction.* They were extracting something, taking something from the baby. What? Why? It seemed so—

Her thoughts were suddenly shattered when she heard a loud buzzing sound coming from the operating room, an instrument that sounded like a dentist's drill. Then she heard the sickening tearing sound of a blade cutting into bone. A wave of images of what Chyles and Acer were doing to that baby swept through her, images so repulsive that she couldn't suffer them internally any longer. She doubled over with pain and fell against the cages, the contents of her stomach spilling onto the floor.

Suddenly the dogs began barking and jumping against the walls of their cages. Through the noise, Laura heard the motor of the drill in the other room suddenly stop. They knew she was here.

30

Laura scrambled down the hall, her stomach making it difficult for her to run. There wasn't much light to guide her, but her eyes were accustomed to the darkness now and she could see most of what was in front of her. The hall led to a stairway. She hurried up, tripping once, scraping her knees and palms. When she reached the top, she saw a door ahead of her, a thin line of light glowing under it. She rushed over and fell against it, out of breath. Her body was shaking with fear. She hesitated a moment and listened for the sound of someone following her. In the distance behind her, she heard the clatter of shoes on the concrete, the sound of someone running.

She grasped the doorknob, praying that it wouldn't be locked. It turned in her hands. She pulled open the door and staggered out. Bright light stung her eyes. She smelled only disinfectant up here, which made it a little easier for her to breathe. But she knew she wasn't safe yet, not until she was out of the building and away from here.

She looked around and realized she was standing in the hallway just outside the delivery rooms. A loud slapping noise behind her startled her. She wheeled around to see what it was, and realized it was just the door closing. On the door was the sign saying PATHOLOGY——PHYSICIANS ONLY.

She remembered now seeing Dr. Acer go through this same door just after Charlotte Wheeler delivered her baby. Acer had been carrying something that night, and from the size and shape of it, Laura suddenly realized it could have been a baby.

Was it Michael? Had they done something to him, and was that why he seemed abnormal now? But she had seen Charlotte's baby shortly afterward and he had no scar on his scalp—or anywhere else. There would have been scars if they had done to him what they were doing to the baby downstairs.

The more she tried to figure it out, the less sense it made. She just wanted to get out of here, reason it out later, just leave before they—*before they what?* Every fiber in her body now told her that they were dangerous.

She hurried toward the double doors that led out of the delivery area. Two nurses came out of one of the supply rooms off the hallway and looked at her curiously.

"Excuse me," one of them said. "Patients aren't allowed back here."

"I'm sorry," Laura said, barely getting the words out. She hurried past them.

"Ma'am," the nurse said, calling after her, noticing that she was unsteady and pale. "Ma'am, are you all right?"

Laura couldn't answer. Without even glancing back, she raised her hand and gave a slight wave. She hurried to the end of the hall and threw open the double doors.

She saw Roy, the security guard, at the end of the hall, talking on the beige clinic phone. He hung up and started up the hall, his movements very deliberate, as though he was searching for something—*for her.* When he saw her in the doorway, he quickened his pace and came toward her.

"Mrs. Fielding," he said.

Laura froze, not sure what to do. She couldn't go back into the delivery area, because Chyles would be coming up from the basement at any moment. She had to go toward the lobby. She had to get to her car, get away from here.

"I'm glad I found you," Roy said. "I just talked to Dr. Acer on the phone. She and Dr. Chyles are looking for you."

Roy didn't seem threatening at all, Laura noticed, which

led her to believe that maybe he didn't know. She had no idea which staff members were involved in what Chyles and Acer were doing, but Roy seemed innocent. She took a deep breath and steadied herself, thinking perhaps she could get past him. Telling him what she had just seen was out of the question, she realized. He would only think she was delirious. What she needed to do right now was just get away from here. Later, she could decide what to do, whom to tell.

Roy was still coming toward her. "They wanted to talk to you about something," he said.

"I know," she said. "I—I just talked to the nurse." She pointed to the doors behind her, then walked past Roy, heading toward the lobby. "All taken care of," she said. She could feel him watching her. It was difficult for her not to start running.

"Mrs. Fielding," Roy called out.

Laura kept walking.

"Mrs. Fielding," he said again.

Laura heard his heavy shoes start up the hall after her. She glanced over her shoulder, ready to sprint for the door if he started running.

"You mean you just talked to the nurse just now?" Roy asked.

"Yes, just a second ago."

She heard her voice crack with fear, but Roy didn't seem to notice.

"Whatever it was they wanted is straightened out?"

"All set." Laura forced herself to smile. "Thanks."

"Have a nice day, Mrs. Fielding," he said and walked to the water fountain.

Laura managed to maintain a steady gait until she rounded the corner into the lobby. Out of sight of the guard, she raced out the door and across the parking lot.

She slid into her car and slammed the door. She swatted at the lock several times, finally engaging it. She was gasping for air, taking short, quick breaths. Her head felt as if it was filling with blood, like it would burst. Perspiration dripped down her face.

When she took out the key and tried to put it in the ignition, it slipped from her fingers and fell to the floor. Her hands were sweaty and trembling. She glanced over her shoulder at the clinic entrance. Through the glass doors, she saw Chyles rushing across the lobby. Roy hurried up behind him.

She bent forward and patted the floor for the key. Her stomach made it awkward for her to reach down, but finally she found it. As she struggled to put it in the ignition, she checked the rear-view mirror and saw Chyles rush out of the building and scan the parking lot. Roy came out behind him and pointed out Laura's car. Chyles started forward.

Laura realized she had the key upside down, so she turned it over and stuck it in the ignition. The car started right away. Even before she had the car in gear, she stepped on the accelerator. When the transmission finally engaged, the tires squealed and the car lurched forward. She barely missed two other cars as the car fishtailed and sped across the parking lot and down the road.

Peering one last time in the rear-view mirror, she saw Chyles standing in the parking lot, watching her. Even from this distance, she could see the look of desperation on his face.

31

When Laura rushed into the house, she tripped over the cat and fell against the wall. The cat screeched, startling her. Laura's heart was already racing. She struggled to breathe. She felt the baby move inside her, a sensation that only heightened her fear.

She looked around the house, confused and in a daze. She wasn't sure what to do. She looked out the window. No one was out there, but instead of putting her at ease, that frightened her. Her isolation meant no one was here to help her. No one would see if something happened.

She rushed over to her desk and grabbed the phone. Her hand was unsteady as she dialed. On the second ring, the machine answered. Dan wasn't home.

"Damn it!"

She hung up without leaving a message and dialed his studio but again got the answering machine.

"Goddamn it, Dan, where are you?"

The machine beeped.

"Dan, it's me!" she said, the words coming out in a rush. "There's a problem—the baby—the clinic— I have to get out of here. Call me—no, I'm coming home. I'm leaving right now. I'll call you—"

She started to cry into the phone.

"Oh, God," she whispered. "Dan, I'm scared," she said. "The babies . . ."

She managed to get hold of herself and stopped crying. She wiped her nose, rubbed the tears from her cheeks. "I don't know what to do," she said. "We have to do something—when I get there, we'll do something—I don't know—I'll be there tonight."

She hung up and staggered upstairs to pack a bag. Her legs were aching now. She felt nauseated again, but there was nothing left in her stomach to throw up. The baby was there, she thought. She was very conscious of the baby being there, right alongside the sensation of nausea.

Her suitcase was in the back of the closet. As she pulled it out, several dresses came off their hangers. She flung them aside and carried the suitcase to the bed. She tried to open it, but it was locked. Her hands clammy and trembling, she dialed the combination and pulled at the latch, but it wouldn't open.

"Damn it!"

She tried again to unlock it, but her thumb kept slipping off the brass rollers. Finally, she shoved it off the bed and rushed back to the closet. On the top shelf was a shopping bag she had gotten from the maternity shop in Montgomery. She pulled that down and started stuffing clothes into it, paying little attention to which items she was taking or how she was packing them. She knew she was in danger. Every second counted. She had to get out. Her whole body was shaking violently now.

As she stuffed the last few items into the bag and turned quickly to get some shoes, the bottom of the bag ripped out and everything fell to the floor. Her emotions finally overwhelmed her and she started crying. She dropped to her knees and began picking things up, but she realized she was wasting time. She didn't need clothes; she needed only to get away from here as quickly as possible, so she left everything on the floor and struggled to get up.

Her stomach made it difficult for her to stand. She had to pull herself up by the handle of the closet door. She felt the baby again as she doddered out of the room toward the steps. She was about to go downstairs when Dr. Chyles stepped into view below.

For a moment, she and Chyles just stared at each other, neither of them speaking. Laura was frightened and confused, not sure what to do. Chyles looked at her calmly.

"We have to talk, Laura," he said.

"Stay away from me!"

In panic, she glanced back at the bedroom only a few steps away. She was sure she could make it there and lock the door before Chyles could get upstairs. "Just stay away!" she screamed. "I swear, I'll call the police!"

As she said this, she realized he could have taken the phone off the hook downstairs, making it impossible for her to call for help. "I already called Dan," she said, hoping to frighten him. "He's on his way over here right now."

"I'm not going to do anything to hurt you, Laura. I just want to talk."

"I don't want to talk to you."

"I think you do, Laura."

"I said I don't!"

"You saw something today, didn't you, Laura?"

The way he kept repeating her name, speaking in a calm,

hypnotic manner, made her even more nervous. It was the way he had spoken to her since she arrived at the clinic, the way he had always allayed her fears, constantly reassuring her that everything would be all right. Now she understood what he really had been doing all along: deceiving her, deceiving everybody. And right now he was trying to deceive her again, to persuade her that everything was all right. He wanted her to lower her defenses so he could strike.

"Go away," she said. "I'm warning you."

"You don't understand what you saw, Laura. I want to explain it to you. Maybe I can put your mind at ease."

She shook her head, not letting herself be tricked by him this time. "No. I want you to go," she said. "I'm going to call the police right now."

"There's no need for that, Laura."

"I will! I swear to God I will if you don't leave!"

"I'm going to leave. I promise you that. And I'm not going to hurt you. What could I possibly do to hurt you? I'm a doctor, Laura. My life is committed to helping people, to bringing new life into the world. I made it possible for you to have a baby, didn't I? And for many other women too. Does that sound like someone who's dangerous? I don't know what you're thinking, but I'm not a bad person, Laura. I couldn't hurt you or anybody else."

"Just leave. Dan is coming. He'll be here any minute. I called him."

"You just called him, and he'll be here any minute?" He smiled, a friendly, harmless smile. "Come on now, Laura, he couldn't possibly come all the way from New Orleans that quickly."

"He's not in New Orleans. He's in town. In Collier. At the diner. I called him there. He's on his way. He'll be right here, so you'd better go."

Chyles sighed. He looked like a frustrated parent trying to keep his patience. "Okay. Wherever he is," he said, "it doesn't matter. We're just talking, right? No harm in that."

"I want you to go. Right now! *Please!*"

"I know you don't want to do anything to hurt anyone," he said. "You don't want to jeopardize all the wonderful things we're doing for so many people at the clinic. You're just a little afraid because you don't understand what you saw today, and that's understandable. I just want to help you understand."

"I understand completely. I know what I saw."

"I don't think you do, Laura. It's very complicated. Things aren't always what they appear to be."

"I saw that baby."

Chyles hesitated. He moved forward to the bottom step.

"Stop!" Laura screamed, ready to run toward the bedroom. "Stop or I'll call the police!"

"Relax, Laura. I'm just going to sit down."

Slowly, he lowered himself onto the step with a weary moan.

"I'm just a little tired," he said with a lightness that succeeded in allaying her momentary fear. He chuckled. "It's been an eventful morning, to say the least, wouldn't you agree?"

She didn't answer.

He took a deep breath, then went on. "So it was you who went to see Jeremy last week, wasn't it?" he asked.

She considered denying it, but then realized there was no sense in doing that. He knew. Sorenson must have described her, or Chyles had recognized the car. He had known all along. But she knew things too, and now she wanted him to understand that.

"I know all about you, Dr. Nefayre," she said, speaking his name as though it was an evil curse. "And I know about Erin Archembeau and the cloning. I know everything."

He nodded and gave her the kind of look one gives a formidable opponent in a chess match. "You certainly do know a lot, Laura," he said. "But you don't know everything."

"I know enough."

"Do you know that Jeremy should be dead?" Chyles stared up at her in silence, letting that sink in. Then he said, "Children suffering the affliction he has don't normally live as long as he has. Did you know that?"

Laura managed a nod. Sorenson had explained that.

"Do you know why Jeremy is still alive?" Chyles asked.

Laura stared at him, saying nothing. She felt a little less tense now that he was sitting, a little less threatened, but she reminded herself not to be tricked by him. He was like a cobra that swayed and quivered before his prey, hypnotizing it into letting down its guard. Then he would strike. But she wouldn't let that happen. She told herself to stay alert, to be ready to run to the bedroom if he should move one inch.

"He's alive today," Chyles said, "and improving every day, because of the work I'm doing at the New Life Center. You didn't realize that, did you?"

His words didn't make sense to her. He was cloning babies. It was still difficult for her to accept, but everything she found pointed to that. He *was* cloning babies. But she didn't understand what that had to do with prolonging his son's life.

"No, I guess you had no way of knowing," Chyles said. "Would you like to know how my work at the clinic has helped Jeremy, how it's kept him alive this long?"

She still didn't answer, but she was listening intently. She wanted to understand.

"I've been trying a special treatment on him," he said.

"Sorenson told me about transfusions," she said.

He smiled and nodded. Hearing her speak to him renewed his hope that he could convince her of the virtue of his work.

"Yes, that's exactly right, Laura. I've been giving Jeremy transfusions. Do you know what kind of transfusions?"

She shook her head. Sorenson didn't even know.

"Let me see. How's the best way to explain this?" He looked off for a moment to reflect and find the right words to make her understand. "Have you ever heard of fetal-tissue research, Laura?" he asked.

She had heard a little about it, but she didn't know much. From what she remembered reading somewhere, it involved scientists' using aborted fetuses to find cures for various diseases. Because it was controversial, the government halted all funding for such research for several years. She was pretty sure it had begun funding again recently.

"Without going into too much detail," Chyles said, "basically we've learned that if we inject brain cells from fetuses into the brains of patients with certain genetic abnormalities, namely enzyme deficiencies, the sick patient often sees a reversal in the deficiency. Fetal cells are still growing, whereas mature cells have stopped. This growth of new cells replaces the deficit in the recipient. It's a lot more complicated than that, but that's pretty much how it works. The benefits of this type of therapy have proven to be quite miraculous, really. You'd be surprised, Laura. You'd be impressed by the good it's done. From what I know of you, I honestly believe you would. You're an intelligent, caring woman. I believe you would encourage progress like this that can help so many suffering children."

He paused a moment to let it sink in, then he continued.

"Jeremy has a deficiency of the enzyme alpha-iduronidase. I think you saw for yourself the effect that this deficiency has on his physical appearance. You'd have to agree that it's a tragic situation, a horrible way to live. It's also a horrible way to die, Laura. But there are many other symptoms that you can't see from the outside—such as Jeremy's liver and spleen. Without sufficient quantities of alpha-iduronidase, they would grow too large for his body. That alone could kill him, if the damage it does to his heart doesn't kill him first. Did you see his eyes?" he asked.

She shook her head. "He was asleep," she said quietly.

"I wish you could have been there while he was awake. You would have seen that he really is a wonderful child. If you could only get to know him, I'm sure you'd fall in love with him instantly."

His voice cracked now and he had to pause a moment to regain his composure.

"The deficiency causes his eyes to become clouded," he said. "He was almost blind before we began the transfusions. Since then, he's regained some vision but not as much as I'd have liked. His vision will improve more, though. I'm very hopeful of that. He's still completely deaf, however, and I don't know if we can reverse that. We're not going to give up hope, though. His mental retardation," Chyles said, looking somber, "well, it's still too early to know if the treatments can reverse that as well. I wish you could have seen him a year ago. He was so much worse. It's hard to appreciate how much the transfusions have helped him unless you saw him before."

As he spoke of the transfusions, it suddenly occurred to Laura what he was doing, what the transfusions were.

"You're taking brain tissue from babies and giving them to Jeremy, aren't you?" she said. "That's why Charlotte's son didn't seem normal. That's why Jenny's niece is the way she is. You did something to their brains."

"No. Of course not!" He looked stunned by the accusation. "My God, Laura," he said. "What do you think I am? I would never do anything like that."

Laura felt more confused now than she had been before. Watching the shocked reaction on his face, she believed he was telling the truth about Charlotte's baby and Jenny's niece. But if that wasn't what he was doing, then what was he doing?

"But I saw your wife with that baby," she said.

"That's not what we're doing at all, Laura. You misunderstand completely. I'm glad now that we're having this talk so I can clear up your misconceptions."

"I saw!" she yelled, her anger stemming from confusion, from the chaos in her head. "I *saw* your wife cut into that baby's head! That was someone's baby and you took out some of its brain. I know you did."

"You're wrong."

"But I *saw* it!"

"You did see something, Laura, but you don't understand what you saw. Let me try to explain. First of all, that wasn't anyone's baby."

"Do you think I'm stupid? I saw it. I saw the baby."

"Not the woman's baby. That's not what you saw. That woman's baby left the operating room with the nurses immediately after delivery. It was cleaned up, weighed and measured, examined to make sure it was healthy, then it was brought directly to its mother. That was not the woman's baby you saw."

"I know what I saw, and I saw that baby."

"What you saw," Chyles said, pausing a moment to find the right words, "was a secondary issuance of the woman's geniture."

"Geniture? Secondary issuance? That's double-talk. You're not saying anything."

"What I'm trying to explain to you, Laura, is that the woman who delivered this morning has her baby. You can go to the clinic right now and see her holding her baby. I promise you she has her baby and her baby is just fine. We didn't touch her baby. What we kept was the subsequent birth."

"Subsequent birth? You mean a second baby?"

"Do you remember when you and your husband first came to the clinic to see if I could help you? I explained that after the delivery I sometimes have to sedate the patient to deliver the placenta?"

"That wasn't a placenta. That was a baby."

"In a manner of speaking, yes."

"That woman had twins, and you kept one of the babies?"

"No. Not twins."

At last Laura put it all together, what she had seen in the basement, what she had read on Chyles's computer, what Chyles was saying now.

"You mean she gave birth to clones?" she whispered.

Chyles answered with a silent nod.

Neither of them spoke for several seconds, then Chyles said, "So you see, she got her baby, the baby she came here for. And Jeremy will get the fetal cells he needs. Everyone wins. Do you see my point?"

"You're crazy," Laura said. "You're insane. You killed that baby."

"Laura, it wasn't anyone's baby."

"It belonged to the woman who gave birth to it! For God's sake, it was a baby!"

"No, she has her baby. I told you that. You ask her and she'll tell you that she has her baby. She didn't want two babies."

"But she had two babies! You killed that baby!"

Quietly but firmly he said, "As did you, Laura."

His words stunned her. For a moment, she couldn't respond. Then she said, "What are you talking about? I didn't kill any babies."

"I think you know what I'm referring to."

"No, I don't. I never killed any babies."

"Didn't you?"

"No! And I don't—"

Suddenly she realized what he was referring to.

Chyles, seeing the realization in her face now, nodded and said, "Yes, your abortion."

"That's not even close to being the same thing," she said, but her voice lacked conviction.

"How is it different, Laura? You destroyed an unwanted baby six months before delivery. How is that different from what I'm doing? Aside from time of delivery, how is one different from the other?"

"Time," she said. "That's exactly the difference. The baby was alive when you did it!"

"You're deceiving yourself if you think your baby wasn't alive when *you* did it, Laura. You've seen the sonogram of your own baby. Didn't it have a beating heart? They have beating hearts when they're only six weeks old. And they move too. Doesn't yours move, Laura? They have beating hearts; they move. If that isn't enough to be alive, what is?"

"It's completely different. They can't live without the mother's body sustaining them. After they're born, they don't need the mother to sustain them."

"Don't they? Oh, I think they do. They definitely do. They need their mothers' milk or they need someone to give them a bottle. Either way, they cannot survive on their own. They're just as dependent on their mother after they're born as they are for the nine months before they're born. So let me ask you, why is it okay for you to sacrifice that life to further your legal career and not okay for me to use it to keep my son alive? Which reason is more noble? You tell me."

"You're twisting everything."

"No, Laura. I'm not. I believe that deep down in your heart, you know that I'm right."

"I don't know that. No, I don't know that at all."

"You think Jeremy should die, then? Is that it?"

"I didn't say that."

"Because he's mentally and physically handicapped, you think his life doesn't mean enough to keep him alive. He's not even worth an aborted fetus."

"I didn't say that, and that's not what we're talking about. These aren't aborted fetuses you're using. They're babies, living babies."

"And Jeremy isn't alive?"

"One doesn't have anything to do with the other."

"And that justifies your sentencing him to death?"

"I'm not sentencing him to anything."

"If he doesn't get the brain cells he needs, he will die. It's that simple. The only way I can get the particular cells that will help him is to extract them from fetuses."

"Can't you use aborted fetuses?"

"I need fetuses that have matured to the third trimester. Without getting into the technical reasons, there are genetic changes that occur in the brain in the third trimester. My research has shown that this is when the cells are most effective for Jeremy's affliction. There's no other way to keep him alive. These are the facts, Laura. The cells I'm using are from fetuses that I have created myself. These babies wouldn't exist if it weren't for me, for my cloning procedure. So I don't see how it is I'm stealing them from anyone. If I don't do this, Jeremy dies. So you tell me what I should do. You make the call."

"I'm not going to make any call."

"Oh, but you will be—by whatever you decide to do. Jeremy's life is in your hands now. It's up to you to either give him life or to kill him. If you call the police, you might as well just save time and call Jeremy directly. You can tell him yourself that you're going to kill him."

"You're the one who's killing, not me."

"Tell yourself that. It'll make it easier for you. But you and I both know that your actions will bring about Jeremy's death. Don't you understand that all I want, all I'm asking, is to keep my son alive and to make his life a little better, to make him healthy and happy? Is that any different from what you want for your child? I made it possible for you to have a child. I'm asking the same thing from you now. Help me keep my son. That's all. Don't kill my little boy."

Laura felt weak and more confused than ever. Her legs wouldn't support her anymore, so she lowered herself to the top step.

"The babies," she said, struggling to talk. "Charlotte's son, Jenny's niece, the one from the party: there's something wrong with them. Don't tell me there isn't, because I saw them; I know they're not normal."

Chyles sighed and nodded. "Yes," he admitted. "The first baby to be born is not always the product of the primary embryo. And I've noticed that in a few cases they've been developing a little more slowly than normal. But that's just for the first few months. That corrects itself with time. The baby catches up."

"The one from the party was already a year old."

"Talk to his parents now. I'll give you their phone number. You'll see that he's developing fine now."

"It's more than just developing slowly. There's something wrong with them besides that. They seem to be—I don't know—less emotional, less attached. Less human," she said, the words making her shudder.

"I don't agree, Laura."

"I've seen them!"

"I'm not going to argue with you, Laura. If you say it's so, then all right."

"That's important!"

Chyles didn't say anything.

"It's because they're clones, isn't it?" she asked. "How can you clone a personality? How can you clone emotions? You gave Charlotte and Paula babies that weren't even real babies. They don't feel anything, do they? There's nothing inside. What are they going to grow up to be? My God, I can't believe this is happening."

"There is a way to tell," he said.

"I can tell just by looking at them, interacting with them."

"No, I mean there is a way to tell which is the primary and which is the secondary as soon as they're born."

He waited a moment to allow this to sink in.

"There's a chromosomal test I can do," he said. "It will allow me to determine which is the secondary fetus. I haven't been able to do it in the past because I've had to maintain discretion. But with your child," he said, pausing a beat to make sure she was listening, to make sure she understood what he was offering her, "with your child, we can be absolutely sure."

"Mine?"

"You're carrying a secondary fetus too, Laura."

Her shock would not let her respond right away. Finally, she whispered, "My baby is going to be like—" She was too frightened to finish.

"Not if we test it," Chyles said. "We can make sure you get the right one."

"You want to take my baby?"

"Only the clone. Unless you want them both. We can say that we didn't realize there was a second baby until we did another sonogram. And then when we deliver it—"

"Wait a minute. You think I'm going to stay here? You think I'm going to keep going to your clinic? No way. I'm leaving here. I'm going back to New Orleans today."

"If you leave here, you'll lose both babies."

"What are you talking about?"

"You won't be able to carry them without the hormone therapy I've been giving you. That's one of the side effects of the cloning procedure."

"I don't believe you."

"You're pregnant only because I'm helping you. If you leave here and stop the injections, you'll miscarry. It's that simple. If you call the police and they do something to me so that I can't continue what I'm doing, you'll lose your child, and I'll lose Jeremy, and many of the other women at the clinic will miscarry. So you see, it's not only Jeremy's life that's at stake, Laura. Many lives depend on what you do now, including your own baby's."

32

As soon as Chyles left, Laura was on the phone. First she called the Collier Public Library's reference desk and asked if they had a phone book for Montgomery. They did, the woman said, and she agreed to check the listing for obstetricians. She gave Laura a list of fourteen doctors and their phone numbers. Laura called them one by one until she found one who would see her this afternoon, a doctor named Morris Echols.

Next she called her doctor in New Orleans. She gave the secretary Dr. Echols's number in Montgomery and asked her to fax her medical records.

"I thought you were seeing Dr. Chyles at the New Life Center," the secretary said.

"I'm seeing Dr. Echols about something else. He needs my medical history today. It's very important. Can you fax it right away?"

"Of course, Mrs. Fielding. But are you feeling—?"

Laura hung up before the woman could finish her question. She had too many questions of her own and far too few answers.

By the time she left for Montgomery, Dan still hadn't returned her call. Perhaps he was still angry about the abortion and didn't want to talk to her, she thought. Was he angry enough that he never wanted to see her again?

She waited for an hour and a half before Dr. Echols could see her. It was almost five when she went back to the examination room. As the doctor reviewed her medical history, she said very little. Occasionally, he asked a question. She answer tersely, yes or no. She was here to listen, not to talk.

After he examined her, he gave her a sonogram and confirmed that she was carrying two babies. Laura remembered her first sonogram, remembered seeing the second baby, remembered Chyles's telling her that it was just the placenta. How could she have been so blind?

Looking at it now on the ultrasound monitor, she trembled. She became acutely aware that her baby was sharing her womb with that—that what? What was it? She didn't know what it was. But she knew it wasn't a baby like her baby was. But it was there, in her womb beside her real baby. The thought of her baby and the *other* fighting each other for precious life brought a sudden wave of nausea.

Dr. Echols completed his examination. After Laura got dressed, they met again in his office.

"Well, everything appears to be going well," he said. He scanned her chart as he spoke.

"Are you sure?" she asked.

"Oh, yes. You're doing excellently. The babies are doing quite well."

"Can I carry the baby to term, Doctor?"

"The bab*ies,* you mean. Well, that's a difficult question to answer, but considering how well you've done so far, I don't see why we can't be optimistic. I would say yes, barring any unforeseen complications, I believe you can carry the babies to term."

His words came as a relief. She felt some of the pressure leave her now. "Then we don't need to do anything special to make sure?" she asked.

"No."

"That's great." And she started to smile.

But then he said, "Whatever you've been doing, that's what we should continue doing. I wouldn't change a thing."

Laura trembled. "What—what do you mean?"

"Whatever course you've been following the last five months, you should continue that. It's worked this long; I wouldn't change it. I don't have the records from your current doctor, so I don't know what treatment you've been undergoing, but it seems to be working just fine for you."

"But if I stop, what'll happen?"

"If you stop what?"

"My doctor's been giving me hormone shots. If I stop getting the shots, will I lose the baby? I mean, the babies?"

"Why would you want to stop? Are you having an adverse reaction to them?"

"I—I don't know. I just want to stop. I think I should. What would happen if I did?"

"I can't tell you that. I don't know what kind of hormones you're taking, but I have to reiterate what I said before. If things are going smoothly, I wouldn't change now. Would you like me to talk to your doctor? Maybe we can—"

"No, don't do that," Laura said quickly. Chyles wouldn't tell this doctor what he was doing, and she was afraid that Chyles would do something to harm the babies if he knew she talked to Echols. She steadied herself and said, "There's no reason to talk to him. There's no real problem with the shots."

"Well, all I can say is that whatever treatment he's been giving you seems to be working quite well. I would strongly recommend against changing course now, unless you're experiencing problems, in which case—"

"No," Laura said quietly.

She realized now that she had no way of knowing if Chyles had been lying when he warned that if she left the clinic and discontinued the injections, she would lose the babies.

But there might be another other option, she thought.

"Let me ask you something else, Doctor," she said. She took a breath to steel herself and said, "Can I deliver now?"

Echols was stunned by the question. "What was that?"

"Deliver the baby—the babies. Can I deliver them now? Today?"

Echols chuckled. "You can't be serious, Mrs. Fielding."

"Is it possible? That's all I want to know."

Echols came around the desk and sat in the chair next to her. "Mrs. Fielding," he said, sounding patronizing. "You're not the first mother to become impatient and wish she didn't have to wait the full term before her babies were born. But I assure you, the time will pass much more quickly than you think, and afterward, you may even wish you could relive these months over again. My advice to you is to try not to dwell on the discomfort and on your eagerness to have your babies, and try to enjoy the pregnancy itself as much as possible."

"I just want to know if I can deliver the babies now or not. Would they survive? Just tell me, please."

"The answer is no."

"No, I can't, or no, I shouldn't?"

"No, you can't, and no, you shouldn't. What I'm trying to explain to you is that what you're going through is quite common."

"No, it isn't."

"Mrs. Fielding—"

"You don't know what I'm going through, so don't tell me what I'm going through!"

Echols backed off a little, surprised by her outburst. Laura managed to calm down.

"I'm sorry," she said. "All I want to know is if the babies can survive now. Out of the womb. If I had them today, could they survive?"

"You can't deliver now, Mrs. Fielding."

"Just tell me yes or no!" She stopped to catch her breath and calm down. "Please," she said. "Just tell me. If I delivered now, could the babies survive? Hypothetically speaking."

"Hypothetically speaking," he said, clearly uncomfortable discussing this, "if you delivered now—and that's a big if, which we still need to talk about—but if you did, let me see." He paused to check her chart and consider his answer. "You're in your twenty-third week, a little more than halfway through your pregnancy. At this point, your babies weigh less than a pound. If you were in a hospital with a neonatal intensive care unit set up to care for babies who are that premature, then it's possible that your babies could survive. But the chances are low. *Very* low. It would be a huge risk. At best, only about twenty percent of babies that age survive."

As the words hit her, Laura had to hold tightly to the chair, her body shaking in horror.

"Are you sure?" she said.

"Yes, but you're not going to deliver today, Mrs. Fielding. You're not going to deliver for many weeks, so you shouldn't even think about that."

Laura couldn't say anything. She couldn't even look at him anymore.

"Are you afraid that you're going to lose the babies?" Echols asked. "Is that it, Mrs. Fielding?"

Her mind was flooded with thoughts and emotions, too many for her to process.

"If that's what you're worried about," Echols said, "you shouldn't be. Let me assure you, from what I can see, the babies should be just fine. You should be able to carry them to term."

"No," Laura whispered.

"Mrs. Fielding, don't take this the wrong way, but maybe you should consider speaking with someone who can help you deal with the psychological aspects of your pregnancy."

Chyles had control of her, she realized. She would have to go back to him. She would have to continue treatment at his clinic. If not, she might lose her baby, and she could not bear to give up this child. She had given up a baby 13 years ago; she could not do that again. Stopping the shots now would be tantamount to aborting this baby, and she couldn't do that. Dan had been so upset when he'd learned that she'd had the abortion 13 years earlier. How would he react if she caused him to lose this one too? No, she couldn't possibly risk losing this baby. Whatever it took to keep it, that's what she would have to do.

"Mrs. Fielding?" Echols was saying.

Laura realized that he had been speaking to her, but she hadn't heard a word he said. Her thoughts were elsewhere. She realized there was only one other solution.

She looked up at him and asked, "How long—" She stopped because her heart was racing. She swallowed hard, then continued. "How old must the babies be before they can survive?"

Echols sighed and shook his head, not wanting to pursue this any further. "Mrs. Fielding—"

"Please."

"I really don't think it's healthy for you to dwell on this."

"Just tell me, *please!*" She steadied herself and said, "You said that at twenty-three weeks, the survival rate is twenty percent. Does it go up as the babies get older?"

"Yes."

"Tell me. Tell me the numbers." In her profession, she worked with numbers all the time. She could understand numbers. She would know what to do if she could reduce this problem to numbers.

"It's not that cut and dry, Mrs. Fielding."

"You must have some idea. You didn't pull twenty percent out of a hat. You must know approximately what the odds are as the babies get older."

"Very approximate," he said.

"That's okay. I just need to know."

He blew out a breath of resignation and quietly said, "Let's see, at about twenty-five weeks, the babies should weigh close to one pound. At that stage, probably only half of the babies survive."

"Half?" Half meant that one of the babies could survive, she reasoned. She felt a sudden rush of hope. *Her* baby would survive. Chyles's baby, the clone, would die. That would be all right. That would solve everything.

But then she thought, *What if Chyles's baby is the one that survives? What if all I'm left with is a lifeless child like Charlotte's?* She couldn't bear to think of that.

"No," she said out loud, shaking her head. She looked up at Echols. "How about older?" she asked.

"At twenty-eight or twenty-nine weeks," Echols said, "the babies would weigh more. At that point, the survival rate goes up to the seventy-five percent range, possibly even as high as ninety percent. But the babies really do much better after thirty-two weeks—"

"Twenty-eight weeks?" Laura said, cutting him off. She had heard what she needed and she wanted to make sure. "The odds are very good at twenty-eight weeks, right?"

"Yes, at twenty-eight, most babies survive. However . . ."

Laura stopped listening. Five more weeks, she thought. She had to continue at Chyles's clinic for five more weeks, long enough to ensure that her baby would survive, *her* baby, the real baby. She had to find another doctor willing to do the delivery, but she would deal with that in five weeks. By early January, this would all be over, she would be home in New Orleans, and she and Dan would have their baby.

Bab*ies,* she reminded herself again.

Her baby. And the *other.* She was still confused about that. In a way, it too was her baby. But in another way, it wasn't, not really. She thought about Charlotte's son, about Jenny's niece, about the baby at the birthday party last summer. If that was how the *other* would be, she wasn't sure she wanted it. She wasn't sure she could love it. Charlotte's baby seemed to be barely alive. Laura couldn't help question if it—and the one inside her own womb right now—if they were even human.

Souls can't be cloned, she told herself. *The essence of what makes us more than just biological entities, more than plant life or bacteria, can't be recreated in a laboratory.*

And yet one of them, one of what Chyles called the secondary issuance, was growing inside her, alongside the baby she and Dan had created. She could not ignore that it was a part of her. She could not just kill it. And she felt bad now that she had wished it would be born dead, that God would take care of it so she didn't have to deal with it.

Yes, it was her baby. And that made it difficult for her to know what to do with it. But for right now, she knew what had to be done.

"Thank you, Doctor," she told Echols as she got up to leave. "You've been a big help."

"I really feel you should talk to someone, Mrs. Fielding."

"Yes, I will. I definitely will. I know exactly who I have to talk to."

33

It was after 8:00 when she got back to Collier. She called the clinic, but the outpatient wing was closed. The answering service took her name and number, and within five minutes, the phone rang. It was Dr. Chyles.

"Okay," she said.

"You're doing the right thing, Laura. For you and Dan, and for Jeremy."

"You can do a test, you said, right? You can tell which one is the real baby?"

"Yes, I can. Are you going to keep one or both?"

"My God," she said, her breath suddenly leaving her. She couldn't believe she was discussing this. "I don't know yet," she said, barely able to get the words out.

"Well, whatever you decide," he said, "we'll work it out so no one questions it. Tell me something, though. Does your husband know?"

"Why?" she said, an edge to her voice now. She still didn't trust him.

"You know him better than I do. Will he understand?"

"I'll worry about that," she said and hung up.

The phone rang again at 10:55. Laura was sitting in the living room, hugging her knees, shivering. She knew it was Dan calling. For the last three hours, she had been trying to decide what to tell him. The time had come.

She picked up the phone. "Hello?"

236

"Laura, are you all right?" Dan said. He sounded worried.

"I'm okay," she whispered.

"I just got your message. What's wrong? What's going on? You said there was a problem with the baby? What's happening, Laura?"

She took a breath to steady herself. "The baby's okay," she said.

"Are you sure? Are you positive?"

"Yes."

"Are *you* okay?"

"Yeah, I'm okay too."

"What happened, then? What's wrong? Your message scared me to death. I thought there was a problem with the baby."

"No, the baby is fine. I'm fine."

"I don't understand. You left a message saying you were leaving there. You said all kinds of things that didn't make sense. And your doctor called me today too—your doctor here in New Orleans. She said you had your records faxed to a doctor in Montgomery. Is something wrong? What's going on there?"

"I'm sorry about the message. I was a little—a little crazy then, I guess. I'm okay now. I just needed to talk to you."

He was silent for a moment, and when he spoke again, he sounded apologetic.

"Is it about what happened Friday?" he asked. "If it is, I want to say—" He hesitated, struggling for words. "It was wrong for me to do what I did, Laura. I shouldn't have acted like I did. I shouldn't have left and I shouldn't have gotten so angry."

"I don't blame you," she said.

"I do. That wasn't the right way to react. I lost control and I shouldn't have. You can understand, though, can't you?"

"I understand, yes."

"I'm not trying to justify what I did, but it hurt me and I guess I wanted to hurt you back. That was wrong. I realize that now. I've been thinking about it a lot since Friday. That's about all I have been thinking about." He took a breath, then said, "We can put it behind us, can't we? I mean, it was a long time ago. At this point, it doesn't matter whether it was right or wrong. It can't be undone."

"I wish it could."

"That's not what's important now. What's important now is that we're going to have a baby. That's what really matters. I want us to be together, to be a family. I don't want to do anything that'll ruin that for us. What I'm trying to say, Laura, is I'm sorry. I really am."

"I'm sorry too. For everything."

"I love you," he said. "What happened before isn't important. That was a long time ago. That's over. We're going to have our baby now, and as far as I'm concerned, this is the only baby that matters. It's going to be our life now—the three of us. I just want us to be happy together."

"That's all I want. I love you too, Dan," she said. "And don't worry, I'm not going to let anything interfere with our having this baby."

"You're all right now?"

"Yes."

"You're not leaving there, are you?"

"No."

"Good, because I don't want to get there and find out that you're gone."

"You're coming up here?"

"Thanksgiving is Thursday, isn't it? Everything I have to give thanks for is up there. You bet I'm coming up there. I'm going to leave tomorrow morning, first thing, and I'm going to stay with you through next weekend."

"That would be wonderful if you could stay."

"I realized these last few days that there's nothing I want more than to be with you. If I couldn't, I don't know what I'd do. I don't even want to think about that. Do you still have the champagne?"

"It's probably flat now."

"I don't care. Put it on ice and we'll celebrate when I get there tomorrow. And find out from Chyles if the baby's a boy or a girl. And tell him to get it right this time. I want to know if my kid's going to grow up to look like me or you. For its sake, I hope it looks like you. I couldn't ask for a more beautiful kid than that."

"I hope it isn't as full of bull as you are," Laura said, hearing herself laugh. She was beginning to feel a little stronger now, a little less afraid. Having Dan come up here would definitely help. She might even be able to explain everything to him once he was here, but she certainly couldn't do it over the phone.

"Come early," she said. "So we can talk."

"I'll be there around one or two. We'll have lunch together if you don't mind waiting."

"I'll be waiting."

"I love you," he said again, and the words flowed into her aching head like medicine.

"I love you too."

34

The next morning, Tuesday, Laura felt uneasy about going to the clinic, about seeing Chyles, but she was more fearful of what would happen to the baby if she didn't go. She could not risk losing it. After last night's conversation with Dan, she was even more sure of this. Maybe their marriage would withstand the abortion from 13 years before. But if she took this baby from him as well, his love for her could not endure.

The clinic seemed disturbingly quiet when she walked in. Maybe it was always like this, she thought, but this morning, she noticed it more than before. The lobby was empty, the halls absent of patients and scurrying nurses. She heard the faint hiss of the wind outside and that was all.

She started toward the outpatient wing but stopped and looked up the hall in the other direction, toward the maternity ward. She had a few minutes before her appointment. She wanted to make sure of something.

When she started down the hall, she saw the security guard come around the corner from the cafeteria, carrying a steaming cup of coffee.

"Morning, Mrs. Fielding," Roy said.

"Good morning."

"Did Dr. Chyles get in touch with you again? He was still looking for you after I saw you yesterday."

"Yes, we spoke."

"That's good. I'll tell you what, he was so ticked off at me for not stopping you when I saw you, I thought he was going to have a cow. Must've been real important what he wanted to talk to you about."

Laura just nodded, walked past him and on to the maternity ward. As she approached the nurses' station, she noticed that she was shivering. She was nervous about what she would find.

"Can I help you?" the nurse said.

"A woman delivered yesterday morning."

"You must mean Mrs. Parker. Shirley Parker. She's the only one who delivered this week."

"Yes. Mrs. Parker. Could you tell me what room she's in?"

"Sure. Four-A." She pointed up the hall.

"Do you think she's awake now?"

"I know she is. Mr. Parker just went in a few minutes ago. I brought the baby in myself."

"How is the baby?"

"She's doing just fine."

Laura headed up the hall toward Mrs. Parker's room. The door was half open. She stayed in the hall and peeked into the room. Shirley Parker was in bed. Her husband sat on the mattress next to her and between them was the baby.

The tiny girl was wrapped in a white blanket, but Laura could see her face clearly. She had a rosy glow and bright, vibrant eyes. Even from this far away, Laura could tell that she was fine. She wasn't one of Chyles's babies. She was the real thing.

The mother and father looked full of joy as they doted on the baby. Laura felt tears well in her eyes. She wanted that to be her and Dan with their baby, their *real* baby. She told herself that things could work out. If they got the right baby, things could definitely work out for them.

But what about the other baby? she asked herself.

She hadn't yet been able to resolve her mixed feelings about it. She could not deny that it was her child, that it came from inside her. But also she could not forget that it was not a normal baby, that it might not even be fully human.

In the examination room, the nurse checked Laura as usual then drew blood and left. As Laura waited for her shots, she turned and looked at the picture over the desk, the seascape taken somewhere near Vancouver. It brought thoughts of Erin Archembeau.

According to Catherine McKay, the lawyer in Seattle, Erin's son killed a puppy when he was 3 years old. Neighbors claimed the boy wasn't normal, and Laura believed that. But killing a puppy? She found that difficult to digest.

She couldn't imagine Charlotte's son or Jenny's niece killing a dog, but she reminded herself that Erin's son had been much older. Chyles had assured her that the cloned babies would become normal as they aged, that their development would catch up with the other children within months. But if Erin's son was typical of these babies when they matured, Laura wondered just how abnormal they would eventually become.

She thought about them 20 years from now, as adults, fully grown men and women, and what they might be capable of. The thought made her tremble.

There was a knock at the door and Chyles came in. Even though he had examined her just yesterday and wasn't scheduled to see her for another week, she wasn't surprised to see him this morning.

"Good morning, Laura," he said.

She just nodded.

He came in, carrying the syringes and the hormone solution for her injections. He set the tray on the table, then examined her briefly. Neither of them spoke. She avoided looking at him directly. When he finished examining her and began to prepare the injections, he finally spoke.

"I'm glad you made the choice you did," he said.

"I didn't see that I had a choice." She did not even try to hide the anger in her voice. "What else could I do?"

Chyles did not respond.

Still thinking about Erin Archembeau's son, she said, "You're sure you can tell which baby is which, right?"

"Definitely."

"You can make sure we get the right baby?"

"It's a simple test. There's no problem there. Have you decided to take just the one?"

"I'm going to discuss it with Dan tonight."

"You haven't talked with him about it yet, have you?"

She shook her head, feeling a little ashamed that she hadn't, but she told herself that she had done the right thing. How could she possibly break news like this to him over the phone? They needed to be face to face when she told him. That afternoon, she would do it, and then they would decide whether to keep both babies or just one, the real one.

"Do you think it's a good idea to tell him?" Chyles said. "Do you think he'll understand?"

"I'll worry about that," she said, irritated that he was intruding in her private life. "You just make sure nothing happens to my babies," she said. "I'll take care of my husband."

As he gave her the injections, pain shot through her arm, pain that was more in her head than in her flesh, she told herself, but pain that was real. Her arm felt like it was burning as he depressed the plunger. She winced and closed her eyes, not wanting to see Chyles next to her. Her head filled again with the image of acid burning her real baby. In her mind, its tiny mouth spread open and screamed in silence for her to save it.

* * *

It was half past noon. Laura was in the kitchen cleaning chicken to grill for lunch with Dan in an hour or two. She kept checking the clock, wishing Dan were already here, wishing he already knew, wishing she didn't have to endure this all alone.

The cat scratched at the back door, wanting to come in. When Laura went to open it, she felt a dull ache in her stomach. It wasn't the sensation of the baby moving; she had felt that enough now to know the difference. Nor was it the type of nausea she had experienced months before, when she suffered morning sickness. This was different, a feeling of discomfort that was new.

And it wasn't in her mind this time, she knew—not like at the clinic when Chyles gave her the shots. This was real. She didn't know what it was, didn't know why she was feeling pain now, and that worried her, but the ache passed quickly and she decided it was probably nothing significant.

As she walked back to the sink to continue cleaning the chicken, she became dizzy and had to hold onto the counter to steady herself. The lightheadedness lasted only a few moments, but it left her with a throbbing headache behind her eyes. Her heart felt like it was racing.

She tried to continue cleaning the chicken, but her headache kept getting worse and she began having chest pains. She decided to sit down for a little while. She had plenty of time to finish cooking before Dan arrived. A few minutes of rest would do her good.

She went into the living room and sat by the window. Looking out at the house across the street, she saw a Blazer pull into the driveway. The truck had Florida tags and Laura recognized it as the husband's truck. He hurried around to the passenger side and helped his wife out. She was still in her first trimester and barely showing, but the pregnancy seemed to be taking its toll. The woman looked tired and weak. Probably morning sickness, Laura thought. It would pass quickly. Then everything would seem fine. If only they knew the truth, knew what she was really carrying.

Thoughts of Charlotte's son and Jenny's niece came to mind again, making her headache even worse and her heart beat faster. She shuddered when she thought about the second baby inside her. Why couldn't she be carrying just the one baby? Why did everything have to go so wrong?

Dan would know what to do. Together they would figure this out, make things right. She wished he would hurry up and get there. *He must be in Alabama by now,* she thought. *He probably passed Mobile more than an hour ago.* She looked up the street, hoping to see his car heading her way, but the street was empty.

The couple renting Charlotte's old house had gone inside. Outside, it looked desolate. The grass was dormant brown. Most of the trees were bare. The sun was hidden today and the wind blew dead leaves and a yellowed newspaper across the driveway.

She felt isolated, vulnerable. A thought came to her suddenly, like a chilling whisper in her brain. *Chyles can get to you if he wants. He can silence you at will. There is nothing to stop him.*

She turned away from the window and shook that thought from her head. *You're overreacting,* she told herself. *You're being paranoid.* She assured herself that no one was going to *get* her. Chyles was a doctor, not a gangster, not a hit man. He didn't "rub out" patients who learned what he was doing.

No, what he does is threaten the lives of their babies. With that power, he doesn't have to worry about being exposed.

Dan's car was still nowhere in sight. Sitting there watching for it became too nerve wracking, so Laura went back to the kitchen and got a glass of water, hoping it would calm her nerves. As she stood at the sink, her dizziness returned, nausea again unsettled her stomach, and her heart pounded so fiercely that she began to wonder if she were having a heart attack. She sat at the table, closed her eyes, and rested her head in her hands until the discomfort gradually receded.

She dismissed her concerns about a heart attack, but she could not deny that the way she was suddenly feeling was odd. She had never felt this way before. She was having trouble breathing now, and she was damp with perspiration. Even though the house was chilly, she was sweating. She wondered if she was coming down with a flu or something.

She stood up to look out the front window again, hoping to see Dan pulling into the driveway. But as soon as she was standing, she felt strangely lightheaded. The ache in her chest became a sudden stabbing pain, so fierce that she doubled over and for a moment could not move or even breathe. She held on to the chair to steady herself.

Straining, she managed to draw a breath of cold air. It stung as it entered her lungs. She looked up and the room seemed to be swaying, as though it were a boat far out to sea, rough sea, the kind of sea Chyles favored in his photographs.

And suddenly it dawned on her.

Chyles.

The injections.

He gave me something!

Panic rushed through her as she realized he might have poisoned her. Not *might* have. *Must* have! This feeling of sickness wasn't normal. This feeling wasn't right. The shots this morning must have been something other than the hormones.

He's trying to kill me!

No, it can't be, she told herself. They had agreed, made a pact. She wouldn't tell, and in return, he would help her have a healthy baby.

She stood by the table in a confused daze, clutching the chair for support, trying to convince herself that she was mistaken, that there had to be a logical explanation, and with each second she thought this, with each unconvincing excuse she proffered, the pain became worse, the dizziness became worse. Her eyesight began to fail her. Within seconds, she was barely able to stand.

"Oh my God," she said out loud, realizing it was true: he was trying to kill her.

She saw the blurry outline of the phone across the room. It looked such a long distance away. She strained to draw another breath, then staggered away from the table. As soon as she took her hands away from the chair, she nearly collapsed. Her right hand found the counter and she held on to it for support. She felt like she was going to throw up; she felt like she was going to pass out. Her legs were barely functioning.

She focused on the phone again, five feet away. Pausing a moment to gather her strength, she thrust herself toward it. Her body slammed against the wall, knocking the receiver off the hook and onto the floor. She leaned against the wall, her eyes closed, her head spinning.

Her heart began to race. She thought again that she was having a heart attack. Sweat soaked through her clothes. Her hands were clammy and weak, her eyes barely able to trace the cord from the phone to the receiver on the floor. Grasping the cord, she pulled it toward her. The receiver felt heavy, but she managed to hold on to it. She squinted to see the numbers on the dial. The 9 was easy to find. She pressed it.

A crippling pain shot through her stomach now, a pain so severe she screamed. Her legs buckled. She grabbed the phone in a futile attempt to hold herself up, but the plastic casing broke off the phone and she fell to the floor.

She could barely breathe now. Her strength was quickly draining from her body. She stared up at the phone. She had to get help quickly or she would die—Chyles would have succeeded in silencing her forever.

Gathering the last wisps of strength, she pushed herself up, holding on to the wall the entire time. Her vision was so blurred she had to position her face directly in front of the dial plate on the phone. Straining to see, she found the 1. Her hand was numb when she raised it. She couldn't feel the button under her finger. She pressed it twice, then collapsed to her knees. The receiver fell to the floor. She didn't have the strength to pick it up again.

"Nine-one-one emergency," a woman's voice said over the phone.

Laura was too weak even to plead for help. She crumpled forward and landed face down on the floor. The last thing she saw as she lost consciousness was the earless cat staring at her from the corner of the room.

35

At 2:00 in the afternoon, Dan pulled into the driveway and parked beside Laura's car. Because of the tractor-trailer that had overturned on I-10 just west of Mobile, the drive had taken him longer than he had expected. An hour earlier, when he had stopped for gas on the highway, he had tried to call to let Laura know that he'd be late, but the line had been busy. It had still been busy after he'd finished pumping gas too. He'd waited at the truck stop for a few minutes longer, tried one more time, then left.

Now, as he turned off the engine, he hoped she hadn't been worried. He remembered how badly she had handled her friend Jenny's death. Because he was driving and because Jenny died in a car accident, Laura probably worried even more. When she didn't hear from him, she might have thought he was in an accident. He hoped it hadn't made her too nervous. He thought now that perhaps he should have stopped again and tried to call her. If his being late had made her worry, he vowed to make it up to her somehow.

When he walked up onto the porch, he found the front door locked. He searched his pockets for the key, thinking how he had so much to make up for already, after the way he'd acted Friday. He had been wrong. It had taken the last weekend for him to realize that no one else in his life mattered as much as she did, she and the baby. He did not want to lose them.

247

He unlocked the door and went in. The lights were off, there was no radio or TV playing, no creaking of the old floorboards upstairs, no sound at all except the faint whisper of wind outside rattling the windowpanes. It appeared that no one was home, but Laura's car was parked in the driveway and Dan knew she was expecting him.

She might be upstairs sleeping, he thought. He remembered how tired she had sounded on the phone last night, as if she hadn't been sleeping well. It made him sick to think how much he had hurt her.

Quietly, he went upstairs to check on Laura but found the bedroom empty. He looked in the bathroom, but she wasn't there either. "Laura?" he called out. "Honey?" He checked the other rooms upstairs, then came back downstairs. "Laura? Honey, it's me."

There was no answer.

He went into the kitchen and noticed right away that the phone was broken. The plastic casing was on the counter and was cracked. The receiver was hung up, but he could see the inner workings of the phone. He picked up the receiver and listened for a dial tone, thinking maybe this was why the phone had been busy when he called, but there was a dial tone. It appeared to be working, but he couldn't understand how the casing broke.

He had replaced the receiver and started to turn, when something suddenly leaped from the window sill, catching him by surprise. Startled, he yelled and jumped back. A cat scurried across the linoleum to the back door and scratched it, wanting to go out.

"Damn!" Dan said, taking a few deep breaths to calm his heart. He looked across the kitchen and saw that it was the same earless cat he had run over a month ago. "I thought you were dead!" He just stared at the cat, wondering if it were possible that he hadn't killed it when he ran over it. It must be, he reasoned, because there it was, still very much alive. He opened the door and the cat hurried out. "Don't get any ideas of moving back to New Orleans with us," he said. "You're not welcome in our house."

Dan followed the cat outside and looked around the yard, calling Laura's name. It was chilly out here and oddly silent.

He watched the cat scamper into the tall grass and disappear. Feeling strangely uneasy, he went back inside and tried to figure out where Laura could be. He returned to the living room and looked around for a note but couldn't find one. He went to the window to double-check whether her car was here. He saw it right beside his, just as he'd thought he had before. So where was she? he wondered.

He noticed the house across the street. That was the only place she could be. *Must be commiserating with a fellow preggo,* he thought with a chuckle, feeling a little more at ease now. He decided to give her a few minutes, long enough for him to have a cold beer and use the bathroom. He hoped she'd notice his car in the driveway and come home. If she didn't, he'd have to go over there and get her, but he dreaded having to make polite conversation with the neighbors. He wanted to be alone with his wife. He wanted to hold her, to show her how much he loved her, how much she meant to him, she and the baby. He promised himself that he would make Thanksgiving special for her.

While he was in the bathroom, the phone rang. "That figures," he said. "Hold on!" He tried to hurry to finish, thinking it might be Laura, but before he could get out, the phone stopped ringing. Whoever it was hung up after the fourth ring.

"Damn it."

He just finished washing his hands when the phone rang again. He rushed to Laura's desk to answer it, but when he grabbed the receiver, he heard only a dial tone. There was one more ring, then the fax machine started printing.

Disappointed that it wasn't Laura calling from across the street, Dan went to the kitchen while the fax was printing, and grabbed a can of Budweiser from the refrigerator. When he came back to Laura's desk, the first sheet was printed and the second sheet was starting to go through the fax. Curious, he picked up the first sheet of paper.

It was a cover sheet. It indicated that the fax was from someone named Catherine McKay at Conner, Lipman. It sounded like the name of a law firm. Something for work, he assumed. He noticed that the address was in Seattle, and he wondered what kind of business Laura's firm did in Washington state. Some boring tax stuff, he figured.

As the second sheet printed, he picked up his beer and took a long drink. His throat was dry from the drive. He went back to the window to see if Laura was coming back from across the street yet.

Behind him, the fax continued to hum as it printed. He went back to the desk, wondering if Laura had the phone number for the people across the street written down somewhere. He could call her and let her know he was here; that way he wouldn't have to go over there and make idle conversation with the pregnant neighbor.

He found several phone numbers scribbled on scraps of paper, but since he didn't even know the names of the people across the street, he had no way of knowing if one of these was their number. He gave up that idea and turned his attention back to the fax machine. There was nothing else to do while he waited for Laura to come home.

The second sheet finished printing now. He figured Laura wouldn't mind if he took a quick look, so he picked up the paper and started to read.

It was a photocopy of a newspaper article. The headline read: HEALTH MINISTRY PROBES DEATHS AT FERTILITY CLINIC. The words hit him like a blow to the chest, momentarily taking his breath away. His heart began to race as he started to read.

36

Laura's consciousness flickered on and off like a light with a loose circuit. She was vaguely conscious of the paramedics' pulling her out of the ambulance and carrying her out in a cold wind. She could hear the wail of a siren and wished someone would turn it off. Her body felt weightless. She seemed to have no control over it. She could not move.

Sharp pains sliced through her stomach and chest each time the gurney jostled. She wished someone would make the pain go away. She barely opened her eyes, but she saw gray sky. The paramedics wheeled her into the building now, the gurney jostling again as the wheels caught on the threshold.

She realized she was in the hospital now. They would understand what Chyles had done. They would know how to treat her. Some of her fear receded, but she kept thinking about her baby. Would they know how to save the baby?

The gurney suddenly stopped. She felt cold. The wind from outside was still hitting her. She realized she was still near the door.

Someone approached and touched her arm, then that person felt her throat. She felt the cold metal of a stethoscope against her chest. She strained to turn and focus on the person beside her, the doctor checking her vital signs, but before she could see, the gurney began moving again.

Ceiling panels flashed past above her, the flat white surface interrupted every few seconds by a bright fluorescent fixture. She caught a glimpse of the paramedic at the foot of the gurney. He was rushing her down the hall. A nurse standing and watching the stretcher go by flashed in and out of view. Laura thought she heard the faint voice of a woman say, "Poor thing."

She lost consciousness.

When she awoke, she was staring up at a bank of bright lights. She was in the operating room. A face appeared over her, a woman with long hair and a green surgical mask.

"Everything is going to be all right, Mrs. Fielding," the woman said. "You're going to be okay."

She felt a blood-pressure cuff constrict around her arm. A needle pierced the skin on the other arm. Someone hung an IV beside her. More faces appeared above, surgical masks with businesslike eyes above them staring down at her. Her head fogged, and all the activity left her disoriented. The pain in her chest was back, along with a sick feeling in her stomach.

Voices buzzed around her, at first sounding more like insect noises than distinguishable words, but slowly they took on character and she began to comprehend some of what was being said.

"BP is one-ninety over one-ten."

"Pulse one-oh-eight."

"Twenty milligrams Normodyne," a man ordered. "Fifty lidocaine."

There was a hint of familiarity in the voice, Laura thought, but she heard the man speak for only an instant and her head was so clouded and her attention so focused on the pain that she couldn't be sure she knew him.

She moaned when they touched her. As the pain became worse, her body convulsed. Two nurses quickly held her down.

"Ten milligrams of morphine," the doctor shouted.

A moment later, Laura felt a needle pierce her arm and realized they were giving her something for the pain. The chatter continued around her, most of it indecipherable. She understood that they were medical people, that they were treating her, reversing what Dr. Chyles had done.

She hoped it wasn't too late.

The next time she was sentient, she noticed that much of the pain had receded, but with it, she felt a loss of control over her body and a dulling in her head. It must be the drugs, she realized. She didn't mind it, as long as the pain was gone.

Each time she opened her eyes and was aware of her surroundings, she picked up some of what was being said around her. Most of it was medical jargon, making little sense to her. But she heard one phrase spoken clearly.

". . . acute toxemia . . ."

The rest of what the doctor said disappeared amid all the activity in the room, but the word *toxemia* reverberated through her brain. That was what Dana Aaron had died from.

Laura tried to speak, to tell the doctors and nurses what was happening, but all that came out of her mouth were unintelligible mumblings. The painkiller they had given her had deadened her ability to communicate.

She reached up and tried to grab someone, anyone.

The doctor pushed her hand down, then opened her eyelid with his thumb and shined a light in her eyeball.

"Just relax," he told her. "Everything's going to be all right."

Again, she thought his voice sounded familiar, but she could not place it. Instead of the familiarity reassuring her, she found it somehow disturbing.

"Ellen, start your IV now," the doctor said. "I want to keep her sedated."

"Five milligrams Versed IM," a woman's voice ordered. "Start an IV, two hundred milligrams pentobarbitol sodium."

She tried again to speak, but the drugs flowing through her body made it impossible for her to do anything but mumble. The male doctor quickly hushed her and held her arms down on the examination table.

"Hurry up with that sedative," he shouted impatiently.

Laura felt a needle jab into her arm again. She turned and saw a nurse giving her an injection. The anesthesiologist was setting up the IV drip. Her face was hidden behind a mask, but Laura could see her eyes. They were cold, unemotional.

"Everything's going to be okay," she told Laura, but the tone of her voice was not at all reassuring.

And, like the male doctor's voice, Laura thought this woman's voice was also familiar.

"I want to operate right away," the doctor said.

The sureness in his voice gave Laura hope. This man seemed to know what to do. He sounded confident. He must understand what's wrong. He must know what Chyles had done.

"Give the Versed fifteen minutes," the anesthesiologist said. "Maybe twenty. She'll be out by the time we scrub."

Laura's vision was becoming blurry as the painkiller and sedative gradually took effect. But she could still see the two doctors standing over her, their faces covered by surgical masks.

"We need to deliver the baby," the doctor told two other nurses standing near the table. "The baby is what's putting the stress on her body, and that's what caused her condition."

Laura wanted to ask if it was too soon, if the baby could survive, but she couldn't make the words come out. All she could do was moan. No one was paying attention.

She watched as the doctor peeled off his latex gloves and tossed them aside.

"Let's scrub," he told the anesthesiologist.

She nodded.

As he told the nurses to prepare for surgery, he pulled down the surgical mask that had been concealing his face. Laura's vision was bleary and the bright lights above made it difficult for her to see at first, but she blinked some of the fog from her eyes and squinted so she could make out the doctor's face. In the last moment before he walked away, she finally saw him clearly.

The anesthesiologist took off her mask as well. Laura's breath left her in a sudden flush of horror as she watched Dr. Chyles and Dr. Acer walk toward the scrub room to prepare for surgery.

37

The date on the article was August 3, 1993. The newspaper was the *Vancouver Sun*. Dan stood in front of Laura's desk, engrossed in the article that had come from her fax machine.

BURNABY—On Tuesday, the British Columbia Department of Health and Welfare in conjunction with the Canadian Medical Association announced a joint investigation into the Narrows Point Center for Assisted Reproduction. The action was taken in response to concerns arising from the deaths of Marie Bruneau and Sharon Caswell, patients of the clinic, which specializes in helping infertile couples.

Bruneau and Caswell died earlier this year from complications due to toxemia, a dangerous hypertensive condition associated with pregnancy.

Less than five percent of all pregnant women in Canada experience some degree of toxemia. Among its symptoms are high blood pressure, excessive weight gain, blurry vision, painful headaches and stomach discomfort. Most cases are mild and, if detected early, easily treated with medication and bed rest. However, if the disease is severe, it can lead to the death of the baby or to stroke or kidney damage and eventually death in the mother. The causes of toxemia are not fully known.

Dan glanced again at the cover sheet that came with the fax. It didn't make sense that a law firm in Seattle would fax this article to Laura. If it had to do with her job, why wasn't it about taxes?

It must not have anything to do with work, he decided. Since it was about pregnant women it seemed more likely that Laura was interested in it for personal reasons. But why? Why these women? Why this clinic? Why Vancouver, Canada?

Then he remembered that Laura's writer friend had gone to Vancouver shortly before her death. Laura had mentioned it after the funeral. She had been very interested in why Jenny had gone to Vancouver. He had a vague recollection of someone else going to Vancouver, months ago. *No, not going there—but coming from there. That's right, the woman who died in a car crash near Chyles's house. Wasn't she from Vancouver?* Dan thought.

The fax machine was still humming, printing the second sheet. Dan looked again at the first sheet and, his interest piqued, read on.

> Attorneys representing the families of Bruneau and Caswell have accused Dr. Lloyd Nefayre, the reproductive endocrinologist who ran the Narrows Point clinic, of causing the women's condition. They claim that the hormone given to the patients by Nefayre to assist infertile women in conceiving and carrying a baby to term was not safe.
>
> Doctors working with the DHW have been examining the hormone in their labs but so far have not been able to determine exactly what it is and if it is dangerous. According to a DHW spokesperson, Nefayre is not cooperating with the investigation.

Dan started to get nervous.

He thought back to the first visit he and Laura had made to the New Life Center here in Collier. He couldn't remember exactly what Dr. Chyles had told them, but he was sure Chyles had said something about using hormone supplements. Could they be anything like the ones this Canadian doctor had used, the ones that might have caused two women to die?

He wondered if that was what Laura had been looking into, if that was what had made her come unglued yesterday on the phone.

He read the last paragraph.

> Several attempts by *The Sun* to contact Dr. Nefayre were unsuccessful. The Narrows Point clinic stopped operating in July, and Dr. Nefayre is no longer practicing in the Vancouver area.

The whole thing troubled Dan. A Seattle law firm wouldn't fax this to Laura unless she had requested it, and she wouldn't have requested it unless there was a good reason. Why was she interested in a doctor in Canada, in patients up there? It had to have something to do with her own condition.

The second sheet came out of the fax machine now. Dan grabbed it quickly. It was a photocopy of another newspaper article, this one dated January 11, 1994. The headline read HEALTH MINISTRY, CMA REVOKES LICENSE OF BABY DOCTOR. Dan started reading.

OTTAWA—The Canadian Medical Association and the Ministry of Health announced yesterday that the medical license of Vancouver reproductive endocrinologist Lloyd Nefayre would be permanently revoked, effective immediately.

The action was taken as part of an agreement reached between Nefayre, the CMA, and the Department of Health and Welfare. The DHW had been investigating Nefayre and his Burnaby infertility clinic in connection with the deaths of two patients.

Families of the patients allege that the supplemental hormone that Nefayre prescribed for the women caused toxemia, leading to stroke in Sharon Caswell and heart failure in Marie Bruneau. Families of both women have settled civil suits against Nefayre out of court. Details of those settlements were not made public.

Still unsettled is litigation brought by several other former patients who claim that the drugs used by Nefayre caused their babies to be physically deformed. One child was born with only eight fingers, another without the ocular nerves that carry signals from the retina to the brain, leaving the child blind.

The DHW has not been able to determine

whether the synthetic hormone was the cause of the deformities. Tests are still being conducted. No criminal action has been taken against Nefayre. It is believed that he has left British Columbia and may be living in Europe or in the United States.

Investigations into the possible involvement of his wife, Dr. Florence Nefayre, an anesthesiologist at the Narrows Point clinic, are still under way. No ruling has yet been made regarding her medical privileges in Canada.

Beside the text of the article was a grainy black-and-white photograph. The quality of the picture was poor after the faxing done by the Seattle law firm. The man in the photo, pictured getting into his car, was barely visible; the photo was obviously taken at night.

But even though the quality of the picture was poor, Dan recognized the man. The caption underneath said LLOYD NEFAYRE, but the face was unmistakably that of Dr. Norman Chyles.

38

Slowly, with each drip through the IV, Laura could feel her senses leaving her. She realized that if she was to do anything, she would have to do it now. In a matter of minutes, it would be too late for her.

She forced her head sideways and strained to see across the operating room. Two nurses were standing at a counter, preparing surgical instruments. One moment they were blurry, the next moment clear, then blurry again as Laura struggled to maintain focus. One of the nurses picked up a plastic bottle and shook it.

"We're going to need more Betadine," she told the other nurse.

"I'll get it."

"Get some extra towels while you're at it—both sizes. And we're probably going to need Paige to assist. See if you can find her, stat. Chyles wants to operate right away."

"You bet."

"I'm going to take the cesarean tray to the autoclave," she said, picking up a tray of instruments and following the other nurse out the door.

The operating room was suddenly silent. Laura swung her eyes around to see if anyone else was in here. The movement of her pupils made her dizzy, but she saw that she was alone.

She strained to turn her head so she could see the IV hanging beside her. Clear liquid dripped from the bag into the catheter. With her eyes, she followed the tube down to the table, over her shoulder and into the needle in her left arm. Acer had secured the needle in place with several strips of white medical tape. Laura realized she needed to remove it, and she needed to do it right away.

She could feel herself succumbing to the sedative. Her right arm had gone completely numb. It did not respond when she tried to move it. It took all of her strength just to inch it off the table. She brought it across her body, gasping from the effort, perspiration dripping down her face.

After only a few seconds, she could not hold her arm up any longer and let it fall to her stomach. She had to stop a moment to catch her breath and gather enough strength to continue. She swallowed hard. Her throat was parched. Sharp pains pierced her stomach and chest again.

She turned her head just enough to see the doors across the room. No one was coming yet. But she told herself again that she had to hurry. She didn't know how many of the nurses were involved in what Chyles was doing, but she knew she couldn't trust anyone. She needed to get to a phone and call the police.

She pulled her arm the rest of the way and dropped it over the left side of her body. Her fingers touched the plastic tubing. She traced it down to the needle in her arm and grasped it as tightly as her limp hand would allow. When she pulled the first time, the tape resisted. She caught her breath, then tried again, yanking as hard as she could.

The tape sounded like it was tearing as it slowly came off and the needle slid out of her vein. Blood began seeping out, but Laura wasn't concerned with that. The blood flow was slow. She would be all right.

She feared that too much of the sedative was in her system already. She was beginning to feel sleepy, her body drained of all strength. It was a strain just to maintain consciousness. She didn't know how she was going to get out of there, but she knew she had no other choice. She told herself that she could do it.

Breathing was difficult for her now. She wanted to sleep, just for a minute. That would give her a chance to regain enough strength to walk. But she knew that with each passing second, Chyles could return, and then it would be too late.

With her right arm still draped across her body and her right hand hanging over the edge of the table, she grasped the side of the table and tried to pull herself up. At the same time, she forced her legs over the side. They dropped with very little control and dangled above the floor. Her shoulders and head came up. Blades of pain cut into her stomach and chest, so fierce that she could not move. The pain finally receded, leaving nausea and dizziness.

She had to sit at the edge of the table for a few moments, knowing that if she tried to stand immediately, she would only fall and hurt herself and probably never get out. She twisted her head just enough to see the doors, swimming in her blurred vision. They were still closed. The room was still empty. But for how long?

She could not delay any longer. Still feeling unsure of herself, she slid off the edge of the table. Her feet hit the floor hard, and for an instant, her legs felt like they would buckle, but she managed to hold on and remain upright. The tiles felt like ice beneath her bare feet. Her toes went numb immediately.

Holding the table for support, she turned herself around and scanned the room again. The doors looked like they were a mile away. She drew several frail breaths, hoping the room would settle down, but it kept pitching from side to side like a boat in a storm.

She staggered away from the table. Although the doorway was straight ahead, she couldn't stop herself from zigzagging across the room, colliding with the wall twice. She knocked a box of gloves and a stack of gauze sponges to the floor, but she managed to stay on her feet.

Out of breath, she fell against the doors. She eased them open an inch and peered out. The hall outside the operating room seemed empty, but her vision wasn't good enough for her to be sure. Still, she had no choice. This was the only way out, and she had to get out.

She was beginning to feel a little steadier now, but she was still dizzy and weak, still nauseated. The morphine suppressed much of the pain in her stomach and chest. Her arms and legs were beginning to respond to commands from her brain. Her brain too was becoming clearer.

Slowly, she pushed open the door just wide enough for her to slip out. She heard voices coming from one of the rooms somewhere off the corridor, but there was no one in the hallway itself. She hesitated a moment, deciding which way to go. The double doors leading to the lobby were straight ahead, but that was the direction the voices were coming from. She couldn't go there.

Just then, the door to the scrub room opened electrically and she saw Dr. Chyles step out into the hall. He was looking over his shoulder, talking to Dr. Acer, who was coming out behind him. Quickly, Laura stumbled out of the operating room and ducked to the side. In front of her was the door marked: PATHOLOGY—PHYSICIANS ONLY. She clutched the doorknob and found it unlocked, so she tugged open the door and slipped through.

Silently, she eased the door closed behind her, and now darkness surrounded her. The faint scent of formaldehyde was apparent with the first breath she took. As it filled her lungs, the image of the tiny gray body Chyles and Acer had dissected yesterday came to her mind.

She did not want to go back into the basement; it filled her with horror. But she remembered that the hallway below led to Chyles's office in the outpatient wing. The office had phones. She could call the police. There was also an exit there. If she could make it to that part of the clinic, she was sure she could escape.

It was her only chance to get out of the clinic alive.

Pausing for just a moment to catch her breath and let her heart settle, she felt her way along the wall to the steps, then started down.

39

Dan threw the curtain aside and peered out the window at the house across the street. *Laura has to be there,* he thought. *Where else could she be?*

He had to make sure. He had to talk to her. After reading the newspaper clippings that had been faxed to her, he needed assurance that everything was all right with Laura. He shuddered when he thought about women dying, about deformed babies. The message Laura had left on his answering machine yesterday played over and over in his head now.

There's a problem—the baby—the clinic—I have to get

out of here. Call me—no, I'm coming home. I'm leaving right now. I'll call you—

Her words had made no sense then, but now, suddenly, their meaning was painfully clear. Somehow she had learned about Chyles, even without the faxes that came today.

Oh, God . . . she had whispered over the phone yesterday. *Dan, I'm scared. The babies . . .*

Those last two words had echoed with fear.

The babies . . . the babies . . . the babies . . .

He hurried back to the desk, deciding to call the people across the street to make sure Laura was there. The fax machine was still printing. He noticed the headline on this article. It read THREE-YEAR-OLD BOY KILLS DOG.

Dan hesitated, struck by this, unable to make sense of it, but he didn't wait for the fax machine to finish printing. He didn't have time to read it now. He felt an urgent need to find Laura.

He began searching the desk for the phone number of the people across the street. He didn't know their name, but he remembered Laura mentioning once that they were Filipino. But what did a Filipino name sound like? He had no idea. He was looking without even knowing what he was looking for.

Then he remembered that Laura had told him that the *wife* was Filipino; the husband wasn't. He was American, in the navy. But Dan didn't know if he was Italian or Polish or Irish, what his name sounded like. It could be almost anything. He picked up a few pieces of paper from the desk and looked for a name with a military rank on it, thinking that might be the name of the husband, but he didn't find anything like that.

He took a quick look at the fax machine again. The fax with the story about the boy who killed a dog was finished and now another sheet was starting to print. Dan grabbed the dog story and skimmed through it quickly. There was no mention of a fertility clinic or a doctor named Nefayre. He didn't see how this had any connection to the other faxes, didn't understand why Laura would be interested in this. He didn't understand any of it, but the articles were troubling.

He dropped the fax and went back to the window, hoping to see Laura coming across the street, but there was no one outside. He couldn't wait any longer. He hurried out the front door, off the porch, and down the driveway. There weren't any cars, so he ran across the street and up to the neighbors' door. The bell chimed "Dixie" when he pressed it.

A moment later, a tall, sinewy man with a crew cut and wearing a polo shirt with a Buffalo Bills insignia on it opened the door.

"Isn't that the most ridiculous doorbell you ever heard?" the man said.

Dan forced himself to smile and nod. The man had a New York accent. In the background, Dan could hear the television.

"So, what can I do for you, guy?" the man said.

"I'm Dan Fielding." He pointed behind him and said, "My wife, Laura, is staying across the street."

The man's expression changed suddenly, from a look of polite tolerance one might give to a salesman who comes to the door to a look of concern and sympathy.

"Oh," the man said. "Hi. How is your wife?"

"Good. Is she here by any chance?"

"Here?" The man seemed bewildered by the question.

"I just drove up from New Orleans. Her car's in the driveway, but she's not in the house," Dan said. "I thought she might have come here to visit." He laughed uneasily, sensing that something was very definitely wrong. "Where else could she be? You're the only neighbors around."

The man's wife came up behind him now, a shy, young, Filipino woman.

"Honey, this is Dan Fielding," the man said. "The husband of the woman across the street."

Her expression changed, matching the sympathetic look of her husband.

"You haven't heard, then?" the man said.

"Heard what?"

"Your wife—a little while ago, they took her away in an ambulance."

"Took her away? Who took her? Where? What happened?"

"We don't know what happened; we just saw the ambulance come. Your wife must have called them. I walked over afterward, when the paramedics were taking her out. She was unconscious."

"What did they say? Is she all right?"

"I really don't know. I'm sorry."

"Where did they take her? Where's the hospital around here?"

"The hospital's in the next county, but they didn't take her there. Apparently, they called her doctor, or he called them or something—whatever it was, he told them to bring her straight to the clinic."

"Dr. Chyles told them that?"

"Yeah, I guess. She is one of his patients, isn't she? I think my wife has seen her at the clinic once or twice, haven't you, honey?"

"The paramedics didn't say what was wrong with her?" Dan asked.

"Someone said something about toxic or toxins or something like that, but I didn't catch exactly what they were saying."

"Toxemia? Is that what they said?"

"Yeah, that sounds like what they said. Do you know what that is? I sure don't."

"Yeah, I know what that is," Dan said. "She's definitely at the clinic, then?"

"That's where they said they were taking her. I hope she's all right."

"Thanks," Dan said and hurried away. By the time he reached the street, the man's words, combined with the faxes he had read a few minutes earlier, turned his concern to panic. He broke into a run, sprinting to his car and driving away without stopping to lock the house. The clinic was a 10-minute drive from the house. He hoped to God he wasn't too late.

40

The effects of the sedative continued to diminish as Laura staggered deeper into the basement, but she was still weak and tired. She wished she could find a safe corner somewhere, curl up, and go to sleep for a few minutes, but she knew that if she did, she probably would never awaken. She had to fight her exhaustion, fight her desire to sleep.

The morphine too was wearing off, and with each step she took, the pain in her stomach steadily worsened. Her lungs burned with each breath of air she drew. The odor of formaldehyde down here assaulted her senses. She tried not to dwell on the jars filled with dismembered baby body parts she would soon encounter, tried not to think about the newborn whose dissection she had witnessed.

She followed the same passageway she had used the day before to escape from Chyles, only now she was running deeper into the basement, not away from it. Today, there was even less light. There was a dim glow further ahead, but it offered almost no illumination here. She had to feel her way along the walls.

Finally, she saw the entrance to the laboratory ahead where a small light was burning. She hesitated, wondering if someone was in there. Both Chyles and Acer were upstairs, she knew. She still wasn't sure how many others, if any, knew about this place. But if someone else was here now, someone who was participating in killing babies with Chyles, it would be dangerous for her to continue ahead.

She stopped in the darkness and listened for sounds of movement, any indication that someone might be in the lab. Her own breathing sounded loud all of a sudden. She could hear her heart beating rapidly.

The quiet and stillness unsettled her. Perhaps no one was here, but she remembered those deformed, cloned animals, and all those body parts floating in the jars, and that baby they had dissected, and she dreaded going back in there.

Suddenly, she heard the muffled sound of a door closing behind her. She turned and peered into the blackness, not able to see even a foot away. As the sound of the door faded, the basement became silent again. She questioned if that really had been a door she heard. Maybe it was the boiler kicking in or something else having to do with the building's power plant.

Then, from the darkness, came the sound of shoes descending stairs, a steady, ominous tap that grew louder with each step. She knew in an instant that it was Chyles.

She turned and, ignoring her fear of the lab ahead, raced up the passageway toward the dim light. Footsteps hurried behind her, coming at her much faster than she could run. She nearly fell through the doorway into the lab, out of breath. She was filled with panic.

A small lamp on one of the tables had been left on, illuminating the jars and the body parts floating inside. She tried not to look at them as she staggered across the room toward the doorway that led up to Chyles's office. But she was not even close to that doorway when she heard footsteps coming toward her quickly. They were loud now. He was only seconds away from reaching the lab.

She didn't have enough time to escape through the doorway. He would surely see her before she could get to his office. The doorway leading to the operating room was much closer. She hastily decided to go there and stumbled down that passage just as Chyles reached the lab.

Struggling to remain on her feet, she hurried past the refrigerator room, but she was unsure of where she was going. She realized suddenly that there was no door leading out of the room. All she could do now was hide and hope Chyles assumed she had already gone.

As she looked around for a safe place to hide, she heard Chyles's footsteps stop. The lab behind her became silent. She too stopped, realizing that Chyles was out there listening for her movements. She was barefoot and could move without making noise, but she was still frightened that he might hear her. She held her breath and wished she could somehow quiet her heart.

She heard the scrape of leather soles on the tile floor in the lab, Chyles moving slowly out there. He was searching for her. No longer running after her, now he was searching slowly, methodically. Her body trembled. She could feel herself about to cry in desperation, but she fought to restrain her tears. She had to control her fear if she wanted to survive.

She heard him move something in the lab, a chair or table. He was searching thoroughly. She had to find a good place to conceal herself, a place where he wouldn't find her, a place where she could hide until he left.

Moving quickly, but being careful not to make any noise, she tiptoed farther down the hall.

Dan drove his car right up to the front entrance of the clinic, the front tires bouncing up onto the sidewalk. He leaped out of the car, then rushed around it, toward the lobby doors. Roy, the guard, stepped outside.

"You can't park there," he told Dan.

"Where's my wife?"

"I don't know who or where your wife is, but I know you can't park there. You're going to have to move the car."

Dan ignored him and rushed into the building. Roy hurried after him.

"Hey, you!"

"They brought her here in an ambulance a little while ago," Dan said as he crossed the lobby and headed up the hall toward the outpatient clinic. "Laura Fielding. I have to find her."

"Oh, you're Mrs. Fielding's husband. You're going the wrong way. She's down there," he said, pointing to the other hall.

Dan turned and ran past the guard, down the hallway toward the maternity ward and the delivery rooms. "Where is she?" Dan shouted, leaving Roy far behind.

"They brought her to the operating room, but you can't go in there. Dr. Chyles is operating on her right now."

"Call an ambulance," Dan told him.

"Huh?"

"Call an ambulance. I'm taking my wife out of here!"

"Mr. Fielding, wait!"

Dan shoved open the double doors that said STERILE AREA—AUTHORIZED PERSONNEL ONLY. Straight ahead were the two operating rooms. He saw a nurse carrying medical supplies toward one of the rooms. Dan hurried toward her.

"You! Nurse!" he shouted, still far away. "Where's my wife? Is she in there?" he asked, pointing to the operating room.

The nurse looked at him, confused, not sure what to say.

"Laura Fielding," Dan said. "Is she in there? Listen to me, I want you to tell Chyles that I don't want him operating on her. I have an ambulance coming. I'm going to take her out of here."

Roy burst through the double doors behind Dan, out of breath from running. "Mr. Fielding, wait," he said, gasping for air. "You can't be in here."

Dan ignored him and said to the nurse, "Go in there and tell Chyles to stop. I don't want him operating on my wife."

The nurse didn't know what to do.

Roy came closer. "Mr. Fielding, you really can't be back here."

"Did you call for an ambulance?"

"I'm going to have to ask you to leave this area."

"Just call for a goddamn ambulance!" Dan shouted.

Another nurse, an older woman, came out of a supply room now. She had the manner of someone in charge. "What's all the shouting out here?" she said. "What's going on?"

Dan rushed over to her. "I want my wife out of that operating room right now!"

"Calm down, sir."

"Don't tell me to calm down! I don't want Chyles operating on my wife!"

"There are other patients here, and if you insist on yelling," she said, glancing at Roy, "I'm going to have to—"

"Don't look at him! You look at me! I'm going to keep yelling until you start listening!"

"I am listening."

"Good. Chyles is not going to operate on my wife. Do you understand me?"

Roy came over and started to put his hand on Dan's shoulder, but Dan pulled away quickly.

"Come on, Mr. Fielding. This isn't helping any of us."

"Will you for Christ's sake call an ambulance?!"

"I'm not going to call an ambulance. I am going to ask you to calm down and come with me to the waiting room, or I'm afraid I'm going to have to—"

"Like hell you are," Dan said. He started up the hall toward the operating rooms. "I'm going to get my wife out of here right now."

"Mr. Fielding!"

Dr. Acer came out of the operating room. "What's going on out here?" she asked. Seeing Dan, she quickly said, "You're not supposed to be here. You have to go."

"I'm not going anywhere," Dan said. "I know about you and your husband. I know about Vancouver. I want my wife out of here right now, or I'm going to call the police!"

Acer's eyes darted from Dan to the nurses to Roy and back to Dan. She looked frightened. She didn't answer him.

"I'm warning you!" Dan shouted.

Roy hurried over and grabbed Dan, holding him back.

While the two men started struggling, Dr. Acer stepped over and pulled the revolver from Roy's holster. As soon as Roy felt it being removed, he let go of Dan and whirled around. Acer leveled the gun at Dan. Roy lunged to get the gun just as Acer squeezed the trigger.

The gunshot echoed through the hall. One of the nurses screamed. Dan lunged forward. Roy clutched his side and crumpled to the floor. Acer watched, shocked. She saw Dan coming at her and started to raise the gun again, but Dan grabbed her and pushed her arm aside. The gun went off again, the bullet plugging the ceiling. Dan drove his fist into her chin, a punch that unloaded the full force of his fury and fear. He felt her bony chin crack. Her head snapped back and she fell to the floor, her skull hitting hard, knocking her unconscious. The gun skidded across the floor. Dan picked it up.

"Take care of him," he told the nurses, pointing to Roy, who was on the floor, wincing in pain, blood spilling from the wound in his side.

"And for God's sake, someone call an ambulance! And call the police too!"

He stepped over Roy and ran into the operating room. It was empty. He rushed back out into the hall. "Where's my wife?"

The nurses were on the floor with Roy, trying to help him. They didn't hear Dan. He was about to scream at them to get their attention when he noticed a trail of blood on the floor leading from the operating room to the door marked PATHOLOGY—PHYSICIANS ONLY. Something inside him, a deep fear, told him that this was Laura's blood.

He ran to the door and found it unlocked. There was more blood smeared on the door knob. *How bad is she?* he thought, frightened.

"Oh, God, don't let me be too late."

He pulled open the door and rushed into the darkness. He almost fell when he reached the steps, but he caught the rail and stopped himself from tumbling headfirst down the stairs. It was so dark that he couldn't tell what was below, but he was sure Laura was down there. Unable to see, he hastily descended into the blackness.

42

Cold panic rushed through Laura as she heard Chyles step into the room. He moved slowly, stopping after each step, pausing to look and listen. Her eyes were accustomed to the darkness now and she saw the outline of his body come deeper into the room. He held something in his hand. It was hard to see, but she thought it looked like a knife.

He took another step into the room. The animals around her stirred slightly, wakened by the movement. She was sure Chyles hadn't heard what she had done a moment ago. If he had, he would have rushed in here sooner. All he knew was that she was somewhere in the darkness of the basement. He was being cautious. But she was running out of time.

He flipped the switch, flooding the room in light. Laura pressed herself back against the wall, hoping he couldn't see her here. She began to fear her plan might not work. The odds seemed so small now. She had no weapon. All she could do was run, and in her condition, she couldn't even do that very well. It wouldn't take him long to recover and catch up with her. But what else could she do?

He moved to the center of the room, the spot where she had vomited yesterday. She pressed herself deeper into the tiny space, hoping her stomach wasn't sticking out too far. She tried to draw it in. The baby must have sensed the tensing of her body, because she felt it move inside her.

The sensation of the life in her womb made it clear that she was not only fighting for her own life but for her baby's as well—the real baby—and the other one too. That one mattered too. She wished she could tell herself otherwise, but her heart knew the truth. As revolting and frightening as the image of the other baby was, she could not deny that it was still her baby, that it was from her body, from her egg and Dan's sperm. It depended on her to protect it also. And while her sense of reason told her to let it die, her maternal instinct beseeched her to preserve its life.

"Laura?" Chyles whispered.

His voice sounded like the breath of a snake. She cringed as her name reverberated through the room, burning into her brain as though his voice were a toxic venom sprayed into her ears.

"I know you're in here," he said.

As she pressed herself flatter against the wall, trying desperately to keep from being seen, she felt something in her stomach, a pain she feared was a contraction.

No, God, not now, not yet. She could not go into labor now, here.

The animals moved about in their cages as Chyles's voice was beginning to arouse them. He stepped farther into the room; she pressed herself back farther. She could barely see him now, but she could see the object he held out in front of him. She shuddered as she realized it was a scalpel.

She slid her right arm into the narrow space. How heavy would it be, she wondered. She hoped not too heavy for her to move. Her plan depended on her being able to move it.

It wasn't yet time, she decided. He needed to get closer.

"I won't hurt you, Laura," Chyles said. "I promise. I just want to deliver the babies. They need to be delivered now or they'll die—both of them. And you'll die too. You need to let me deliver the babies."

She watched him take another step into the room. He looked around carefully. Another foot or so and he would be able to see her. It was almost time.

"Do you want your babies to die, Laura?" he asked.

He took another step.

"Do you want to risk—"

She directed all her strength to her arm and thrust the cage forward, shrieking as she did it. Chyles turned toward the sound. The cage toppled forward, taking with it the one above and below. She had removed the safety catches when she first came in and now the doors sprang open and the dogs inside, startled by the sudden movement, rushed out. The top cage hit Chyles's shoulder, knocking him to one knee. The dogs started barking and rushing around, exciting the rest of the animals in the room. She had unlocked as many of the cages as she could when she had come in. Now a dozen dogs and cats were knocking open their doors and rushing out.

Laura moved quickly along the wall, reaching behind the second stack of cages and pushing them toward Chyles. These hit him square in the back, knocking him to the floor. Dogs were running everywhere. A cat leaped at Laura, frightening her. She swatted it, knocking it against the wall, then she squeezed out past the fallen cages and stumbled toward the door, almost tripping over the animals.

"Goddamn you!" Chyles yelled, struggling to get up.

Laura staggered out into the hall and rushed toward the lab, where the light was still glowing, illuminating the baby parts floating in jars. She headed for the door that led to Chyles's office. The animals were scrambling all around her.

She heard someone approaching now from the other door, the one that led back to the operating rooms. Thinking that it was Dr. Acer, she pushed herself to move faster, bumping into a lab stool and then into a table, knocking over a rack of test tubes. The crashing sound as the glass hit the floor seemed as loud as a gunshot. She burst into tears in frustration and fear. Adrenaline pushed her forward even though her legs seemed to stop working. She fell against the doorjamb and started to run through the dark passageway.

"Wait! Laura!"

She recognized the voice immediately. With relief, she turned and saw Dan hurrying into the room, struggling to avoid the animals rushing all around him. He was carrying a pistol. At the sight of him, she surrendered to her pain and fatigue and sank to the floor, sobbing uncontrollably. His face was full of concern as he rushed around the lab table toward her.

Dan didn't see him coming. His eyes were fixed on Laura and he was still concentrating on not tripping over the animals. When she looked up as Dan was approaching, all she saw was a blur. Chyles moved so quickly that Laura didn't have time to warn Dan.

She screamed as Chyles slashed at Dan with the scalpel, slicing through his shirt and ripping open his back. Dan whirled around to defend himself, blood spraying from the wound as he did, but Chyles was already wielding the scalpel again. The blade sliced into Dan's forearm, cutting tendon and muscle, crippling Dan's hand. As Chyles sliced with the scalpel a third time, cutting open Dan's chest, Dan fell backward, losing his grip on the gun. It skidded across the tile floor, out of reach.

Dan fell against the wall, breaking the shelves and knocking dozens of jars to the floor. Glass shattered. Formaldehyde sprayed everywhere. Laura saw a tiny heart and the loose shreds of a brain slide across the lab amid the scurrying animals. Chyles rushed at Dan, who was already weak and struggling to stay on his feet. Dan raised his good arm to cover himself as Chyles slashed again, opening a deep laceration in his forearm. Blood splattered everywhere.

Chyles drove his knee into Dan's groin. Dan crumpled forward, landing hard on his knees. He looked overcome with pain, unable to defend himself. Chyles grabbed a fistful of his hair and yanked Dan's head back, exposing his neck. Then he raised the scalpel again to slash Dan's throat.

Laura reacted without thinking. Lunging forward, she grabbed the pistol on the floor. She had been frozen with fear before this moment, but that very same fear that had paralyzed her now pushed her to do something to help the man she loved. She raised the gun. Chyles's arm started to move toward Dan's throat. With an uncontrolled scream, she fired.

The bullet struck Chyles in the ribs. The impact spun him around and knocked him into the wall. He was facing her now. He released Dan's hair and Dan again crumpled to the floor. Chyles tried to cover the bullet wound in his side with one hand, but his other hand still clutched desperately to the scalpel. Breathing was difficult for him, and each breath he drew was painful. He inhaled short, wet gasps as blood filled his lungs.

He stared across the room at Laura. His face was ghastly white now, his eyes looking dead already. A trickle of blood dripped from his mouth and streaked down his chin. He struggled to stay on his feet as he staggered toward her.

"Don't," Laura said in a frightened whimper, the pistol shaking in her outstretched hands.

He looked at her, confused, and struggled to speak. His voice was faint.

"I gave you a baby," he said with resentment.

He raised the scalpel over his head, his face twisted from the effort. It seemed as though he were lifting a ton of steel instead of the weightless surgical instrument.

"Don't," Laura pleaded.

He came forward, so slowly at first that Laura was sure he would collapse before he reached her. But then he came faster, in what seemed more like falling than walking. His face was consumed with rage as his arm came down toward her.

"I won't let you kill my son!" he screamed.

Laura fired a bullet into his chest. The bullet halted him. His arm dropped to his side, but he did not fall. He glared at her, surprise and anger drawing the last color from his face. He struggled to lift his arm again. Then he took a feeble step toward her. She fired again. This time, the bullet sent him to the floor.

For a brief moment, he tried to crawl toward her, still clutching the scalpel. But then he stopped. His arm went limp; his head fell to the floor. A moment later, his hand spread open and released the scalpel.

EPILOGUE

———◆———

When Laura awakened, Dan was sitting in the chair by
the window. His shirt was unbuttoned and draped over his
shoulders. A white bandage circled his chest. Another
bandage covered part of his left forearm. His right arm was
completely wrapped and resting in a sling.

Laura felt sluggish from the drugs they had given her. Her
mouth was dry, her throat swollen. A dull ache rose slowly
in her pelvic area, an ache that was deep with memories.

Dan saw that she was awake and he came over. The safety
rail was up, so he lowered it and sat on the edge of the bed.
He took her hand gently and bent over and kissed her. The
warmth of his lips against her skin felt good.

"Hi, honey," he whispered. "How do you feel?"

"All right. I guess." It hurt her to talk. He gave her the
glass of water from the table beside the bed and she drank a
little through the straw. "That's better," she said.

He leaned close and kissed her again. "I love you so
much," he said.

She felt weak, but she managed to put one arm around
him and hold him. His nearness assured her that everything
would be all right.

"How are you feeling?" she asked, fingering the gauze
bandage around his chest.

He dismissed his own injuries. "I'm fine."

He looked like he hadn't slept in days. His skin had little

color. He seemed to have lost several pounds, mostly in his face. "You look terrible," she said.

"And you're the most beautiful sight I've ever seen," he said.

She laughed.

They stared at each other for a moment, just smiling, holding hands, thankful to be alive, thankful to be together.

At last, she had to ask.

"The delivery . . . ?" she said.

Dan was about to speak when someone knocked at the door. A doctor poked his head into the room.

"I see you're awake, Mrs. Fielding. How are you feeling?"

Laura shrugged. The doctor came to the bed and examined her briefly, listening to her heart and checking her blood pressure and pulse. Dan watched anxiously.

"She is okay, isn't she, Doctor?" he asked, sounding worried.

"I'd say she's doing just fine."

Dan sighed and squeezed Laura's hand to reassure her. But she didn't share his relief. She was filled with dread as she thought of the delivery. She had an indescribable sensation in her womb, something between pain and numbness.

"What happened?" she asked.

The doctor didn't seem to understand the question at first, but when Laura's eyes drifted to her stomach, he realized what she was talking about.

"You mean the babies?" he said. The doctor took a deep breath. "We had to deliver them early."

"Honey." Dan squeezed her hand again. "We had *twins*. Two girls," he said in a low, grave voice. Laura realized instantly that something had happened, something bad. She feared the worst.

Dan said, "Did you know you were going to have twins?"

She nodded in contrite silence.

"You should have told me," he said. She saw that he wasn't angry with her, but he was somber, troubled.

"I should have," she said quietly.

Dan held Laura's hand tightly. But now his grip felt different. She could tell that he was afraid.

"Honey, we have to be prepared," he said. "In case they . . ." He glanced at the doctor, caught on the next word. Finally, he looked back at Laura and said, "There's a chance that one of the babies may not survive. A good chance."

Laura held tightly to Dan's hand as she looked over at the doctor. "Tell me . . ." she said.

The doctor hesitated, measuring how much she could stand to hear. Finally, he said, "I explained to your husband earlier that with babies born as early as yours, there's always a risk of complications. Both babies are extremely small and vulnerable right now. They're in a special section of our neonatal intensive care unit. It's still too early to tell."

Laura listened silently, nodding when the doctor finished. What he was saying came as no surprise to her. She had heard of the dangers of a premature delivery from Dr. Echols in Montgomery. Her conversation with Echols was still vivid in her thoughts. She remembered him telling her of the risks of delivering early, remembered thinking that because the risks were so high, only one baby would survive. But which baby would be the one to live? She had feared the answer to that question when she was with Echols, when it had only been a possibility. Now that it was really happening, she was terrified.

She looked at the doctor again. There was so much stirring in her mind that she could not form her thoughts into a coherent question. "Are they—? I mean, is one of them . . . is one different?" she asked.

The doctor nodded. "One is considerably weaker than the other, yes. She's the one we're most concerned with. We're doing everything we can."

Dan strained to stretch his right arm out of the sling so he could hold Laura with both hands. "Honey," he said, his voice reflecting his own fear and concern. "They don't think she'll make it through the day."

A dozen thoughts came at once, horrifying thoughts, hopeful thoughts. One baby was weaker. Wouldn't that be the one Chyles had created? It wasn't real; it wasn't human. Wouldn't that mean it had to be the weaker, it had to be the one that would die?

Or was it the stronger one? Did Chyles engineer his baby so that it would be stronger, so that it would be able to survive any dangerous delivery? Could his baby have stolen the nourishment from the real baby? Could the real baby be the one close to death, killed by Chyles's . . . monster?

"Oh, God . . ." she whispered.

Dan held her more tightly. "They'll save one," he said. "We'll have a baby, Laura. I know we will."

She couldn't speak, thoughts of what that baby would be continuing to torment her.

The doctor stepped a little closer.

"I want to make sure you both understand," he said, "that even if one of the babies survives, there's a chance that she'll have some developmental problems. Many babies born as prematurely as yours develop varying degrees of deficits. These deficits can be mild, such as hearing or visual loss, poor coordination, minor learning disabilities—certainly challenges for the child, but a more or less normal life would still be possible."

Laura saw that Dan was watching her instead of listening to the doctor. He knew all this already. When he noticed her looking at him, he nodded, trying to appear reassuring. But did he know it *all?* she thought. Did he really understand? The look in his eyes told her that he did not.

"However," the doctor continued, "the disabilities may also be more serious. Much more serious." He paused for a moment, allowing his words to settle in slowly. Then he said, "The baby could be severely retarded. I don't want to scare you, but it's important that you understand that this is a possibility."

Laura still could not speak.

Dan said, "We understand, Doctor."

He told them that he would come see them again later, as soon as he knew more about the babies. After he left, Dan let out a long, tired breath. He looked exasperated, but somehow he was still optimistic.

"It's going to be all right," he told Laura. He brushed the hair off her forehead, then leaned over and kissed her. "Whatever happens," he said, "we'll deal with it."

Laura tried to hold in her emotions, but tears began leaking from her eyes.

"It's going to be okay," Dan whispered again, his voice low and soothing. He wiped her cheeks, then kissed her again. "I know it's hard," he said. "But we have to face this. We have to be strong."

"You don't understand," she said, her voice so low she wasn't even sure Dan heard her.

"I do understand, Laura. I know that the baby may be . . ." He struggled for a word that wouldn't sound too harsh. "She may have problems," he said. "I realize this. But we have to accept it. When we decided to have a baby, there never was a guarantee that she would be perfect. But she's our baby, and that's all that matters. We'll love her and we'll do whatever we can to help her. I know it won't be easy, but nothing worthwhile ever is."

"Dan . . ."

"Laura, medical science is coming up with advances all the time," he said. "There's so much that doctors can do nowadays. The fact that you even got pregnant in the first place is proof of that. They'll find ways to help our daughter. We just have to put our faith in the specialists."

"No!" Laura said in a weak, desperate plea. She looked up at him and shook her head as his words dripped like acid into her brain. "No more specialists."

"Honey, listen to me," he said. "We have to trust the people who know. If they can help our little girl, we have to let them."

"Chyles . . ." she said, shuddering in terror as the name hissed from her lips. "What if they're like Chyles?"

"They won't be."

"We don't know that. We can't be sure."

"We'll get the best doctors there are. She'll have the best care anybody could possibly have. I promise you."

Laura shook her head, frightened of what he was saying, frightened of what might happen . . .

Dan's eyes became glassy with tears now. "Honey," he said, his voice breaking with emotion. "I wanted to have a family with you for so long. Now we finally have a daughter.

That's what's important—nothing else. We're going to make a good life for our little girl. We're going to love her no matter what, no matter how she turns out. My God, she's our baby. She's from us. How can we not love her?"

Laura just closed her eyes and tried to make it all go away. If only their problems were as easy to solve as Dan made them sound. If only Dan understood the real horror facing them. But he didn't. He couldn't. *She* knew, though. She knew what was really at stake. One day, they would take the newborn home, but what would that newborn be? She could not ignore the fact that it might not even be human. And if it was not human, what then? Would they have the strength to do what was necessary? Dan would not, she knew, which left only her. Could she do it? She asked herself that over and over. Could she do it?

The answer horrified her.

"God help us," she whispered.